Living Soul

By

S.B. Niccum

Living Soul
By S.B. Niccum

©2012 by S.B Niccum

Cover Design: Laura J. Miller
www.AnAuthorsArt.com

Published by: TreasureLine Publishing
www.TreasureLinePublishing.com

ISBN: 978-1-61752-125-6

Also available in eBook publication

www.sbniccum.com
www.TreasureLinePublishing.com

The following is a work of fiction. Names, characters, places, and incidents are fictitious or used fictitiously. Any resemblance to real persons, living or dead, to factual events or to businesses is coincidental and unintentional.

Printed in the United States of America

For my children and their children.
Something to remember me by.

I would like to thank my husband for encouraging, and supporting me while I chase my dreams. I can write love stories because of his love for me. Also, I would like to thank my children for their willingness to not talk to me while I finish up my writing, early in the morning.

A big, big thanks to my mother, who has been my biggest supporter, reader, reviewer and sounding board. I don't think I can stress my thanks to her enough—not without tearing-up.

I would also like to thank from the bottom of my heart, Larry Sidwell, who has spent many meticulous hours editing all my books. I'd also like to thank Erin Cantwell, Jodie Jarvis, Naomi DeLaTorre and Amy Goggans. I love you all so very much! Thank you, thank you, thank you, for your patience in helping me with proofreading, for taking the time out of your busy schedules, for being willing to work under a deadline, for being honest and kind, and good friends.

Also, Linda Boulanger, for always being a keystroke away. For being my publisher, for guiding me through the murky waters of the business, and for being my advocate and a good friend.

Jamie Grant, your covers speak for themselves. Thank you so much for your patience and advice.

I'd also like to thank Norris Niccum and Larry Sidwell, for being my Military experts.

Mandie O'Steen Stevens, thank you for the blog tours and all the favors and hard work you do.

Carleene Heidenreich and Libby Bruton, thank you for letting me use your names fictionally. And to McKenzie, Kim, Madison Ottley for babysitting, so I could finish up this book.

To all the readers that I consider friends now, thank you for buying, reading, reviewing, rating and telling your friends about my work. None of this would be possible without your help.

Living Soul

Remember who you were.

"Our birth is but a sleep and a forgetting;
The soul that rises with us, our life's Star,
Hath had elsewhere its setting
And cometh from afar:
Not in entire forgetfulness,
And not in utter nakedness,
But trailing clouds of glory do we come
From God, who is our home:
Heaven lies about us in our infancy."

~William Wordsworth~

"Ode Intimations of Immortality from
Recollections of Early Childhood."

"And the Lord God formed man of the dust of the ground, and breathed into his nostrils the breath of life; and man became a Living Soul."

Genesis 2:7

Prologue

Crouching in the corner of the small shower, right where she had been placed, the child shivers and rocks herself back and forth. If only her eyes were open, she would see that she's encircled in unearthly light, but instead she just feels cold.

The woman wraps her arms protectively around the child's shoulders, but the child trembles, and pulls back.

Stopping her ears with her hands, the child tries to shut out the noises that frighten her, yet still, she hears it all—the shouting, the screaming, two shots, then a third—then nothing.

"It'll all be okay, I promise. I will never leave your side. You hear me?" the woman whispers, and the child nods while suppressing a sob.

"Shh … shh … " the woman soothes, then starts to sing that same lullaby that she has sung to her since birth.

"Duérmete mi niña, duérmete mi amor, duérmete pedazo de mi corazón."

Part I ~ The Dream
Chapter 1

I sat up in bed trembling. My heart still raced and I panted from the adrenaline rush. Disappointed, I looked all around me hoping to find some trace of him, but everything had vanished into thin air. Though the room was dark I could still discern my foster brother's shape, on his bed, sleeping soundly. My alarm clock showed 5 a.m. and a dull headache started to form behind my eyes. That dream felt so real—so much so, that I wanted to cry in desperation.

Hoping to recapture the last few moments of that dream, I closed my eyes and focused on his face. We had talked almost all night about ourselves, right here on my rooftop, where Dorian and I go to watch the sunset. Dreams don't have to make sense, I guess, or be rooted to what reality dictates. That's the beauty of them; they can be as surreal as we can think them up to be. Yet this dream … it was different. He told me things, things about his family that I could have never dreamed up. In turn, I told him about my life at Charlotte's.

He had inched his way toward me little by little, until we were a mere fraction of an inch away from each other. I woke up right when his lips were brushing against mine, and the vexation I felt for not being able to finish that dream soured my stomach. I knew that falling back asleep was a lost cause, so I got up and took advantage of the bathroom before Agatha took it all for herself.

I love to take shower baths—that's when I plug the tub and let it fill up with the showerhead water instead of from the faucet—I like the feel of the water droplets on my scalp. Right now, it was helping with my headache. After a relaxing moment or two, I reached for my aromatherapy bag and took out my favorite oil— jasmine. I counted as ten drops touched the water then added five drops of mint and five of rosemary—to wake me up. After swirling the water around a few times, I sunk down in the water, leaving only my nose out to breathe. Little by little, my tight muscles relaxed and my mind started easing itself into a peaceful state.

I often use these rare quiet moments as a time for introspection. I like to look within because I always feel like part of me is missing. I keep hoping that one of these days I'll unlock the mystery within, if I look hard enough.

For example, who were my parents, and why can't I remember them? The first five years of my life have somehow been completely erased from my memory. Joe, my foster dad says that a lot of kids like me had some pretty bad experiences before being placed in foster care, and the only way they can deal with them is to block them. That must be why I remember nothing, not even what my parents look like. No one will tell me if they are even still alive or if they were bums or addicts, or just plain neglectful. I simply don't remember.

I don't even know what my racial background is, though I am pretty sure I'm Hispanic because apparently, I speak Spanish. I found this out last year during Spanish class one day. The teacher thought I was being a smart aleck when I spoke the language without even realizing it. I tried to explain to him that I didn't know I could speak Spanish, but the whole class laughed, making things worse. I got detention for that. Later I found out that Agatha had been in his class the previous hour and the teacher feared that I was a troublemaker just like her, and that's why I got the short end.

Agatha is my vile foster sister. She was already living with Charlotte and Joe when I came. At first I thought that perhaps she was mad that she had to share the limelight with me, but I quickly realized that she didn't care about that. In fact, I'm not really sure what she cares about—not people—that's for sure. She antagonizes everyone she comes in contact with, and pretty much hates everyone, except for me—she loathes me. From what I can tell, her meanness doesn't come from insecurities, nor is it a front that she puts on to keep people away. I think that she truly is cold, calculating, conniving and cruel. I see it in her eyes; she delights in the pain of others, and in her control over them. It's weird. If I didn't know her, I would be inclined to say that no one is wholly bad or good—but I do know her—and because of it, I am of the opinion that some of us may simply come into this world with pre-formed dispositions.

As a child she was curious looking, in a Gollum sort of way, with thin blond hair that laid flat against her head, and big blue eyes—too big for her face—that glared uncomfortably long at people. Now, her hair is drab and mousy looking, and though her face has balanced out some, her scowling eyes still manage to unnerve people. Her hard demeanor doesn't help make people at ease, either, but she doesn't seem to care about what others think of her. She certainly has no friends, but she doesn't seem to care.

"Dang!" The water stopped all at once and I was left sitting in a pool of lukewarm water. Joe never should have told her where the main water shut off was. He thought that Agatha was just worried about what to do in an emergency—she wasn't. She just wanted to know the quickest way to get me out of the bathroom. Before I was fully dressed, Agatha was picking the lock and barging in.

"Get out," she said dryly.

"I'm not done yet."

She came in anyway, headed straight for my aromatherapy bag, and started taking out its contents. I was in the process of making my own scented lotion by mixing the essential oils with olive oil, as my aromatherapy kit suggested. I got this kit for Christmas and I use it every day; I love the way the oils smell, so pure and uncomplicated.

"You are so weird! Why do you mix this stuff?" Agatha asked as she winced at the frankincense. "They smell awful!" She opened her hand and let the bottle drop; I caught it before it hit the ground and splattered all over.

"That's all perfume is … these scents all mixed together. I just like to mix them myself."

Agatha was picking up the patchouli and smelling it, when I noticed a small trace of ink on her forearm, like part of a tattoo. I lifted her sleeve and she jerked back. Then, she smirked and pulled up her sleeve, exposing the Wiccan symbol.

"Oh … so it's official now," I told her. I took the patchouli away from her, before she used up the whole bottle.

"Very funny! But you would make an excellent witch too. You can make the potions and I can make the spells." She opened her already large eyes even larger.

"No thanks," I told her as I gathered my stuff. "What is Charlotte going to say when she sees that?"

Agatha shrugged and looked generally uninterested. "I'll curse you if you tell her. I can do that you know," she added for good measure.

Wrapping the towel tightly around my head, I grabbed my belongings and left without saying anything else. This, I've learned, is the best way to deal with Agatha. Over time I've learned a few rules of engagement. Rule number one is to not engage her—period. Number two, if conversation can't be avoided—be short, to the point, and end it. And rule number three, don't let anything she says or does get to you, or at least don't show the fact that it got to you. Agatha's reward is the pain she sees in someone's eyes; particularly mine. It almost seems as if she was put on this Earth for the sole purpose of vexing me.

Our power struggles started the day I got to Charlotte's house and they have never stopped. It was instant enmity between us, like oil and water in a hot pan. I knew she was evil, but naïve as I was, I gave her the benefit of the doubt a few times and paid dearly each time. The last time I trusted her, I learned my lesson for good and I haven't had a slip-up since. That incident was four years ago; she volunteered to give me a pedicure. Little did I know that they made metal files! She jabbed the sharp pointy end under my toenail and to this day it looks weird. Charlotte thought it was an accident, but I never saw how she could think that, since the thing was stuck half way up my toenail!

While she's an all out tyrant at home, at school she's pretty much an angry loner who everyone avoids. I, on the other hand, have a few good friends. They are nice and pretend like I'm really part of the gang, even though I know that I am the outsider.

A foster kid is something of an anomaly. We are all part of "the system" and anyone who is part of "the system" is bound to have problems. I'm sure that my problems have to do with those missing first five years of life. There's bound to be problems lurking there that I have no conscious clue about.

My closest friend at school is Brandy. She's the youngest of the Bradford kids, Ben, Brooke and Brandy. All three are blond, beautiful and popular; except for Brandy who is too shy and too nice to play the high school games needed to get ahead in the popularity scale. Then there's Wes, our pet. I know that's rude to call him that, but he is. At least he follows us around like one. He is cute, a swimmer and a soccer player, and when he is not following us around, he is with his teammates. Wes is one of those guys who are full of energy—A.D.H.D. energy. He's smart, but aloof, and doesn't keep the fact that he has a crush on me hidden very well. Sadly I don't care for him that way. I say sadly, because my sights are set way too high on a junior named Alex Preston.

Not only does half the female student body have a crush on him as well, but he has a girlfriend—Eugenia, Genie for short. She's tall and willowy, beautiful, rich, and a total snob. She took special notice of me early on and has me on her most-wanted-for-humiliation list. Between Genie and Agatha, I get my fair share of grief. But the difference between Agatha and Genie lies in motive—Agatha has none and Genie thinks she does.

It all started my freshman year. I was late for class because I had been talking with Brandy. We had just realized that we had most of our classes together and our lockers were next to each other too. I was running down the hall and hastily turned into my Civics class, only to realize that the teacher was late too. I slowed down and breathed a sigh of relief when something made me turn my head. It was something strong, like a magnet that pulled my head to my left. That's when I first saw him. He looked up the moment I turned to face him. It felt like I had tunnel vision and I just couldn't look away, even though I knew I was staring, and that I was making a fool of myself.

Suddenly, the tunnel vision turned into something else. It was like fast-forwarding a movie—he was sitting across the room—then in an instant he was right in front of me, his lips arching into a smile, as he bent down to kiss me. It felt like a memory, an echo, and a promise. His thoughts were in my head, and as familiar to me as my own, we were thinking the same thing: *I can't wait!* We were feeling the same thing too—frustration—pure and undiluted, to the point of torment. We were eager to feel more than just emotions; we wanted to touch … to experience.

Goosebumps ran up and down my body, when my foot caught on a desk, and I tripped, effectively ending the trance. Yet the feeling remained as I bit my lip to keep from screaming, not so much in pain, as exasperation over the loss of that moment.

He stood up suddenly, making his chair screech loudly. Fortunately, I regained my balance before I landed on my face. He asked me if I was all right and I nodded numbly. Then I took the first empty seat I could find and tried to regain my composure. I didn't dare turn my head to see him again. I was still reeling in from whatever that was, when, to my infinite aggravation, Agatha walked into the classroom. When she saw me she sneered and made sure she knocked me on the head with her backpack as she passed me.

"You are in my seat, pizza face!" she snarled to a shy girl that was sitting in the back of the room. Then she grabbed the girl's backpack and threw it toward the front of the classroom. The girl got up to retrieve her bag and Agatha sat down in her seat with a snigger. I got up too, and picked up the girl's bag for her.

"Here, you can have my seat," I mumbled apologetically. The girl nodded and her eyes welled up with tears. I shot Agatha a dirty look. She was such a beast! As I looked around for another seat, I noticed that Alex was on his feet, this time for real, holding the back of a chair that was near him. He tried to look casual, but I could tell that he was pleased with me. I tried to not stare as I walked to his side, but it was inevitable and I couldn't get my eyes to obey.

For the rest of the year we kept the same seats, and Alex made sure he had a foot or a hand on that same seat, so that no one else would take it. Rumors of this got around to Genie, and that's when I became her favorite joke. I was, after all, perfect for that—poor, unassuming, a foster kid with a disputable past, who lived with Agatha, of all people, in a rundown old house on the wrong side of town.

Genie never really worried me though; I could read her like an open book. I could read most people, but she was particularly easy. She shone with seething jealousy and insecurity—dark green and murky red. To think that she would see *me* as a threat to her relationship was ludicrous and somewhat flattering. Far from making me feel bad, her taunts led me to believe that perhaps she did have something to worry about. But if she did, Alex never mentioned it to me. We spent the rest of the year in that class and he never said more than two words to me.

This year has been no different, with the exception that his locker was next to Brandy's and mine. I have enjoyed looking at his face almost every day, and this has been the highlight of my days— my life, really. Our conversations have now grown to include a nod, a hello or a good-bye.

Half the girls in my school belong to the Ben Bradford fan club, Brandy's brother, and the other half to the Alex Preston fan club. Brandy knows that I belong to the latter, and regularly elbows me in the ribs when he notices me. We giggle, and sigh, and daydream that perhaps one day Alex will be available and out of Genie's hypnotic control. But last night's dream was no daydream. This dream was unlike anything else I've ever experienced. It was vivid and life-like. I could have sworn that I was really having a conversation with Alex Preston. On my rooftop, all night long.

Chapter 2

I felt odd at school all day, like I was under a spell of sorts. I found it hard to focus in class and felt tired; the kind of tired that you feel in your chest and makes your legs feel like lead.

At lunchtime, I found my locker surrounded by people. Wes and his friends were talking with Brandy, and Alex was there too, talking with his pals. I squared my shoulders and took a deep breath as I walked right in between them to reach my locker. None of Alex's friends took notice of me, but Alex did. I could feel his gaze burrowing a trail of heat into the side of my face. I could feel a red streak rising from the base of my neck to the top of my ears. It touched my cheeks until they were so red that I felt like I was suffocating. I tried to focus on my lock's combination, but I kept messing up and having to start over. "Get a grip!" I muttered through clenched teeth. He did vexing things like this sometimes, and I couldn't help wonder if he did them out of sport or actual interest.

Wes shoved me slightly in a form of greeting, but being shaky already, I lost my balance. Alex caught me before I hit the ground and his proximity gave me hot chills—if that was possible.

"Thanks," I mumbled.

"No problem." His voice sent new chills through my body and I shivered. This amused him and I felt him smile. I shot him an exasperated look as I straightened out and smoothed my crumpled shirt.

"Oh! If it isn't Foster Freak!" Genie taunted as she approached the scene with her pack of cheerleaders in stilettos. "Where do you shop, Foster-Care? I think my dad wore that shirt in the seventies!" she taunted, and draped herself over Alex's shoulders, fumigating the area with her designer perfume. The smell was so strong that I couldn't help cough a few times as the fumes went straight to my head, accentuating my already existing headache.

"Don't listen to her Tess!" Brooke, Brandy's sister, who was part of the Genie pack, stepped forward. "Besides, retro is coming back," she added, then rolled her eyes, knowing that she had made it worse for me. At this comment, Genie broke out into an exaggerated laugh. Brooke was actually pretty decent. She usually tried to take my side, but I think it was mostly because her sister hung around with me.

I winced at the pain in my head, and felt Alex's reassuring hand on my shoulder. "Are you sure you're okay? You look a bit pale." His eyes looked genuinely concerned and something else … not sure what, but I could swear that he was trying to convey something to me, but I just couldn't fathom what.

"I'm fine! I'm just allergic to insecure cheerleaders."

Alex chuckled, and noticing this, Genie stopped her forced laughter abruptly and zeroed in on me. "What did you say, you little …"

"Genie! How old are you?" Alex scolded and turned her by the shoulders and pushed her down the hall. Before following her crowd, Brooke mouthed an apology to me and smiled at her sister.

"Wow! They really have it out for you, don't they? What did you ever do to get on her bad side?" Wes commented.

"Nothing," Brandy said defensively. "Genie is a jerk and that's all there is to it! She looked back at the direction the popular pack was going. "Like it's Tess' fault she's in foster care!"

With my back against my locker, I slid all the way to the ground and ripped a bite out of my sandwich. The little group that surrounded me joined me on the floor where we ended up having our lunch. Their lively conversations didn't interest me today; my mind was still caught up in that dream.

In the fall I had tried out for the swim team and made it. Wes and I have practice together every day after school and then his mom gives me a ride home. Swimming always clears my head. I love it! I had never had any formal instruction before, so when I tried out, I didn't even know if I could make it to the other end of the pool, but I did. One could say I took to swimming like a fish to water. It felt natural and I always feel better after a good practice. Sometimes I think through problems and some other times I just let my mind go blank; it almost feels as if my brain goes to sleep for the hour of practice.

It was no different today. As I swam I let all my frustrations out in the water and they melted away in the wake of my kicks.

When I got home I felt serene again and ready to face the dread that is life at Charlotte's. But as I entered my room I found a brand new problem sprawled on the floor. Dorian was on the floor, crying. Not wailing like when he has a fit, but weeping, the most pitiful and sad cry I had ever heard. In the eight years that I've known him, I've never seen him cry. He has thrown fits and screamed so much that he's passed out from sheer exhaustion, but he's never cried.

Dropping my bag on the floor, I rushed to his side and wrapped my arms around him. Immediately I was flooded with his emotions. I could feel his pain so keenly that it almost overwhelmed me. I don't know why, but I can sense what other people feel, almost to the point that I feel it myself. This time though … I didn't need to have empathy to know what this felt like. In fact, his grief overwhelmed me because I could relate. I've often felt the same way. His anguish though, was far deeper than mine and compounded by his knowledge of his limitations and his disability. I could express myself—he couldn't.

Dorian is autistic and savant. He hardly ever talks and often has tantrums, though they seem to be getting less frequent as he grows up. He's a year younger than me and came to live with us just two years after I got here. I share a room with him, much against all state regulations, but there was no other way … so Charlotte relented. She didn't want to send Dorian back, because children with special needs bring in more money—and Charlotte is in it for the money. She's open about this with us, but would kill us if we told anyone.

Dorian's first day with us was very interesting. At the time, I was sharing this room with Agatha, and Dorian was going to get the recently vacated bedroom. But Dorian would have nothing to do with that room; he clawed and screamed until he passed out from the exertion. He wouldn't go to anybody or let anyone come near him—except for me.

When he first saw Agatha, his eyes grew big with fear and he took refuge behind me. I thought he showed excellent judgment, but Charlotte saw it as him being difficult, and declared him "the hardest money ever earned." Then she confirmed herself a saint for taking on such children, and left me to handle the situation.

Agatha loved being feared. It always encouraged her when she saw fear in someone's eyes. She tried to torment Dorian by coming closer to me, with hands in clawing shape and teeth bared, while emitting a low growl. Dorian whimpered like a wounded animal. This made my blood boil, so from that moment, I took it upon myself to protect him from Agatha. I feel it's my duty because I know her way of thinking and for some strange reason, I feel uniquely qualified to deal with her.

By nature, I'm not violent, but when she was in range I lifted one of my legs up and with the base of my foot I pushed her as hard as I could on the stomach. As she was going down, I grabbed Dorian's hand and his little bag and barricaded us both in my bedroom. Agatha pounded on the door until Charlotte could bear the noise no more and had to get involved. On seeing that Dorian was determined to stay with me and in this room only, she made Agatha take the spare room. Dorian and I have been here ever since.

"If you two insist on being together, then—then—I make you personally responsible for him. *You* keep him out of trouble!" Charlotte shouted, as if any of it was my fault. So from that day on, Charlotte relinquished all responsibility of Dorian to me—then a seven year old—and has basked in the warm glow of sainthood ever since.

The room Dorian and I share is the smallest and the most uncomfortable room in the house. It's like a little attic that has been transformed into a bedroom, just so Charlotte could fit more kids in the house and run her "Foster Care" business. But Dorian and I like the room; it has some perks that can't be denied. It's secluded and has a tiny window that looks out onto the roof of the wrap-around porch, where Dorian and I like to sit and hang out…and where Alex visited me last night…in my dream.

Dorian doesn't let anyone touch him but me, and he's not very talkative. He expresses himself through his drawings, which are highly detailed renditions of things or people he has either only seen once or never seen at all. He only draws with No. 2 pencils and crisp, white, unused, Hammermill copy paper that he carries around everywhere he goes. He is black, tall for his age, skinny, and has been bounced around from foster home to foster home since he was a baby, this being the longest home he's been in his whole life.

On the floor, he rocked his body back and forth rhythmically as he often did when having one of his fits. But this one, I could tell was different. He seemed beaten. His hands were covering his face, and a gray shroud surrounded him. I tried to lift his head, but he wouldn't let me see him.

With effort, I pulled him to my chest and held him tight, rocking along with him. As I did all this, I felt like I was in a movie, when they move in slow motion. Everything around me felt strangely familiar. I felt destined for this moment, and I knew what would happen next as if I had done this very same thing in another life.

"I'll always take care of you," I told him, and as I was saying those words I felt an echo within me. Like déjà vu, but different.

I knew the cause of this breakdown; it was long coming. He had borne the burden of loneliness far too long, and today ... he met his quota. Like me, he had no family. Like me, he got no love, and like me, he was all alone in this world. That is an overwhelming feeling for anyone—and much greater for a kid like him.

Hot tears sprung to my own eyes as I held him; I could feel his pain, my pain...our pain. We were all alone, and in less than three years I would be turned out of this house and I would have to fend for myself for the rest of my life. I didn't have relatives waiting for me. I didn't have friends that had promised to help me out—I had nothing, and neither did he. What would become of me? What would become of Dorian? What would become of us?

My heart filled with love toward him, sisterly and maternal love all at once. I realized that he was the only person in the world that I loved like family. This caused some more tears to fall, as I understood the full significance of it. Then it hit me! I guess they call it an epiphany—when you realize something all at once. *I* was his family and *I* would take care of him. But to accomplish this, I would have to sacrifice all the normal teenage games, dramas, and dreams.

The thought sobered me and my tears dried up. My breathing became steady and filled with determination. I could see a path forming before me, a path that did not include parties and proms; but study and preparation. I would have to be ready for the realities that would greet Dorian and me right after high school. I had no money for college, so I would need to get scholarships and a few loans too. I had no idea how I would accomplish all of this, but I would have to find out, and quickly. All of a sudden, I realized that three years might not be enough time, but that was all I had, because once I turned eighteen I would be homeless … me … homeless.

The image of being a vagrant in rags filled me with a stubborn determination to do all in my power to become a successful person and to provide for us. His past might have been miserable, and so might his present, but his future would not be—not if I could help it!

Once the resolution was made, the trance I was in ended. The path had been shown to me. Now it was up to me to put it into effect.

During History, Brandy and I had braided friendship bracelets. We had made enough to supply the whole school with one, but I only kept two, and they were identical. I grabbed the bracelets out of my backpack and put one in Dorian's hand.

"I want you to take this. It is a sister bracelet, I have a brother bracelet—see?" I showed him the other bracelet as I slipped it onto my wrist. "This means we are family and that we're not alone. You'll come and live with me when you turn eighteen and we'll be a family, okay?" He nodded in response.

I held him until his sobs subsided, then we crawled out the window and sat in our spot on the roof. Winter was ending and the crisp night had a warm spring breeze blowing our way. Tonight we were rewarded not only with a clear star-filled sky, but with one of those huge, full, Texas moons as well. I set us up with all the necessary items: my homework, his pencils, paper, and the radio—tuned to his favorite radio station. Dorian refused to listen to any type of music other than classical, so that's what we listened to every night.

In silence we listened to the fluid sounds of Copeland's Appalachian Spring—fitting for this time of year. Dorian seemed satisfied by my earlier proposition, but now I was anxious. I had made him a promise, and now, I had to fulfill it!

He looked more at ease, as his No. 2 pencil moved fast across the page. He was lost in a world of his own, his tongue stuck out of the corner of his mouth, and his eyes were moving almost as fast as his hand. I looked at my books and picked them up with a new respect. From now on, these books would be my life. No more foolish dreams of Alex, no more friendship bracelets, no more fun. I had a full ride scholarship to get and I only had two years and four months to get it.

The rest of my sophomore year ended quite uneventfully. I did manage to get my grades up, and finished with a sparkling 4.0! I also did fairly well in swimming, which only meant longer practices for me next year. This made Wes extremely happy, since he had improved his times as well. It was with great pride that he told me that he would drive me home after practice next year, because by then he would have his license.

While he walked me home from swimming, he talked my ear off about his dilemma between soccer and swimming. Apparently he had to choose one or the other and was at a crossroads. I listened, not so much attentively as obligingly, to his plight. It seemed somehow ridiculous to me now, that such a thing would bring so much distress to his life. …But I guess that's what normal teenagers worry about. His plight only made me feel more distant from him and my peers, but of course, I couldn't tell him that.

Whenever possible I tried to keep my foster life and my school life separate, not out of shame, but sanity. Besides, I knew that the realities of my life would shock them and would cause them to pity me. I knew their lives were not perfect, but they were a marked improvement over mine.

Wes goes home every day to a house full of boys, where the dad coaches the many Little League teams and the mom provides large amounts of food to keep her boys happily buzzing around her kitchen. Brandy goes home to a large house, plays tennis with her mom on their backyard court, and eats organic tofu for dinner.

I on the other hand, ride the bus to Charlotte's, with Agatha tormenting me the whole way. Then I do my laundry, clean the bathrooms and the kitchen, and cook Hamburger Helper for dinner, all while trying to ignore Agatha's snide remarks and purposeful hindrances to my cleaning efforts, just to get me in trouble with Charlotte.

None of my friends from school would ever imagine what the intricacies of living with Agatha are. At school no one likes her and she is a loner, her mousy blond hair is always dirty, and she never, ever smiles. At home, however, she is a tyrant. She ruins, steals, or vandalizes anything that she can get her hands on. I have learned to keep careful track of all my belongings and have them under lock and key. I have to hastily do my and Dorian's laundry so that Agatha doesn't put bleach or something in with our wash to ruin it. I also have to keep her physically away from Dorian, because he is an easy target for her.

On the dining room wall, Charlotte has an impressive chore chart that she proudly displays, but which is completely ignored by Agatha. Charlotte is afraid to confront her on this score so somehow I have been stuck with all her chores as well. Dinner has always been my job, ever since, well … ever since Agatha laced our food with laxatives and other things that have made us sick. So Dorian and I cover the chore chart, while Agatha walks around and messes things up on purpose.

This is my world, and I can't be blamed for keeping it from my friends. They wouldn't understand it. They would feel sorry for me, then they would treat me differently and I'm already different enough. School is my only link to the real world and if I want to have some semblance of a normal teenage life, I need to keep the two worlds separate.

Sometimes, though, the two worlds collide. Earlier this year, Brandy and I were having lunch by our lockers—we hated the cafeteria because it smelled funny—and I had noticed that down the hall, a new group of girls had started gathering there for lunch as well. One of them was a huge girl named Amanda, who didn't just act like a pig, but was one in a previous life. She wasn't just big, she was buff too, and most likely stronger than half the football team.

I saw Agatha pass by with her usual scowl on her face. I ignored her, as always, but then I looked up with a jerk. I had that odd feeling I got now and then, like déjà vu on steroids. I looked down the hall and I noticed that Amanda was looking like a bull about to charge; only Agatha didn't see it.

I've never been too concerned about Agatha's safety, but I couldn't stop myself. The whole scene seemed strangely familiar to me, as if I had seen the whole thing before in a movie, and my feet seemed to be moving without my conscious permission. Still, I was too late. As Agatha walked by Amanda, the latter stuck her arm out and Agatha got knocked to the ground, hitting the floor hard.

Several students let out a groan at the sound of Agatha's head hitting the floor. Agatha was down and not moving. I didn't know what to say or do, yet my legs rushed me to the scene. Amanda had her back turned to me, so I tapped her on the shoulder. She turned around and when she saw me, she cocked her head to one side and zeroed in on me as her next victim.

On the floor, Agatha was now regaining consciousness. When she saw Amanda, she sprung to her feet with the agility of a cheetah, and leapt on to Amanda's back, knocking her off balance. Some teachers came to break up the fight and I backed away, glad that I didn't have to take one for Agatha, of all people.

When I got back to my lunch spot, Brandy was beside herself. She couldn't understand why I had to get involved; I could've been hurt! Not to mention, all for Agatha? This was one of those few times where my two worlds collided—my odd home-life, filled with unexplainable phenomena—and my normal school life. I couldn't explain exactly why I did it, why I felt like I was destined to be there, to live through that event … or re-live it. I simply couldn't explain it, because I couldn't understand it myself. So I just shrugged, and no doubt Brandy thinks me odd for it.

Chapter 3

A friendship between Agatha and Amanda ensued from that fight—a strange and parasitical friendship. I'm still not too clear on the details, but from that day on, Amanda has come to Charlotte's often, and grunts a greeting at me, like a trained dog. And since summer started, she comes by a lot more often.

I hate summers! All summertime means to me is house arrest, or rather, room arrest. The TV is always monopolized by Charlotte during the day or by Joe when he gets home from one of his two jobs. Poor Joe. I actually really like him. He is a sweet simple man who works as a security guard and a janitor for a big office building downtown. He's like a big teddy bear, loyal and kind, and bends over backwards to provide for Charlotte, but she doesn't appreciate him. All she ever does is complain about how ugly their house is and how she has to put up with all these brats because of him. Joe ignores her insults and shoots apologetic glances in my direction. He has a way of seeing the good in others, though he often struggles for good adjectives when it comes to Agatha.

My summers usually consist of chores, reading, and trips to the air-conditioned library. This summer will be no different, I expect.

"I found a job for you!" Charlotte announced as she barged into my room. She was grinning from ear to ear. "The Anderson's both work and have four children. I was talking to Gwen Anderson at the Salon, and she was telling me how expensive day care is, so I told her you would watch the kids! You'll get paid of course."

My jaw almost dislocated, it fell open so wide. Those kids are hellions!

"Now, I know I should have asked you first, but I know how bored you get. Besides, they live just down the street from that fancy Sports Club with the water slides; she said that you would have to take the kids there once a day because they have swimming lessons there. You'll have access to the pool and I know how you love to swim!" she added with a perky tone.

"Come on Tess; don't look at me like that," she scolded. "It's about time you earned some money. Why, when I was your age, I bought all my own clothes!"

Oh … so that's the real issue here! If Charlotte was anything, she was frugal. It wasn't my boredom that she was worried about; it was the expense of my school clothes! I didn't bother asking her if she had found a job for Agatha as well, I knew the answer to that. Agatha would laugh in her face if Charlotte told her to get a job.

"O.K. Charlotte, I'll take the job. Does this mean I pay for all my school clothes this fall?" I said, without the slightest hint of an attitude. But she narrowed her eyes and shot me a venomous look.

"You ungrateful little—. See if I help you out anymore!" She stormed out, and slammed the door so hard a picture fell and broke.

I laughed somewhat cynically, and then went back to taking mental refuge in my current read *Persuasion,* by Jane Austen.

I was no Mary Poppins, and the Anderson kids were no angels, but we did get used to each other and, toward the end of the summer, we did become friends. Going to the gym every day was what saved me. They offered free childcare for two hours every day, and I took full advantage of it. So, while the older kids had their swimming lessons, and the gym's day care staff was watching the younger kids, I worked out, swam, and read.

"*Great Expectations*? I don't think I've read that one, is it any good?"

My heart got lodged in my throat when I heard that voice. I didn't lower the book right away because I was sure my face was bright red. I gulped in some air and tried to steady my breathing before I casually let the book drop.

"You would love it!" I said, trying to sound confident. Alex was standing in my sun, but he emanated his own light, so I still had to shield my eyes.

"Maybe I'll read that next," he said, with a casual smile.

The glare was so blinding, I had to squint as he sat down at the end of my lawn chair. My heart was beating wildly, as it was always this way when he got near me, or when I saw him from a distance, or when I thought about him, or—it was always this way where Alex was concerned. And now … here he was, sitting on my lawn chair, wearing a smile, a tan and a Rip Curl swim suit!

"How's your summer been so far?" he asked as he casually moved one arm over my legs and leaned into it.

I swallowed the lump in my throat and tried to verbalize my summer, but it came out disjointed. "I—I've been working." I stammered.

"Oh yeah, where at?"

"Charlotte got me a job as a nanny for a family she knows."

"Oh …" he looked around for evidence.

"The two oldest are over there," I signaled to two children having a lesson. "The other two are in the play area, and I am on a lunch break." I smiled.

"Good! You deserve one, I'm sure." He blinked and I noticed how bleached his eyelashes had gotten with the sun.

"So what have you been doing?" I asked in what I hoped would be a casual confident voice.

"Oh…" he looked sheepishly down at his feet. "Nothing much…"

I raised my eyebrows and he smiled, dimples forming as he did so.

"I've been sailing with my grandfather," he admitted, and now I knew why he was embarrassed. It wasn't the fact that he was spending time with his grandpa that embarrassed him; it was the sailing part. He didn't want to sound like a snob. Somehow, he knew my life sucked and was sensitive about it.

How did I know this? I don't know, but I was sure of it. In fact most times people don't have to explain themselves to me; I understand them—unless they purposely try to hide something, and even then I know that they are hiding something.

"That sounds so fun!" I remarked cheerfully, making sure he knew I was happy for him. "Someday I'd like to go to the ocean."

"You've never been to the ocean?"

"No."

His eyes grew big and amazed; he couldn't fathom someone not seeing the ocean before. "Haven't Charlotte and Joe ever gone to Galveston or something?"

How did he know about Charlotte and Joe? "They have. I'm sure, but as a foster child, I can't leave the county." I said matter-of-fact.

His mouth fell open. "Are you serious? The county?"

I nodded and felt worse for him than I did for me. "It's okay. In two years I'll be eighteen and I'll leave the county for sure," I explained. Then I saw Genie's gym-fit figure looming behind him. Her friends surrounded her. They were all wearing skimpy bikinis and she was sporting shiny belly ring. They told Alex that they couldn't play volleyball without him and to hurry up. He turned back to me and as he straightened up he let his hand rest on my foot. He made the tiniest stroking movement on the bridge of my foot, toward my ankle, before he lifted his hand and got up to leave. Instinctively my heart skipped a beat and my stomach filled with butterflies.

"Hope to see you again soon!" he said before he left. I waved at him, fully ignoring Genie's murderous glare.

That night I had another one of those dreams. Alex was standing on the deck of a sailboat about twenty-five feet long. The boat was in good shape, but it looked older, like it had been well used for a few decades. He was fumbling with some ropes but when he saw me, he brightened up and motioned for me to join him.

I floated toward him, propelled by my own desire to be near him.

"Welcome to The Odysseus! And welcome to the Gulf of Mexico!" he said, extending his arms wide.

I took a moment to look all around me and saw the ocean for the first time. The place was strange to me; I had never been here before and had no recollection of ever seeing pictures of this particular spot, so I was shocked by how many details my mind was giving me. Could it be that I had been here with my parents, and I just didn't remember? Dreams were after all, figments of our subconscious mind.

"So this is where you spend your summers?"

"This is where my summers begin. There—" he pointed to open ocean, *"is where I spend my summers."*

"Where do you go?"

"Mexico, the Caribbean islands, Jamaica and when I graduate, we're going all the way to Brazil!"

"Are you serious? Isn't that a little scary? I mean ... what if you get stranded? What if you run out of food or water? What if a storm came? What—" He interrupted me by standing in front of me and pulling a long strand of hair away from my shoulders. This simple movement on his part rendered me completely awestruck and mute.

"It's no scarier than driving down the freeway during rush hour, and no worse than being stranded in Amarillo without food or water in the middle of a dust storm!" he smiled wryly. I narrowed my eyes in reply and he insisted on disarming me by moving his hands down my neck to my shoulders.

"If only this were real," I sighed.

A look of frustration that mirrored mine crossed his face before he dropped his gaze, and without saying anything else, started the motor. *"Where do you want to go?"*

"Hmm ... are you allowed to cross the Atlantic?"

"In real life? No. But in dreams ... we can go anywhere in our dreams, right?"

"Right," I smiled and sat down next to him as he steered the boat out of the marina. *"What else would you do? If you could do anything you wanted to."*

"Fly. I would want to fly. Not just to get places, I would rather sail for that. But I would fly just for the experience of flying."

"I flew to your boat just now."

"Yeah ... you did!" His eyes narrowed and he pursed up lips as if he were concocting some plan. *"Let's do it! Let's fly!"* He grabbed my hand and pulled me straight up. We flew over the ocean, hand-in-hand, sometimes high up and through the clouds and

then down, and almost flush with the surface of the water. At one point, I told him that I always wanted to go deep sea diving, so we submerged ourselves below. But right as we were about to reach the bottom, a strange ringing sound startled us. We looked at each other, perplexed—then, just like that he vanished. My eyes opened once more to the cruel reality of my bedroom, and another day of babysitting.

That fall Charlotte made good on the promise to let me buy my own clothes. Part of me was glad, because I thought I would be able to afford to go to an actual store and not the nearest thrift store. But I soon realized that if I wanted to save for a mode of transportation that would liberate me from the bus, my meager earnings would not be enough to buy me new clothes to last the entire school year.

This was not all together a bad thing for me, because while I tried to do my best with second hand clothes, I discovered something new—my own style. I'm not quite sure how it all happened, but as I was making my rounds at the thrift store, I started seeing how I could alter the clothes to make better outfits out of them.

"Charlotte?"

"What!" She snarled, thinking that I was going to ask her to buy me something.

"Do you have a sewing machine?"

She looked at me blinking for a while. I wasn't sure if her fake eyelashes were loose or if she was trying to process my question.

"I do," she said curtly.

"May I borrow it?"

"What for? You don't know how to use it," she said, turning back to the racks.

"It has instructions, doesn't it?"

"You'll get yourself hurt, and then you'll come crying to me."

"If I get hurt I promise not to come crying to you," I said, without an attitude, but she didn't buy it.

"You'll break it," she insisted.

"If I break it, I'll get it fixed."

"What do you want with it anyway?"

"I want to make alterations."

She inspected the basket full of clothes I had with one raised eyebrow, and then grunted "Fine."

Charlotte was a curious creature; she was almost six feet tall and very fleshy. I say fleshy because, though overweight, she still had a shapely figure, which she brazenly flaunted. She wore tights in winter with short skirts that barely covered her bottom. In the summer she dispense with the tights, which was even more unsettling. Her shirts were always V-neck and showed vast amounts of cleavage.

She usually wore her hair slicked back in a ponytail, and attached a different hairpiece end to it every day. Sometimes it was a long, shiny, blond tail, while some other days it was a smooth chignon twist. Recently she had purchased some of those messy looking knots, with strands of straight hair poking out in every direction. Occasionally, she would wear her natural hair down, and though thin and scanty, she would style those few hairs with obsession. She always wore too much eye makeup and perfume, and her fake square nails tips were as ever changing as her fake hair.

While my own physical appearance remained pretty much the same—straight, long, almost black hair—with no variation to it other than the occasional difference in how I parted it, Agatha went through an all-out metamorphosis. It started slowly at first, but it has escalated to the point that she has become a different creature. To start with, she spent the summer indoors, getting paler and gaunter looking than usual. Then, she and Amanda made some interesting new friends, with whom she only associated after dark. One day she came home with her lower lip pierced and her nose pierced. Charlotte and Joe almost had a heart attack, but there was nothing they could say or do. A week later, she came home with a blunt, uneven haircut and jet-black hair. Then she made a large investment in makeup. This would have been a joyous moment for Charlotte, except for the color—all of it was black—with the exclusion of a blood red liner that she sometimes used to underline her eyes.

Presently, she was walking the rows of the thrift store, knocking down hangers that held anything pink or yellow, and taking only the black or gray items. Charlotte didn't like confrontations with Agatha, so she said nothing and paid for the clothes.

I worked tirelessly on my experimental wardrobe; I made some mistakes, but nothing that couldn't be fixed. I realized that I had a knack for this type of thing, and couldn't wait to show off my new creations.

When school started, I displayed my best outfits first, and Brandy was very impressed. Soon, I gained a solid reputation for being fashionable and every now and then, I found a girl copying some accessory of my invention. This pleased me greatly, and only fueled my passion for my newfound pastime.

Meanwhile, the year passed as normally as it could. I got out of bed every day, simply because I knew I would see Alex at school. I swam every day, I studied every evening and spent my weekends at the sewing machine disassembling old clothes and reassembling them into cool new stuff. I also signed up for a sewing class at school and learned to read patterns for dresses, skirts and pants.

The only distressing thing in my life was Wes. He was hell-bent on taking me out, and I could not, in good conscience do it. I discussed this with Brandy and she couldn't understand why I didn't like him. Wes was a cute guy, with curly dark brown hair that was stylishly long, past his ears. He had brown, puppy dog eyes and an easy smile. But my heart just wasn't in it; my heart was fully vested in a fantasy. I felt silly, of course. I didn't have a chance in a million with Alex, but I stubbornly held out hope. To add insult to injury, one day, while I was making an exchange of books at my locker, I managed to make things worse—if they ever were better between Alex and I.

Genie and a few of her friends were surrounding Alex, who

was at his locker. They were making fun of him, saying how predictable he was and how he always ordered the same thing at lunch. Then they rattled off the things that he would order at the different restaurants they frequented. At this restaurant, he would always order this, and at that restaurant, he would always order that.

I let a glance slip toward him, and he gave me a fleeting look in reply. In that brief look I could sense the dread and annoyance he felt right then. Perversely, I was happy about this.

"I've known Alex since we were kids, and he is an open book. He couldn't surprise me if he tried." Genie winked cockily at Alex, then directed a smug look in my direction.

"There are things you don't know about me, Genie, trust me," he murmured soberly.

"Oh yeah, like what? Let me guess … you want to sail around the world?"

"He wants to fly around the world," I mumbled under my breath, but somehow, I was heard and all eyes turned on me, Alex's included. But his look was not what I expected; he looked shocked and guarded. I shrugged and made a hopeless grimace. I left amid a chorus of laughter from Eugenia and her cronies, my face burning with shame.

"Sailing, flying, and deep sea diving with Alex—dream. School—real life," I repeated to myself with reproach. *"Please keep those two straight, or you'll look insane!"* I thought, while in the distance I could still hear Genie's forced laughter over my unsolicited, ridiculous comment.

Chapter 4

As I stood in the pouring rain and stared into the empty parking lot I could think of nothing but my own idiocy. How could I have forgotten that Wes could not give me a ride tonight? How could it have slipped my mind all together until this very moment … when it was infinitely too late? After a meet, I usually get a ride home with Wes, but earlier in the week he had told me that he wouldn't be able to this time.

The whole place had cleared out faster than I could have imagined; and I was left standing alone in the shadows of the parking lot as the last of the staff closed up the building. I felt dumb asking them for a ride, so I ventured out and started walking, not too sure where I was headed. As my luck would have it, it started to rain—not just a little, a lot—in sheets, like a waterfall. I was soaked in minutes and felt as awful as I looked. I walked in the direction where the most streetlights were and regretted not asking someone for a ride. What was wrong with me? Why did I just let a building full of people leave me stranded here?

I had no idea how to get home. Calling Charlotte at this point would be suicidal, but so would be to venture these unknown streets on my own. I had no idea where I was, and as terrible as I am with directions, I had no idea how to tell her to get here. She would have to look up on the website to see where tonight's meet was and she would not be happy about having to go this extra mile for me.

Under the merciless rain, I got to the intersection and looked both ways. This part of town looked like an industrial area with large parking lots and no people. In the distance I could see the lights of a gas station, so I took off running toward it. Once inside, I asked for the phone. The attendant looked at me narrowly, sizing me up in an unsettling manner. I dialed, the phone rang and Agatha answered. I told her to put Charlotte on the phone but she said that Charlotte was out and then hung up.

"Can I make another call?" I asked the attendant, who was

blatantly staring and swishing a wad of tobacco from one side of his bottom lip to the other. The glint in his eyes made me feel uneasy, so I did my best to not look so pathetic and tried to appear to be in control.

"This ain't prison," he responded as he spit some tobacco in a cup. He wiped a trickle of dark spit from his chin with the back of his hand.

I stared at him uncomprehendingly.

"You get more than one call—provided it be local," he added and grinned, exposing his slimy yellow teeth with bits of chew stuck to them.

I called again, but this time the phone rang and rang with no answer so I knew that Agatha must have disconnected the jack. I stopped trying that venue, and tried Joe's cell phone instead, but it went to voicemail. At night he worked as a janitor for some office buildings downtown, and would, most likely not hear me over the noise of his vacuum.

As I started out of the gas station, the guy working there asked me if I needed anything else. I told him I didn't, and walked away. A shiver went through me as I stepped back out into the rain. I debated going back in, but I could feel the attendant's eyes still trained on me, making me uncomfortable. However, the lonely street and the zooming cars didn't seem to offer any more comfort. This was indeed a pickle if I'd ever been in one. No. A pickle would have been earlier, at the aquatic center, while there were normal people around. This was no longer a pickle, or a jam, or even a quandary. This was a real life and death situation that I couldn't fix on my own.

As I let this last thought sink in, a tear slid down my wet cheek. I started to get cold, and felt attacked by all kinds of fears and what if's. Would I become another picture on a mailer of missing and abducted children? Who would turn Heaven and Hell to find me? Who would hang pictures of me in the streets and who would insist on talking to the media, offering a reward for me? No one. Right then an unspeakable feeling of worthlessness invaded me, followed by the miserable thought that always lingered in the back of my mind—that I was all alone and no one cared for me. Anguish ripped through my frame and I started to shake uncontrollably, but I walked on. In the distance I saw a bus bench. I walked toward it, and as I did so, I once again entered one of those weird reveries of mine.

I walked and shivered, as if I were in a dream. Part of me felt detached, and part of me was still very aware of my perilous situation, but I felt destined for this. Was this to be a turning point in my life?

My tears were now mingled with the rain. I was soaked, cold, and shaking so much that my muscles ached. The rain was loud, but I could swear I heard whispers. I turned and saw nothing. I reached the bus bench, sat down listlessly, pulled my legs up to my chest and wept bitterly. Cars drove by, and I felt like they were slowing down to look at me. I didn't want to think of what could happen to me if someone… Instead I cried, even harder, giving full sway to my wretchedness and the flood of emotions I held inside. It was now my turn to have a meltdown; unfortunately Dorian was not here to help me out.

I was glad that the pelting of the rain was loud and covered up my wailing; yet now and then I could swear that I heard zooming sounds … or voices—not loud—more like hisses and murmurs. I turned around and found no one there. "No … " I groaned, "not those voices! I can't hear those voices!" I was either crazy or highly imaginative, but every now and then, I'd swear I heard voices. Not in my head, but real audible murmurs that whizzed past me like a gust of wind.

In my anguish and fear, my thoughts oddly turned to Alex. I'm not sure why or what exactly I thought about; I just thought of him and a pleading escaped my lips. "Help me, please!"

A low cloud clung to the ground, and stayed there disturbed only by the sporadic passing cars. *"Tessss … sss … Tesss … "* I turned again, recognizing the fact that this time I heard my name, and still nothing—or rather, no one was there. My skin bristled and an awful empty feeling gripped my stomach. I couldn't stop the shaking, and my teeth clattered in spite of my efforts to stop them.

Help of the helpless, Lord, abide with me ... The words from the hymn that was sung at Charlotte's church came to mind. I repeated that verse over and over in my head like a prayer—hoping to get rid of that awful taunting feeling—but instead it laughed. I rocked back and forth in the fetal position like Dorian and the hiss mocked me, and reaffirmed my misgivings about my situation.

Behind my closed eyelids I could see the glare of a car's high beams. Several cars had driven by, but this one stopped. My heart started pounding even faster. I shook from head to foot and I could feel a fruitless scream building up inside of me, one that I would let out, but would go unheard. I didn't want to see who it was; I wanted to pretend that this was not happening, that it was all a nightmare. I tried not to think of what would happen to me now; I tried to ignore the voices, but they got louder and louder. Soon I'd be forgotten and become a sad statistic. How long will the nightmare take? I would have to run for it. *"That's my last recourse,"* I thought.

"Tess?"

I heard his voice but I thought my mind was playing tricks on me, so I didn't answer. Instead I kept rocking back and forth, like Dorian does. *"Runnn ..."* the vicious hiss sounded in my ear. I thought perhaps I should do just that, but I couldn't get my legs to move. Then I heard a car door slam and the roar of an idle engine, then footsteps coming closer. I instinctively jerked back when I felt a human presence near me.

"Tess ... it's me, Alex."

"Run, Tesss ... run!" the taunting voice dared me. But instead of listening to it, I raised my head up above my knees just enough to see who was in front of me, and I saw him. It was really him in the flesh, standing there with an outstretched hand! Without thinking twice I threw myself into his chest, and wrapped my arms around his neck. He held me tight and tried to soothe me. After a few minutes, he gently pulled my hair back and pressed his cheek against mine. "You're Okay, Tess ... you are safe now," he whispered in my ear and stroked my hair.

Slowly I stopped shaking and I willed my jaw to relax. He

scooped me up like a baby and carried me to his car. I didn't want to release him, but I had to in order to get into his Jeep. I was still shivering and tears still streamed down my face. I didn't want to look into his eyes for fear of crying some more, but I knew that he was inspecting me, looking for outward signs of abuse.

"What are you doing here, Tess?" he asked with concern. "Did—did something or someone … "

"No," I told him evenly, to make sure he knew I wasn't lying. "I had a swim meet nearby and I forgot to get a ride back."

He looked at me for another long while and then looked around to make sure there really were no bad guys to chase away. He was completely drenched by now, but didn't seem to notice.

"You're sure you're okay?"

I nodded.

"Have you had dinner yet?" he asked after another long pause.

I looked up at him, surprised at him for not rebuking me in any way for being such an idiot. "No." I shook my head and noticed for the first time how empty my stomach really was.

"Good! I haven't either and I know just where two wet and hungry people can go to dinner at this hour," he smiled ruefully. He leaned in, strapped my seatbelt on, then shut the door. He took one last look around before he came around and got in. He was about to put the jeep in gear, when he stopped and turned toward me, placing one hand over mine. "Why didn't you call someone?"

"I tried," I said miserably, turning to face him. His eyes were intent on mine as he mulled something over in his mind. He seemed puzzled about something, I narrowed my eyes questioningly and something passed between us.

For a split second I felt like I had looked into his eyes this same way for eons. I felt a closeness to him that seemed to transcend time and space, if that were possible. His hand tightened around mine and I knew that he felt that timeless familiarity as well. I could see it in his eyes, but this strange exchange only seemed to add to the confusion he already felt, so he brushed off his stupor and dismissed the thought.

"You know," he said as he released my hand and put the Jeep

in gear. "I was on my way home from my dad's office downtown." When I didn't respond, he shot a questioning look my way. Was this comment supposed to mean something to me? Perhaps he didn't know how terrible I was with directions.

"Oh yeah? Well I don't even know where I am. I'm awful with directions; I mean … I get lost inside our school." He laughed out loud and it was music in my ears.

He proceeded to ask me all kinds of questions about how I had gotten there in the first place and why Agatha or Charlotte wouldn't help me. He seemed to want to settle something in his head, but the crease between his eyes told me he couldn't.

"It's a miracle that you found me at all."

"It is," he said, and turned to look at me again with something like awe in his eyes.

"Thank you."

"It's weird you know. I never come this way—never—but I did tonight."

An involuntary chill ran through my body, and by the looks of it, another chill went through his as well. I wanted to reach over and hug him, but I had to settle with hugging my own cold torso. He turned up the heater and patted my knee. Oh how I loved him! This was no crush…I loved him! My whole body and soul told me so, and he had a stupid girlfriend. Stealing boyfriends away from others seemed like something that I wouldn't stoop to doing. Even if I could do it, there were no guarantees that Alex would fall for someone like me. He was gorgeous, rich, popular, and normal—I was not.

He drove us to his grandfather's house, who lived alone in a small house. He received us warmly, and seemed quite unconcerned about the whole situation. It was as if this kind of thing happened to him all the time.

Alex called his grandfather "Admiral" because he was a retired Navy Admiral. He was a large, corpulent man who looked like he had been very strong his whole life, but now limped a little, and had lost some of his muscle weight. He was a widower, having lost his wife to cancer five years ago.

"Tess, you say? What a fine name, were you named after someone in particular?" the Admiral asked.

"I don't know." I shrugged, and Alex wrapped a dry blanket around my shoulders. "I don't remember anything about my parents. I don't even know if I'm an orphan."

"Really?" the Admiral said with interest. Then he looked at Alex. "Son, you both need dry clothes. Why don't you go get some of Katie's clothes so Tess can change? You should go change too." He then turned to me. "We'll stick your clothes in the dryer and have you back to yourself in no time."

At times like these I was glad that my hair was straight and easy to manage. I brushed it out a few time and left it down, so it could dry faster. Thanks to swimming, I had all my toiletries in my backpack, so I was able to apply some cover-up under my puffy eyes. I hardly ever wore makeup, and I thought I would overdo it if I went for it now. So after I changed into Katie's dry clothes, I checked my overall appearance one last time in the mirror and called it sufficient.

Katie was Alex's sister. She was a year younger than me. She was tall for her age and I was probably a little short, so we were about the same size, and her clothes fit me well.

When I came out of the bathroom, I was greeted by the best smell ever! I didn't even know what it was, but it smelled good, and my stomach gave a lurch.

"How do you like your steak, Tess?" Alex yelled from the kitchen casually, as if he had done it a hundred times. My hungry stomach now had butterflies and my heart skipped a beat. He popped his head around the corner and looked at me expectantly. "Rare, medium, or well?"

I shrugged, "Medium, I guess." No one had ever asked me that question before, and I had no idea what he was talking about. At Charlotte's, dinner comes out of a box or the microwave and more likely than not, I'm the one making it for Dorian and me.

He seemed to understand my puzzled look and yelled, "medium!" to his grandfather. "Charlotte doesn't cook steak?"

I snorted and left it at that.

He took my hand, led me to the living room and sat me on the couch. He grabbed an old hand knitted blanket and wrapped me in it like a mummy. I couldn't help but laugh at his over protective efforts; no one had ever done that much for me in my life! I felt kind of strange, but thought that I could certainly get used to this type of treatment.

"What about you? You got wet too," I pointed out.

"Not as long as you did." Then he looked at me intently and I turned red. He smiled, understanding my feelings and tried to change the subject. He was sitting directly in front of me on the coffee table. Then he reached down and grabbed one of my bare feet. My eyes almost popped out of their sockets and I was rewarded with those dimples that formed on his face when he smiled.

"May I?" he asked politely. "Your feet are icy cold. Let me warm them up."

From the kitchen we could hear the Admiral whistling an old tune that sounded vaguely familiar. My interest must have shown on my face because Alex asked me what I was thinking.

"That song … it sounds familiar."

"It does?"

He was right, my feet were cold and his warm hands brought the circulation back to my toes. But that melody … it was bothering me. I had heard it before. Then it dawned on me, Dorian and I had heard a radio concert, paying homage to an Irish singer.

"Estelle!" I said, finally remembering the famous song and the singer's story. She had been the nanny of two opera singers. When her employers realized that she could sing, they trained her. Her voice was not cut out for opera, but they helped her get her start as a Celtic singer.

Alex had stopped rubbing my feet and was looking at me with astonishment.

"I listen to a lot of Classical music. Dorian … my foster brother … he has to listen to this show on the radio every night," I explained. "They feature mostly classical music composers, but every now and then they'll feature someone else. There was a segment one night, on Celtic music, and they featured a singer named Estelle. Her voice was so captivating, so clear. I wrote her name down and then bought some of her songs. Her voice reminds me of—of—" What *did* her voice remind me of?

By now the Admiral had stopped his whistling and was looking at me just as astonished as Alex was.

"What? Did I say something wrong?" I asked.

"Heaven. Her voice is just like an Angel's," the Admiral finished.

"Yes … I guess so." I shrugged, a little uncomfortable by the looks on their faces.

"Here, I want to show you something." Alex extended a hand to me as he rose. I took it with delight and noticed how he didn't let go of it once I was on my feet.

He led me to a wall in the living room that was filled with framed pictures. "This is Estelle," he said, pointing to a portrait of a beautiful redhead with milky skin and dark brown eyes.

I stared at her for a long while. She looked so beautiful, so vulnerable, and so … familiar. I couldn't get my eyes off her, and Alex noticed this with curiosity.

"She was my great grandmother." Alex's voice was barely above a whisper.

"Really?" I turned to face him, not realizing how close to me he was. This sent my mind into a whirl and I felt a little dizzy. His hand was still holding mine, and he tightened the hold on it. I had the most intense desire to kiss him. I don't know if I got closer, or if he did, but we were fractions away from each other, when we heard the Admiral call us from the kitchen. We both jolted back a little and he released my hand. He then placed the palm of his hand on my back and led me to the kitchen. He pulled a chair out for me. I sat down, and he pushed me in a little—another first for me.

During dinner, the Admiral told us about his childhood. How Estelle, his mother, was a single mother and how he never met his father. Estelle wouldn't talk about him either. He mentioned this, perhaps in an attempt to sympathize with the fact that I had no parents. He also explained that, growing up; he was always getting into fights.

One day he even ended up in jail for getting in a street fight, and his mom had to bail him out. When they got home, she told him that he was wasting his strength in useless pursuits. She was always rather mild and soft spoken, but this time he saw an intensity in her eyes that he had never seen before. She told him that we were all given gifts, and it was up to us to use them wisely. She told him that he was born a warrior, and the world needed them just as much as engineers or musicians. Estelle told him to find a good cause and fight for it, or he would waste away like his father had. This had been the first and only mention of his father that she ever made. The Admiral vowed then, that he never wanted to see that look on her face again, so he joined the Navy that same day.

While he expounded on his life story, I felt myself transported to a different time. I could actually see the events of his own life unfolding, and my heart warmed toward this big guy in front of me. For the first time, I felt a twinge of jealousy and I wanted him in my life—a bear of a grandfather who loved me and protected me.

"How about you, Tess, do you have any family at all?" the Admiral asked between bites.

"Just Dorian," I said simply. "We have adopted each other, because we have no one else. When I turn eighteen I'll have to leave foster care and fend for Dorian and myself. He has special needs and I don't know how he could take care of himself. They might put him in a group home, but I don't want him to end up there." The Admiral nodded his head and Alex looked intently at me. "I want to go to college too, so I'll have to get scholarships and loans."

"What do you want to study?" the Admiral asked.

"Fashion Design, I think," I said, not really sure of where that had come from. I had never really thought that far, but it sounded like a good plan. I did enjoy altering my own clothes and I felt a hunger for knowledge and skill in that area. Just as I said it, the idea seemed to take material shape before me and I was now sure that I would do this thing.

Alex remained pensive and somewhat glum throughout the

whole conversation, and hardly looked at me.

"Where will you guys live while you're in college and Dorian's out of foster care?"

That, I had not thought of yet. "I don't know, I would probably have to rent an apartment or something," I replied, but the truth was that I had no idea how I was going to pull this off. My plans had only gone as far as me getting good grades so I could get scholarships and go to college. The details escaped me.

The Admiral smiled and reached a big hand over to pat my shoulder. "Well you can always count on my help. I like you Tess, and I would be happy to lend you a hand."

My eyes got instantly moist, and I fought back the urge to cry. How I would love to take full advantage of his offer!

"How was your steak?" Alex asked. His voice sounded melancholy.

"It was delicious! I can honestly say that I've never had better." Knowing that I had never had steak before, they both laughed. Then the Admiral picked up our plates and excused himself to an adjoining room to watch a game.

"Did you like *Great Expectations*?" Alex asked out of the blue. He sounded a little downhearted, but I couldn't tell why. He seemed to be hiding something from me, or was protecting me from something—I couldn't tell.

"Yes, it's one of my favorites."

"How many times have you read it?" he asked and his mood brightened a little.

"Not as many times as I've read *Jane Eyre*. What do you like to read?"

"I grew up sailing with my grandpa. We'd leave for weeks at a time and there's no T.V on the boat, so we read a lot. When I was little he used to read to me *Arabian Nights*, *The Odyssey* and *The Iliad*. We still read out loud to each other; it's a tradition that we can't seem to break away from. Lately we've been reading Dumas, but Dickens we haven't read yet," he smirked, remembering something. "We have a strict adventure books only policy," he added with a smile.

A mental image of a young Alex with the Admiral, on the deck of my imaginary sailboat dressed like pirates having a mock sword fight popped into my head. This made me chuckle and I wondered if the thing I imagined might have actually occurred on one of their sailing trips. Then that melancholy feeling came back. I promptly brushed it aside for fear the tears that I was trying to keep at bay, would overflow.

"Well … I'm prejudiced; I tend to like all the stories about orphans. But I would like to read Dumas next, which—"

"*The Count of Monte Cristo*," he said, not letting me finish. "He was sort of orphaned," he grinned.

"I'll have to check that one out."

"No need. Here, you can have my copy." He thumbed through the bookcase and handed me a well-worn hard cover copy of the book.

I looked up at him intending to smile, but those tears escaped and fell down my cheek, betraying my emotions. I looked down and tried to blink them away, but Alex beat me to it and gently wiped a few tears away.

"I'm sorry," I apologized. "I don't know why … "

He lifted my face and looked tenderly into my eyes. I couldn't quite wrap my mind around my own feelings at that point; all I knew for sure was that I loved him, and that he had a girlfriend.

Alex must have been thinking about his girlfriend too, because he slowly dropped his hand and turned ashen.

"I should probably get you home now," he said softly.

I nodded, much against my own will. I didn't want this night to end, but reality was calling me back to Hell.

Chapter 5

Agatha had now fully embraced the whole Goth thing. She never left her room anymore, not even to watch her favorite reality TV shows with Charlotte. Her wardrobe now consisted wholly of black or gray items and black, lace-up, leather boots. Her music had lost all melody to it and was mainly made up of jarring noises. She had a little group of followers, that frequented her room, and they never spoke to anyone—ever.

I was looking forward to the next day of school, but I was apprehensive. I wondered how my relationship with Alex had changed—if at all. The anticipation of what might happen today had my stomach all in knots, and because of this I paid no attention to Agatha and her coven's odd behavior as I entered the school. She was leaning against a corner of the entrance with them and she was wearing her "hungry vampire" contacts that made her irises look black. She had accentuated her vampirish look by dying two strands of hair around her face blood red. I chuckled as I saw her, and shook my head. She seemed to be especially pleased today because she made no comment as I passed her. But immediately, I noticed an even bigger threat.

Genie and her gang of sparkly cheerleaders were blocking my way to my locker. I looked up and smiled impertinently at her. She called me some obscene name and everyone around me froze in place. All the students instinctively knew that high school history was now in the making and that they would be able to call themselves official witness.

I didn't respond to her insult, but I didn't look away either. I just stared at her, no smile this time. I was suddenly very aware of her freshly manicured nails with embedded rhinestones.

"He's taken," Genie informed me, sounding like a spoiled socialite who was having a bad hair day.

"Who?" I asked without flinching.

"*My* boyfriend, Alex."

I probably shouldn't have done this, but a smile crossed my face; I couldn't help it. She was so insecure! But truth be told, if she was worried, I was glad.

She started coming toward me, her eyes blazing and her jaw set. I didn't want to hit anyone and I certainly didn't want to get hit. I was planning on ducking and I hoped that her stilettos wouldn't be sturdy enough to support her if she took a swing at me. Suddenly I realized that some more people were coming at me from behind.

"You want to fight, Barbie?" Agatha called from behind me. I turned and saw her and her little band of vampires looking bloodthirstily at the Cheering squad. "I'd like to reserve the right to beat you up," Agatha sneered.

Genie's sparkly swat team promptly turned and walked away, digging their high heels angrily into the tiled hallway floor as they went. I didn't bother thanking Agatha; that would have only encouraged her to make me do some chore for her later. Luckily she left without asking for any thanks. Instead, I heard them laugh and make fun of the cheerleaders as they walked away.

Brandy and her sister had witnessed the whole thing from the sidelines and they stared at me, open mouthed, as I approached.

"Sometimes I think that Genie has mental problems," Brooke said with contempt. I shrugged.

"She *is* psycho, Brooke! Why does she pick on Tess? Why would she ever think that Tess is a threat to her?" Brandy demanded of her sister. Brooke didn't respond; she just looked at me with a raised eyebrow.

"Threat or not, if Genie ever bothers you again Tess, and your Fairy-goth-mother is not there to protect you, you can count on me!" Brooke added. We all burst out laughing at her comment, right as Alex came to his locker. He looked livid, I thought the look was for me, but the moment he saw me, his face softened.

"I'm sorry, Tess—I—" He shook his head unable to put his thoughts into words. "I'm so sorry, are you OK?"

"Yes," I said coolly and looked away. I didn't know why he was dating her before, but if he continued to date her now—. He must have caught my meaning because he straightened up, nodded once, retrieved his things, and left.

I felt sorry about my tone the minute he was gone, but I still felt somewhat betrayed by his actions. I knew he liked me, he knew I liked him, but his girlfriend had some strange hold on him and there didn't seem to be anything I could do about it.

Later that day, I accepted Wes's standing invitation to go out, and resolved to get over Alex, one way or another.

The days seemed to blend into each other. I could hardly tell when one ended and another one began. There were only a few variations to my life; the first was a weekend job I got at a local boutique that sold essential oils. The store was on Historic Main St. where all the shops had been remodeled to look like you were stepping back in time about two hundred years. The shop was called The Apothecary and, thanks to this job, I was able to save up enough money to procure for myself a mode of transportation. It was nothing fancy, just an old, aqua colored scooter that got me around town, when the weather allowed it. The other break from monotony came on my seventeenth birthday, by way of an unexpected gift from Dorian.

The gift was made more meaningful by the fact that it was of his own making. It was a collection of his drawings, four to be exact. The first one was a portrait of a lady I had never seen before. I asked him who she was, but got no answer; he just peered at the drawing with his blank stare and gave me no hint. The second one was of him and me embracing each other on the floor, just like we did on the day I told him that we were family.

The third picture was of a house, two stories high, rectangular in shape and very symmetrical with four windows, two on each side and two "A" shaped eaves over the top windows. Red terracotta tiles formed the roof, and the walls looked like stucco or cement. The four windows were framed by wrought iron balconies, which were adorned with cascading red geraniums. The front door looked solid and wide, and the heavily treed landscape looked like no place I've ever seen. In front of the house was a dock, where a sailboat named "Odysseus" was docked.

The fourth picture completely unnerved me. This picture was of me, sitting on a bus bench, with my hands to my face as if crying, and rain coming down hard all around me. Behind me, and floating just a few feet from the ground, were three shadowy figures. They had cynical, tormenting smiles on their disfigured faces as they bent over me. Part of their essence was spread out like smoke and wrapped itself around me, so that I was completely engulfed by them.

"The voices …" I whispered and shivered. "Could this be?" I looked at Dorian for an explanation, but he gave none. Once he was satisfied that I had seen all the pictures, he simply went back to his bed and resumed his next project.

My relationship with Alex during school was distant for a while, but then it slowly reverted back to what it used to be—a kind look and a polite sentence or two. His relationship with Genie seemed to go through a similar pattern, but I didn't ask and he didn't tell me. I was pretty sure they were still together, though he seemed annoyed at her all the time. She never came to his locker anymore and I was glad of that. In fact, I had no further encounters with her at all. She avoided me and I avoided her, too.

Wes tried hard to win my heart with all kinds of fun activities, but I could tell that my icy disposition was frustrating him. I didn't think I was icy by nature. In fact, I knew that I wasn't because of the dreams; I'm never icy with Alex in my dreams.

These dreams have actually been a source of great concern for me lately. I'm angry at my weakness when it comes to Alex and I fear that if I continue with this obsession I will lose my sanity altogether. Already there have been days when I can't tell if I'm dreaming or if I'm awake when I see him. He might smile at me in the hallway and I read all kinds of things into that smile that I know are not there in real life. But I can't help it, come nightfall, all I can think of while crawling in bed, is of *him*. My last thoughts as I lose consciousness are of him and whether or not I'll see him in my head that night.

Not all dreams are the vivid dreams where we talk for hours, hold each other, and sail. Some are two-dimensional and lack the same intensity and depth. So what are those other dreams? Why the difference?

As I turned the last page of *The Count of Monte Cristo*, a tear slid down my cheek. I read the book as slowly as I could, so as to prolong the inevitable—giving it back. In my hands I held a part of him, something he touched ... something he loved. I tried to picture him sitting on a boat, reading under the baking hot sun, surrounded by blue ocean water, just like the color of his eyes.

"Tess! Tess! Over here!" Just as I had imagined him, Alex stood on the deck of The Odysseus. I glided to him as if flying was second nature. Once my foot touched the deck, Alex extended one arm and helped me get on board. *"I knew you'd come today."*

"How?"

"You looked ... conflicted today." He wrapped his arm around my shoulders and squeezed me tightly against his torso.

I smiled and wished that the real Alex had noticed. But I didn't say anything; if these dreams were a delusion, I wanted them ... I needed them.

"You still look conflicted."

I took in a deep breath and felt as alive and as free as ever.

"It's nothing, nothing that matters now anyway. So ... where are you taking me this time?" I inquired, impishly.

"I was thinking we could skirt the shore to Florida, and see how far we get."

I shrugged, not particularly concerned over our destination. Then it hit me. My destination. The heaviness of my own future hung over me like an anvil waiting to drop. Had I been right to promise Dorian that I would take care of him? How was I going to accomplish this? The Admiral had brought up a very crucial kink in my plans; what would I do with Dorian while I went to school?

"That's it! There it is again!" Alex pointed to my face.

"What?" I asked somewhat defensively.

"That worried look. I hate seeing that on your face."

I shook my head, and tried not to spoil this fleeting moment with Alex with my personal baggage. But he looked like he was not going to drop it, so I relented. I told him of my dilemma, and how I can't stand not having a clear picture of how I was going to work things out for us. *"Not going to school is out of the question. But I might have to postpone it."* I said with dismay, and felt like crying.

In an instant he was by my side, wrapping his arms around me and pulling me to his chest, like he did that night, out in the rain.

"I could—"

"No!" I cut him short. There was no way I would let him help me. I wasn't sure why I felt so strongly about this, he wasn't even real! But there was something inside of me that rejected the idea completely. *"I have to do this on my own."*

"We can't do everything on our own! You're just a kid, Tess. At some point you'll have to depend on someone."

"I can do this," I said with a certainty that came out of nowhere. *"How about you, Alex? What will you do after high school?"* I asked, moving the subject away from myself.

"I'm going to join the military and I'm going to learn to fly." He looked up at the sky and watched with envy as a seagull flew by.

"I thought you wanted to go to college?" I frowned.

"I do ... and I will. I can do both."

"You don't strike me as the type who would join the military."

He raised one eyebrow. *"And what is the type?"*

"I don't know ... someone like me. Someone who can't afford college."

"Well, I don't know why others join the military. But I'm doing it because I love my country and our way of life, and I'm willing to fight to keep it that way." He stuck his chest out and looked as determined as ever. *"I know no one expects this of me, I know that everyone thinks I'm just a spoiled rich kid who's going to join a fraternity and breeze through college simply because my father,*

and his father, are alumni at Harvard." He looked pensive for a moment. *"Not that I like war or anything, but a voluntary army needs to be made up of people who want justice, people with convictions."* He looked down at his hands and fidgeted with his fingers. His words sounded like they came straight from the Admiral's mouth.

"So ... what will you do after the military; or are you making the military your career?" I asked, changing the subject.

"I'm not going to be a career soldier like my grandfather, but I still want to serve."

"Peace Corps, policeman, fire fighter?" I suggested.

"Politician," he replied with a teasing smile, but I could tell he was dead serious.

I nodded and stuck out my lip. *"I can see it."*

"My other grandfather is a Senator, but he's not running for reelection this year. I think he's finally going to retire. He and my father never got along; they butted heads on everything. When my dad didn't follow in his political footsteps, it created a huge rift. But I want to give it a go."

We had been sitting on the bow of the ship, with our legs dangling over the edge while the water splashed up on them. He still held my hand, and presently, he picked it up and brought it up to his lips for a kiss. Suddenly, I felt my body being shaken with force by someone back in reality. I stretched out one hand to him as I floated away, until he faded completely and I was aware of my real surroundings once again.

Bent over me was Dorian, who was pale and shivering. My head ached around my temples, a common side effect of these dreams.

"What's wrong, Dorian?"

Half relieved and half faint, he dropped onto his bed, and laid his head on his pillow. Instinctively, I touched his forehead and noticed that it was hot and clammy. I looked around the room, hoping to find a clue as to what to do, but found none. I told him to stay put while I got Charlotte and he nodded as he closed his eyes.

He had the flu. Apparently half the school had it too, and the halls looked eerily empty as I walked them that day. I was glad for it, in a way. My head hurt so bad that I welcomed the silence. So I stayed at my locker for lunch, and pulled out Alex's book with the intention of giving it back when I saw him. But, as soon as I was comfortably sitting on the floor, I felt my eyes getting heavy, and slumber creeping in.

Alex was glad that there was almost no one around today. "I'll just have a quiet lunch by my locker today," he thought ruefully, knowing full well who he would find there. However, he found his reason asleep on the floor with her head on her bag, a sandwich in one hand and his book in the other.

He couldn't help suppress a smile; she looked spent … and beautiful. So beautiful in fact, that she looked like a work of art, with her silky dark hair spilling over her shoulders, covering part of her smooth olive skin. Her thick eyelashes framed her closed lids and her rosy lips were slightly parted. He stared at those lips for a moment, then sat down next to her with frustration. He pulled out his own lunch and started breaking chunks out of it. Out of his bag, he retrieved *Great Expectations*, but settled on looking at the cover and thinking, instead of reading.

Stealing another glance in her direction he struggled with his own feelings. She had wedged herself quite deeply into his heart, and he didn't even know how. From the start he was attracted to her and felt for her what he had never felt for Genie. Then, the dreams … they didn't help him at all. How could he remain aloof when he had those dreams?

Chapter 6

"Hmm ... " Celeste floated above the two with arms crossed and a scowl on her face.

"Is she yours?" Estelle asked as she hurriedly floated down the hall, her tunic flowing and swirling behind her with light.

"Yes, she's mine. How about the boy? Is he yours?" Celeste could not hide her contempt as she placed her fists on her waist.

"He is. Alex is my great-grandson," Estelle said with obvious pride. But Celeste let out a contemptuous huff and crossed her arms again.

"Are you related to her?" Estelle asked cheerily, not catching Celeste's obvious hints.

"She's my grand-daughter, Tess."

"Tess ... yes ... " Estelle got a faraway look and nodded, then her face brightened and her eyes opened wide. *"Is your name Celeste?"*

"Yes," Celeste said distrustfully. *"Why?"*

Estelle almost hugged her, but settled to jumping and clapping her hands instead. *"Oh goodness! You have no idea how long I've been looking for you! And to think you were right here all along! Celeste, as I live well not live per say ... "* Upon Celeste's annoyed look Estelle composed herself and stretched out her hand. *"Hi, my name is Estelle, and I've been looking for you! I was asked to give you a message."* She bit her lip and looked expectantly at Celeste.

"Sent by who and what message?"

"By them." Estelle dropped the hand and pointed to Tess who slept and Alex who sat pondering.

"By them?"

"Yes! Before they were born and before I died! You see, I had the ability to see spirits while I was alive. I saw them on a few occasions, but the last time they came to me, they asked me to look for Celeste, you, and tell you that they wanted to be together,"

Estelle said triumphantly and felt like a burden had just been lifted off her shoulders. But Celeste looked unconvinced and eyed her suspiciously.

"You could see spirits?"

"Yes, while I was alive."

"And they ... " she pointed specifically to the two mortals in front of her, *"came to you before you died, just to tell you that they wanted to be together?"*

Estelle nodded vigorously.

"O—kay." Celeste thought about all the implications that this news conveyed. She knew that there were unborn spirits, but she had never encountered one. The reason for this might simply be because they inhabited another realm of existence. This might have seemed farfetched to her at one time, but not anymore. Since she'd died, she had learned a few things. First, everyone has gifts and some were more pronounced than others. Didn't her own son see her after she passed? And Tess herself, didn't she hear her—before ... when she used to speak to her? And second, there were different realms of existence; she inhabited one right now—something she never knew until she passed. So why not another realm, inhabited by those who have not been born yet! Heavens! She might have a slew of people in that realm that she knows, or used to know. ... So why couldn't she remember it?

"I know it sounds a bit crazy, but it's true! I swear it! They came to me the very night that he was born. They were in a hurry and were very distressed at the thought that they might soon forget everything."

"Forget everything? Is that why I can't remember?" Celeste asked now with interest.

"I've been told that we all had to cross a veil of sorts before we're born that erases all memories of our existence prior to mortal life."

"You don't say? Well, I always thought that there must be another piece to the puzzle. I guess I need to sign up for the 'Spiritual Progression' class when I get back."

"That's precisely the class I took!" Estelle declared with satisfaction.

"So about these two…what are we to do?" Celeste asked, now warmed to the spirit next to her.

"I suppose we figure out a way of getting them together."

"He is dating that spoiled girl … Eugenia!"

"And now she is dating someone too." Estelle pointed out.

"Only because her feelings got hurt. He should break up with that Genie girl and ask Tess out."

"It's not that simple. He feels that his parents expect him to marry Genie. Their parents are best friends … they've joked about this 'arranged marriage' since they were little."

"Ahh, por favor!" Celeste threw her hands up in the air in frustration and paced the space right in front of Alex and Tess, looking like a blurry glow light.

"I know! I've tried to tell him. He's coming around though. Look at him and tell me he doesn't like her."

Celeste stopped her pacing and narrowed her eyes, inspecting Alex closely. Then she straightened up and pursed her lips. *"Well … if we are going to make this happen, we'll have to put our minds together."*

"Agreed!" Estelle extended her arm and Celeste took it with a grin. Like two fairies, the two matriarchs floated arm in arm down the hall, deep in conversation, leaving a shimmery trail of light behind them.

The jarring bell woke me up with a start, and as I straightened up I bumped into something—Alex. "Alex!" I squeaked rather breathlessly. "What—?" I looked around, disoriented. Was I awake or still dreaming? It occurred to me right then that this double life of mine was getting increasingly complicated.

Alex smiled sweetly and the dimples showed up again. "Good morning."

I bit my lips and straightened my hair, then my uneaten sandwich fell from my lap, making a mess of ham, cheese and lettuce on the floor. Hastily I tried to clean up my mess and found Alex's hand reaching over and helping me.

"Here, let me help you. You look a bit groggy still," he smiled again.

Embarrassed, I let him help me and I watched as he cleaned up and threw the mess away. Then he came back to my side and offered me his own lunch. "No, thank you," I insisted.

He pushed it forward. "Come on, you need to eat. You have practice after school and you'll sink if you don't have food in you. Besides, this is my second sandwich, I ate one already."

His kindness touched me and my feelings for him bubbled up to the surface—dang! How am I supposed to stay mad at him? "OK, thank you, but won't you be hungry?"

He shook his head. "I'm not that hungry today." Then he looked away, looking lost in thought.

By now the hallway began to fill with students, and we got a few stares as they passed.

"Did you have a rough night last night?" Alex asked, turning his attention back to me.

I looked at him, but my look was more like a stare. How much like my dreams, he was! How real those dreams were! But of course they are not real, and disclosing the fact that I dream of him almost every night was out of the question. "Just a dream." I sighed.

"A bad dream?"

"No, just a dream. I—have you ever had a dream so real that you felt like you were actually living it?"

One of his eyebrows rose high above the other and he peered into my own eyes with intensity. "I think so, why?" he asked mysteriously.

I shrugged. "Well, because when I dream those very intense dreams, I wake up more tired than when I fell asleep, that's all." By now the second bell had rung and the hallway was clearing of students who were now in their classrooms. I reached for my bag and started to get up, but as I did so, *The Count of Monte Cristo* book fell to the floor. "Oh, here, I meant to give this back to you."

Alex was getting up too and looked down at the book. "Did you like it?"

"I loved it!"

He smiled a tight smile and took the book from my hands. Our fingers overlapped for a second, sending electric shocks up my arm. He noticed this, because he looked up at me with intensity again. He opened his mouth to speak, but didn't. Instead he turned from me and stalked off without another word. He left in his wake, a trail of frustration that I myself, shared. To my infinite chagrin, I didn't see him again. I worried that I had offended him somehow, but for the life of me, I didn't know how.

A few weeks later, Dorian came up to me with a postcard. He sat on my bed looking eager, pushing the postcard under my line of vision. The picture on the postcard was of a beautiful painting done by Thomas Kinkade. It was an iron gate that was partially opened and all around it were luscious flowers and shrubs. I was mesmerized by this beautiful work of art; I looked up at Dorian, and turned the postcard over. It was an invitation for two to a Thomas Kindade art exposition in downtown Dallas, that weekend.

"You want to go?" I asked Dorian.

He smiled broadly and nodded. "Together," he said.

"I might get lost though, and it will be late when it's done. Do you mind if we get Wes to drive us?"

Dorian was clearly disappointed by this suggestion, but he didn't refuse. "I want to go," he reiterated stubbornly, which I took to mean "do what you have to do to get me there."

The next day at school I put before Wes and his friends this grand plan for a group date, where we went to an art exhibit and then out to dinner somewhere downtown. I knew this last part would be appealing to Wes and his buddies, and they readily agreed. Wes was also glad to see me take the initiative on my end, and let me know so with a smile. Far from making me feel good, that smile cut straight through my heart. I was using him.

I saw a strange look cross Brandy's usual happy face and I

knew then that she was annoyed with me. She was cold toward me for the rest of the day, and my entreaties had no effect on her.

On Friday night, seven of us crowded into Wes' Suburban and made our way to the art exhibit. I tried to smooth things over with Brandy again, and she seemed more receptive, but I could tell that she still held a sliver of resentment there, and I couldn't blame her. She was right in being angry. In fact, I wished that Wes would be angry too, but he wasn't. He was filled with hope for the evening.

Once we got there, the group dislodged, leaving Dorian, Wes, and me, alone. Dorian took his time at each picture, and I did too, which only made Wes antsy. His constant need for action was stifled here. Soon his constant fidgeting and sulking got to me, and I started to get annoyed. I pulled him aside and leveled with him. If he gave us a little bit of time alone, then we would join the rest of the group. Wes seemed relieved by this suggestion and was glad to move on. He spotted Brandy and her date ahead, and hurried to catch up with them. Once he was gone, my relief was almost palpable, and I turned my attention back to Dorian and the pictures before me.

Dorian would get so close to some pictures that his nose would almost touch the canvas. Then he would take a few steps back and study it anew. I could tell that he saw things in those paintings that I didn't. I could see that he was learning something and taking in a lot more than just a beautiful image.

"I know you can draw this, but do you think you could use colors too?" I asked him.

He looked thoughtful for a moment, then he shook his head, no.

"It says here that he is called 'The Painter of Light'. I can see why. All of his pictures are drenched in sunlight, lamplight or the glow of a fire."

Dorian nodded, and then moved to the next picture. One particular painting across the aisle caught my eye, I crossed to see it and stood there looking intently at it for a while. There seemed to be something familiar about it, but I couldn't quite tell what. It was a white gazebo with a lilac colored wisteria creeping up on it. The picture mesmerized me and I almost felt transported there. I felt like I was floating somewhere above it, looking down.

"What does it remind you of?" His voice startled me and sent my heart racing, pumping blood through my veins so fast that it flushed my face.

"I don't know, but it looks familiar somehow." I closed my eyes and tried to steady my breathing before turning.

When I turned, I found him to be much closer than I anticipated. I raised my gaze and looked into his eyes. There was pain in them. They looked hurt and there was a trace of anger in them as well. I looked at him questioningly, but he didn't explain. He seemed to be caught in some internal struggle of his own.

"Where's your boyfriend," he asked curtly.

"He's … I don't know," I said looking around, not so much looking for Wes, as making sure he wasn't around. "I wanted to come here with Dorian, but … "

He stared hard into my eyes. He seemed to be trying to find something there, but was not succeeding. Then he softened a little and all I could see was pain. He seemed to emanate pain from his person.

"Did you sleep better last night?"

"Yes," I told him suspiciously.

"Good, glad to hear it." We stared at each other for a few seconds without talking.

"I came here with my family," he said, changing the subject. " … My mom is an artist and loves Thomas Kinkade. She makes us come to all her favorite artists' exhibits."

"That's nice. Dorian wanted to come and see it too, but I seem to have lost him," I said looking around me fruitlessly. Then Alex moved in closer, if that was possible, giving me little room to move between him and the painting.

"Ah, there you are!" a woman exclaimed.

Both Alex and I jerked our heads up at the same time. I tucked my nervous hands behind my back, and as I did this, they brushed against Alex's hands for a very distracting moment.

"Mom, this is Tess; a friend from school," Alex said casually while his fingers found their way back to mine.

"Hi," I said hoarsely.

The woman came closer and was soon followed by a man, no doubt Alex's father, and Katie, his little sister. Meanwhile the tips of Alex's fingers interlaced themselves with mine, I felt all the blood drain from my face and I knew I looked ashen. For a few glorious seconds our hands were fully entangled, but regretfully I had to let go of this most unusual display of closeness, to shake Mr. Preston's extended hand.

"Oh look, Dane! Doesn't that picture look exactly like that the gazebo my parents had in the Waco house?" Alex's mom, Valerie, exclaimed.

"You're right, almost exactly! We got engaged under that gazebo," Dane explained to us, turning with a smile. "We kissed for the first time under it too," he added, with a cocky smile, and kissed his wife on the cheek. She smiled back and without turning she reached for his hand and they entwined their fingers casually. I looked at their hands with envy, then stole a glance back at Alex, who mirrored my frustration.

Chapter 7

Seconds later we were ambushed by Wes, Brandy, and her date, who had had enough of the paintings. Wes made a beeline to my side and claimed me by wrapping his arms around my waist. I could see the change in Alex right away; his look had reverted back to that former, cool, pained stare. I tried to apologize with my eyes, but he wouldn't have it. He was mad now and it showed.

"I—need to find Dorian," I told Wes and the group at large. "I'll be right back."

I stole away from the group almost at a dead run while blinking back the oncoming tears. When I found Dorian, he could tell that I was distressed and I could swear he knew why. He smiled tenderly, almost knowingly, then he put his arm around my shoulder and squeezed a bit. He usually didn't appreciate this type of closeness, but he didn't seem to mind this time, so like this we made our way back to the group.

Dorian had grown so much in the last year. He was about six feet tall, still thin, but muscular. At his school he had started playing some sports, and he found that he enjoyed running track a lot. This, perhaps accounted for his toned muscles.

When we got back to the group, Dorian seemed like a different person. Usually he's reserved and doesn't like to interact with people, especially new people, but he responded well to Alex and his family. He shook hands with all of them, something he never does. He even smiled, but he still couldn't bring himself to look them in the eye—though I have to say he tried.

"We heard you are an artist yourself, Dorian," Dane said.

Dorian shifted his eyes and looked down, shyly. I stole a quizzical glance toward Alex but he only gave me a cold look in return. I had told Alex about Dorian on that night that he found me in the storm and he had apparently he told his parents about it too. The thought of them discussing Dorian and me around their kitchen table; left me feeling a bit uncertain. What was said? What did they think of us? Did they pity us?

"I would love to see some of your work," Valerie said with a motherly smile.

She was a beautiful woman, tall and fit, with dark brown hair that was stylishly cut short. Her eyes were her most striking feature, being almost violet. She was dressed in nice designer clothes, but not over the top. Katie had inherited much of her mother's beauty, but her eyes were lighter colored, like Alex's. Katie had dark hair like her mother and had her father's sweet expression. Alex was a good mix of the two; he had his father's build, tall broad shoulders, light brown hair and Caribbean blue eyes. He also had those dimples when he smiled, and I could see now that he got those from his father as well.

By now the rest of our group found us and insisted that they had seen every picture there was to see and that they were ready to eat.

"What do you say, buddy? Should we go get some food?" Wes slapped Dorian on the back and wrapped one arm around him, Dorian jerked away from him and sidestepped to put some distance between them. "Whoa!" Wes exclaimed, throwing his hands up in the air, as if he had been charged with an undeserved foul.

"It's OK! He doesn't like to be touched," I explained. But Wes looked unconvinced. "I'm the only one who can touch him," I explained again and tried to soothe Dorian, who was now rocking back and forth, and hitting his face with his fists.

Alex's dad, stepped forward too, but evaluated the situation from a safe distance.

"Wanna go home, home, home!" Dorian's voice was gaining crescendo, making people turn and stare.

"Look Wes, you're going to have to take us home," I told him, and he looked positively crestfallen. Right then, displeased murmurs from our group rose up.

"I'll take him home," Alex asserted through the noise. I looked at him, and his eyes still looked hard.

"Yes, we'll take him home, Tess. Don't worry," Dane reiterated.

I shook my head, "I appreciate it, but he won't go without me," I looked pleadingly at Wes.

"Then we'll take you both home, and your friends can go on without you," Valerie said with a firm voice that sounded more like a command than a suggestion.

Wes had no option but to agree to this. He kissed my cheek and whispered, "I'll call you later." Brandy shot me a reproachful look before turning on her heels and walking away. What? Did she think I orchestrated this?

Katie made sure to let me ride in the back of the Preston's SUV with her brother. Her intentions were so transparent that no one was fooled—not even Dorian, who by now had miraculously regained his composure. I was feeling, relieved, nervous, excited, angry, and puzzled—all wound up in a tight little bundle. Alex was wound tight too; I could feel his unease as he snapped his seatbelt. Everyone was quiet, so I broke the silence, by thanking them for their kindness.

Dane immediately said that it was no problem at all and that they were on their way home anyway. Then the car fell silent again, and my heart sank with dread.

"So, did you read *Great Expectations*? I asked Alex quietly, almost in a whisper.

He turned his head and frowned. I returned his frown and looked down, wounded.

"It was a good book," he finally answered, dryly.

"I really liked *The Count of Monte Cristo*," I said, trying hard to make the conversation more pleasant.

"Yes, you told me that already."

I looked back at him, stung by his coarseness.

"*Great Expectations* has two endings, does it not?" Alex's dad said from the driver's seat.

"Yes, Charles Dickens' publisher didn't like the first ending, so he asked for another." I said.

"Well, I agree with the publisher; no use in reading a book if it's going to end badly. It sours the whole story," Alex put in as he looked out his window.

"But real life doesn't always end well," I interjected.

"People don't read fiction to get reality; they read it to escape it," he added without turning.

"The first ending doesn't necessarily end badly; it's open-ended in my opinion," Dane looked at us through the rear view mirror.

"Estelle clearly rejects him," Alex stated.

"That's a matter of opinion," I countered.

"Estelle… my grandmother's name was Estelle," Valerie said, trying to change the subject. "She was a popular Celtic singer, in her time."

"Yes, I heard that," I said choking on a few tears.

"Tess is a fan," Alex offered. His voice seemed gentler now.

"Really? You've heard of her?" Valerie turned to look at me.

"We heard her on the radio," Dorian spoke up, in an uncharacteristic bout of talkativeness.

Dane looked at him through the rear view mirror and smiled at him. Valerie smiled too, and began to tell us all about how her grandmother was discovered, and her path to stardom.

Alex seemed to relax a bit in his seat; he even turned and looked at me. I ventured a look as well, but we said nothing.

"She didn't get your emails!" Celeste shouted in Alex's ear.

"That Agatha girl is the Devil's spawn, I swear!" Estelle said with disgust while shaking her head.

"She really is. No doubt about it!" Celeste agreed emphatically. *"How she hacked into Tess' email is despicable! I swear if I ever get a hold of one of those Cast-outs … I wish we could expose her somehow."*

"Hacked?"

"Yes, that's what they call it when someone breaks into electronic data."

"Oh—" Estelle nodded. *"Well, she does whatever they tell her, that's for sure. Why doesn't Tess get one of those … um … cell phones like all the other kids?"*

Celeste shook her head, *"Tess hates cell phones! Besides, she can't afford them. She's saving up her money."* She looked down at the couple in the back seat, each looking out their respective windows, each wrapped up in their own misery. *"Were you really a singer?"* Celeste asked in a sudden change of subject.

"Yes, I was."

"Oh, I would love to hear you sing."

"Really? Here? Now?"

"Of course, why not?"

I wasn't sure why, but I felt a chill that gave me goose bumps and then heard the faint noise of hushed whispers. I shuddered again, and Alex turned away from his window to look at me. I didn't turn—my eyes were welling up with tears that I didn't want him to see.

He shifted in his seat, then I felt the tips of his fingers brushing against mine again. Without turning, I inched my own fingers toward his until our hands were once again intertwined. Right then the vehicle seemed to fill with music; a sweet bright tinkling like sound that flowed in the air like an enchanted water fall that with each drop made a crystalline type song. The sound seemed to pacify all inside the car. Dorian took his pencil and paper out from his backpack and his hand started moving fast across the page.

On Monday, before first period I found Alex waiting for me by his locker. He looked lost in thought and he watched me approach with an apologetic look on his face.

"I really did like the book," he said remorsefully. "I'm sorry for being such a jerk the other night," he added.

"It's okay," I lied.

"Can I ask you a question about Dorian?"

I nodded, a bit taken back by his request.

"Did you see the picture he drew for my mom?"

"No." In fact I didn't even know he had given her a picture.

"Has he ever ... drawn a picture for you?" he asked suspiciously.

"A few, why?" I immediately thought of the pictures that he had given me on my last birthday, but I didn't want go into the details of those pictures. They were very important to me, bordering on sacred. There was a mystical magic to them. They brought more questions than answers. Alex wanted were answers, and I had none.

Alex started to speak, but then stopped himself. He did this a few times until he finally decided on something. "Has he ever seen a picture of Estelle?"

"Estelle, your great-grandmother?" I asked. He nodded. "I don't think so. The first time I saw her picture was at your grandfather's house, but I don't think *he's* ever seen one. Why?"

"He drew her," Alex said plainly.

I nodded for a moment, how was I supposed to explain to Alex the complexities that I take for granted. How am I supposed to tell him that my life is filled with inexplicable phenomena; from pictures of things that a boy could not possibly know about, to reliving things that never happened but feel like they have, and hearing whispers of people who are not there? I hate to admit these things, even to myself, but they happened and I simply could not explain them.

"He … does things like that sometimes," I finally said, hoping to leave it at that.

"What has he drawn for you?"

"A woman … that I've never seen before," I said bluntly.

"Who do you think it is?" he insisted.

"No idea."

"Does she look like you? Could it be your mother?"

The thought had occurred to me, but she really looked nothing like me, with the exception of the eyes. "She's blond … we do have similar eyes, but who knows," I shrugged.

"What else?" He looked genuinely interested now.

I sighed, and wondered whether I should reveal to him what I considered to be too close to my heart. "A house that I've never seen before, with a dock in front of it." Then the image of the picture came to my mind, and I remembered how there was a boat named The Odysseus docked in front of it, just like the boat from my dreams.

"A dock?" he asked with interest. "What else?"

I shook my head, there were too many people around us now, and I was bordering on tears, again. I wiped my blurry eyes with my hand and looked at him pleadingly. I wanted to tell him but not now, not here, and not like this.

"I can't … " I shook my head.

"It's okay. You don't have to tell me," he looked crestfallen. Then smiled sympathetically and started to walk away.

"Alex!" I called before he got too far, "I like happy endings too."

He turned and looked back at me, with a faint smile forming on his face. He stared at me for a long while. "Trouble is… they don't come until the end," he said with intensity.

"The end of what?"

"A very long, dramatic story." Alex flashed a quick, sad smile then turned and walked away.

Chapter 8

I never liked riddles much, so it was a mystery to me why I liked Alex so much. Everything about him was a riddle when it came to me. Sometimes he would ignore me and other times he acted like he wanted to kiss me right then and there. Some days we could talk like he was my best friend, and then others, he was so mad at me he his jaw would tense up, and he looked as if it took a great deal of self-control to keep from screaming. But no matter what mood he happened to be in, one thing remained a constant— my complete adoration of him.

What makes the needle of a compass always point North? I know it has to do with magnetism. Well…whatever pulls that needle North is what pulls me toward Alex. He is my North. I'm lost without him, and this realization has finally made me feel intensely guilty.

It is painfully obvious to me now, that I don't love Wes, and that I never will. But I'm a coward, and with Wes, one thing is for sure, he likes me—a lot. The other painful realization was that high school was coming to an end for Alex, and that perhaps I would never see him again.

This distasteful thought, I pushed aside. I couldn't process that into my life. I had to hold on to the hope that perhaps one day …

Prom was right around the corner, and Wes looked so sad when he asked me to go, that I had to say yes. Brandy had forgiven me somewhat, especially since she was a bit preoccupied with her own guy problems. She was asked to go to the prom by a senior who had recently transferred to the school. He had created quite a stir among the female student body, and singled Brandy out, who seemed to be the only girl—besides myself—who didn't care about him in the least.

"He gives me the creeps," she confided during lunch.

Wes nodded thoughtfully, "Yeah, I know what you mean. There's something fishy about that guy. Why don't you insist on coming with us?"

I immediately agreed to it and told her that I would go with her when she broke the news to him.

"If he doesn't agree, you can be my second date!" Wes beamed, sticking his chest out and looking grand. "I'll dress like James Bond," he added, making what he thought would be a Bond-ish face.

After school, Brandy told me that the deed was done by way of a note during one of the classes she had with the guy. He apparently shrugged, in aloof response.

"You'll have to come and get ready with me. My mom makes a big fuss about prom night-day."

I looked at her uncomprehendingly and she expounded. "Prom night-day is an excuse to pamper ourselves all day long. My mom says that it's practice time for your wedding day, so we girls spend the day exfoliating, getting pedicures, manicures, and facials, then we start on the hair. It's an all day event!"

"That actually sounds like fun! But I'm afraid of pedicures."

Brandy laughed, knowing the story about Agatha and the metal file. "No, I mean it, I don't let anyone near my toes now," I assured her in all seriousness.

Prom day at Brandy's was the most fun I'd had in a long time, quite possibly, ever. Her mom had a stylist and a masseuse come to her house to give us the full spa treatment. I declined the pedicure, and got a lesson instead, on how to do my own toes.

When word got out that I had made my own prom dress, and that I was somewhat of a gifted fashionista, everyone—stylist, masseuse and all—gathered around me for the unveiling of my dress. It was in fact one of my best "Frankenstein" efforts. It consisted of several thrift-store dresses, all taken apart and put back together in quite a magical way. It was still very formal, but with a deliberate tattered look that made it fabulous. The ripped layers of taffeta from an old eighties dress, were cut diagonally making overlapping flat ruffles in three different muted shades of green. The top was angled as well with only one strap over my left shoulder, and cascading beads attached to the top by a taffeta flower, with the beads hanging all the way down past my waist.

I showed them how the beads could be worn down, or tossed around to the other side, as a necklace or scarf. The beads were threaded through a thin satin ribbon that matched the color of the dress. Once I was done explaining my dress, and the many ways to wear the beads, I noticed that the room was in complete silence.

I looked around me, worried that only I thought this was cool, but by the look on their faces, I surmised that the silence was really awe.

"Tess … " Brandy's mom said breathlessly, "This is amazing! You know how to sew like this?" She looked at the seams and the careful stitching on the hems of every layer. Then she let her fingers touch the beads slightly and looked up at me with a new found respect. "You're going to be a designer," she stated. It was perhaps the best compliment I could have received too, because I wanted to be a designer, and she was the type of woman who knew about fashion.

Slowly the others, Brandy, Brooke, the stylist and the masseuse approached the dress and started making all kinds of comments. "You're like one of those artists that turn trash into art!" one said, "But with dresses!" said another.

Then, Brooke asked if I could alter her dress, because there was something that she didn't like about it. Her mom insisted that there was no time for that now, but I took a look at it any way. In fact, I ended up giving finishing touches to both, Brooke's and Brandy's dress while I waited for my facial to dry. After a few hours at the sewing machine, both their dresses had the 'Tess' stamp of approval along with their own.

Once we finished getting dressed and the stylist was tucking the last strands of hair into place, I realized that perhaps this was going to be the best part of prom. During the course of the day, Brooke had let it slip—casually or not, I couldn't tell—that Alex and Genie had broken up a few months ago. She said, though, that they were still going to prom together because Genie made him promise to, as a parting favor of sorts. I knew that Genie had done this as a way of getting back at me, but I made no comment and pretended to not be interested in the least about this information.

But the reality was that I was very much interested. In fact, that explained his annoyance over my still being with Wes. Why didn't he tell me, I wonder? I realized then, that I let an involuntary sigh escape me, and several knowing looks darted my way.

After meeting Brandy's date, I realized why he gave her the creeps. He was handsome and he knew it, but behind his chiseled features was a hard, cold, and even cruel demeanor. If he were into Gothic chicks I would have set him up with Agatha. But, as it turned out, he found an equal at the dance—Genie. She had showed up with Alex, merely to vex me. But she had an agenda that night and it included Brandy's date. As soon as the two schemers saw each other, they left their dates in complete limbo and spent a wonderful evening together.

Wes, of course, turned himself into James Bond and demanded that Brandy be his date too. She accepted, a bit embarrassed, but seemed to forget all her woes as soon as Wes had us spinning, one on each of his arms, on the dance floor. While we twirled, my eyes scanned the room for signs of Alex. I found him sitting alone at a table, doodling on the tablecloth. I wanted to run to him, but that would require me to break up with Wes really quick—and that was not to be easily done. After a few more songs, I lost sight of Alex, so I used this opportunity to excuse myself under some mumbled pretext, and took off to look for him.

I saw a pair of large French doors that opened up to a terrace and, pulled by a strange force, I went straight to them. Once outside, my feet didn't feel like they moved at all, yet they guided me all the way around to the end of the balcony. At the very end, hidden by the shadows, I saw him with his forearms resting on the balustrade, looking out into the open.

"You look stunning," Alex stated without turning. I moved forward, feeling like I was floating toward him, much like I did in my dreams. As I got near, he straightened and turned toward me. He waited until I was within arms' reach, then stepped in closer. He examined the edge of one of my ruffles by sliding his finger softly under the fabric. "Is this of your making?"

I nodded.

"How do you do it?"

"Um … well … first—"

He chuckled, "I don't particularly care to know about sewing, though it is remarkable. What I mean is; how do you do all of it? How do you spin a web so fine and firm that—" he paused, looking for the right words. I looked up at him incredulously, not really sure what he meant to say. Was he implying that I was forcing him to like me? That he felt trapped and wanted to escape? Because that's what I think about when I think of a spider and its web.

"—that has me spell-bound. How do you manage to disturb my dreams?" I frowned, not sure of whether he liked his dreams disturbed or not. Besides, he was often in my dreams and I never thought of them as disturbing or upsetting. In fact, if I ever dreamed of anything else, I would feel disturbed.

He gave me a crooked smile, then kissed my forehead and wrapped one arm around my waist, extending the other. "May I have this dance?"

I readily agreed and ventured to rest my head on his chest. I could hear his steady heartbeat and my own soon fell in step with his. Wherever his body touched mine, I felt swirls of magic energy and light, spreading to the rest of my body; making me feel tingly and lightheaded. The tiles under our feet seemed to melt, the music evaporated and I felt as if we floated in mid-air—dancing only to the beat of our hearts and the music of the cicadas.

I don't know how much time passed, but the next thing I knew, our eyes were locked. His lips were coming closer to mine and I could feel their warmth. His eyes were piercing mine with an intensity that made my knees weak and they would have given out from under me if it wasn't for the hold he had on me.

Disturbed … I guess I did feel disturbed, but I liked it. Was that what he meant? His lips brushed teasingly against mine, and he smiled ruefully, knowing what he was doing to me and relishing his torture.

"Tess! Are you out here?" Wes' voice wrung through the air, freezing us both in place. Brandy whispered something, and Wes answered her, then they both resumed their calling for me.

Alex looked at me still, but his eyes were cold, like the evening at the art exhibit. "Your boyfriend is calling you," he stated, not moving away or releasing me at all. His lips still brushed against mine slightly as he spoke, but this time they were reproachful, not playful. I responded by not moving and tightening my grip on him. I simply refused to let him go. I wanted to tell him that I was about to break up with Wes, that this night was the last night I went out with him—just like he did with Eugenia. But the words wouldn't come. I knew that they were insufficient, that what I was doing was wrong; that I had been using Wes, and that my behavior was cowardly.

"Tess? Tess!" They had walked in the opposite direction for now, but they would soon walk back this way.

Alex's eyes softened and then looked pleadingly into mine. He bent slightly and bridged the small gap, giving me a brief preview of what could have been a great first kiss. All too soon his lips moved away, leaving me once again, disturbed—in yet a different way.

With one hand on the railing of the veranda, he swung his torso over the edge and jumped down into the darkness. I rushed to the side and bent over the edge, suddenly worried because the drop seemed to be quite steep. But he landed safely on both feet and walked away with his tuxedo jacket slung over his shoulder as if he had done that a million times before.

Disappointed, I turned away from the spot, and walked back to the main entrance of the balcony. For a short moment, I had been Cinderella, but now I had to come back to reality. I would waste no more time. I would end it with Wes, but what I found as I turned the corner was not at all what I expected.

The sight was only shocking for a split second, then it seemed hilarious to me. A burst of laughter escaped my lips and I quickly stopped my mouth, but I was unable to control the onslaught of laughter that rippled through me. Wes and Brandy, with fingers tangled in each other's hair, were kissing. The moment they heard me laugh, they froze in place with a look of astonishment on their faces. This made me laugh even more, and a fresh new wave hit me so hard that I reached for the veranda for support.

They stared at me speechlessly for a long while, and then Brandy started to cry. This sobered me up a bit, and I tried to rein in my amusement so I could explain myself.

"No, Brandy, don't cry please, this is all my fault."

She stared at me through reddened eyes. "I'm sorry. I'm a horrible friend, I—I—"

"Nonsense, this is all my fault," I insisted.

"Why do you keep saying that, Tess?" Wes asked in a hoarse whisper.

"Because, Wes, I should have seen this sooner. I've been a poor excuse for a girlfriend to you and this whole time … " I looked at Brandy and realized all the little instances that should have clued me in. But I was so engrossed in my own insecurities that I didn't notice them. "I don't know why you put up with me this long Wes, I really don't. We should have broken up a long time ago, but I was a coward."

Wes narrowed his eyes and tried to follow my train of thought, but he didn't seem to quite grasp it. "Why were you a coward?"

"Because … " how was I going to say this without hurting his feelings?

"Because of Alex Preston," Brandy said succinctly.

Wes looked momentarily at Brandy, then back to me, when it dawned on him. "You … and Alex Preston?" He stared in disbelief, "You were dating me to make him jealous?"

"No! Not, really. Not to make him jealous. I wanted to get over him. I wanted to move on."

"Get over him? I never knew you guys dated?" Wes' head

seemed to be spinning.

"Well ... no, we never really did date, but," I shrugged. "I don't know ... we've ... " I was at a loss for words. What *did* Alex and I have? And how could I ever explain it?

Wes narrowed his eyes again then stretched his head toward the direction I had just come from. "Who were you out here with?"

I turned pink and looked down, embarrassed. I could tell that they exchanged glances. I looked up and Wes had a cross between a frown and a crooked smile. He saw the irony in it too.

"Is Alex still back there?" he asked.

"No, he jumped off the balcony when he heard you coming." Immediately Wes and Brandy looked over the edge of the balcony, thinking the same thing I had thought initially—that the drop was too far.

"It's only four feet," I explained.

"Did you kiss him?" Brandy asked, now feeling less guilty.

I turned pink again.

"She did!" Wes exclaimed; his voice was a mixture of vindication and accusation.

"Not like you guys! ... We would have though, if you hadn't come out."

"Well I'm—" Wes started to complain, but Brandy cut him short.

"It's obvious none of us are blameless, so let's wipe the slate clean," Brandy suggested.

To this we all agreed. Then remorseful, Wes added, "Well ... let's go find Alex. I suppose we can still save the evening if we get Alex back for you."

Wes paraded us both out of the dance hall, making sure he kissed us both on the cheek for added effect. I rushed down the entrance staircase and searched the parking lot. They helped me too, but Alex was nowhere to be found. He was gone.

In defeat, I slumped down on one of the steps of the entrance. I didn't feel like Cinderella any more, I felt like her shoe. Left behind and   forsaken.

Chapter 9

In vain I waited for Alex to call or make an appearance of sorts. But after a whole month went by, I lost all hope. I hated him for it! How could he? There was no question now of how he felt—he liked me! I was sure of it, so why didn't he call? The mounting frustration I felt over this was immense. There were days when I vowed that I would never love anyone ever again, and other days when I worried that perhaps I was being too harsh, and that there was a good reason for his silence. Maybe he was sailing with his grandfather and had no access to a phone—but why didn't he leave me a message before he left? I tried to rationalize his behavior any way I could, but I came up empty. By the end of summer there was only one true answer—he was purposely staying away.

I frantically kept busy, working two jobs: one as a lifeguard and the other at The Apothecary. I also started reading *Les Miserables* because that's exactly how I felt, miserable. Like a vulture smelling blood, Agatha seemed to know about my internal struggles and she reveled in it, but expressed her interest in my agony in a curious manner. She didn't exacerbate the situation. Instead she did something far worse—she was nice. This roused even more suspicion on my part. She was never nice. Nice was simply not part of her being. Distrustfully I avoided her and kept all communications to a minimum. I knew she was up to something. She was like that snake from *The Jungle Book*, who, while it wrapped itself around you, hissed, "trusssst in meee," then it ate you!

Finally, one day, toward the end of the summer, she made her move. I was cleaning the kitchen, putting dishes away, and making some tea in the process, when she sulked in and leaned casually against the counter. She was wearing contacts again, not the hungry vampire black, but the non-vegetarian vampire red. Her hair was all shaved now, except for two tufts of red and black strands by her face. On her skull she had a huge Third Eye tattoo, with a pyramid behind it, the symbol for "the illuminati". She reeked of heavy incense and tobacco and what's worse; she looked engulfed by a dark shroud. I didn't want to stare at her, but all the light seemed to be gone from her and the shroud looked like it was expanding as she stood there. Tendrils of darkness stretched out from her and toward me.

Instinctively I stepped away, and this seemed humorous to her. I picked up my towel and kept drying and putting away the dishes, but the darkness was expanding. Soon I started hearing hisses—unintelligible words, but despairing in meaning. They were just like the sounds I heard that rainy night at the bus stop.

"I know you can hear them," was all she said. I ignored her as usual, but she stood still and stared at me like a ghoul.

"I have no clue what you are saying, and I don't care to know either," I told her.

"I can tell them to talk to you so loud that they will drive you crazy," she said calmly.

"Listening to you does the job just fine."

"Very well, have it your way," she said. She turned to walk away, then stopped abruptly and turned to face me once more. "Your gift is very rare; you should embrace it, like I have. I can teach you how. We can find out what happened to your parents. We can find out what happened to Alex." Then she left, but not without leaving part of her darkness behind her. As promised, they were louder.

I still couldn't decipher the words, but I knew what they were trying to tell me. They wanted me to know how alone I really was, how despised by all, and how forsaken I was. Deep inside of me I knew they were lying, but they brought many good points to mind, starting with Alex and his disappearance, continuing on with how happy Wes was now with Brandy and how they never called me anymore. Then they jumped on my biggest doubt of all—my parent's love for me. *"Weee ... know ... "* they breathed out as they passed close by my ear. *"Summonnnn ... usss ... "* they continued as they coiled themselves around me. Taking in a deep breath and with a determined step, I knocked on Agatha's door.

She opened her door with a self-satisfied look on her face. "Told 'ya," she said and opened her door wide enough for me to pass. Her room was hideous. Posters and graffiti littered the walls, everything was strewn around the room and there was no natural light coming in from the large window. Agatha had hung a black sheet of fabric on top of the existing curtains, thus completely covering any cracks where the sun might possibly penetrate.

"Nice," I told her sarcastically.

"I thought you were here to get answers, not to decorate."

I turned and looked at her, no longer sure that she could help me. But I had to admit that the voices had left me alone the moment I entered Agatha's cavernous dungeon. In one hand Agatha was holding an Ouija board, and in the other hand a thick pillar candle. I lowered my eyelids and raised my eyebrows. "Are you serious?" I asked.

"Very. I'll have you know, that this is the most efficient way to summon spirits from the other side. I know it's now considered cliché, but it's a tool that works well and I refuse to stop using it simply because every horror movie uses it as a prop. Maybe once I'm more … experienced, I can summon them without the board, but for now this will do. Are you ready?"

I knew I should walk away right then and there, but my curiosity was piqued. They said they could tell me about my parents, whoever they were. "So who are we calling, exactly?"

"The spirits that surround us," she stated simply and with her foot she cleared a spot on the ground for us to sit. Then she laid the board down and lit the candle. "They have been around since the world began. They know everything."

"So what have you asked them?"

Agatha snorted a laugh, "like you, I started by asking them about my parents."

" … And?"

"Not much to tell there."

I stared at her with a probing look, "What else?"

"At first I was like you, wanting to know things about my past. I lived with my grandmother until she died. Then I entered the system," she said matter-of-factually, folding her legs like an Indian. This was the closest thing to bonding that we had ever done. "I wanted to know about my mom and why she left me with the old hag," she snorted. "Apparently she liked to live in the fast lane, and I was slowing her down. She died, in a ditch, of an overdose. My dad … the spirits said that he too came to an untimely death, never knowing that he had fathered a child." She shrugged, as if none of that mattered to her, as if the tragic lives of her parents were inconsequential to her. Maybe they were.

"Then, I wanted to know about my present," she continued with a chuckle, "like a test, you know. Then I started asking about the future, small things like, 'tell me what will happen today at school'." She looked up and smiled, "That day that Eugenia was about to beat you up, that was the first time I had inquired about the future. I was told of Eugenia's intentions. That's why I was ready." She nodded with pride, as if that was a great moment in her life. "So, ready?" She opened her eyes wide, looking deranged.

No. I wasn't. But I nodded briefly instead, and swallowed the lump in my throat. I kept feeling like I should get up—even now—and walk away, but I didn't. Agatha closed her eyes and took in a deep breath. "Double, double, toil and trouble … " she started.

"Okay, that's it. I'm outta here." I started to get up, but she laughed and pulled me down.

"Relax, will you? I was just kidding. I've been dying to use that on someone who was actually conscious during English class."

I looked at her evenly. "Doesn't that tell you something about your friends?"

"They're not my friends, and they don't need to be smart. They just need to be obedient," she protested. She closed her eyes again and took in a few more breaths before she started mumbling something in some foreign language. Then, she opened her eyes and rolled her eyeballs back, exposing the white—creepy, but somewhat amusing.

I shook my head; this was a load of—. Right then the candlelight started to flicker, an odd thing since there was no movement of air at all in this room.

"They're here," Agatha whispered, closing her eyes again, and inhaling deeply. "They want to talk to you, Tess." She placed her hand on the cursor and with her eyes closed guided it toward the letter K, then I-L-L.

"But you are moving it," I said to Agatha, in spite of the goose bumps that I had on my arm. In a dramatic display, Agatha raised her hands up, letting go of the cursor and the thing kept moving on its own toward E-D. KILLED, it spelled.

"What? They were killed? By who? Who killed them?" My heart was now racing, and a consuming need for information flooded my mind. I could see why people got addicted to this thing; it was real! Was it?

Upon my request for more information, Agatha mumbled some cheesy summon, asking the spirits that be, to grace me once again with an answer. She then grabbed some smooth pebbles and shook them in her hand. She dramatically let them drop on the board, and they scattered in an odd manner to spell F-A-T-H-E-R.

"No," I gasped and covered my mouth. "It can't be."

"We didn't end up here because our parents were stellar people, Tess," Agatha said soothingly. But I shook my head. It couldn't be. That wasn't right, I knew it wasn't right. They were lying!

A terrible laugh sounded in my ear, and I could hear it now so clearly that it froze my blood. My eyes grew big and I looked up at Agatha to see if she heard it too; she did. She tried to look as if it didn't scare her, but it did. I could see that part of her was glad I was sharing this nightmare with her, just to have someone who understood this burden. But there was another part of Agatha that was slowly surfacing before my eyes that was glad for my misery because she enjoyed it.

I stopped my ears, hoping that the awful evil laugh would not reach me, but it was in vain. I stood up and rushed out of her room with the darkness and the laughter trailing behind me. *"We can tell youuu ... the truth ... you can know what happened that night ... we know ... "* I started running up the stairs and tripped half way up, landing hard on my chin. They laughed even louder now. I got up and kept going. The race to my room seemed interminable, but as soon as I crossed the threshold of my room, a shiver went through me and a thunderous voice said, *"Depart!"*

Dorian seemed to know that something was on my mind, because he followed me with his eyes as I paced the room like a grenade about to go off. As usual he said nothing, but looked up at me questioningly.

"I can hear them, Dorian," I told him, without any other explanation. "I don't know who or what they are, but I can definitely hear them. Does this mean that I'm a freak like Agatha?

A wide grin crossed his face, making him look very handsome and quite grown-up. He didn't have to say a word. I knew what he was thinking, *"Not a freak like Agatha, a freak like me."*

"You're not a freak," I told him and then sat by his side. "You're special."

I curled up in bed with him and he stretched next to me. He covered my shivering arms with his blanket and draped one arm over me. For the most part Dorian didn't seem to like human contact, so I appreciated this grand gesture. I read that Autistic kids are ultra sensitive and all their senses are heightened, so things that wouldn't bother us bothered them. Smells or visual stimuli and a simple touch may be heightened for them. But none of these things seemed to bother him right now or if they did, he found a way to deal with them. We lay in silence for a long while as I tried to come to terms with what had just happened. Dorian's silence was soothing to me; we could have whole silent conversations like this. They were more like assisted introspection for me—I don't know what they were to him.

After a while I told him what happened. He listened, and was silent, but his silence conveyed a message—*you'll be all right*. And I believed him.

That night I had the first dream in months. Sadly, it wasn't about Alex, it was about today. In my dream I saw the events of the afternoon unfolding as a third party floating from above. To begin with I see myself drying the dishes, and Agatha coming to talk to me. As she leaves me in the kitchen, I see the shadows attack me;

but from this perspective, I can see them zooming all around me like cords of darkness that bind me, almost squelching my own light.

Then I see myself going into Agatha's room with an odd determination. The shadows are still there, but hovering and no longer bothering me. Agatha starts her chanting and the shadows start circling and the shapeless faces in the shadows look happy. Not in a good way, but happy in a cruel and malicious way.

Once she's done with her chanting, the distorted shadows start churning and swirling madly; the candle light flickers and some of them enter Agatha through her open mouth. She starts moving the board and spells KILLED. She shudders and the shadows exit her body the same way they went in. She looks sick to her stomach but tries to hide it. Then I call her on it, and the shadows gather thickly into one large mass that keeps growing and growing invisibly right before us. The mass of dark shadows take the shape of a demonic looking dragon and manages to move the pebbles and spell the word, FATHER. Then the dragon rears its ugly disfigured face at me and appears to peer into my freaked out face. It loves it!

I get up and start running up the stairs, with the dragon at my heels. It stretches its claw-like fingers and tries to snatch me, but miraculously, it misses. As I pass through the threshold of my bedroom, I also pass through a gigantic winged figure that blocks the entrance to my bedroom. He is almost too big to be inside this house, and is pearly white, with long feathered wings.

Somehow, I pass through him, and I see myself shivering, then the creature extends his enormous arm and stops the dragon by declaring: *"Depart!"*

Immediately the dragon explodes into thousands of smaller black pieces before retreating back down the stairs like a swarm of locusts, and enters Agatha's bedroom through the gap under her door.

"There's work for you to do, Tess," a soft purring voice says. *"This is part of your mission."* I turn my head toward the sound, and I see a golden face unlike any other. The face is that of a human, but slightly feline. Her tawny eyes are cat like and her skin

shines like gold and fire mixed together. I startled when I see her, in spite of the fact that she doesn't frighten me. I am just surprised to see her there, so close to me. There is something strangely familiar about her too. For a split second, I even feel relief at the sight of her, but then she starts to fade.

"Wait!" I tell her, *"I know you ... "*

"Remember, Tess ... it's what you were trained for. It's your mission, your responsibility ... your destiny," she says then fades completely out of view.

I woke up feeling rested and oddly at peace. But the night wasn't over; in fact it was only 3 a.m. *"Go to Agatha's room!"* I felt the command in my head. It reverberated in my thoughts over and over again until I felt compelled to get up. Before I even realized it, I was passing the threshold of my door again, and shivering—again. I turned to inspect the doorway, half expecting, half-hoping to see the huge winged man standing guard, but all I saw was my rickety old wood door with all its usual marks and scuffs.

My feet directed me down the stairs and I stopped right outside of Agatha's door. It was locked, but the lock would not be hard to pick. All I needed was a nail. Oddly, I found one on the floor right by my feet. "Strange," I mumbled, "I swear it wasn't there before."

The lock gave way and soon I found myself inside Agatha's room, again. What I was doing here of all places was beyond me. Why did I feel so compelled to be here? Agatha was dead asleep on her bed; so much so that she actually looked dead. Only the faintest movement of her chest gave any indication of life.

Her room looked more disheveled than it had looked earlier. Her clothes looked as if they had all been taken out of their drawers and thrown every which way. It also smelled gross, an odd combination of incense and something acid and metallic, which made my stomach turn. Her desk had a laptop that I hadn't noticed before. I don't know how she ever managed to afford it; she didn't have a job. Next to it were scattered papers, scribbles and tarot cards. I touched the mouse-pad and the dormant screen came to life displaying the title, "Corpus Hermeticum". My eyes automatically went to a paper that was placed right next to the computer, upon which were scribbled the same words, plus some other comments; "Astrology: magic has a natural power that comes from the stars. Powers come when sacrificing to the Source." Then below that, the words "Enneads, Neo-Platonism, Rasputin," and "Khlysts—only through ecstasy can we experience closeness to the Source." This was underlined several times.

I had no idea what all this meant, but I surmised that she was doing some sort of research on some ancient type of magic or astrology mixed up with some weird mystic-orthodox society. As I turned away from the computer and scanned the room one more time, my eyes caught sight of something that was sticking out from underneath her bed. It was half covered by her underwear, which I flung out of the way with one of her pencils.

I don't know why this item caught my eye, but it did. It was very old. The leather binding was falling apart, the pages yellow and thick, and roughly cut. Unsure of what I was doing, but certain that this was what I had come in here for—I tucked the book under my arm, placed the pencil back where I found it, and locked the door behind me—holding my breath as the door clicked shut.

Once inside my own room I climbed out the window and waited for my normal heart rate to return, before opening it. Most of the writings seemed to be in another language that I couldn't decipher at all. There were pictures in it as well—pictures of horned demons, dissected animals, and the grossest human anatomy ever— with drawings of limbs that looked as if they had been ripped out then sliced open. I closed the book with a thud, sickened by it, and I set it aside, wanting to put as much distance as I could between it and me.

The night was heavy with humidity, promising another three-digit day as soon as the sun rose, but for the time being, the air felt cool. As I drew my knees up against my chest, I looked up at the stars. They were bright and the moon looked beautiful as the sunlight only touched one side of it, leaving the other in semi-darkness. I loved looking at the night sky and I loved looking at the moon. I always felt an odd longing and a yearning when I did this.

Why would that be, I wonder? Why would I long for a place as foreign as the stars?

On top of the roof stood a massive white winged creature, his skin irradiated a polished marble white glow and his chiseled arms were crossed over his bare chest. Beside him, a golden creature landed softly, tucking her leathery bat-like wings behind her back. She was equally impressive and emanated a fiery glow.

"Is she asleep yet?"

"Shh … not yet. Almost, though," the white giant said quietly, as he stretched one of his huge feathered wings out and shook it a little as if stretching out a stiff leg. He eyed the golden figure beside him and smiled. "It's like she's your baby."

"She is, in a way," the golden creature sighed. "I just hope the training I gave her was enough. I personally chose each one of her classes, and missions. What if—"

"You did great, Dayspring. No human was ever more prepared … well … maybe not 'no human' … there might have been a few others … but the point is, Tess was ready. She is ready. This is the right time and she'll make the right choices. Just wait and see."

"I hope you're right, Kerubiel. Or our wedding will be indefinitely postponed," Dayspring added smugly.

"Well, you know me! Always willing to help out when it comes to you…and yours," he beamed and eyed Tess. "Just tell me what—"

"Just take her to bed," Dayspring said with a roll of her eyes. As she sauntered down the roof with feline agility and picked up the book that was lying on the roof, a flame shot out of the palm of her hand that consumed the book in an instant.

Kerubiel lifted Tess' body as one who would pick up a porcelain doll, and started for the tiny window. He soon realized that he would never fit through the opening, but he tried nonetheless. He tried going in head first, but his wings got stuck on the window sill, then he tried fitting one of his wings first, but his shoulder blade, torso and neck wouldn't fit either. Dayspring stifled a laugh. She suggested that he hand Tess to her, then go inside the other way and she could hand Tess to him through the window. This he did, amid repressed laughter and some other awkward moments. Finally, Kerubiel managed to put the sleeping Tess down on her bed, and tucked her in with the tenderness of a father.

I opened my eyes when I felt the glow of the sun behind my eyelids. My bedroom window was open and light was streaming in hot and bright. It's amazing to me how the sun, a star so far away from us, could give so much light and heat. And how, on a day like today, that star could give off so much heat that it will drive people indoors, just to escape it. Yet in winter its glow will feel so far away that it will barely provide any heat at all. Who designed this? Who orchestrated the whole thing? Surely it wasn't all coincidence; surely all of this was not a random act of nature. Laws can exist, but someone, something has to set them in motion—nothing just happens without someone first starting the chain of events.

I hopped out of my bed, and took inventory of my body and realized that I felt more rested than I had in a long time. Brushing off a faint feeling of disorientation, I squatted down and retrieved my valise from under my bed. This little suitcase was with me when I came to Charlotte's home, and it contained all my most valued possessions. They weren't many, and most of them had no monetary value, but they were my treasures. The little suitcase itself was a treasure, because it was one of the few items that I have from the first five years of my life—the mystery years. It was light brown imitation leather, with a map of the world on the outside. Every time I opened it, it smelled familiar, but the smell would only take me back so far. It smelled of love and happiness, but then there was a block, a huge gap that cut the fleeting memory short. This feeling was incongruous with the despairing picture that was put before me last night. How can love and happiness end up in murder? I shook my head and opened the suitcase.

Inside it I kept a satin sachet with the pearl earrings I was wearing on the day I came to Charlotte's. They were real pearls, because they were gritty against my teeth. Someone bought these for me; someone who loved me gave me these. Surely a child of five is not just given pearl earrings if they are not treasured in some way.

The other items in my valise were more mementos than anything else—papers that I wrote for school with shiny A's on them, swimming ribbons, report cards, my social security card, my prom dress that Alex touched, admired and held as we danced. And finally, the valise held the pictures that Dorian gave me.

These pictures I took out to bring with me outside onto the roof—then I remembered! Last night! Didn't I go back into Agatha's room last night? I rushed to the window and looked at the spot, where I clearly remember setting a strange book down. But the book was gone. Did Dorian take it? He was already gone, but I doubt that he took it. He never veers from his routine enough to even come out here to look. He wakes up, eats breakfast, then showers, gets dressed, and, depending on the day, starts on his chores, or goes to school. The sound of the lawnmower below told me that he was sticking to his chore schedule, so he wouldn't have taken it. He wouldn't even have gone out the window.

So where was it? I would have heard Agatha if she had tried to retrieve it; the whole neighborhood would have heard her! Did I dream that? Was it all just a bizarre dream? I've had plenty of those.

I looked down to the pictures in my hands…the woman, the house with the sailboat, me sitting on the bus bench and Alex in front of me with the trailing dark figures behind me…. Tears came easily enough, blurring my vision and stinging my hot cheeks.

"Heee ... hasss aaaa gfft ... " a familiar, soothing voice zoomed past me. I froze in place, and shivered in spite of the heat. I rubbed my arms, trying to get rid of the goose bumps on my skin, and my eyes immediately stopped producing tears.

"Like you," the same voice uttered somewhere off to my left,

so I turned abruptly to look at it, but there was nothing there.

"Who said that?" No! Not again, I thought.

"Don't be afraid, Tess. I'm her."

My eyes reverted instinctively to the drawing of the woman, the one with the gray eyes. I picked up the paper and studied it closely. *"That's right. That's me,"* she said.

"Who are you? What are you?" I asked, much against my better judgment, but curious.

"Your Guardian Angel."

Chapter 10

Chills filled my frame again. I tried to say something, like "am I dreaming?" or "am I losing my mind?" but no words would come.

"You have a gift, like Dorian, but different. You see...he can see things in his head, things that have happened or will happen, or that simply exist—like me."

"Am I related to you?"

"I can't tell you that. All I can say is that I've been watching over you since the day you were born."

"So you know my parents? You can tell me what happened to them, why I'm here, in foster care—"

"No, I'm sorry. I can't tell you that either."

"Then what are you good for?" I reproached. "If I'm going to hallucinate, then let's make it interesting. Let's come up with a good story and some answers."

"Ha!" she retorted, with something like an attitude. *"You did not just say that! I can leave, you know. I don't have to hover over you day and night, keeping you safe. Heaven knows the lengths I've gone to make your life easier, smoother, and happier, in spite of your circumstances. But if you don't think I'm any good then I'll just ... "*

"Okay, Okay, I get it!" I laughed. Not only was an Angel talking to me, but she was nagging me! "Let's start over. What can you tell me? Can you tell me your name?"

"Yes," she sounded somewhat mollified, but not entirely forgiving.

" ... And it is?"

"Celeste"

"Celeste. You pronounced it differently than what I expected. You said it in Spanish, with the short `e at the end."

"Nothing gets past you, does it? Yes, I do say it in Spanish, because I was from Spain. It means 'light blue' like the sky."

"Or like your eyes," I said with awe, while looking at the

picture of her. The name seemed to fit her perfectly and a fleeting memory crossed my mind's eye. It was an image of Celeste laughing. She was surrounded by light against an orange rocky backdrop. For that instant, she was no longer black and white, like on the paper. She was bright, her eyes were light blue-gray and her golden hair framed her face. Her laughter was intoxicating, and she made us all laugh. … Made *us all* laugh? I tried to go back and pull that memory forward again, but it was gone. For that split second, that memory seemed so real! For that second I felt differently, like I was part of something, something big, a greater … something … a large group of … some ones. And why did Alex come to mind right now?

"Yes, like my eyes. But I can't tell you much more about me. My life is not what's important here. You are. Now, since the cat is out of the bag, I decided to just come forward and introduce myself. Besides, I need to teach you how to focus your gift, so you don't drive yourself nuts and so you don't get yourself in trouble, like Agatha has. Not that she wasn't looking for it, but that's her deal."

"What—what are you talking about? What trouble?"

"Well, simply this. You can hear voices from other realms of existence. That's why we are having this conversation."

I nodded, and she sounded like she was pacing right in front of me. *"Once someone who is clairaudient realizes this, the floodgates are open. Your conscious mind will no longer block the sounds from the other realms and they will come in torrents. Since you can't see us, only hear us, you won't be able to distinguish who is who—until it's too late. You need to be taught certain techniques that will help you discern who to listen to and who to ignore. Do you follow?"*

"Yes. But could you stop pacing, it's giving me a headache."

"Humph!"

"Sorry, but it's true. It's not like I can hear you perfectly, you are hard to hear and then if you pace … "

"OK! I'll stop pacing! De tal palo, tal astilla," she murmured.

"What?"

"Nothing. Did you get what I just told you?"

"Yes, I'll go nuts if I don't learn to listen to the right kind of spirits. But how can I tell which ones are good spirits and which are bad?"

"I'm getting to that! But first I need you to understand something about the afterlife. Most spirits of the afterlife are not roaming around haunting people and such. For the most part, that is a total farce, a Hollywood thing. The spirits of the dead stay on our side, unless they break the rules—very bad—or are sent, like me, to watch over someone.

"Cast-outs on the other hand, are the ones that like to impersonate the dead and haunt people ... and that type of stuff. They pretend to be disembodied spirits and fool 'sensitive' people into doing all kinds of stuff and believing all kinds of things."

"What are cast-outs?" I asked, remembering the dream and the feelings I had last night when I was talking with Agatha.

"Cast-outs are the ones you need to watch out for, because they also know everything there is to know about you. They know your weaknesses and use them against you. They will say and do anything to make you miserable, and that is all they are after—misery. Not even I am immune to them. Like you, I have to be very careful of who I listen to."

I nodded, remembering last night and how they were so quick to know my own weakness—my past and what happened with my parents. "So what do disembodied spirits, like you, do all day?"

"That, querida, I can't tell you."

"Oh, come on! Who am I going to tell? It's not like I'll go to any of my friends and tell them that I just had a conversation with my Guardian Angel."

All was quiet for a moment and I wasn't sure if she had left or if she was thinking, but then she seemed to sigh, and quite possibly sit next to me, because I felt a chill on my left.

"OK, but this information is for your ears only, comprendes?" I nodded solemnly and, though I've never been a scout, I gave her the promise nonetheless.

"The realm of the dead is technically, here," she said in a low whisper.

"Here as in, here on Earth?" I asked.

"Yes, here on Earth, but mortals can't see us and we can't see

mortals, unless we get special permission or break a few hundred rules."

"So, disembodied spirits *can* cross over into the mortal realm?"

"*Technically, yes, but seldom do they do it. There's simply no need unless we sign up and get Angelic training. Even if disembodied spirits wanted their life back, crossing over into the mortal realm is torturous,*" she sighed. "*Try to imagine how frustrating it would be for you to be right next to someone you love, yet be completely ignored by them.*"

It wasn't hard for me to picture this; I knew all too well how it felt to be ignored by someone I loved. Alex was ignoring me in much the same way.

"*Add to that frustration, the fact that your situation will not change for a long, long time—not until that person dies too! It's miserable, trust me,*" she sounded like she had experience with this, so I simply nodded. "*Even I, who have been trained for Angelic work, still struggle with it. For those who manage to slip through without the preparation and the understanding it's—it's—Hell.*"

"Are you saying that that is what Hell is?"

"*That's one form of Hell. Heaven and Hell are not destinations per-se, not at this point, not before we're judged. When people die, they die exactly as they were when they were alive. Nothing changes. Their thoughts, their fears, their troubles, those all die with them, and their mental anguish does not diminish nor go away simply because they lose their bodies. On the contrary, those problems simply increase! Now they have no body and no way to fix those problems.*" She was silent for another long moment, then continued. "*Well, you asked about what we do and then I went off on a tangent.*" She made a clicking noise with her tongue in clear disapproval of herself. "*You see? I'm going to get in trouble!*"

"Sorry."

"*All I can tell you is what I do and nothing more.*"

"Fair enough."

"*I learn and work.*"

"That's it?"

"*Basically. When I first crossed over, I had a big joyous*

reunion with all my loved ones that were on that side. We talked and caught up for quite a while, then they showed me around."

"I thought you said that the other side was here?"

"It is, but it doesn't look like Earth does now, at least not all of it," she sighed again, this time with frustration. *"He told me it would be difficult, and now I see why!"*

"Who? What?"

"Shush! Let me think." She was quiet for a long while and I started tapping my foot impatiently. *"I'm doing my best here! It's just hard to explain things without revealing too much, okay?"*

"Okay," I answered defensively. This Angel was nothing like I would have expected. She treated me with familiarity and contempt. She wasn't as cryptic as I would have imagined and she brought with her an air of … joviality.

"Where I stay," she continued treading carefully, *"Spirit Earth, there are a lot of schools—universities, really. We go to these universities to learn about everything and anything we want to. I recently took a botany class, and attended a lecture and a performance taught by Bach."*

"The *Johann Sebastian Bach?"* I asked incredulously.

"Yes, of course, who else? You should hear Handel's 'Hallelujah Chorus' in heaven!"

"Wow…I never thought about concerts in heaven. Who else plays?"

"Well, anyone who wants to, I suppose. But my husband and I like a certain type of music, so we only attend those we care to hear."

"So you and your husband spend your time going to concerts?"

"Tonta, no! We do go to some, but that's not all we do. I already told you, we go to classes; we learn—intellectually—learn things. You can't pick up a new hobby here, but you can intellectually learn all you want. We can take classes from Shakespeare and Cervantes, Cicero, Galileo, Socrates, Mother Teresa, even Moses teaches!"

"Are you serious?"

"Of course! They teach us all they know, plus, they learn from

us too! It's very interesting. But there are limits to what we can learn, and these limits are frustrating. For example, because we have no body, we can't improve on a skill that would require your physical body. If I were to sit at a spiritual piano, my fingers would not move any faster than they did on the day I died! So progression is limited to those of spiritual and intellectual pursuits."

"Huh, that's interesting." I pondered on that for a while. By now the sun was higher in the sky, and was burning my skin. I looked at my watch and realized that in an hour I would have to be at work. Celeste must have noticed this, because she started pacing again, and complained that we had wasted precious time talking nonsense. "I don't think it was nonsense," I disagreed, "I thought it was interesting!"

"You would! But the problem is that the most important thing for you to know, you don't yet know. Listen. I was sent to teach you how to tell the difference between good spirits—who, like me are Angels, and the cast-outs. Escuchas?"

"Yes, I hear you."

"Bien. It's really rather simple, but you have to focus. The key lies in how you feel inside when spirits or even mortals are around you. Try not to be swayed by what they say or how they present themselves. Look within, how do you feel? While we spoke, how did you feel?"

"I felt good. Happy!"

"Now think back to how you felt when those Cast-outs were after you last night." I thought and I remember feeling tormented by them. When I told her this, she added that it wouldn't always be such a stark contrast. Sometimes it would be subtler—like a general feeling that something is amiss. Then she told me that I needed to work on tuning myself to the right sort of spirits; she said that the more tuned I was to good, the less I would hear the bad ones.

"I don't know how to do that, Celeste," I told her flatly.

"Think of it as tuning a radio. Some channels are nothing but static while others come in clear. Spend time tuning into the voices that are clearly good—that make you feel at peace. And when you come across a bad voice, tune it out! Eventually it will become full

of static and you'll avoid it naturally."

I nodded slowly, trying to digest all that information.

"Oh! One more thing! A voice may come along that sounds ... familiar, or even is familiar. The voice might confuse you, or it might not be a voice that makes you feel particularly bad. If this ever happens, just remember, the voice of a good spirit would never interfere with your own life. A Guardian Angel, like me, would never infringe on your life or consume your mortal time. Do you understand?"

"I'm not sure," I shrugged, feeling overwhelmed by all of it. I waited for a while for her response, but she remained quiet, so quiet and so still that I wasn't sure anymore if she was still here. "Celeste?"

"Yes, I'm here ... I was just ... never mind. Listen, all you have to remember is that a good spirit who has been sent from the Eternals, will not ruin your life or demand you spend all your time with them. That would be a haunting, and we good spirits do not haunt mortals."

The rest of the summer flew by. I worked two jobs and enjoyed the occasional quip from Celeste, who seemed to be on duty quite a bit. She said that cast-outs were after me, now that they knew that I could hear them, and that she was shooing them off for me. At first I found this to be a bit unsettling, but as the weeks wore on, the whole situation seemed more commonplace, and I found Celeste's company soothing.

The fall and school came all too soon, and life fell, more or less, back into its usual monotony. This year, I had no Alex to look forward to, so the only thing that kept me motivated to move forward and do something, was my promise to Dorian. Wes and Brandy were inseparable. They loved each other, and they emitted a radiant light when they were together. It was good to see them so happy, but I have to admit that sometimes I felt a twinge of jealousy. Not because of

Wes, but over their happiness. They tried to include me as much as possible, but being around them all the time could be downright unbearable sometimes. I would often make up excuses during school, to skip out and be alone. For weekend activities, they stopped trying altogether, after the third month of consecutive refusals. I was now officially a loner—not just a loner—but a weird loner at that.

Celeste made sure I was thoroughly nagged about this, whenever she came by. With the experience of a lifetime behind her, she pestered me endlessly about needing to go out more and having more fun with my friends. After a while, even she gave up, and eventually took to giving me ideas on my clothes designing. She had lived during the Second World War era, so she had me doing research on clothing from the 30's and 40's. I was able to design several pieces based on that time period that I really liked. One of the dresses I made, Brandy's mom ended up buying. She was one of my most devoted fans, and promised to help me become a designer in any way possible. I wasn't sure what she could do for me, but it was nice to know that someone out there cared about my future.

Agatha had changed too, since that day that she pulled out the Ouija board for me and revealed to me the whole thing about the voices. She looked ashen and sicklier than ever; she hardly needed to wear her white makeup anymore. She appeared gaunt and had dark purple circles under her eyes. Charlotte even noticed, asking me if I thought Agatha was doing drugs or something. I told her that I had no clue—which I didn't. But in fact, I thought I knew what was going on; it was just too creepy to say it out loud. Agatha was being haunted.

Chapter 11

Celeste, who could see clearly what went on in the unseen world of spirits, assured me that cast-out spirits constantly surrounded Agatha. These spirits were the true undead, the real devils. Their only goal was to demoralize, depress and ultimately destroy us at any cost. There were times, when they would converge on me with such malicious fortitude that they would succeed in getting through to me, and I would hear them almost as clearly as I heard Celeste. Fortunately, my room was like a sanctuary, and the moment I would step across the threshold of my bedroom, I was safe. Dorian, however, seemed to remain impervious to them; almost as if he carried his own invisible winged giant with him wherever he went.

In the safety of this little bedroom of ours, Dorian and I spent a great deal of time. Here I set up Charlotte's sewing machine, which, in an unprecedented gesture of kindness, she gifted me. I was very grateful to her for this, because it was a good machine and it would have cost me a lot of money to buy one this good.

To even out the score, I made her a dress that she could wear to church on Sundays. It was a Charlotte dress, not at all something that I would ever consider to my taste, but I knew that she would like it—and she did. This turned over a new leaf in our relationship, and we now regarded each other on more equal footing.

She still wasn't my mother nor my friend, but she was an ally. She no longer took Agatha's side on everything, and she treated me with more respect and consideration than ever. She was still Charlotte, still looking on the financial side of everything, so she still reminded me that once I turned eighteen, I was supposed to be out of her house.

She did concede to let me stay until graduation day, because I would turn eighteen a few months before school let out. But she was planning on having more foster kids come the moment I was gone, so I would have to vacate on that precise day.

"I've missed you," Alex crooned. I was standing inside a room I'd never been in. It was sparsely decorated in shades of blue-gray in a modern minimalist way. I looked around and saw clues that led me to believe that perhaps this was Alex's bedroom.

"I've missed you too." More than words could say. Even in dream form he seemed so real. He moved like Alex, he talked and acted just like him, and I had no clue what he was about to say. If dreams are part of my imagination, shouldn't I be able to change them?

A wild thought crossed my mind and I thought I would test this theory of mine. He was following me with his eyes and he seemed to be questioning my impish look.

"I just found out I can hear spirits," I blurted out.

His eyebrows shot up, then came down, forming a frown. *"What do you mean by spirits?"*

"Just that. I hear voices from other realms of existence. Today, I had a whole conversation with my Guardian Angel. Her name is Celeste." I sat down on the edge of his bed and crossed my legs while reclining back onto his mattress. *"Oh, and get this! Dorian drew her!"*

"You mean the picture of that lady you told me about?"

"What?" How did he know about that? Oh, that's right! I told the real Alex that Dorian had drawn me a picture of a woman, after he asked me about *"Estelle ... "*

"That's right, he drew my great-grandmother, Estelle. So how do you know that the lady in the picture is your Guardian Angel?"

"She told me. She tells me lots of things, all the time! In fact, she won't shut up. She nags and nags and bosses me around all day long."

Alex started laughing. *"That doesn't sound like fun. I wonder if I have a Guardian Angel?"*

"I'm sure you do. Next time I see you in real life, I'll tune in and see who turns up."

"You're serious."

"Very." Then I did get serious. *"Do you think I'm crazy?"*

He paced the space right at the foot of his bed a few times, as he mulled the question over in his head. I watched him with interest, having no idea what he was about to say, but wishing he would say, "no, you're not crazy." Instead he crossed his arms over his chest and tapped his lips with one finger. *"My sister says she can understand animals,"* he said suddenly, taking me by complete surprise. I had no clue he would say that. *"One summer, when we were kids, we went outside with nets and glass jars to catch butterflies. I caught a whole bunch and handed them to her, because she was crazy about them."* He paused and looked at me with one eyebrow raised. *"She grabbed the glass jar full of fluttering butterflies and she dropped it! Then put her hands up to her ears and started screaming, saying that the butterflies were shrieking and crying!*

"She made me let every single one of them go and swears to this day that she heard those butterflies."

"Really?" I was sitting on the edge of his bed and he was now sitting on a chair that he had scooted to the foot of his bed. As he spoke, I got so into the story that, as I leaned forward, we were inches from each other.

"Dorian draws pictures of people he can't possibly know. My mom predicts the future and I—I hullucinate about you." His last words were soft, almost like a tingle against my lips.

This made me laugh, and I backed away. *"But you're wrong. I'm the one who hallucinates about you."*

"Tess! Tess! Wake up!"

"Oh, be quiet Celeste! I'm dreaming."

Alex smirked and scooted his chair forward, then placed his hands on my knees and slowly inched his way over me.

"You get off her!" Celeste shouted. Something shimmery and white, zoomed past me, and pushed Alex back down on his chair.

"What the—? he started to say, when all it went dark.

"What's eating at him?" Valerie bent slightly and whispered in her daughter's ear. "He's been so … so … "

"Despondent," Katie summed up.

"Yes, despondent. Do you know why?"

Katie sighed, she knew why; she had gotten the whole thing out of Alex while he visited from school last month. But he made her swear that she wouldn't tell anyone, not even their parents. This she couldn't understand. Why the secrecy? But out of respect to him, she had kept her promise. But he looked worse now, more so than ever; and she wondered if he didn't know what was good for him anymore. "Why don't you ask him?"

"I have, but he doesn't say anything! I think it has something to do with a girl, but … he won't tell me who or why."

Kate sighed again. "Just keep pestering him; you'll wear him down eventually." They walked in silence for a while. The sound of Christmas music filled in for conversation and the twinkling of the many Christmas lights reflected off their faces. Alex walked briskly ahead, not bothering to look at any of the store windows. They were supposed to be looking for gifts for the Admiral, Dane, and for the church Christmas Charity. Every year, they had been assigned a particular family, but this year, the committee had decided to make a list of all the ages, and genders and split that list among the members of the congregation that wanted to contribute. Valerie had chosen teen-age girls, because she figured that Katie would be an asset in helping her find suitable gifts for them. Katie, however, was not like most teen-age girls, and was failing miserably at the whole gift thing.

While it's highly understood that most teen-age girls are into make-up and clothes, Katie was into animals. In fact she couldn't fathom what the attraction of painting your face "to attract members of the opposite sex," was. She merely understood human behavior, from the animal kingdom point of view, and to her, painting your face was akin to peacocks fluffing and extending their tails. But since in the animal kingdom it is traditionally the male's job to do all the fluffing and showing off, she decided to take the same approach and let the guys show off for her. This point of view had been expressed to her parents; Dane had accepted this with much relief, but Valerie couldn't help feel a twinge of sadness over the lack of "girl time" with her daughter.

"I don't think that a card stating that we donated money to an animal preservation program will cut it," Valerie said in frustration, after Katie shrugged indifferently at the sight of a pile of diverse accessories.

"You know who would be great at this? Tess!" Katie said brightly and loud enough for Alex to hear from the door.

"Tess?" Valerie inquired. "That girl we took home after the art gallery?"

Katie nodded, and Alex shot her daggers with his eyes. "She's into fashion big time! She designed her prom dress last spring. She designs all her clothes, for that matter."

"Really? How wonderful! You know, she is one of the girls we need to buy a present for. Charlotte puts her foster kids' names in the charity every year, and I seem to remember seeing it again this year. You know her, right, Alex?"

Alex's face was now ashen and slightly angry, but Valerie ignored him and continued with her verbal musings. "What should we get her? Hmm … fashion design, huh?" She tapped her lips with her finger. "Well, she might need drawing supplies. You need to be able to sketch well to design clothes. Oh, Katie! Remember her foster brother? Maybe we should buy him—"

Alex walked away fuming and Valerie took exception to that.

"Oh no, he didn't!" Valerie protested. Alex had succeeded in angering his mother who was now on an intercept course.

"Listen son, I don't know what your deal is but—" she stopped, noticing the pain behind his eyes. "What is it? Look, Alex, I'm not the psychiatrist in the family, but I can tell when something is wrong. You might be surprised to know that I can be very understanding when I want to, and I really want to understand you right now."

Alex looked down, then back up at his mother's violet eyes. "She's not just a foster kid," Alex stated through gritted teeth. Valerie cocked her head to one side and stared at her son for a moment. Then a smile crossed her face, " … you like her!"

Alex closed his eyes and exhaled, trying to compose himself, before he lashed out. He had no idea why he felt so irritated at his mother. Of course she didn't know about Tess, he hadn't told her anything. Of course she would think of Tess as just a foster kid. She was one after all. But the stigma that the word carried irritated him. Eugenia had teased her mercilessly about being a foster kid, and he was angry, mostly with himself for allowing that to happen. And now, his mother's tone when she said, "you like her!" like it was amusing to her, infuriated him. He didn't just like her, he loved her! He thought of no one else! And he had to stay away from her.

Valerie tried to read her son's expression, but it was riddled with contradictory emotions. "Alex, it's okay for you to like her. I thought she was lovely."

"I know it's OK for me to like her, mom. It's not that."

"Then what?"

"You won't understand."

"Does your grandfather understand?"

Alex looked away. This was a sore subject with his mom. At times she would get slightly jealous of the fact that he confided in his grandpa more than he did with her. "Yes, he does," he said, waiting for the storm to unleash. But it didn't. Instead, Valerie smiled and patted his head.

"Well, as long as you have someone to talk to about this. I know your grandpa will never lead you astray. He loves you and wants nothing but your happiness. Just remember that I'm a woman, and I understand the way women think. Women warfare is far different than the kind your grandpa has learned about," she said, then walked on ahead. "If she's into fashion, then we need to get her some clothes."

"No," Alex howled.

"Fabric?"

He shook his head and stalked off. Valerie, and the mute Katie, pursued him with brisk steps and side-glances until he made a sudden stop in front of a bookstore. Shrugging, they followed him in and made themselves scarce while he wandered down the classics aisle. Not ten minutes had gone by before he was walking out with a large brown bag in hand and a big smile—for a change.

Every Christmas Charlotte put our names in the church's charity list. It was embarrassing, but I suppose better than nothing. Charlotte was not going to spend her own money on us, so we had grown up on the kindness of the community. When I was younger, the gifts were adequate, but as I grew up, the gifts got worse—or rather less enticing. This year I volunteered to help wrap gifts, and I finally realized why the gifts I got were always so random.

People from the congregation were assigned to a family or an age group, and then would buy things. Only one year did I get lucky and received a truly great gift. It was my freshman year, and I got an aromatherapy kit. It was a gift donated by my current employer, Libby, from The Apothecary and thanks to that gift, I later got the job. I told Libby that I was the one who got the kit that she had donated, and how much I loved it! She hired me on the spot, and we have been great friends ever since. But for the most part, Christmas morning was not something we particularly looked forward to.

This year, I volunteered to wrap the little kid's toys, because I know they are more likely to love any toy they get. Also because the organizers think that I, as a recipient, should stay as far away from the teen table as possible. In the mean time I'm getting a taste of what the other side of the spectrum is like. I've come to find out that those who donate gifts actually agonize over what the recipients will think; they do hope that what they bought will please some unfortunate child. As one who has been on the receiving end, I, of course lie, and assure those who ask that the gifts will be appreciated and cherished.

The whole process is organized chaos. Working under the constant din of Christmas music and sparse North Pole decorations, the volunteers line several rows of rectangular tables arranged end to end. Each table has a gender and age group assigned, and the volunteers form an assembly line. One measures and cuts the paper, another folds, and yet another tapes. A fourth person applies the bow and a fifth writes the age group on the sticker and drops the gift in a huge bin. Those who deliver the gifts pick them at random from the bins and put them in boxes with the family's name on them. Those boxes are delivered on Christmas Eve by yet another large group of volunteers. It's impossible to get personal under these circumstances, and now I understand.

Once the last gift was wrapped and in the right bin, the large group of volunteers sang a carol, and shared hot cocoa. I stayed with the people from my table, which consisted of grandmotherly-type ladies who told a great deal of jokes while they wrapped, and were members of a crochet group that I said I would be interested in joining.

There were so many people roaming around that I hadn't noticed until the hot cocoa was passed around, that Valerie and Katie Preston were there too. All of a sudden all the blood drained from my face, and strangely, I felt like I should run away. All I could think of was that dream that I had last night, where I confessed to Alex that I heard voices; then Celeste's sudden intrusion in the dream. I still wasn't sure what that was all about. She hadn't turned up yet so I couldn't ask her.

My grandma group noticed my odd behavior and started with their inquiries. I told them that I had forgotten that I had to work, so after hugging them all and promising to join them at their next crochet club meeting, I left.

Chapter 12

At Charlotte's, no one wakes up early on Christmas morning. When we were children, Charlotte would threaten to take all our toys away if we woke them up before 9 a.m. to open gifts. Now no one even wants to wake up early. In fact, Charlotte has to coerce us with all kinds of threats to come down at all.

This year though, Charlotte must have been in a good mood, because she woke us up, not with threats, but with the smell of sausage and biscuits with gravy. Once she had us all in the kitchen, she cynically announced that we had to open presents before eating. Agatha rolled her eyes and walked right past the tree, heading back to her room, but Joe stopped her and sat her down. Usually she would have made some rude display at being touched at all, but she was still acting weird, so she simply flopped herself down on the floor and fell back asleep.

Joe gave his customary short speech of all the things we should be grateful for; it was really more of a Thanksgiving speech, but he always delivered it on Christmas morning, leaving Thanksgiving wide open to football. After waking Agatha back up, we opened gifts, one at a time. Under the tree there were the customary gifts, wrapped with cheap paper and stick-on bows; but this year there was one gift that was different. This one was expertly wrapped with expensive, thick paper and had an actual cloth ribbon tied around it. The present itself looked beautiful, like a decoration. Once Joe reached for Charlotte's gift, we all noticed it, and even Agatha seemed to perk up at the sight of it. Charlotte opened her gift first; it was a gift card to a local spa. Joe got a new suit for church. He hated suits, but he would wear it nonetheless. Then Joe reached for another present, being careful to avoid the "nice" one, announcing that it was for Dorian. It was two country music CD's. He stared at them blankly. I put my hand on his knee to reassure him that I had gotten him a present and it was waiting for him upstairs.

Up next was Agatha, who shot me a hateful look when she was

given the second to last present—a box of popcorn and the movie "Becoming Jane". She pocketed the popcorn, and tossed the movie back under the tree, then laid back on the floor, and promptly fell back asleep. I couldn't possibly fathom who would take the time to wrap a present like this. Perhaps it was Brandy's mom, or maybe …

All my anxiety over who might give me this present disappeared the moment I opened the box—all the while being careful not to rip the pretty paper. In the bottom of the box, under several layers of fluffy tissue paper, lay a leather-bound, gilded, ribbon marked copy of *Jane Eyre*.

I reached down and retrieved the book with care. I could feel all eyes on me, or rather the object I was about to reveal. I keenly felt their disappointment at the sight of the book, and their amazement at my joy. Agatha snorted and got up to leave, making sure she stepped on the tissue paper and her movie. Charlotte announced that breakfast was ready, and Joe followed her. I gathered up my box and went back up to my room, while Dorian followed Joe and the smells of sausage and biscuits.

"Your life will be a living Hell," Agatha warned as I passed her bedroom on my way up the stairs. "They know all about you, and they know how to crush you!"

I froze in place. The hairs on the back of my neck bristled, sending chills up and down my spine. I had no doubt that she spoke the truth, yet something inside of me burned. It was anger, not toward Agatha, but toward those unseen voices that haunted her. I was sure that they were using her. She was guilty of listening and heeding everything they said, but I hated the voices more than I hated Agatha.

"They will ruin your life too, if you keep seeking them out," I cautioned.

"Ha! Since when do you care?"

"Just saying," I shrugged, then walked up to my room.

"They'll help me be who I was meant to be!"

"No they won't. They'll use you, then they'll ruin you." I said without turning.

In the privacy of my room and with my heart racing, I

inspected the beautiful hardcover copy of my most favorite book in the whole entire world. With misty eyes I traced the cover and turned a few leaves. This wasn't just a book, it was a message … he loved me—I hoped. At the very least, he was thinking about me. *He loved me.*

For the rest of the day I felt like a caged lion. I kept pacing my room back and forth, trying to decide whether I should go to his house and thank him for it, or not. There was no note of any kind, no dedication—nothing. What if the gift wasn't from him after all? Then I would be making a total fool of myself. If only Celeste were here! I might be able to coax her into telling me who sent this! I wonder what Christmas in Heaven is like?

Suddenly there was an odd sound downstairs. It was like a gasp and a thud. I rushed out of my room and down the stairs to find Agatha's bedroom door opened and Charlotte on the floor recovering from some sort of fainting spell. Joe was there in an instant as well. "What's wrong?" he inquired. Charlotte was mute, but managed to point inside Agatha's room. Joe and I peeked in, and stared at the same time.

Against the already depressing backdrop of graffiti and vandalized furniture, hanging from the ceiling fan, was a dead cat. Agatha and her belongings, however, were nowhere to be found. Her window was ajar, indicating that she left from there. Both Joe and I stared in dumb amazement at the cat and the room. Finally, Charlotte regained her composure, rushed to the phone and called the police.

Two Officers came. One of them looked familiar, but I couldn't quite place him. Because Agatha was still a minor, an Amber Alert was issued, and a detailed investigation into her disappearance was underway. They asked for a list of her friends, this list was short. In fact, I only knew Amanda by name, the others I always referred to as—her coven. The Officer that looked familiar bit his lip and suppressed a laugh when I said this. Then he quickly recovered and handed me a business card. "Just in case you remember any names," he said, with steady eyes that seemed to burn into mine. I took the card and inspected it. "John Lovell,

Detective", it said in big bold letters.

The Officers wanted to question us all separately, but when it was Dorian's turn, I explained that he didn't talk to anyone. Both Charlotte and Joe verified this and added that I seemed to be the only one who could ever understand him. Cold sweat broke out on Charlotte's forehead after this; she feared that the Officers would figure out that Dorian and I shared a room. The detectives noticed Charlotte's sudden uncomfortable shifting of her body, and one of them was about to ask more questions when Officer Lovell sent him back to Agatha's room to look for further signs of a possible forced entry.

I was next to be interviewed, so the others went to the kitchen to wait for me. Without wasting any time, Officer Lovell started questioning me about Agatha. My answers were short; the fact was I didn't know Agatha that well.

"Why do you think she did that to the cat? Was she in the habit of killing animals?"

"I don't know, to both questions," I told him. He stared at me a bit longer, clearly wanting me to expand my answer. "I wouldn't put it past her," I added, to please him and to seem like a "willing" witness.

"Why?"

"Well ... you saw her room. She's deranged. We've never gotten along, not from day one. We avoided each other like the plague."

"I think you know more about Agatha than you're letting on," he stated calmly.

I shrugged, and then thought of the book. But that was a dream—a very real dream—but a dream nonetheless. Besides, even if it had been real, the book was gone. I guess I could tell him about the voices…but then he'd have me committed. I sighed. This was an impossible situation.

"Look, she was mental, okay? I'm not one hundred percent sure, but I think she dabbled in witchcraft, voodoo and other weird stuff. She also mentioned to me once or twice that she could hear voices. She's probably schizophrenic."

"Her bedroom wall would certainly attest to that," he added calmly and jotted some things down on a pad of paper. He then looked back up at me and studied me carefully for a few seconds. "What did she say the voices said?"

"She didn't tell me what they said. She just said that she could hear them and that they got loud," I said, and for the first time in my life I felt a bit sorry for her. Was Agatha schizophrenic or was she being haunted? If she was schizophrenic, then maybe I was too—I heard voices.

"So you two didn't get along," he verified.

"No—Yes. We did not get along!"

Detective Lovell studied my face, then narrowed his eyes. "You are taking this rather coolly."

I shrugged again. What was I supposed to say? I wasn't sad she left. I wouldn't wish her any harm, but I certainly wasn't going to hold a vigil in her name.

He stared at me sharply for a few seconds. "So what do you think about the note?"

"The note? What note?"

His brown eyes dug into mine with alarm. "You didn't see the note attached to the cat's neck?"

"No," I said, breathlessly. "What did it say?"

"Tess. It said, Tess."

Agatha's disappearance marked a new beginning for me. All the happiness and hope that I had felt from my Christmas gift was gone. I no longer felt sure of what was real around me anymore. Celeste tried to convince me that she was real, but that only depressed me more, so she left. School turned into an endless cycle of days that blended into each other, I dropped swimming because I had lost whatever it was that propelled me forward. I still studied and got good grades, but I did that for Dorian, not me.

I joined the crochet group with the grandmas because it was

soothing and they didn't make me talk. They were happy, content women who mothered me with tea and pastries. They never asked about my gloominess. They just taught me the crafts of knitting and crochet, and reminisced about the past. I loved to hear them talk about their lives; they reminded me of Celeste. But Celeste was not real, I decided. And even if she were real, she was dead and not part of this realm, and I was better off without her. My life was complicated enough without voices from the great beyond.

The room that Agatha had occupied for so long was eventually remodeled and a new girl came to occupy it. Charlotte tried to move me in there, but Dorian refused to share a room with another boy, so our sleeping arrangement remained the same, and magically undisturbed by all of the state workers. The new girl, Meg, was nice. She had been in and out of foster care due to her mom's drug addiction. Now, her mom was in prison for good, and Meg was finally free to start her life.

Though only twelve years old, Meg knew a lot more about life than most girls do at that age. She and Charlotte hit it off right away, and for the first time, I saw Charlotte in the mother role. She seemed to take it right up with Meg, no nagging about the cost of having foster children in the house, no thrift-store shopping, no indifference, and no charity Christmas gifts ... Charlotte just took Meg under her wing and kept her there for herself.

I wasn't jealous, I was glad. I had Dorian, so I didn't need Charlotte. Perhaps, if I had bonded with Charlotte, I would have never taken to Dorian like I did, and I wouldn't trade that for anything. All in all, our home life did improve with Agatha's departure and Meg's arrival. Charlotte's house felt more like a home. Meals were now shared, and conversations started up naturally. Meg was giggly and frivolous, and by springtime, she was a mini-Charlotte, down to the fake nails and hair. Joe was thrilled about this, and was as indulgent as ever. Even I joined in the doting and gifted Meg one of my latest creations—a rag doll with crocheted clothes.

The idea of making rag dolls came to me during a crochet meeting. One of the ladies showed me a doll she'd had since childhood. It was a homemade version of Raggedy Ann. It was so lovely, that I spent the weekend making one out of scraps. Then I crocheted the clothes and the end product was adorable. I made several of them after that, and with the help of the crochet ladies; I soon had a whole collection. After I let Meg choose one, I donated the rest to the local Foster care office so they could be given to kids who, like me, entered the system young and empty-handed. This was a great success, and the state workers were soon requesting more. Now the crochet club had a mission and a purpose that we all took to heart.

I did join my friends a few times for movies and parties, but truth be told, I didn't have that much fun. Wes and Brandy were still my best friends at school and we had lunch together every day, but I always felt out of place and detached from normal teen-age life. They sympathized with me, but they couldn't understand the extent of my feelings. They didn't have vivid dreams that blurred reality, they didn't hear voices from the dead and they didn't have a death threat looming over their heads—but I did.

School also reminded me of Alex. I saw his sister often, but we never said much to each other besides a warm 'Hello' or a smile. Her presence inevitably reminded me of Alex, and I would feel a pang in my chest and a knot in my stomach that left me slightly queasy.

Only one time, toward the end of the school year, did she and I talk. I was parking my scooter when I saw Amanda and the rest of Agatha's now stranded coven standing by Katie, who looked like she was crying. They were all looking at something on the ground in front of them. I couldn't tell what it was, so I ran to Katie's side to see what was the matter.

They were looking at a cat that was going berserk, jumping up and down and twisting around like it was possessed. I would have thought it somewhat funny looking, had I not been threatened with that hanging cat. Katie certainly didn't think it was funny and she was desperately trying to snatch the crazy cat from its torturers, but every time she tried to pick it up Amanda would stop her and push her out of the way.

"What's wrong with that cat?" I asked.

"Catnip," Amanda boasted, then laughed rather diabolically.

"She's not having fun. It's torturous for her!" Katie pleaded. "Please, let me wash her now."

"Did the cat tell you that, Miss Doolittle?" one of the other freaks sneered.

"Leave her alone!" I said, stepping forward.

"Or what?" A rather greasy looking boy with yellow teeth taunted.

I didn't respond to him directly, instead I glowered at Amanda with the most vicious scowl I could muster. Then it occurred to me that Amanda *knew* about me. I was sure that Agatha had confided in her about my so-called gift. Trusting my gut on this, I stepped forward ignoring the crazy cat. "She knows," I said unflinchingly and nodded my head toward Amanda.

I was right. Amanda knew about my … abilities so she started backing away, not wanting to experience what Agatha had given her a preview of. There were few things a big bully like Amanda feared, and Agatha had figured that out—devilish voices from other realms of existence—was one of them.

"Come on, let's go," Amanda called out. The stragglers exchanged a few puzzled looks, then obeyed.

As soon as they were a few steps away, Katie reached down and picked up the writhing cat. "Thanks," she sighed. "I'll have to take her to the bathroom and wash her off."

"Will it be OK?"

"Yeah, I just need to rinse the catnip off. Then she'll be fine." She wiped a tear away and gave me a quick hug with her spare arm. "Why was she so afraid of you?"

"I grew up with Agatha, remember? Amanda knows I can hold my own," I said, hoping that she would leave it at that. Luckily she did.

Chapter 13

I woke up on Graduation day to a hot spring morning, dreading the layers of clothing with the added cap and gown. My bags were packed, and Dorian looked glum, but he knew this day was coming. I had been preparing him for my departure from Charlotte's for a long time. He had enough composure not to freak out like he had on other occasions; he knew I would come back for him in one year. But it was still sad and hard—harder than I thought. I hadn't planned on feeling this way. For years all I could think about was getting out of this hole and taking Dorian with me. But I had not anticipated on "this hole" becoming my home, nor had I fully realized that Dorian would have to stay behind for a whole year.

Since I was to be officially homeless as of today, I had lined up a job as a summer camp counselor and lifeguard. They offered room and board, which consisted of stuffy wooden cabins to be shared with five other counselors, camp food, that I'm sure was disgusting. Either way, it was a roof over my head until I could move into my dorm room.

I had been accepted to five different schools in Texas and most of them offered me a full ride scholarship. I had my crochet group to thank for that. They each wrote recommendation letters and pulled the many strings they had around the state. Their high remarks, along with my good grades and my impressive, though not perfect, swimming background, got me the scholarships. It also helped that I was chosen as Valedictorian. This honor, though, seemed somewhat fishy to me. Not that I didn't have the grades to back it up, but it just so happened that one of my crochet grandmas was my Principal's mother—something I didn't know until I got the good news.

Regardless, here I was, about to leave my home and Dorian to fulfill a goal that was three years in the making. Then I was to start phase two of my goal. It wasn't hard to pick a school. I only wanted to get into one of them—the one where Alex was. My stomach filled with butterflies at the thought of seeing him again. I imagined all kinds of different ways in which I would run into him, or happen to share a class with him, or simply look him up—this was what made me nervous and my hands feel sweaty—not the speech I was about to give.

I had spent a long time on this speech, mostly because I didn't know what to say. I had finally achieved my ultimate goal, and that's all I ever really cared about. I had no nostalgic view of high school. Sure, I had a few friends that I would miss, but not enough to be reduced to tears, like some were. All I wanted to do was to get my diploma and leave so I could go jump into some large body of water to cool off—gown and all.

The commencement ceremony was to take place outdoors, in the football stadium. At ten o'clock the heat had already reached an intolerable degree. From the platform where I sat I could see my classmates. Most were excitedly talking and hugging each other, while their parents filed in, taking pictures and decorating their graduates with huge ribbons, leis and other ornaments. I would have no pictures of this event, no leis, no ribbons … not that I wanted them. I had invited my foster family of course, but Charlotte hadn't thought to bring a camera and Joe looked crabby from the heat. Dorian sat indifferent, drawing, while Meg looked around her, in complete giddiness at the sight of all the high school boys.

Once the ceremony started, I thought I would melt right on the spot. Several people spoke before me. All the while an odd feeling of bitterness crept inside of me. It could have been the relentless heat, but I couldn't suppress the bitterness. I had no room to be bitter; all in all, life had been good to me. I had gotten what I wanted, a college acceptance and a scholarship. But I didn't want to be here. Being here only seemed to remind me of all the things I didn't have and never would have—a real family.

My name was announced, and I swallowed the bad taste in my mouth. I got up and looked around at the people before me and mustered a fake smile. All eyes were on me, but no one cared. I could tell that everyone's mind was on something else. Dorian cared, but he wasn't looking, he was drawing. Joe was loosening a button on his shirt collar; Charlotte was fussing with Meg's hair and Meg had her gaze fixed on a boy that was sitting nearby.

I took in a deep breath and started my carefully crafted speech. I was told to speak for ten minutes, but I could tell that I would lose everyone after three. No one wanted to be here any longer than was absolutely necessary. I began to recite my memorized words; they were eloquent and witty, inspirational and wise, but the more I spoke the more I hated being here and the more resentment I felt. Who were these people that pretended to look at me? No one was listening. No one cared.

The anger beneath the surface was hard to hide; I struggled to sound happy and excited, but I knew I was failing. Suddenly, as I looked over the audience, a bright light started to shine in my face. It was really bright, like the glare from the sun reflecting from a mirror. I shielded my eyes for a second, and then tried to blink away the brightness, but it was useless. I continued my speech in spite of that light, and a new feeling crept over me. I need to be near that light.

Some sort of rebellion welled up inside of me, and I felt the intense urge to take off running toward that light. So with one last planned joke, I ended my five-minute speech. I could see the relief that registered in every face, once they realized that I was done and now the actual graduation would start. I turned from the podium and walked off toward my spot among my peers, on the grass. But just as I was nearing my spot, I saw that light again and instead of taking my seat; I kept on walking toward it. I didn't know what it was, but it beckoned me, so I went. No one noticed me, no one cared that the valedictorian didn't take her seat as expected. Every eye was now on the principal who, to the sound of the band in the background, was about to start calling names.

As I walked, I tossed my cap and shed my gown. I didn't know what I was doing exactly, but I was so hot and the only thing that sounded good at that moment was water, not just to drink, but also to dive into. Then there was that light; it was coming from the very back, behind all the parents. The closer I got, the better I could see it. There was someone inside the light; it had the shape of a man.

My heart skipped a beat and my limbs tingled and wobbled as I made my way to it.

"You did it," he said with a crooked smile.

I nodded dumbly.

"So what now?"

I shrugged, "I was thinking of jumping into the lake," I said, my voice barely above a whisper and my heart pounding so fast that I found it hard to breathe.

"That sounds like a great idea! Do you mind if I join you?"

My breath caught in my throat and I felt both hot and cold at the same time. I wasn't sure what to say. I was mad at him, furious really, but I couldn't surface the anger that I had felt this whole year. All I wanted to do was fall into his arms and stay there forever.

"You're not going to walk?" He motioned toward my cap and gown on the ground.

"No"

"Are you going to the party later?"

"No"

"Do you want to come with me?" His smile was cocky, and that made me angry.

"You're a jerk, you know that." His smile vanished and he didn't respond. "You could have called me or something," I said, then I remembered his Christmas gift. That should count for "something". "Thanks for the book," I added, more remorseful now.

"You knew it was from me?" He smiled, pleased.

"Yeah … who else?"

"I'm sorry for the silent treatment. I had my reasons."

I snorted. What kind of superior comment was that?

"I'll tell you what they were, but not here." He stretched out his arm and wrapped it around my shoulders. I let myself be led like this to the deserted parking lot. He had already placed my scooter into the back of his jeep—how presumptuous! I told him this much and he turned me around to face him. He looked serious, and his eyes showed desperation, like time was running out.

"I know you're mad Tess, you have every right to be. But it wouldn't have worked if I had warned you."

"Warned me of what? Desertion?"

"Yes—no," he shook his head in frustration. "I never deserted you, Tess. I stayed away so you could do this." He waved is hand toward the stadium where my class was receiving their diplomas. I looked back at him with a blank stare. "I didn't want to get in your way, I didn't want to be a distraction and ruin your plans," he continued.

"How would you have been a distraction? How could you ruin my plans? Do you know what it was like for me this last year? Do you realize how much…" I couldn't finish. To say anything else would be to reveal too much. We only shared one short kiss, but I loved him, I loved him to the point of tears—tears that soon appeared.

Alex stepped in closer and cupped my face in his hands. "Shh, shh," he soothed. "I'm sorry Tess; it was hard for me too."

"Ha!" I laughed bitterly and shook my face from his hands. He didn't know what hard was. He had a loving family, and a home. I had a death threat and a hot cabin to look forward to.

"It was hard, Tess, but do you really think I'm that heartless? I did this for us, for our future." His eyes were intent on mine as his hands slid from my face to my shoulders.

I frowned in confusion at his comment and tried really hard to not let my knees buckle.

"Don't you see? If we had picked up right where we left off at that dance, you wouldn't have accomplished all of this."

"And why not?" I asked, with my wounded pride resurfacing my anger. "You don't think I could have handled a boyfriend and good grades?"

"No," he said flatly. "Good grades, maybe, but not this. Not Valedictorian and five scholarships. You wouldn't have started a charity and given six ladies a purpose to their lonely lives. I would have monopolized all your spare time; we would have spent every evening on the phone planning our next weekend.

"It would have been fun—no—heaven, but what if you didn't

get a scholarship? What then? How would you have paid for college? Would you have let me pay for you? I would, I could. I have a hefty trust fund, you know."

I shook my head humbly. I would have never let him pay for my school.

"So you could have gotten a job, and saved up," he continued with a pleading tone, "but would have had to put college on the back-burner and that was your dream! Eventually this could have become a source of bitterness between us. I didn't want that."

His logic was perfect, and wise beyond his years. I looked up at him, now understanding his point. He slid his hand under my chin and with his thumb he stroked my lips. "Then there's this," he let the words drift. "This would have been another problem altogether. This would have made us both fail out of school. I guarantee it!" He mumbled as his lips brushed against mine.

"Yeah, right!"

"Oh, you doubt me? You don't think this is distracting in the least?" He trailed his fingertips down my neck, my shoulders, then and my arm until he entwined his fingers with mine. This simple and gentle gesture sent my heart racing, and my breathing into irregular gasps. I tried to resist the urge to kiss him, but without my permission, my lips parted and my arms wrapped tightly around his neck. To drive his point home he pressed me against his jeep, giving me no option but to give in—not that I objected in the least.

I never thought of a kiss as a means of communication, but I found that this kiss was just that. It spoke of frustration and desire—pent up passion that was just now finding a release—like when you shake a pop bottle and you finally open up the cap. These feelings were now gushing out like fizz, and our kiss spoke of that. My mind reeled with scenes of his face, flashes of him and his smile, all things that I've never seen in real life—scenes that must have happened in my dreams or ... somewhere else—some place hazy and ethereal.

Then his words made a whole lot of sense. He was right. If this passion had been unleashed a moment too soon, it would have consumed us both. *Now* was the right time for us.

"So do you still blame me?" he asked sheepishly, as he pulled back a bit, giving me time to catch my breath.

"Blame you?" I felt dazed, drunk with adrenaline. Looking at him was like heaven, and I wanted to spend the rest of my life looking at him. "Blame you for caring enough to let me grow up?"

"Yeah," he smiled.

"I guess I don't. But if you ever—" He didn't let me finish, and I forgot what I was about to say the moment his lips touched mine again.

Chapter 14

From graduation, Alex drove us to the local marina, where we boarded a sailboat.

"Is it the Odysseus?" I asked as he helped me into it. He froze mid stride, then gently lowered me in.

"The Odysseus? How do you know about the Odysseus?" he asked with suspicion. Just then I realized what I had done. I had gotten dreams and reality mixed up! I knew this would happen one day! I bit my lip and closed my eyes, hoping that the boat would swallow me whole. His eyes were huge and looked questioningly back at me.

"The Odysseus is my grandfather's boat. It's moored in Galveston," he said cautiously while his mind processed what I had just asked.

"Oh, then maybe that's where I heard about it?"

"No, we didn't talk about the Odysseus at my grandfather's house that night." His turquoise eyes burrowed into mine. I swallowed hard, and remembered the dreams, several really, where we sailed in the open ocean on board the Odysseus. Then I remembered the picture that Dorian drew for me. The house, with the sailboat docked in front, bearing the same name. … . Could this be? Did he really have a boat named The Odysseus? I thought I had used that name in my dreams, because of the picture. So if the boat was real … then …

"Tess, honestly, how do you know?" he insisted with intensity, but I was petrified and mortified all at the same time. Part of me was trying to make sense of the fact that I had gotten the name right, and the other part of me was hoping to forget all about it.

"I don't know," I lied. I needed time to think through this. He stared at me still, chewing the inside of his cheek while I bit my lower lip. We were at a standstill. Someone had to make the next move, and it sure wasn't going to be me.

He nodded slowly and backed away. He looked disappointed,

which was interesting. "Why?" I asked, now curious myself at his behavior.

While untying ropes and pushing us off the marina, he seemed to mull the simple question over. He drove us in silence out of the no-wake zone, then killed the motor and unfurled the main sail. "What if I told you that I've been dreaming of you for the past three years?" he said as he tightened some ropes. "What if I told you that the dreams I've had of you were so real, that—"

"—that they made you unsure of what reality is?" I finished.

"Yeah," he replied, and peered into my eyes. "In my dreams, I've taken you on board the Odysseus to all the islands and places I've been. We've even gone deep sea diving—"

"—without any diving equipment?" I completed his sentence again. We stared at each other wordlessly for a few moments. Then he rushed to grab the tiller, to avoid some oncoming boats. Once we were safely going in the right direction, he waved me over to him. I sat next to him, looking out toward the water. It was amazing to think that we were still in the same town where I grew up. Being out here felt like a different world. And being here with the actual physical version of Alex was downright mind-boggling. I waited for him to say something else, but he didn't. He had made his move, now it was my turn.

"I've had those dreams too," I finally confessed. Alex nodded and placed his free hand over mine, then slowly started tangling his fingers with mine. This reminded me of that time at the art gallery, and how this simple touch sent shivers up and down my frame— they did so again. We made no sound for a long time, we just sailed. Only the wind and the water splashing against the sides of the boat broke the silence. My mind, however, was far from silent; it was in fact, filled with anxiety, excitement and eagerness. A million thoughts crowded in there all at once. Could this be? Could those dreams have been real? No. They couldn't have been real, but they could have been shared—couldn't they?

"How's Celeste?"

"I've banned her. She was driving me nuts," I said with a laugh, and then realized too late to what I had just admitted. I turned my head and looked horrified into his eyes. His face wore a smirk from ear to ear, but his expression of "got'ya," was too much for me. I turned my head and buried it in my hands.

Instantly he pulled my hands down and drew me to him. "So, it's true. It's all true."

I nodded, admitting to it all. It might as well come out; eventually he would have had to know. Better to have it out now, before I got too involved. Before I fell too deeply in love with him. Ha! Who was I fooling? I already loved him too much. How could this get any worse?

"Here I was all this time thinking I was crazy for fantasizing and obsessing about you. I thought I was mental!"

I looked up at him through blurry eyes from crying. "You thought *you* were mental?"

He nodded. "Of course. At least now I know that we're both mental! If I end up being committed to a hospital, I'll just make sure they put us in the same wing." I laughed, releasing all the tension that I had been holding inside.

"What—what about … Celeste?" I asked, wanting redemption from that bit of craziness too.

"She's the one Dorian drew, right? Your Guardian Angel?"

I nodded.

"I saw her," he stated, and I remembered that the last time I shared a dream with Alex, I had seen that flash of light. At the time I thought I was just dreaming and getting my wires crossed, but now…this was new.

"Great! Add something else to the paranormal list!" I exclaimed. "You actually saw her face?"

He nodded. "She didn't look very happy with me."

"But how?" I wondered. This was getting complicated. Even now I started to doubt whether I was really here with Alex or dreaming again.

"So … it's true then? What you told me that night?"

I exhaled and nodded.

"You can hear her?"

I nodded again. He pursed up his lips and mirrored my motion.

"So… what now?"

He flashed a smile that quickly faded into a more serious look. "I see dead people."

I shoved him and he laughed. "Well … I did. Didn't I?" His look was something between consternation and elation.

"I talk to dead people," I offered sympathetically.

"Well, it's weird … but I think I like it. Who wants to be normal anyway?" He stretched his hand and, grabbing mine, pulled me toward him. A shadow passed over his face as he did so.

"What, what is it?"

He didn't answer. Instead he turned me around and pulled me tightly against his torso. I burrowed my back into his chest and looked out as we sailed toward a secluded cove.

"You know, I've only seen the ocean through your eyes." I mentioned after some time.

"I guess that's right."

"How do you think that works?"

"The dreams?"

I nodded and he shook his head. "Who knows how anything like that works? How does Dorian do what he does? How does my mom know that certain things are going to happen before they actually do?

"My dad says that we only use about 10 % of our brains, so what's the rest of it for? What if these special abilities are simply parts of the brain that go unused in most people? Maybe we're just more evolved."

"I like that," I said absentmindedly. "More evolved. Sounds better than crazy."

We had now reached an inlet and Alex released me to go let the anchor down. "Katie left a swim suit for you to wear down in the cabin. You can go change if you'd like," he suggested as he pulled his shirt off and tossed it casually on the seat.

I tried not to ogle, but I'm afraid that I did. He smiled, and tiny crow's feet appeared in the corners of his eyes. I liked them almost as much as his dimples. My cheeks burned crimson, and I hurried down into the cabin. When I returned it as Alex's turn to stare.

Katie had good taste, good taste. Her swimsuit was a simple, yet classy. It was a white tankini with black trim. Accustomed only to wearing Speedos, I shifted my weight uncomfortably for a few minutes, and then dove overboard.

The water was just a few degrees cooler than the outside temperature, but it was refreshing enough. When I came up for air, Alex was tying a knot around a huge inner tube that he threw in before jumping in himself.

He deliberately floated up right in front of me and shook his head to one side, flicking water from his hair in my face. This action on his part provoked a water fight of sorts that inevitably ended with my hands pulled behind my back and his face inches from mine. I felt a greedy sense of entitlement come over me, so I freed my arms from his grasp and wrapped them around his neck. The last thing I saw was a smile stealing across his face, before our lips touched.

A picture is worth a thousand words, they say. I would change that saying to *a kiss is worth a thousand words*, because this second kiss said things that cannot be uttered. It spoke of understanding, acceptance, and tenderness. Next it became deep, revealing our true feelings—feelings that we had for each other, but had never uttered out loud before. It spoke of a deep rooted bond that we knew existed—not just because of the recent dreams we had shared, but because of something much, much older—something inexplicably ancient. And it also spoke of a promise, that this would certainly not be the last kiss, but the first of many more yet to come. Our lips moved apart at the same moment. This kiss had summed up almost all we had to say—all but one thing.

"I love you," we both breathed out at the same time. Neither one of us was surprised to hear those words fall from the other's lips. There were no other explanations needed, and nothing else to add. It was a simple fact, and it had to be stated.

Alex reached for the rope that held the tube without taking his eyes off of me. He wore a crooked smile as he did this, and once he had the tube in his hands he jumped up onto it and extended his hand for me to take. He sat me across his lap and I wrapped my arms around his neck, resting my head on his chest. We stayed like this for some time. He stroked my hair and kissed the top of my head, while I drank in every ounce of this moment.

"Oh ... look at them Max!" Celeste said enviously as Tess and Alex indulged in a kiss.

"Celeste ... we should go," Max whispered.

But Celeste didn't budge. She missed those days so much.

"Celeste, this is private. How would you have liked it if they had watched us ... " Max encouraged, but Celeste was not moving. *"Come on, honey. It's bordering on haunting."* Celeste was enthralled now, and jealousy started to creep inside her.

"Celeste!" Max yelled.

A sound, a voice, sent chills through my veins and made me jump. I knew what that voice was. I looked around me with alarm. Was Celeste watching us? If she weren't already dead, I would have killed her!

Celeste startled and realized what she had done. She leet out a breathless sigh, and shook her head. Max chuckled and put an arm around her. *"I miss it too, mi amor."* And together they rose up.

"What's wrong?" Alex looked perplexed. "Look at you, you have goose bumps."

"Celeste ... " So she hadn't gone away; she was just keeping quiet! This, in a way, was somewhat reassuring, because deep inside I didn't want to lose her—that nosy little ghost!

Alex rubbed my arms, "Celeste? Is she here? Was she ... watching us?" he looked a bit spooked.

"I think so," I said looking around me and straining my ears.

"You know, she didn't look that happy with me the last time I saw her. She did tell me to keep my hands off you."

"Oh, just ignore her! I do."

"Doesn't that defeat the purpose of having a Guardian Angel?"

We had towed ourselves back to the boat and boarded. Alex pulled out a cooler filled with food and cold drinks. He proceeded to spread a blanket on the bow of the ship and set up a cozy little lunch for us. We ate in silence for a while; I would have considered it a comfortable silence, except for the fact that I could feel a weird vibe coming from Alex. I found this to be perplexing. Hadn't we aired out all the weird stuff already?

He slowly chewed a bite of food. He swallowed, and said, "Tess, I have to tell you something. Remember how I told you, in that one dream, that I wanted to join the Navy?"

I nodded in reply.

"Well, I did."

I nodded again, slowly now, and braced myself.

"That's what I've been doing this last year."

"I thought you were in school?"

"I was! I did both."

I stared at him blankly, not sure of what the problem was here. Then it dawned on me. I started to shake my head and a look of pure misery crossed his face.

"I'm sorry," he said with an anguished look on his face.

"I—I didn't know that I'd be deployed so soon."

Tears now filled the rims of my eyes, promising to spill over any second. "When? Where?" I gasped.

Alex closed his eyes and looked down. "I have to report to a base in Fort Worth early tomorrow ... and I can't tell you where I'm going."

Chapter 15

To say that I lost it would be a total understatement. But I didn't completely fall apart either. I was going to save that for tomorrow morning. But cry I did, until my cheeks burned from the sun and the salty tears.

"I promise that we'll be together every minute of every hour until I have to leave. We'll stay up all night, which gives us thirteen hours. That's … " he calculated in his head, "seven-hundred-eighty minutes." I looked at him, swallowing a sob. He was right; we had to make every minute count. My tears would not change anything. I had to pull myself together and enjoy this day … somehow.

"Just one more question, before we make this subject taboo," I asked as I tried to compose myself. He smiled weakly and nodded. "How long will you be gone?"

"A year," he stated and I nodded, swallowing another wave of grief.

After that, I made no more mention of his impending departure, no comment about the fact that our nation was at war and that he would be going into harm's way. I simply tried to live in the here and now, and so did he.

After a few more bites of food, we lay on the bow and, with interlaced fingers, talked and talked, just like we had in our dreams. Only this time I could feel his warmth and his touch. If I could have suspended time, I would have frozen us in this moment forever. There were moments when I wanted to pinch myself, just to make sure this was really happening, that I was really opening my heart and soul to the real Alex, and that he was opening up his soul to me.

He was a deep thinker, and he asked me about things I hadn't really thought about much—like what's the purpose of life, and why are some people born with disabilities? Why can some people pick up an instrument and learn how to use it without instruction, or why did some others have special gifts, like sharing dreams?

Then he told me that he wondered and worried that he was deficient in some way, because he had no defining quality, or gift like I did, or like his sister and mother, or his father who clearly was a gifted psychiatrist. He even thought his grandfather was a gifted soldier, a master strategist, but who was he? What was his gift, his calling?

I thought about this for a moment and the thought came to me, that his gift was subtler—*"wisdom"*.

"You are wise," I told him, not really sure where I got that particular thought from. The word seemed to have fallen into my mind like dew…from heaven. However, once I said it, it made perfect sense. He was wise; he based his decisions on the long-term picture and not just what he wished for at the moment. As we discussed this, I gave him proof of all the instances that I could think of when he had shown wisdom beyond his years. Whenever we got too hot, we jumped in the water to cool off. The afternoon wore away in this most peaceful way, ignoring the dark cloud of his impending departure.

Around five o'clock, Alex received a text from his father saying that we had dinner reservations, and to head back. This we did, and docked right at his backyard dock. The trail that led from the dock to the house was lined with solar lights, and to either side his yard looked perfectly manicured, like a golf course.

"I have to go back to Charlotte's and get my clothes," I told Alex, as we walked up the path.

"Already taken care of," he said smugly.

"How?"

"Katie just got her license and has been dying to drive around and do errands, so I sent her to Charlotte's to pick up some of your clothes."

"But everything is packed up, how would she know which bag has what?"

Alex stopped abruptly and looked at me. "What do you mean, everything is packed up?"

"Just that. I was supposed to move out once I turned eighteen, but they let me stay until graduation. That was today, so I was leaving."

"Where were you going?"

I told him all about my summer job plans, and how they agreed to let me come earlier and help clean up the camp in preparation for the campers. He looked at me with utter shock."

"Well you're not going."

"What do you mean? Of course I am! Where else would I live?" I said defensively.

"You can live here."

"No I can't. Besides, I need to work. I'll need some money for school."

"Work around here," he ordered, and this bristled me.

Just when I was about to tell him exactly what I thought about his orders, his family came out to greet us—well, me, actually. They each took a turn embracing me and telling me how proud they were and so forth. Katie told me that she had picked up all of my belongings and had also brought Dorian. In the background I saw him; he was standing in the kitchen eating a cookie.

Alex immediately proceeded to tell his family about my plans for the summer, and they proposed the same option but more politely. Katie took my side, saying that maybe I wanted to do this, and was not just doing it out of necessity. In reality *I was* doing it out of necessity and would rather not go, but I didn't say it, so they let the issue go.

After we showered and dressed, we boarded the sailboat again, and we all sailed to a restaurant that had its own marina. I was amazed at the fact that we were in the same town, right smack in the middle of Texas. This was indeed a whole different world, and I felt oddly transported to another plane of existence.

After dinner, we sailed as we ate our dessert by the faint glow of golden Christmas lights that Katie had strung along the railings and the mast of the boat. Then, as planned, we tried to stay up all night. We started by taking pictures of each other and then printing them. We then skirted the edge of the lake and talked some more.

Here he managed to convince me to not take the summer job—after he apologized for being bossy. We later took a dip in the hot-tub, and ate more ice-cream. We watched a movie and then—

"Alex … " Dane whispered, shaking Alex slightly, "time to wake up son."

I didn't open my eyes, but I was awake and mad for losing consciousness. The last thing I remember was a conversation about Agatha. We were discussing her in general and we were speculating what had happened with her. We were both very sleepy and our words got fewer and fewer, until all went blank. It didn't seem like we had slept for very long, but I was bitter nonetheless for the loss of those precious minutes together.

Alex got up off the couch, trying not to wake me. Stretching, he mumbled, "Thanks, dad." His father left and Alex bent over me, kissing my cheek.

"Good morning, Beautiful."

My eyes fluttered open at the sound of his voice, and I tried to commit his face to memory. This moment and his face would stay with me forever.

We all ate breakfast in silence. Dorian had been taken back home, but the Admiral was here this morning. He was the only one talking while the rest of us ate in silence.

"Pilots in the Navy have short missions," he explained. "Not like us sailors. Pilots fly in, do their thing, then fly out. End of story. Nothing to worry about."

Valerie snorted in reply.

Once we got to the base, Alex took his time hugging each member of his family and saying some last minute parting words. I was last. He embraced me tightly, then kissed me and cupped my face. "I'll see you in my dreams." He winked, trying to sound cheerful.

Katie, Valerie and I held each other while we watched his plane take off. He was being flown to some secret naval base somewhere. He wasn't allowed to tell us, but it was safe to assume that it would be in harm's way.

The moment his plane left my sight, I felt a knot in my stomach and got a sharp pain in my head, and much like a character in a Jane Austin book, I got sick and swooned. Unfortunately, it wasn't done delicately like in the books where the heroine is so stricken with grief that she takes to her bed for days, needing her forehead to be dabbed now and then with a cool rag. No. Not I. I puked, all over, twice on the way back to the Preston's, and twice at their house. Then I got feverish and passed out. They had no choice but to keep me in their guest bedroom until I recovered.

All I recall from those days are odd, faint conversations, that I'm not sure really happened at all. I vaguely remember Charlotte, bending over me asking, "Is she contagious? Maybe I shouldn't be here." Then Alex, in uniform, telling me, *"I got to my destination ... I have my first mission tomorrow ... are you okay?"* Then Dane, "I hate to say this, but her getting sick has been a good thing for Val. It's been keeping her busy, mothering someone ... she's not falling apart—yet." And Celeste, *"Tess ... everything will be fine."* Then weeping ... someone sitting next to me, weeping a lot. The only thing that they all had in common was the echo. Everything everyone said had an echo that only intensified my headache and made me even sicker.

After three or four days of this delirium, I came out of it. The Prestons were gracious enough to beg me to stay with them and not take the summer job. In private, Dane told me that I would be doing him a personal favor, since his wife had gotten quite attached to me and needed someone to commiserate and gripe with about Alex. I agreed with him, that griping about Alex was all I wanted to do, so it was settled.

Libby gave me my old job back at the aromatherapy store, and I took a second part-time job at a boutique. My crochet group took me in and Valerie joined us, wanting to learn the art. In my spare time, Valerie, Katie and I talked about Alex and, inspired by Valerie's art studio in her home, I started designing my own dress line. It turned out to be one of the best summers I had ever had.

The weeks revolved around the letters we received from Alex. My nights revolved around the brief dreams I shared with him. The dreams were few and far between, because we hardly ever slept at the same time. He never revealed where he was stationed, but it must have been far away, because he was always about to wake up when I was just falling asleep. In our shared dreams I did most the talking. He was interested in what we were all doing. He said that he would write about what he was doing, so I would be eager and surprised when the letters arrived.

In the fall, I headed to college in Alex's Jeep. I was soon settled there, but I returned "home" almost every weekend. Dorian would often be invited to the Preston's during those weekends, so I got to see him quite often. I still worried about what I would do in a few months, when he turned eighteen. I didn't have enough money to pay for housing for both of us. Even with the money he got from the government, it wouldn't be enough. The Admiral had been hinting that he would love a roommate, but I wasn't sure if Dorian would even go for that. I brought up the matter to Dorian a few times, but he never responded and looked most unconcerned about the matter. His behavior only exasperated me more, to the point that I was now getting seriously worried.

"Tess, are you sure you can handle this?"

Agatha smiled. Every time she heard people call her by that name, she got a thrill. Her smile turned cynical. "Of course I can!" She had planned this moment for months now. Everything was in place; all she had to do now was execute the plan. She got in close, pretending to give Carleene a pat on the back, but instead she injected her with an overdose. As Agatha watched her writhe uncomfortably on the floor, she clinically took a mental inventory of the sequence of events that were to follow. She would have to be quick, but she couldn't look to be in a hurry. She had to be perfectly innocuous if this was to work.

After leaving Charlotte's house, Agatha had drifted for a while, only knowing that there were places she wanted to see. When she finally settled in the San Diego area, she came up with a simple idea—steal Tess' identity—only in name of course, because here no one needed any papers. However, living on the streets was only fun for a little while. Then it got boring.

One day, she reached the end of her rope. As Agatha watched a man come out of a black Limo, and enter the back of the club where she usually hung out, she realized that she was an outsider to the real game being played here. This enraged her. If only she still had that book! That book was a gold mine of information.

"You will write your own," the voices promised her, and this gave her hope.

She had quickly become the leader of her little pack of drifters, but this was no longer enough. The truth was, she was a nobody, leading a bunch of losers. That should have been her getting out of that Limo. If she could get the information of the ancients, the information from that book, she should soon be where she wanted to be.

The idea came to her to take a walk down the more respectable parts of town and examine how the world worked there. She learned an important lesson that day. She learned that, though she looked intimidating, she was really a joke to the world at large.

"The most dangerous people don't look it," the voice said.

"But—" she was about to answer out loud, but decided against it. Agatha had learned a thing or two about those voices—they couldn't read her mind. She was going to point out the fact that the voices were the ones that told her to dress this way and come out here in the first place, but then she decided to keep that to herself. Every time she tried to rise against them, they would tear her down. So she started to keep her own mind to herself.

They were right though; if she was going to be taken seriously she had to make some changes, but not here. She needed to start fresh. And to start fresh, she needed money, lots of money. That's when she hatched a plan. All she had to do now was execute it. First, Carleene had to be out of the way. After that, all she had to do was make the drop off in her stead, then the pick-up, take a detour, find two disguises, and she would be free. She knew that she would be followed for part of it, but she was prepared for them.

She took Carleene's place at the exchange point. As expected, the two morons assigned to follow her were a couple of meatheads that looked every inch like the average Hollywood thug. They watched from their car as Agatha made the exchange, then they slowly followed her as she walked away, heading toward the club.

Agatha walked confidently, like nothing was out of the ordinary. She stopped by a gas station, and went into the bathroom. There, hiding behind the stall, she had planted a backpack. She changed into a cycling outfit, complete with a wig and a helmet. She stuffed all her other gear in the backpack, including the money, and slung it over her shoulders. When the two idiots were distracted, she opened the door and walked out casually. She mounted the bicycle that she had stolen earlier and rode away right under their noses. They looked around stupidly, wondering what they had missed. They got out, checked the empty restroom, and finally realized that she had somehow gotten away. After much thought and aimless driving, they put two and two together and started looking for a blond riding a road bicycle.

Agatha rode quickly to a decoy location, a crowded diner. There she had another stash and she changed yet again. Now dressed like a common, frumpy-looking girl with brown hair and glasses, she exited the diner and started walking. A few blocks away, she hailed a cab that took her to the bus station. With a bit of anxiety, she waited until the bus pulled out and carried her safely out of town. After a long nap, she started planning her next move. This bus would take her to Phoenix and there she would begin the permanent changes, including tattoo and piercing removal. Next she would go to Albuquerque and there she would change her hairstyle. She had no intention of hanging around in Texas were she was still wanted, so Oklahoma City was her next stop. There she would shop for new clothes. She thought it would be fun to get pampered in Nashville, so there she would go to a spa to get buffed and made over for her debut in Richmond.

"In Virginia," she thought, "I will start my new life as Carleene. Poor Carleene, she never saw that one coming. Well … that's what she gets I suppose, for hanging out with the wrong crowd," Agatha thought indifferently.

Once Agatha stepped out of the bus in Richmond, she was a new woman. No one would have ever guessed that not even a month ago, the girl with the pixy-short blond hair, perfect make-up, manicured nails, and trendy clothes, was a former homeless Gothic-chick who pushed drugs on the street. Now, armed with her new look, she enrolled in school, got a job and found some roommates.

"Are you two idiots?" Waving his hand, Eros looked at the two men. "Of course you are. I hire idiots, and I get this type of result." He made a movement of the head, which his bodyguards behind him understood to mean, "get rid of them". The other two started backing away, fear registering in their faces. "W—w—we'll find her! We promise we will!"

"Too late," Eros said, unconcerned.

"But—but, we know what she looked like when she left the restroom!"

"She's probably half way to Mexico right now!" Eros said casually, but this gave him an idea. "What did you say her name was?" he asked with new interest.

"Tess DeLeon."

"DeLeon you say?"

The two nodded.

"And she's worked for me for how long?"

"About a year," the two said looking at each other, hoping that maybe this would somehow save them from being maimed.

"Mmm ... DeLeon ... how interesting. I wonder ... " Eros cocked his head again, signaling to his bulldogs that it was now time to teach these morons a lesson. Ignoring the noise behind him, he got up and dialed a number on his cell phone while looking out of his dingy window. "Get the plane ready," he ordered, then hung up. He stared out the window for a few more minutes, and thought some more about the implications of what he was about to do. It would be somewhat risky, but he had to find out.

Chapter 16

For Christmas break I came back to the Preston's home. Dorian was invited for the duration, and for the first time we got to experience a Christmas with gifts from people we knew. Dorian and I made our purchases together and had a great time doing so.

The Prestons had some traditions that they followed, and we got to experience those as well. The only thing that put a damper on it was an anonymous Christmas card that came in the mail, addressed to me. I didn't show it to anyone, not even Dorian, because I knew who it was from. The card looked innocent enough; it was a picture of a cute little cat in a Santa suit. There was no signature. All the card said was, "Have a purrfect Christmas." There was no point in telling them. They wouldn't believe me, and even if they did … what could they do? Agatha was deranged and that's all there was to it. If they did find her, what would they charge her with? Sending a postcard?

Valerie and I had become quite close. We bonded over baby pictures of Alex and by quietly spending hours at our respective hobbies. To pass the time, and keep from falling apart, Valerie painted and I sewed. She set up my things in her studio, and there we spent many quiet hours together.

Katie spent most of her time outdoors, and since she had gotten her license, she had started to volunteer at the zoo, so she was hardly ever home. When Dorian was with us, he too took up a spot in the quiet art studio and did what he always did—sketch. Dane was thrilled to see us thus engaged, and would often reward me with a tight hug. Dorian, who never let anyone touch him, would let Dane shake his hand.

Over Christmas break I finished my first dress from scratch. I did the sketches, the pattern, and sewed the whole thing. I did make some mistakes, but was able to correct them as I went. The final product was a beautiful, formal dress-suit elegant enough for a queen. The material was off-white inlaid with gold. The collar and the cuffs were the most dramatic features, and the body was a form-fitting, mermaid style. Both Valerie and Katie were awestruck by it, and took turns trying it on. Then they insisted that I try it on. I had to admit that it fit me perfectly.

Immediately after this, Valerie took me to the fabric store and insisted that I make dresses for both Katie and her. They each chose fabrics and dresses from my drawings. Katie chose a less formal dress that she wanted to wear to her graduation. Valerie chose a formal dress in the same shade as her eyes, that she said she would wear to a wedding someday.

Nervous now, I set out to make the two new patterns, and hoped that I got them right for my two first customers. I had to go back to school before I finished them, but I dutifully drove back every weekend and worked on them.

"Tess? Tess DeLeon?" A guy dressed in a casual business suit was calling me, waving his hand as I exited my dorm.

I eyed him suspiciously then nodded slightly.

"Oh … good! I can't tell you how hard you are to track down," he said breathlessly. I found this hard to believe, since Agatha had had no problem knowing where I was spending my Christmas break.

The man had wavy, dark brown hair, green-gray eyes, and an easy, winning smile. "I'm Roger Wagner." He stretched out his hand to shake mine.

"Do I know you?"

"Not yet! But you're about to." He smiled. "Is there a place where we can sit and talk?"

"I have a class now."

"You might want to skip it."

"Why?"

"You're going to want to hear what I have to say." He smiled again.

"I don't know … " I hesitated.

"Let me start again." He stretched his hand once more, "I'm Roger Wagner and I'm your cousin."

Eros got to the prison where his half-brother had spent the last fourteen years, but he was too late, Leonardo DeLeon had passed away the previous week. This wasn't altogether bad news, but he was hoping for at least one answer. With Leo gone, his worries were gone as well … unless that little thief was his daughter. If Leo and Irene had a child, she might be the last witness to that careless night. Not to mention, she was now stealing from him! She might be trying to blackmail him. *Well, first things first,* Eros thought.

"Still Mexico, sir?" the pilot asked as he ushered Eros into the jet.

"Yes. We still go as planned."

Seated at the nearest diner I stared at the only person that I have ever known I was related to by blood. He was genial, good-looking; about ten years older than me, and still unmarried but I suspected had no trouble with women.

"Why haven't you looked for me before now?"

"I couldn't, because your father didn't want any of us to have any contact with you." This comment stung and I felt my eyes tearing up, in spite of my efforts to remain calm.

"No, no, no! It's not like that!" Roger reached out with one hand and placed it on mine. "Listen, this is a long, long, story so you're going to have to listen to the whole thing before you start drawing any conclusions."

I nodded, still fighting back the tears. After taking a sip of his Coke, he began.

"Your father's name was Leonardo DeLeon."

"Was?"

"Yes, he passed away recently. Now listen, okay?" I nodded again. "Leo was the only son of Ricardo and Celeste DeLeon."

Chills run up and down my body, "Celeste … " I whispered.

"Yes, Celeste. She was my grandmother too, but she was first married to Maximilliano Montero. They had triplets; one of them is my mother." He paused and took another sip. "After grandpa Max died, Celeste re-married Ricardo—the man that she was engaged to before she eloped with Max."

"Interesting … " I said in a daze.

"Very! Celeste was quite a character!"

I grinned. "I bet she was … Did you know her well?"

"No, not very well. She died when I was very young, but my mom has told me many stories about her." I took a sip of my own drink and Roger took a bite of his taco salad. "Apparently the marriage between Ricardo and Celeste was not a good one. My mom and aunt have told me of their endless fights and Ricardo's long absences. Once he married Celeste, he inherited the historic home and the mill, in Spain—something that he always wanted. He moved Celeste, my mom and her sisters out of their home in Argentina, and bought a beach house in Mexico. Later he bought an agave plantation."

"Like, for nectar?"

"Ha," he laughed, "No. Tequila." He shook his head and grinned. "You just reminded me of Paz!"

"Who's Paz?"

"Our aunt!" He exhaled, releasing some frustration. "Sorry, my fault. My mom and her sisters are The Three Mary's, or Las Tres Marias, the three stars that sit side by side? We call them Orion's Belt here." He looked eagerly back at me, then shrugged when I just stared at him blankly. I liked looking at the stars, but had never bothered to learn their names.

"Like the Big Dipper, they're always there. Three identical little stars, one next to the other … any way … Their real names are, Maria de Amor, that's my mom. Maria de Paz, she's a Nun, and Maria de Luz. She was born last and suffered brain damage during childbirth—she's a fifty-something with the mind of a ten year old."

"Oh," I said sadly.

Roger shook his head and smiled. "She's a sweetie, and you'll love her! She wears pigtails and a tutu every day!" We laughed together and I tried to picture my aunts. I had a family! *I had a family!* I had to let that thought simmer in my mind for a while.

Between bites of food and three Cokes, my cousin told me the whole story of how I came to be in foster care. Apparently my father grew up resenting his father, Ricardo, for abandoning them. When he was seventeen, Ricardo died in Spain, in the arms of his lover. Soon after, they got a visit from an audacious sixteen year old that claimed to be Ricardo's son. Eros was the bastard child of Anabella, an Italian actress, and Ricardo. They were the reason why Ricardo was always so eager to leave Celeste and Leo behind.

Now, Eros came looking for his half of the inheritance, mainly the house in Spain, where he grew up. As could be imagined, my father had no interest in Eros or his claims to the properties, so Eros was asked to leave. After some threats and insults, Eros did leave and my father didn't see him again until after he had married my mother, Irene.

Leo came to the U.S. to study finance at U.C. San Diego, and there he met my mother. She was a pretty Chicana with long black hair and dark chocolate eyes. I longed to see a picture of her, but Roger didn't have one handy. He cursed under his breath for having forgotten to bring any pictures at all, but assured me that he would mail them to me as soon as he got back.

Roger said that the next part of the story he got from my father himself. He said that after he married Irene, Eros showed up again. This time he wasn't asking nicely. Eros threatened my father and Irene, saying that if Leo didn't give him half of everything, they would live to regret it!

My father apparently didn't take him seriously, so they went on with their lives until one day they were pulled over by a cop. Their car was searched, and drugs were found. Of course my parents knew nothing about it. The drugs had been planted there. From then on, my parents were framed, chased, and persecuted by the law and by gangs. Irene was now pregnant, so they moved to Texas and here they were able to live under the radar for a while. They had me, and when I was barely five years old, their luck run out.

Leo said that Eros showed up at their home one evening. He was disgruntled and drunk. He threatened them—again. As a precaution, they hid me in the shower stall of the bathroom while they tried to negotiate with Eros. But Eros was no longer interested in half of the estates; he wanted it all.

"How much money could there be?" I asked.

"A bit," Roger said solemnly, "and you are the sole heir!"

"Me?"

"Who else? You are the only daughter of the only legal heir of the DeLeon family."

"What about you?"

"I'm a Montero, Max's grandson, not a DeLeon," he said taking the last bite and finishing his drink. A waitress came by and offered to refill, but he declined.

"Listen Tess," he said, turning his attention back to me, "this is very serious business. That night, Eros killed your mother, and framed your father for her murder. Leo died in prison for a crime he didn't commit. He was able to arrange for you to grow up in foster care, ignorant of all of this mess, so you could live to adulthood.

He stayed away from you to protect you from Eros. He loved you and your mother more than he loved himself. I loved your father!" Roger's voice turned husky and broke off. "He was my hero while I was growing up. He was fun, full of life and mischief, but in a good way, you know." He tried to take another sip of his drink, then realized it was empty, so he cleared his throat and regained his composure. "I promised him that I would never give up. I will not rest until your father's name is cleared."

"Thank you," I said, but felt so odd. I should be the one tearing up, the one feeling all the anger toward this injustice, but I wasn't. I had always suspected that my parents loved me, but I never had any proof. Now I did and I felt nothing. "How did my father die?" I finally asked.

"Cancer," he said as he placed a bill on the table. "You weren't hungry?" He pointed to my barely touched lunch.

I shook my head and took a sip of my lemonade.

Roger nodded; his face was sympathetic. "After he killed your mother and left your dad with the smoking gun, so to speak, Eros managed to vanish into thin air, and your dad went to prison. Leo never told my mom or her sisters that you existed for fear of Eros coming after you or them. That's why, much to his dismay, he cut himself off from you completely. But don't think he didn't keep tabs on you!"

"He did? How?"

"There was a detective in the force that believed in your father's innocence. They went to college together. He tried to help him out, but the evidence against him, coupled with his previous trumped up charges of drug possession, were too great. Detective Lovell kept an eye on you for him, and then would report to your father when he visited him. John hasn't given up either."

"Detective Lovell? John Lovell?" That was the same guy who came when Agatha disappeared. He had looked familiar to me. Maybe I remembered him.

"Don't you want to know how much money you've inherited?"

"Money! That wretched money! If I had been poor to begin with, none of this would have ever happened. Max and I would have lived to be old together with our children and grandchildren at our side." Celeste mused over me.

So *she's* my grandmother ... my dead grandmother.

Roger was looking at me with interest. "Are you okay? I know I just gave you a lot of information."

"I'm fine. Could you tell me more about my aunts?"

"You don't want to know how much money you have inherited."

I shrugged, and thought about Celeste's words. "Money can't buy you happiness, or family," I declared.

Roger smiled, pleased with my response. "Quite true Tess, quite true. You will love my mom and her sisters. In fact I am willing to bet that they will be all the treasure you ever need."

"Eros, what on earth are you doing here?" Amor said, feeling the hairs on the back of her neck rise.

"Not much. Just thought I'd stop by and say hello to my three big sisters," he said, letting himself in the house. Amor moved aside and hesitantly closed the door. Luz froze the minute she saw Eros and her eyes shifted to her sister.

"Hello Luz. Long time no see," Eros said with a chuckle, at the spectacle of the old woman in a blue tutu and matching hair bows. Luz didn't answer. Instead she averted her eyes to avoid making eye contact with him.

"What do you want?" Amor said tartly, cutting to the chase.

"What, no chit-chat? No catching up? It's been quite a few years. There's really nothing new to tell me about?" Eros said mockingly.

"No."

"I would love some tea please. What is that stuff you guys always drink?" Eros sat himself down on a chair and crossed his legs.

"You are not welcome here."

Eros got up and wandered the room, peeking through doors and all around for signs or evidence of what he was looking for. "Very well, have it your way. I'm looking for her," he said coming to the point.

"Who, Paz?" Amor asked genuinely perplexed.

"No. Not Paz. The girl."

"What girl?"

"Leo's girl. Where is she? I know you've raised her for him." Amor frowned and looked at him questioningly. Eros walked up to Luz and peered into her eyes, knowing that she would not be able to be deceitful. But Luz kept averting his gaze, then finally broke down and started crying.

"She knows something!" he accused.

"All she knows is that you scare her!" Amor said defensively. Now please remove yourself, or I'll have you removed by the local authorities.

"Ha! The local authorities, yeah ... I remember them ... good guys, all of them. I'm not leaving until you tell me where she is."

"Leo has no children. I have no idea what you are talking about." Amor said, angry now.

Eros peered into her face, hoping to extract the truth from her that way. But her face showed nothing but defiance.

"Leo has no child," Amor repeated contritely, "I would know if he did," and she walked back to the door. She opened it and motioned for Eros to pass on through.

"Had a child," Eros corrected. "If Leo had a child you would know," he smiled maliciously. "That's exactly why I'm here. To see where you've hidden her all these years."

"We haven't hidden anyone, certainly not a child. What makes you think that Leo had a child to begin with? And what is all this past tense thing?" Amor was now annoyed and angry.

"You don't know? Leo is dead. I just came from the prison. He died of cancer last week. He refused to get treatment. It must have been very painful."

Amor's eyes burned and filled with tears, but she kept them at bay out of sheer anger and hatred for this cursed imp.

"And I have reason to believe that he had a child, because a Tess DeLeon has crossed my path," Eros added.

"There must be thousands of people with that same last name. You're quite narcissistic aren't you? Everything and everyone revolves around you? Well, for the record, if Leo had a child I would not tell you. But since he never did, I can be honest and put your twisted mind at ease. Now please take your leave before my sister blows you to pieces," Amor said, and motioned with her head, toward the back of the house. Eros turned to look at what she was pointing at, then chuckled at the sight of Luz holding a rifle in her steady hands.

"Oddly, she never misses," Amor said dryly.

Eros laughed and walked out the door, satisfied that perhaps this Tess was not related to him. This was a good thing. Now he could inherit. He had more right to that money than those three harpies did. With a good lawyer he would finally be the sole owner of … well, everything! Even this house!

On his way out of town, he passed an old burnt-down mission that gave him a great idea. "The perfect spot," he mused. Moments later he was making all the necessary arrangements to secure the mission. An opportunity had fallen on his lap weeks earlier, but he had had no place to carry it out. Now, this old abandoned mission would be the perfect place. Mexico was no-man's land these days, and help would be easy to find.

He smiled as he left town. Things were finally working out.

Chapter 17

After lunch, Roger told me more about himself and his family. His mother, Amor, and Paz went to NYU to study, leaving Luz in the sole care of Celeste. There at school, Amor fell in love with Roger Wagner, Sr.

"They were an odd couple to begin with. My mom was—still is—a free spirit, and my dad was and is a very up-tight lawyer. But no one can resist my mother, so two months after they met, they married. Things worked out fine for a while, but after I was born my mother couldn't adjust to life in the city, and my father could not stand the thought of living away from it. They had other disagreements besides that, but they all stemmed from the total lack of compatibility. There really isn't any animosity between them." He paused and took in a long breath. "What you just said about money is exactly what my mom would have said. My father on the other hand … money is all he knows."

"I'm sorry," I told him. He clearly looked like he was still caught in the middle of the 'irreconcilable differences'.

"It's odd, you know, they still love each other and nether has ever re-married." He thought about that for a moment before continuing. "Anyway, my mom moved back to Mexico to help take care of Luz, because by then grandma Celeste had passed." It was so odd to hear him talk so casually about Celeste, *my* Celeste. My ghost.

"I spent my time between Mexico and New York until I was in high school. My father insisted that I attend a private school in New York, and I spent my summers with my mom. By the time I started high school, Aunt Paz was a nun and had asked to be sent to the same town in Mexico where my mom and Luz were living. She took care of Luz at the convent for a while, but Luz was not very happy there, so my mom has been living with her ever since and Paz comes to visit almost every day. Their lives have been the same for years, and I try to visit them as often as I can," he sighed, "but I followed in my father's footsteps and I'm a lawyer too."

I nodded and smiled.

"I did it for your dad," Roger added. "My father was his lawyer, until I became one myself. Your dad always believed in me, and I always believed in him."

I felt a tinge of jealousy toward this close relationship he had with my father. But it was also comforting to know that my dad had such good friends, people like Roger and that detective that believed in him.

"I will write to my mom right away, and take the brunt of her wrath for keeping you a secret all these years. I'll give her your address, if you don't mind, so she can get in touch with you. They will want to meet you right away, so if I were you, I would start packing."

I chuckled.

"One more thing, Tess …well … maybe two. I know you said that you don't care to know how much money you've inherited, but I have to warn you. Between the three estates and the trust fund, there's still a bit of money. Enough, I would say, to kill for. You are now the last thing standing between Eros and what he's always wanted. You might be safe for now, but once he finds out that your dad has passed, and that he still didn't inherit, he's going to move heaven and earth to find out who did. And once he does … "

I nodded solemnly and thought about the note around the cat's neck and the Christmas card. Apparently I now had two death threats! Not bad for a nineteen year old! "So what's the second thing?"

"Get a good accountant."

I wasted no time in jumping in Alex's Jeep and heading back home to tell the Prestons the news. Roger had left me with a stack of legal sized documents that I had signed, officially making me a millionaire! Me! A millionaire! Oddly enough, I kept trying to make myself feel excited about this, but I couldn't. Maybe it was Celeste's unrelenting groans and lamentations that put a damper on the occasion, or maybe it was the threat of death that this money represented. Either way, I finally had enough money to support Dorian, and myself, so, at least that aspect of my life was settled.

"Spend it!" Dane said in response to my news. "Spend it all! If it's the money he's after, what can he possibly do if it's gone?"

Katie brightened up and smiled from ear to ear, "I know how you can spend it! Buy an acre of rainforest!"

"Or set up a trust fund for Dorian," Valerie suggested matter-of-factly. "Pay your schooling in full, gift the house in Mexico to your aunts, donate the plantation in Spain to the city as a museum or something, and sell the house in Argentina. Then buy a shop in town and set up your business as a fashion designer. I bet you could sink all kinds of money into that business!" She winked.

Now, that was an idea … but I was hesitant to blow through a million dollars that quickly. I hadn't even spent a thousand dollars—ever! But they were right, I had to make some decisions and I had to protect Dorian and my aunts. Roger had told me that the only clause in my dad's will was, that I let my aunts live in the home in Mexico for as long as they lived. This I would do without a doubt. In fact, I would put that home in their name, so that they would never feel like they needed to leave.

I had no idea how I would do any of these things, and I felt overwhelmed by it all. This money was already weighing heavily on me, even more than the old burden of not knowing how I would provide for Dorian.

Exhausted, I passed out on my bed, at the Preston's house, but sleep didn't last long. My mind startled at the sound of screams, searing pain, flashes of flames and the panicked looks of three soldiers.

Dear Tess:
When we received Roger's e-mail informing us of your

existence, I can't tell you how thrilled that made us feel. To think that your father had kept you a secret from us all these years! And to think that you had to grow up in foster care, when you had three loving aunts ready and willing to mother and protect you. I'm afraid that poor Roger got quite a scolding from me on the phone, after I read his e-mail. I know he had to keep his client's confidentiality, but still.... We understand the circumstances now, of course, and we know that your father just wanted to do what was best for everyone's safety, but to not even tell us...okay, okay, I'll stop ranting now. Paz tells me I'm ranting.

Needless to say, we want you to come to us as soon as you can manage it. We know that you are currently in school and that you have a scholarship. (Paz says you got your mind from her; she also got a full ride scholarship. She went to Columbia. I went to NYC and had to pay my own way). But if you could just hop on the next flight out as soon as you finish your semester, ~~we demand~~ we would love to meet you.

Love,

... more than you know!

Maria de Amor, Maria de Paz

& Maria de Luz

PS: Bring him. (Luz insisted on writing this herself, I'm not sure what she means.)

I read and reread my aunt's e-mail and tears blurred my vision every time. I felt the love emanating from those pages, a kind of love that I had never had—motherly love. I wrote to Alex right away too, to tell him of the good news. But I knew that he wouldn't get it. I haven't been able to shake the sinking feeling in the pit of my stomach, ever since I had that dream. I felt pain and I perceived his thoughts, *"We're going down, we're going down!"* Those were his thoughts, not mine. To make matters worse I haven't been able to dream of him since then; two agonizing nights have passed with no more information. I feel like Alex's life hangs in the balance and I'm the only one who knows about it, but can't do anything to help him. Even if I said something and was believed…what could we do from here?

When I entered the Preston's kitchen two mornings after the dream, Valerie was sitting on one of the stools stirring a cup of tea absentmindedly. She had dark circles under her eyes and stirring and looked like she had been crying.

"Good morning," I said, clearing my voice.

She looked up and faked a smile, then simply nodded.

"What's wrong?" I asked while reaching for my own cup of tea.

"Sometimes I get bad feelings, and I just can't shake them," she said, rubbing her eyes. "The worst part is … I'm never wrong."

"Is it about Alex?"

She looked up suddenly and fixed her violet eyes on me. "Yes, how—" Chills ran through her and I could see her arms getting goose bumps.

I didn't want to tell her about my dream, but I had to admit that I shared her unease. "I feel like something's wrong too."

Tears filled her eyes, and she slowly nodded. "I knew it! Dane makes me take these pills when I get like this, but I can't feel anything when I take them. I think that I would rather feel this, than feel nothing." She took a sip of her tea, and then stared into the cup.

"You should do what Dane says, though," I suggested, not wanting to go against Dane's professional advice.

She shook her head. "These feelings are not depression. There's a difference. When I get depressed, I feel no reason for my feelings. But there are times when I feel certain that something has happened and that's usually a sign that we need to do something about it."

"What could we possibly do about this?"

She shrugged, "I don't know. Wait, I guess."

But waiting that whole day yielded no answers and I had to get back to school. Dane and Valerie insisted that I take a cell phone with me to school, something that I had thus far been successful in avoiding. I have a huge aversion to cell phones; they might be practical but…so annoying and overrated!

"Mm … assimilation," I thought as I took the loaner phone from Valerie. "Now I can be just like everyone else!" I quipped.

"Now I can reach you if I hear any news!" Valerie responded with a touch of her normal sass.

From that moment on, every time that cell phone rang my heart lodged itself in my throat. But a whole week went by with only check-in calls from Valerie. So naturally toward the end of the week I started to get used to the ring of the phone. But for some reason, when that late Friday night call came, I knew …

"Valerie?" I said, knowing beforehand that it would be her. No one but Valerie ever called me.

"No … it's me, Katie," a soft voice responded.

"What happened?" I whispered, as my blood turned to ice.

"We got the call … his plane went missing."

Alex's jeep, much like a tired horse, seemed to know it was headed home. I didn't pack a thing. I just got into the Jeep and drove. Only as I parked the car in front of the Preston's driveway did I realize this, but shrugged it off at once. I had money now. I could go to the nearest store and buy a whole new wardrobe if I wanted to. I scolded myself for having such frivolous thoughts, and told myself that if I kept thinking that way, I would spend all my inheritance on dumb stuff.

Katie ran out to greet me and threw her arms around my neck. She had been crying and now started afresh.

Inside the house, Valerie was having a meltdown. Dane and the Admiral were there trying to calm her down, but not succeeding.

"I blame you for this," she shouted at her father. "You fed him all those war stories growing up. He joined just to make you proud!"

The Admiral shook his head solemnly. "He wanted to go, Val.

We had a serious discussion about this. He knew what he was doing and he knew that I didn't care what he did with his life as long as he was a man of honor. I specifically told him—"

Valerie shook her head and rolled her eyes, and turned away from her father. She buried her face in her husband's chest and sobbed. Dane acknowledged my entrance with a nod and the Admiral gave me a pathetic smile.

"He's alive." I proclaimed, not knowing where such a powerful statement had come from. But as I said it, I knew it was true. I felt it deep inside. Almost simultaneously, everyone turned to face me. Even Valerie stopped her wailing and looked at me with hope. This family was used to having an oracle, someone who always seemed certain of how things would turn out, but that oracle was currently having a psychotic attack, so someone had to step in.

Later that night, Dane had to sedate his wife, and once she was down, the rest of us held an impromptu council around the kitchen table. It was decided that turns would be taken to watch Valerie around the clock. I was told that it had been a long time since she'd had such a breakdown.

"She was a teenager," the Admiral said solemnly. "It ended badly, and almost succeeded in ending her life."

"If she doesn't improve," Dane said wearily, "she may have to be hospitalized."

"Dane, no!" The Admiral croaked.

"Let's hope we don't have to, but she is insisting on making herself sick over this. She's not listening to reason. She's giving in to the full sway of her emotions and not even considering the fact that Alex might just be fine." He looked at me when he said this, with a grateful smile for my comment earlier.

My prior certainty over my statement had worn off by now, and doubt was creeping in once again. *"If only I could dream of him tonight."* I thought wearily. It was two thirty in the morning and the stress of the day was getting to me.

Dane wrote out a schedule and gave everyone instructions on what to do. Katie and I had the late morning and midday watch hour. The Admiral took the first shift, so Dane could catch a few hours of sleep before he had to go to work.

As my head hit the pillow, I called out to Alex. I laid there trying to reach him, but nothing happened. Then my pleadings turned to a higher power. *"Lord, help him ... I think he's alive ... please ... bring him home."*

"You shall be like an ax in my hands."

"An ax?" My weary mind asked.

"Shall the ax boast itself against him that heweth therewith? Or shall the saw magnify itself against him that shaketh it? As if the rod should shake itself against them that lift it up, or as if the staff should lift up itself, as if it were no wood." a soft firm voice responded. The peace it brought me consumed all the fear and anxiety, and I was soon resting soundly.

Chapter 18

Everyone followed Dane's schedule and Valerie remained under constant surveillance. That meant we followed her into the bathroom and everything. She hated it, of course, but she was sedated, so her temper was subdued.

Later that evening, as the four of us gathered for a bite to eat around the kitchen counter, we heard a knock at the door. We exchanged panicked looks, because a visitor at this hour was unlikely. I could see it in everyone's eyes that for a second all our hearts sank, dreading that it was a visit from men in uniform. Dane went to the door, with all of us on his tail. He inched the door open just a little, then swung it wide with surprise.

"Dorian!" Dane half exclaimed/half breathed out with relief.

"What are you doing here at this hour?" I inquired, as I threw my arms around his neck. He had grown a few inches and looked all grown up. After holding him tight for a moment with his limp arms at his side, it hit me! Today was his eighteenth birthday. A couple of days ago, I had every intention of calling him, and finding out what his plans were and what Charlotte was going to do, but since getting Katie's call, I had forgotten all about it.

I was flooded with guilt and told him so. But he didn't seem to be worried about that. He had a suitcase with him, and there was a cab outside waiting for his fare. I was about to go out and pay the driver, when Dane insisted on doing it himself.

I started to ask Dorian a million questions to which I knew I would get no answers, but with Dorian you just never knew, so I had to try.

"I drew this," he said, handing me a folded piece of paper. It had been folded so many times that it fit perfectly into the palm of his hand.

"Should I call Charlotte? Dane asked, while I unfolded the paper.

"Yeah, we need to at least tell her that I will take care of him from now on," I said, as I focused on the picture. The drawing took up the whole page; there were no empty spaces. At first glance it looked like a jungle and some people seemed to be hiding under thick foliage or resting against the tree trunks. On closer inspection, I could tell that the people were American soldiers—a tiny flag on the uniform on one of the soldiers was clearly visible. Then I saw that the people that were on the ground were not hiding, but lying there, wounded, or dead, I couldn't tell.

Two figures were drawn sitting up. One was a black guy whose leg had a strip of white gauze tied around his thigh, and the other was ... Alex! He looked whole, other than a trickle of blood running down his forehead.

I could feel the blood draining from my head, and my legs giving out. But I refused to be so weak, or to pass out. So I staggered to the nearest chair and leaned against it while I let the wooziness pass. Seeing my reaction Katie came over to my side and looked at the picture. It took her a few moments to see what I saw. She exclaimed, "It's Alex! He's alive!"

The Admiral hurried over too, making loud thuds with his cane as he came, and Dane, who was on the phone, hastily ended his conversation. They all took turns inspecting the drawing.

"Dorian, what does this mean?" Dane asked with what I thought sounded like his psychiatrist voice.

Dorian shrugged. That was all we were going to get out of him, I could tell.

"He does things like this sometimes," I explained for him. "I think that he sees them in his head and has no way of expressing them, other than by drawing them."

"Has he done this before and been right?" the Admiral asked.

"Yes," Kate answered. "He drew a picture of Estelle once, but he's never seen her."

"He's also drawn pictures for me, one specifically that actually took place, but he could have never known about it. In fact," a chill run through me as I spoke, "he must have drawn the picture right as it was happening."

They insisted that I recount the story of that night when I was stranded after the swim meet and had wandered alone in the rain before Alex found me. The Admiral remembered that night, but didn't know about the details leading up to it.

"So you are saying that Dorian had that drawing waiting for you at home, before you even told him anything about what had happened?" the Admiral inquired.

I nodded, "To this day I haven't told Dorian about that night. All he knows is what he's drawn."

The Admiral grabbed the picture again and studied it with more scrutiny. "Then there's got to be something in here that will give us a clue as to where they are," he said, as his eyes searched the paper. He did this for a while, then looked up suddenly. "It could be anywhere, but the military might be able to glean more intelligence out of this. They know where he was headed, and what countries he was flying over, so they might be able to narrow the search down if they give this picture any credence."

"Do you think they would?" Dane asked.

The Admiral shook his head. "It's doubtful that they would, but I have some friends that might humor me."

After discussing this possibility for some time, Dane suggested we all go to bed and get some rest. Dorian was given the room I usually slept in and I was sent to Alex's room. I was expecting Dorian to complain about his accommodations, but he didn't. Today, it seemed, he was full of surprises.

The next day, Dane requested all the pictures that Dorian had drawn for me, and tried to glean any more information he could out of Dorian. The Admiral set to work, trying to reach some of his old acquaintances in the military who owed him favors. He claimed that he had saved their lives, so they owed him this at least. While Katie took care of breakfast and all the household chores, I took my post by Valerie's bed. I brought my homework in with me, hoping to get a few hours of work done, but I soon found my mind drifting in other directions.

"You shall be like an Ax," that soothing voice had said. What was that supposed to mean? I knew from what Celeste had taught me that the voice was good, because it filled me with peace and I

was able to fall asleep. But it was different, too, somehow. I had felt it before … that was it! I had felt it, not heard it! It wasn't a thought that I had, it was a voice in thought form that had been placed in my head. Like when I hear Alex's voice, like telepathy; only…with feelings attached. It seemed to be the most complete form of communication. Words made perfect by the feelings they conveyed. As I thought about this, my mind started to drift yet again, and soon I found my mind being flooded with noise.

"Tess, Tess? Is that you?"

"It's true! You're alive! Why can't I see you?"

"I don't know. Oh, yeah … it's the sack."

"What sack?"

"The one they put over my head."

"Who, why?"

"I don't know who. They speak Spanish, and only in whispers. They put the sack over our heads so we couldn't see where they were taking us."

"Then, why?"

"Don't know that either."

"How long have you been this way? How do you eat or drink?" I asked with alarm.

"Three days … and they've been feeding us our own rations, but they make us keep the sack on our heads. They give us water this way too, not enough though, never enough."

"Oh, Alex…" I groaned. I could feel that he had a headache and a sharp pain on his side. I pointed this out to him and he explained that he must have broken or cracked a rib when they crash-landed the plane.

"You have to tell me where you are. Your grandpa is about to call some of his contacts in the military."

"I don't know where we are now; they've been moving us for a few days. But we were shot down over Venezuela."

"Venezuela? Why?"

"We were flying a Dignitary to a diplomatic meeting. We dropped him off and on our way back we were shot down, probably Guerrilla soldiers … who knows."

"So you're in Venezuela?"

"No, I don't think so. Suarez is pretty sure we've been exchanged somehow, sold or something. She speaks a little Spanish, but she's badly hurt."

"Oh yes, the girl."

"What girl?"

"In the picture, Dorian drew you and two other soldiers. A big guy and a girl."

"Dor—" Suddenly, I felt a sharp pain on the side of my face as if someone had struck me, and woke up with a start. The spot where Alex had received a blow still tingled with pain as if I had been hit myself. Then a new pain surfaced, one in my chest—Alex was somewhere in Central or South America getting a beating right now. To what end? Don't those people know better than to shoot down American planes?

I wanted to hold on to that pain; it was my only connection to his reality right now. But slowly the memory of the pain disappeared.

"What were you dreaming about?" Valerie asked with curiosity. She was sitting up on her bed, with dark maroon circles under her eyes. I regarded her for a moment, unsure of what to tell her that would give her hope and not add further to her distress.

"Alex." I said flatly. "He's alive," I finally told her. "Can't you just feel it, deep inside you, that he is still alive?"

She nodded numbly. "I guess, very deep down inside I do. But I also have this awful feeling that he is in terrible danger, like he's bound or captive."

This, I couldn't dispute. "We'll find him," I assured her. "Dorian came last night. He turned eighteen yesterday, so he came to live with me. I have to get a place for us."

"I will miss having you around. You are the only one who knows how I feel!"

She was right. For some strange reason, I did know just how she felt. Not because I loved Alex—we all loved Alex and worried about him. I knew how Valerie felt, just like I know what Dorian is thinking about and just like I've always known what Agatha's true intentions are. I get people. I see them, and, I see more than just their bodies. I see their natures, their intentions, their light, their … auras?

That's how I knew that Valerie was being irrational in her grief. I knew that she was using this pain to escape reality. She couldn't control it completely, but she knew that if she gave in to the war inside her head, she would have an outlet for her sorrow.

"It's true, I do know how you feel. And I know that you're indulging in your pain right now. By making yourself sick like this, you are adding to their distress, so now they have two people to worry about instead of just one."

Valerie stared at me; a flash of anger crossed her face. Then her features softened, and she nodded. "You're right. But I can't help myself. This—this, whatever this is, rules me."

"She needs to paint," a soft voice suggested. It wasn't Celeste; it was someone else, a high-pitched voice with a thick southern accent.

"Why don't you paint?" I suggested, while rubbing away the goose bumps on my arms. No matter how many times I heard those voices, I always felt goose bumps.

"Paint what?" Valerie said sarcastically.

"Tell her to paint her pain," the woman suggested. I could tell the love that the voice had for Valerie. I could feel the sorrow and compassion she felt for her, and tears came to my eyes. As I delivered the message, I could see a glint in Valerie's eyes. The moisture gathering around the rims told me that, she too, felt that love. Valerie closed her eyes and took in the feeling like a deep breath.

"My mother used to tell me that." Valerie's eyes were red and tears slid softly down her cheek. "How did you think to say that?"

I shrugged and tried to play it down, but Valerie looked at me suspiciously for a while. When she saw that I wasn't going add any more information to this, she got out of bed, took a shower, and got dressed for the day.

When she came into the kitchen, she looked ten times better and more composed. She hugged her father and he in turn held her tightly. All was forgiven and forgotten between them. No words seemed to be necessary; the love they shared healed all wounds.

With Valerie back on her feet, we brought her up to speed. We told her about Dorian's picture and how the Admiral was trying to get someone to take him seriously. But the man he spoke with basically told him, with the utmost respect, that he was crazy. In his best sailor language, the Admiral gave this General a piece of his mind, and then hung up the phone with a thud.

I wanted to share the fact that I knew he was shot down over Cuba, but how? How did I tell them without raising suspicions of my own sanity? Dorian had been tugging at my sleeve. "What?" I asked, a little annoyed.

He looked down and I immediately felt bad for being so short with him. "Sorry, Dorian. What's up?" I said remorsefully.

"Mexico!"

"Mexico?" I searched his face for answers, but I felt too frustrated myself to read his intentions right.

"Don't your aunts live in Mexico?" Katie suggested.

"Oh..." I said, remembering now how my aunt Luz had written, "Bring him," in the e-mail. "I can't go to Mexico right, now Dorian. Alex is missing. I can't just go meet them and feel happy."

"And why not?" Valerie questioned.

I shook my head, then looked at Dorian, "How did you know about Mexico?" I stared into his big brown eyes that looked determined and unyielding. "Never mind, I promise to take you when I go, but I'm not going any time soon." He looked crest fallen as he walked away. I felt bad, but I couldn't imagine going anywhere right now.

The day was long and it brought no new information on Alex. I watched the news and searched the web, hoping to hear some news of a plane crash anywhere in Cuba, or anywhere else for that matter. Valerie painted all day, Dorian drew, the Admiral made calls to everyone he knew, while Katie busied herself with housework.

By mid-afternoon I couldn't stay indoors one more minute, so I announced that I was going for a walk. Valerie said it was a great idea and she joined me. The day didn't feel like winter. It was a mild afternoon that fooled you into thinking that spring would come soon. The street where the Prestons lived was lined with huge houses that had access to the lake. All the front yards were perfectly landscaped and the world, from this angle, looked incredibly prosperous. Walking down this street was like walking in a different world, one where the struggles of every day survival didn't *seem* to exist. But they did; and this made one feel all the more miserable and out of place.

We kept our thoughts to ourselves for quite some time, until Valerie finally spoke up. "I think you should go to Mexico," she said, out of nowhere.

I turned and looked at her a bit shocked.

"Ever since you got that letter from your aunts, I've just have had this feeling that you should go to them right away. I can't explain it," she shrugged, "It's not like you can do anything for him here anyway."

"I can't go now," I said, dismissing the whole thing.

Valerie shook her head emphatically. "If it's me you're worried about—don't be. I really think you should go. This is your family and they are anxious to meet you. We'll call you the minute we hear something."

"I'm not in a frame of mind to go. I do want to meet them, but… meeting them should be a happy occasion, and I just can't go now, feeling the way that I do."

Valerie didn't respond. She knew very well that no one felt like doing anything. We all felt so helpless. Our lives were on hold until Alex was found.

"I dreamed of him," I finally blurted out. I was dying to tell someone, but I wasn't sure who. Valerie turned and looked at me with interest.

"I believe in dreams," she encouraged.

I took in a deep breath. "He was being moved from place to place and had a bag over his head." She stared at me still, and with her eyes she encouraged me to continue. "He seemed okay," I added.

"I've had dreams … very real dreams. Dane says that they are an expression of our subconscious, and I know that they can be that at times … but sometimes they are much more than that. I think that sometimes they can be a conduit to communication that would otherwise be dismissed by the conscious mind."

"I think I believe that, too," I said eagerly, and left it at that, for fear of going too far into things that sounded more supernatural than real.

"Then you believe me when I tell you that I have this very strong feeling that you should go to Mexico and meet your aunts?"

"I believe you, but—"

"We—I, will be fine, if that's still bothering you."

We finished our walk in silence and when we got home we planned the trip. By the end of the day, everything was set. It was also decided that while we were gone, Valerie would do some apartment hunting, so that Dorian and I would have a place to live upon our return.

Chapter 19

We couldn't see the front door to my aunts' house from the curb. A thick, fuchsia bougainvillea hedge covered the view of the house from the street, but there was an open gate that we passed through as we lugged our heavy bags.

We walked down a cobble stone path that was partially covered with scattered white sand. To the sides of the path, the lawn had patches of sand here and there, where the grass was sparse. There were palm trees and colorful overgrown flowerbeds planted at their base. The house looked Colonial, with white stucco walls and a red tile roof. A beautiful fuchsia bougainvillea decorated the entrance, giving the thick wooden front door a welcoming splash of color.

Dorian was beaming; he seemed to love this place already. I looked at him both puzzled and glad, and he responded with an even bigger smile and an unprecedented hug. We knocked on the door, and we could hear from the inside a rush of feet and excited voices. The door was opened suddenly, bringing a gust of salty sea wind inside with it.

"Tess, Dorian?" said a woman, with long, wavy, white-blond hair. She looked like a hippie, with a colorful scarf framing her face, dangling earrings, and the soft, musky and floral smell of patchouli and geranium. Another woman popped her head out from behind the first one. They were each identical, yet somehow different, versions of the other one. "Hi!" she said, tucking herself back behind the first woman.

"Come here!" the first one chided, pulling us both to her in a warm embrace. "Let me give you a big overdue hug!" Before we knew it, we were both squeezed together into a tight embrace. "I'm Maria de Amor, your aunt, Roger's mom. This is Luz," she reached behind her and pulled out her sister. "Aren't you going to give them a hug, Luzita?"

Luz had pigtails and a girlish dress on, with lots of ruffles with a big bow tied in the back. She looked like she was ready for a

Wizard of Oz play at the local theater.

Luzita smiled shyly and refused to give us a hug right away. Though she was identical to her sister, she looked younger—much younger. Her behavior was such that you soon forgot that she was an adult, and naturally thought of her like the child she was.

After a moment she came to my side and gave me a little squeeze. "You smell like jasmine and mint," she declared. Then she went to give Dorian a hug, but stopped herself, looked down with an embarrassed smile, and then retreated to her sister's side.

Inside the house, the floor had large terracotta tiles mixed in with smaller, hand painted tiles. The furniture was thick, rough-hewn walnut. The kitchen opened up to the dining room and the living room, and this main living area had a sprawling, open view of the ocean, separated only by some French doors. From the kitchen window you could see a luscious vegetable garden, and the intoxicating smell of something homemade emanated from the oven.

"What is that wonderful smell?"

"Bread. Luz makes it!" Amor said, as she guided us through the house.

"I've never had homemade bread before."

"Really? That's all I've ever had!" Luz said with amazement.

"Oh, that's not true Luz; you've had plenty of store bought bread. But we do have a family tradition of making our own for everyday use. Our mother, Celeste, enjoyed making it, and taught us how, when we were young." Amor paused, then placing her outstretched arms on my shoulders, added; "now we have to teach you, so you can teach your daughter … some day!"

This last comment brought a pang of sadness to me. A daughter … children … marriage, … Alex … oh, Alex! I tried to swallow the lump in my throat, but I couldn't hide the burning in my eyes, and Amor noticed this.

"I bet Dorian would love to learn," I said, trying to sound cheerful. No sooner had I said this than Luz was at his side and talking to him about all kinds of things. Dorian smiled and nodded, fascinated by her.

The kitchen had a rustic, well used, and old fashioned look to it. It was cute, clean, and homey. It reminded me of a fairy tale kitchen, complete with herbs hanging to dry in bunches from an exposed beam on the ceiling. I walked up to the spices and gently smelled them to see if I recognized any of them.

"These are my collection," Amor commented. I let go of them fearing that I would be disturbing them somehow, but Amor waved her hand in an encouraging manner. "Oh, no, no, you can touch them, go ahead. What I meant to say was that I like to grow herbs, spices and other plants, not just for cooking but for medicinal purposes as well. There are a lot of poor people here that have no access to doctors and I'm an Herbalist, so a lot of people come to me for medicine." She pointed to the hanging clusters, "I'm always drying something so I can turn it into a powder and then into teas or stuff it into capsules for people to take. It's time consuming, but I love it!"

"That's really neat!"

"Yeah, we keep busy around here," Amor made a sweeping motion with her hands. "We have a large garden outside that grows most of our food, and we have chickens and a goat, and we also do a great deal of charity work for Paz's school and the congregation."

"Is she there now?"

"She is. She runs a school for underprivileged girls at the convent."

"I used to live there," Luz put in, and went back to talking to Dorian.

"That's right. Luz lived with Paz in the convent for a little while, but…it didn't work out so well. Apparently, life in a nunnery was not Luz's cup of tea. So I brought her home with me and Roger," Amor said, waving her hair away from her face and releasing a sigh. "Now, tell me all about you. Paz will be here shortly for tea, and we can bring her up to speed then."

"Bring who up to speed?" A flutter of black and white swept into the kitchen. "You must be my beautiful Tess!" Paz said, with an authority that only a principal or a nun could impose.

"I am," I said with a smile, and she hugged me tight in her

boney arms. Paz had the same features as the other two, but she was much thinner, and though kindly, her features were sterner, and she smelled of books and chalk.

"What? No tea yet? Amor, its 3:15 P.M!" Paz mocked as she tapped her watch.

Amor shook her head and shoved the nun out of her way. "There is only one rule you have to follow while you bunk with us," Amor said, as she filled a copper kettle with water. "Tea is at 3 p.m. sharp, every day. We are just as devoted to our afternoon tea as we are to the Pope." Paz crossed herself and nodded in agreement, then led me to the table.

I watched as Amor set five dainty looking cups on five matching saucers, then set a strainer over the set's porcelain kettle and filled it with some strange looking herbs. She handed the tray to her sister, and then started on another that held a sugar bowl, some butter, homemade jam and a generous amount of sliced bread, right out of the oven.

"Now this tea will most likely be unlike any other tea you've had," Amor started. "You see, I make my own mix to boost Antioxidant levels, energy, and immunities. What you'll try today is what we usually have, unless of course one of us needs something special whipped up." She raised her eyebrows and looked at me meaningfully. "Sometimes instead of energy, we might need something to calm us down. Or even knock us out!"

"You can do that?"

Paz laughed. "Oh yes, dear. She most certainly can. Don't worry, all the ingredients are legal, in Mexico of course."

"Stop it, Paz." Amor shook her head, then took the whistling kettle from the stove and poured the water through the strainer. I cranked my neck to get a whiff of the herby, minty aroma that rose from it.

By now my mouth was watering and my stomach gave a lurch. "I'm sure glad I made it right on time for tea then," I joked. Suddenly, an odd feeling came over me—a faint sadness and forlornness. This should have been my home! I could have grown up here, running on that beach and tending that garden.

Then I looked at Dorian, sitting there, listening to whatever Luz was telling him. He looked like he had found his home too. He glowed of peace and contentment here. I let out a sigh. For him, I would do it again, just to see him happy like this. "Thanks for inviting him; he looks happier than I've ever seen him."

My aunts exchanged mysterious looks.

"We are so happy to see you both here, but we had no idea—" Paz started, "that he existed." Amor finished.

"I knew he existed!" Luz protested. "That's why I invited him."

"We didn't know about him until you wrote to us, saying that you would bring him as requested," Paz added in a whisper, like she was telling a secret.

All three of us turned and looked at Luz and Dorian, who were in a world of their own. "What's even stranger still is that he told me that we needed to come to Mexico before I even told him about you guys," I added, now mystified.

"Now that's interesting," Paz mused, taking a sip of her tea. "Excellent as always," she crooned to her sister.

"De nada," Amor acknowledged cordially. "I wonder, " she continued, as she looked at Dorian and Luz, "Could it be that they can see things that we can't? Or receive information that we don't?"

I immediately proceeded, between bites of bread and jam and sips of possibly the best tea I had ever tasted, to tell them about Dorian, his disabilities and his gift. In fact, I poured out my whole life before them, from my earliest memory up to now, complete with Alex's disappearance. It almost seemed as if the tea was laced with a truth serum. My aunts listened attentively, and, with relish, supped on their own tea and buttered bread, topped with homemade plum jam.

Luz and Dorian joined us after a while, but they remained silent. Luz's eyes had been fixed on me while I spoke, but every once in a while they would wander to some spot just over my left shoulder. She looked like she was watching something, so I turned a few times to see what she saw, but there was nothing there. She did this now and then, while I was talking and sometimes she would smile, as if whatever she saw in mid-air was amusing her.

"She has an invisible friend," Amor leaned over and explained when she saw my puzzlement of Luz' behavior. I nodded in acknowledgment, and we continued our conversation. I told them about my life, sparing no details about anyone, including Agatha, Alex, and his family. Then I asked them about my parents and grandparents, and they produced a photo album.

I got to see pictures of my parents, and a few of my grandparents. Celeste looked exactly as Dorian had drawn her. I told my aunts this, and I brought out all the pictures that Dorian had given me. While they looked at Dorian's drawings, I looked at the pictures of my parents. We gasped and marveled in turns as we each saw the photos or the drawings that made up my past.

"What do you suppose these are?" Paz inquired as she pointed to the ominous shadows that hovered over me while I was at the bus station. I hunched my shoulders and shrugged. I didn't want to go into that right now. They understood. It was fine for Dorian or Luz to have quirky gifts, but it was quite different for me to admit to hearing voices.

Paz looked unconvinced, but turned her attention back to the drawings that Amor was shifting through.

"Look here!" Amor exclaimed. "See? That's—" Amor stopped short and Paz shook her head in dumb amazement. "But it can't be!"

"What?" I asked looking up.

"This is our home in Argentina. This is where we grew up!" Amor said, holding the drawing of the house with the dock and the sail boat in front.

"Is there a picture of it?" I asked, as I flipped through some of the pages. Paz stood up and bent over me, flipping some of the pages.

"Here," she paused at one page where there were pictures of three little girls, dressed in identical white dresses, caught in the act of playing tag. "You can't see the whole house, but here is this window, see? And here is the tree he drew here ... this is nothing short of a miracle! I've never seen that boat before though."

"I have," I told her, "it belongs to Alex, or his grandfather, rather."

"Then he will be found," Paz uttered with awe.

This comment caught in my throat and that heavy feeling of dread returned to me.

"She's right," Amor said, "Dorian has been right about everything else he's drawn. Alex will be found. How else will this boat make it all the way there?" She patted my arm while Paz looked at me intensely. We sat and looked at each other like this for some time—in silent acknowledgment of the miracles before us. Instinctively we turned to look at Dorian, who was absentmindedly looking around the room as if he were in heaven.

"Who knows what these two can really do?" Amor murmured with reverence. "For all we know, they can see Angels. Maybe, they were picked to be special because they were better than us. Maybe they are the ones that were sent to help us, and not the other way around."

Paz nodded slowly, and waved her finger affirmatively, "I think you're right, sister."

I had no doubt that Amor was right; Dorian's pictures have been a source of comfort and hope to me all these years. I turned my attention back to the photo album, and through blurry eyes, continued to look at pictures that had parts of the house he drew. My aunts looked like they had a happy childhood, filled with lots of sunshine and river water. Celeste was in many of the pictures, laughing, swimming, playing with her daughters, and tending roses. My aunts told me that she grafted and collected roses from all over the world. The rose garden at the home in Argentina was, at one point, well known and people came from all over just to look at it.

Max, her husband, looked like he was mild and indulgent. He worked as a teacher, and later on was able to get a post teaching at the university, but he died soon after that. Paz told me how his death was rather suspicious; he fell into a well and drowned. "We never did believe it was as simple as that," she added solemnly. "But we've never been able to really piece together any other explanation, except ... "

"What?"

"That he was pushed in," Amor finished. "But that's a bit drastic. Who would have wanted to kill my dad? Everyone loved him!"

I thumbed through several other pages of my aunts' teenage years, but there were no more pictures of Celeste, and there were no pictures of her second husband, Ricardo. I wanted to know more about that, but the time seemed wrong. They were quietly mourning their father again. Their minds were reaching out to him and to the happy memories they still had.

The next sets of pictures were of my dad, Leo. He looked like an imp, a real *Dennis The Menace*, wreaking havoc as he went. Luz especially seemed to be his constant companion. Amor and Paz confirmed my suspicions by saying that she was his accomplice from day one and that she took it very hard when he left for college. In fact, they said that seeing her with Dorian has been the happiest they've seen her since Leo left.

The last few pages had pictures of my father while in college. He looked a lot like Roger did, with wavy brown hair, but his eyes were a lighter gray color. In most pictures he had a cocky, mischievous grin, which made me smile. I mentioned this and my aunts assured me that, though he wasn't conceited, he was very confident and exuded self-assurance everywhere he went.

My mom looked more reserved. She had an exotic beauty, accentuated by her jet-black hair, dark eyes, and high cheekbones. Irene was her name, she was Chicana; a native Californian, and my aunts knew nothing of her family. She had been studying to be a librarian when she met my father; perhaps I inherited my love of books from her.

One of the pictures of my parents caught my attention. It was a group picture taken at the beach. Several young couples were posing in the picture, but one man in particular stood out to me. He had dark brown hair and dark brown eyes, and that kind of forgettable face that was perfectly average. He was standing next to my father, with his arm slung casually around my father's neck, as if they were close friends. But the most remarkable thing about this man was the fact that I knew him.

"Do you know who this is?" I asked my aunts.

They leaned over and looked at to whom I was pointing. They both shook their heads, "Sorry, I don't" Paz said, "Do you?" she asked Amor, who kept shaking her head. "Just a college friend, I suppose."

I stared at that picture. I was sure of who it was, but it was impossible. The man next to my father looked like he was in his twenties, so today he would have to be in his mid-forties at least. But he wasn't. Officer John Lovell had not aged at all in twenty years.

Chapter 20

Interestingly enough, Celeste had not said a single word since I set foot in Mexico. I wasn't sure why. Of all places, her daughters' home should be her favorite place to be. Unless it was too painful; she had mentioned once to me that being around familiar places could be torturous to a disembodied spirit.

The next morning, Dorian and I were given a rundown of how things worked around the house. There were lots of things to do and we were given a list of chores. Laundry was done by hand, just like everything else apparently. I offered to buy Amor a washer and a dryer, and she turned me down flat, saying that washers used up too much water and that life was better when you worked with your hands. "It's good for the soul," she added, as she placed a garden spade in my hand.

At first, weeding didn't look all that appealing. I approached it with trepidation because I didn't want to get my hands too dirty. But as I pulled those obnoxious weeds, my mind began to drift towards Alex and my parents. The pulling and the yanking became somewhat therapeutic as I thought of how short lived my parent's love had been. How unfair for my father to rot in prison, convicted of a crime he didn't commit. Then I thought of Alex and wondered where and how he was.

Involuntary tears of frustration and anger clouded my vision. Would our love be short lived like that of my parents? And how about Celeste? She lost the love of her life early on, too. Did she find love with Ricardo or did she marry him out of loneliness? What would I do if I lost Alex?

Tears were now flowing freely down my cheek and I knew that my face must be stained with dirt as I tried to wipe them away. I stopped weeding when the sun was too hot and the plot I had tackled was weed free. Though filled with sadness, I did feel better. Amor was right; working with your hands was good for the soul.

"Amor needs some vegetables from the garden," Luz said,

startling me. She was standing directly in front of the sun, so her outline shone like an unearthly creature. She was holding a wicker basket out to me with one hand and a lifeless chicken in the other. Shielding my eyes from the glare that encompassed this glorious yet ghastly apparition, I reached for the basket. "Did she say what she needed?"

"Ten tomatoes, two cucumbers, one bell pepper and a small onion," she rattled.

"Okay, I'll fill the order." I smiled.

Satisfied with this, Luz skipped away dangling the chicken. Light flooded my eyes again, blinding me temporarily. *"I'm the light that shineth in the darkness, and the darkness comprehendeth it not,"* the mysterious thought came into my mind. I knew these cryptic messages to be scriptures—they sounded like scriptures anyway. I must have heard them at church, when Charlotte took us, but why was my mind pulling them forward right now?

While I filled the produce order, I decided that I would ask Paz about these messages when she came by this afternoon. She would be able to tell me what they meant, and maybe why my mind kept bringing them up. Was it my mind? These thoughts always seemed so unrelated to my other thoughts. Usually I have a train of thought that connects one thought with another, but these thoughts…they seemed to be placed in my mind, and were not connected to anything else.

Inside the kitchen Amor was busy grinding herbs in the mortar. She looked up at me and smiled brightly. "How was the weeding? Am I working you too hard?"

"No, you were right, it was therapeutic."

"I feel the same way after a good round of weeding. There's something about digging into mother earth with your bare hands that helps me stay rooted," she winked.

"What are you grinding?" I asked, as I started washing the vegetables and digging the dirt out from under my nails.

"It's valerian root, for you, actually. I noticed that your sleep last night was…spotty."

"You could say that," I sighed. "I want to sleep so I can dream of—so I can reach REM, but I can't seem to shut my brain off."

Amor turned and looked sympathetically back at me. "Dream of who—Alex?"

I took in a deep breath and slowly let it out. Amor's patchouli and geranium scent reached me. It was a soothing scent. I wonder if that's why she wears that all the time, to calm those around her? As I exhaled I tried to figure out exactly how much to tell her, if anything at all. Besides Valerie, and then only in a very vague way, I hadn't told anyone, about the dreams. Only Alex and I know how real those dreams are.

"It's okay, you don't have to tell me. Here, let me teach you how to make Celeste's favorite lunch—Gazpacho with a twist."

I handed her ingredients as she blended tomatoes, cucumbers, peppers, onion, garlic and a tablespoon of olive oil into a perfectly smooth texture. She then squeezed a lemon, and diced up an avocado. She ladled the bowls and topped them each with the diced avocado and lemon juice, served it with a side of Mexican tostadas.

"The avocado and the tostadas are the Mexican twist we added when we moved here. My mother loved traditional Spanish food, but along the way she incorporated Italian and Mexican influences. She was known for her cooking everywhere she went. She had a natural knack for it, but she didn't start cooking until after she was married."

"Everyone knows you're a good cook, too," Luz added.

"Thank you, Luzita. I think I inherited that from my mom. We all got something from our parents. Paz got my dad's ability to learn languages easily, and Luz taught herself to play the piano after Dad died."

"Dad taught me," Luz said simply and Amor frowned slightly, as if that didn't jive with her recollection.

With morning chores done, after lunch, everyone took to their own pastimes. Luz sat at the piano and expertly played a sleepy Chopin tune, while Dorian sat on the couch and drew. Amor got back to her herbs, saying that she had a few patients coming by this afternoon. I changed into my swimsuit, grabbed a book and a blanket and headed for the beach. But once I was there, I found that

I couldn't sit there and read. I felt too guilty sitting here, enjoying the beach, while Alex was miserable, so I got up and started running.

At first I found it hard to run on sand, but I soon adjusted and found my pace. This was the first time I had seen the ocean for myself, but I found it … not new. I felt as if I had seen it my whole life. I loved its constancy and endless horizon. I loved its briny air and sticky feel on my skin.

I ran until I could no longer see my blanket and book, then I jumped in the water and swam back, always keeping myself parallel with the shore. Swimming in the ocean was hard, but again, my body got used to it, and soon I felt like there was no other way to swim.

When I got back to my spot, I was physically exhausted and I collapsed on my towel. I reached for my book. Then … *thirst … thirst deep and sticky in my throat. Thirst consumed me and there seemed to be nothing in this world more precious than water.*

"Alex?"

Alex groaned in reply.

"You're in pain."

His breathing was labored, his brain registering pain in his ribcage, his head and several sore muscles. *"You could say that,"* he answered.

"I want to help you. Please, tell me how I can help you!"

"I don't know where we are. I don't think we're in Venezuela any more. I've been in and out of consciousness. I'm pretty sure I heard water."

"Water?"

"Yeah, like splashing against the sides of a boat." He groaned again, and the mention of water made him thirsty again. *"They haven't moved us in a while. We're in a prison of sorts; they have us all in one little room. It only has one tiny window that is up high. We've tried to look through it, but all we can see is another wall about five feet away. It seems desolate. Sometimes we think we can hear street noises, but they're faint and we can never figure out exactly what we're hearing. The climate is mild, so we must be*

somewhere in Central America, but I don't know where."

"Central America? I'm in Mexico, with my aunts!"

"Oh!" he tried to stifle a sharp stab of pain, *"What are they like? Please, tell me about them. I could use the distraction,"* he grunted.

"Alex! For all we know we could be close to each other!" I wanted to shout, to get up, to start moving.

"Tess...Central America may look small on the map, but it's not in real life. Not to mention that many countries are a complete mess right now, ruled by drug lords and guerilla groups. They shot down an American plane and didn't bat an eyelash. What do you think they'll do to you?"

"I speak Spanish, I'll blend in."

He laughed a mirthless laugh, and then coughed. *"Tess, you couldn't blend in in a Miss Universe contest, if you tried."* I felt myself blush, even while still asleep. *"You're blushing,"* he noted. *"Please, promise me you won't do anything stupid, or dangerous. Just—just tell me all about your aunts,"* he pleaded.

With resignation, and mostly because I wanted to bring him some amount of reprieve to his grim situation, I recounted all the events of the past few weeks: Finding Roger, discovering that I had money and that one of my uncles was after it. I also told him about his mom's feeling that I should come to Mexico, and Dorian's positive reaction to being here. Seeing pictures of my family—in particular my parents. Alex listened as attentively as he could amid the many pains he felt all over his body and the intense need for water and food that his mind was conveying to me. My stories, however, seemed to distract him enough to temporarily dull all these needs.

"Tell me more about this uncle of yours who's after your money."

"I don't know much," I told him, playing it down. The last thing he needed right now was to worry about me.

"You need to focus on that right now. You need to figure—" a stab of pain on his side made him groan. *"Someone's coming!"*

"Who?"

*"The goon they've left to look after us. You better go Tess...I
don't want you to worry."*

"No, please!"

"Sorry Tess—"

"Buenos días! Me extrañaron?"

"Who's that?" I asked, at the sound of a strange voice.

"Go Tess, go! I don't want you here while—ow!" Alex
groaned at a brand new pain—a kick to his leg. *"Please, Tess, you
shouldn't be here."*

*"Alex, I don't want to go! Besides, why can't you disconnect?
You have in the past."*

"I don't know—"

"Aquí tengo agua. Quien quiere agua?"

"Agua ... agua ... " one of the soldiers, pleaded.

"Agua?" the man said cynically, then laughed, and by the
sound of splashing water I could only assume that he threw water
on the soldier, rather than give it to him.

*"Vamos, hombre! Dale agua a estos pobres, o se nos van a
morir antes de que podamos venderlos,"* a second voice said.

"Alex, who's that?"

*"I don't know. I've never heard him before. He must be a new
guy. Did you understand what he said?"*

*"Yes, he said to give you guys water, or you would all die
before you were ... sold,"* I translated, and as the words registered,
a chill went through me. Then suddenly, I felt Alex's hair being
pulled back and lukewarm water being poured down his face. I
could feel Alex slipping away from me and into a deeper
consciousness, but not before hearing the voice of the second man,
"Valor, muchacho. Help is on its way!" he whispered.

When I came to, the sun was prickling my skin with its heat,
and my hand was gripping the book I had intended to read, before I
fell asleep. Slowly I straightened myself up into a sitting position
and tried to focus my disoriented mind.

Could it be true? Could that second man be someone who was
trying to help Alex? And what was that he said about selling them?
Who would buy American soldiers? Who would sell them, and

why? I should ask my aunts. They know more about what goes on here in Central America. Maybe there's a group of guerillas that are known to do this. Maybe—as I stood up to go back into the house, I felt a strange chill come over me, and an awful feeling started to surround me. My knees buckled and my strength weakened. A cold claw seemed to be pulling me down, engulfing me in dread and fear. All kinds of vile whispers surrounded me.

"Give up ... he's dead ... jump in the ocean and join him!" the voices suggested, and with the suggestion all hope seemed to drain from me.

From the back deck of the house, I could see Luz, standing there looking back at me with a strange look on her face. Her pigtails looked incongruous with the determined grown-up look on her face. I reached a hand out to her, pleadingly. I tried to call her, but words failed me. It felt as if I was slipping into some overpowering, unseen, dark abyss. Closing her eyes and taking a deep breath, Luz lunged herself forward and charged toward me like a mad bull.

"Leave her alone!" a man's voice demanded. The voice seemed to come with Luz, yet Luz remained mute with a mixed look of sheer terror and determination on her face.

A demonic laughter filled the air, the sound of many voices, speaking in unison hissed, *"You can't stop us! She's been marked. She will be ours."*

"I might not. But the First One can! Depart at once," the stern male voice asserted. Then the laughter started up again, but weaker. The unseen force retreated, releasing me from its unseen grip. My limbs went limp all at once and I crumbled back onto the towel in a heap.

"Are you okay?" Luz asked in her childish voice. I nodded, but I felt weak and mentally strained. "Come on, let's go back to the house, it's almost teatime," the grown little girl said, as she extended one of her arms.

I took her hand and stood up giving myself a minute to make sure my knees wouldn't buckle again. "What was that, Luz?"

She shrugged. "Who was that with you?" She shrugged again,

and once I was safely on the deck, she released me and ran into the house.

"That house has special protection, it shouldn't have happened!"

"You should have been there, Kerubiel!"

"How about you? Why weren't you there?" the Cherub lashed out in frustration. He took a deep breath and his face softened. "Dayspring, you know that I can't go there. Only human spirits are allowed there."

Dayspring looked away, frustrated and angry, but knew that he was right. No one but human Angels were allowed where Luz could see them. Too much could be revealed and then Luz would be responsible for that knowledge—a knowledge that she couldn't understand. But someone had dropped the ball, and she was angry about that. She had asked Kerubiel to keep an eye on Tess for her, because he looked more human than she did. She was afraid that if for some reason Tess ever were to expand her gift, even momentarily, she would be looking at a half-human, half-lion, Seraph. Dayspring knew from personal experience that anyone who had ever seen her on Earth had been shocked, to say the least. Someone even started worshiping her by mistake and created the sphinx. Every time she visited Egypt she was painfully reminded of that mistake.

"Not every human would be scared to see you, Day. If Tess were ever to see you, I think she would just see her old friend and trainer. She might even remember," Kerubiel soothed.

"Excuse me?" Max interrupted, feeling a bit uncomfortable. "I'm sorry, to—to … you called me?" Both Dayspring and Kerubiel turned to face him at the same time. Their forms being so much larger than that of a human, they made an imposing sight to Max, who came exactly up to their middle.

"Yes, Max, we did call you," Kerubiel responded, turning to

Dayspring and silently telling her to go easy on him.

Dayspring nodded in silent reply. She sat on her hind legs in order to look less arresting. "Why isn't Celeste with you?"

"She—she—feels bad."

"We all feel bad about this, but I need to talk to Celeste. She is Tess' Guardian Angel, and she was not at her post. She needs to tell me why."

"I was with my son," Celeste said as she glided forward, head down, trying hard to avoid Dayspring's piercing cat eyes.

"Your leave had expired; you needed to be at your post. Tess was left alone and Legion, of all the hellish creatures, engulfed her!"

"Not to mention—" Dayspring began, but was stopped by Kerubiel who cut in, extending his arm toward Dayspring, who looked too agitated.

"Not to mention that your own daughter saw the creature. I don't know what she thinks of it but—"

" … But it'll have to be addressed somehow." Dayspring finished, with more composure.

"I'm already on it," Max jumped in, "she doesn't want to talk about it, but I know her. She'll come around."

Celeste looked down at her feet and wished she could cry. Producing tears used to be such a simple way to relieve emotions, but now that she no longer had a body, the full force of her emotions had to be dealt with head on with no physical outlet to help it along. "I know what I did was wrong. I thought that she would be okay for a little while longer. I mean … the house is filled with spirits. One of them would surely help her—and one did!" she stammered.

"Thank Heaven that Max was there. But it wasn't his responsibility and now Tess has heard his voice too! I thought we agreed early on that we would try to keep her as ignorant of this realm as possible. I thought we decided that we were going to let her have as normal a life as possible. Now … " Dayspring sighed, "there's little hope of shielding her. She's going to want answers, and you're going to have to deal with her questions."

Celeste nodded grimly. "She's older now, maybe she'll understand better and—" Celeste couldn't finish her sentence. She knew that she had messed up, but she didn't think all of this was her fault. Legion could have just as easily shown up if she had been there.

"You might be right," Dayspring, answered the unuttered words. Her own gift of discernment had been growing and deciphering thoughts was getting easier. "However, it takes them some time to gather up enough cast-outs to form Legion—time that, if you had been there, you could have used to get reinforcements from our side and stopped it. Legion is no trifling matter, Celeste. Legion is so strong that it has the power to control and possess a human. A single human, left to his or her own defenses has very little chance against the Dragon." Dayspring thought of the time when Tess and her clan went against Legion as un-embodied spirits, they had almost lost Henry and barely escaped themselves.

It was obvious that the Second One had not forgotten his promise to Tess, and that he intended on having her, or making her life as torturous as possible. Already he had set several traps in motion for her. This, however, she couldn't share with the Guardian Angel. Things of the premortal realm had to remain veiled—unless remembered by the person, without assistance. After all, Celeste's probation was not over ... even if her mortal life was.

"You're right. I'm sorry. It will not happen again," Celeste said humbly.

"I know ... and I know how hard it is to see your son suffer, but he has to walk his own path. You can help him more by being *here* for his daughter," Dayspring said, mollified.

"I've already ordered reinforcements," Kerubiel announced. "Two of our Aeonian operatives have been assigned to her case."

Chapter 21

Inside, all the tea things were perfectly laid on the table and the whole house smelled like roses.

"Would you leave the French doors open, Tess? I like the breeze," Amor hummed from the kitchen.

Bubbling over the stove was a glass contraption. It had two tubes sticking out of it, and each one was dripping into separate containers.

"What's this?" I asked with interest, as I approached the thing from which the rose aroma was coming.

"A distiller." My aunt grinned, pointing to one of the spouts. "The water comes out of this one, and the oil out of this one," she explained, pointing to the second spout.

"I should know this, I worked selling essential oils for three years, back home."

"Did you really? What else do you do that you haven't told us about?"

"Here I am! Hope you didn't start without me," Paz waltzed in and pulled me in for a tight hug, then jokingly pushed her sister away when she too leaned in for one.

They tried to call Luz for tea, but she refused to come out. It seemed odd to them that she would not want to join us, but they brushed it off for the moment. Somehow I felt bad, almost guilty, as if I were responsible for her odd behavior.

"And what's wrong with you? Did something happen when I sent Luz out to get you?" Amor inquired.

It was now or never. I either told them everything or told them nothing at all. Something inside me said that I should trust them, and that they would understand. Yet … how could they? We just met yesterday.

"What is it, Tess?" Paz asked this time, as she let a lump of sugar plop into her cup of tea.

From the corner of my eye, I watched Luz enter the room

cautiously. She paused when she saw me and regarded me for a moment. Then she scurried to the table and sat down next to Dorian.

"You can hear them," she accused, "I know you can." She looked upset at me, like I was purposely making her look bad in front of her sisters.

I opened my mouth, prepared to speak, but nothing came out. Where would I begin?

"Don't be hard on her, Luzita. She's still trying to understand all of this." Celeste spoke for the first time in a long time. Hearing her startled me, and I noticed that Luz was looking in my direction, but just a few inches over my head. Not seconds later, Luz seemed to be appeased and started pouring Dorian some tea and buttering his toast like she would to an oversized doll at a pretend tea party. I watched with amazement as Dorian submitted to her willingly and even let her hand feed him a piece of toast.

"It's true," I finally said. "Like Luz said, I can hear them."

"Who?" Both Amor and Paz asked at the same time.

"Spirits, voices from other realms of existence. Just now … " my eyes filled with tears and my throat closed up.

"It's okay ... they'll believe you." Both Amor and Paz shuddered and their eyes got misty as if they could sense their mother's presence.

"Your mom, Celeste. I've been able to hear her for some time now." Again. A chill. But this time I felt it too. We were all openly crying now, except for Luz who had a satisfied smile on her face.

Spilling my guts to my aunts over tea was fast becoming my new hobby. I told them everything. Starting with my first dream of Alex, down to all the whispers, and I even included the Ouija Board experience with Agatha. I told them of my dreams where I saw that huge winged creature and those cat eyes looking at me. They listened with rapt attention to everything; I even threw in my gift for knowing what Dorian was thinking and the colors I see when I look at people.

"Anything else?" Paz had asked.

"Yes," I answered solemnly. "I can sew, really well."

This broke the tension in the room and they started laughing.

"It's a gift," Amor sighed, once the laughter had died down.

"I agree," Paz nodded. "After all, the Bible talks about gifts of the spirit, we all have them to one degree or another." She then rattled a long list of gifts that everyone she's ever known has had, including her own sister and her ability to heal people with herbs, and her other sister who perhaps was not crazy, but rather enlightened far beyond that of our own comprehension.

I also took advantage of this time to ask them about who would sell American soldiers. I asked if there were any groups of organized crime that did this. They thought about it. Paz said that kidnappings were almost an every day occurrence, and you were especially targeted if people suspected you had money for a ransom.

"But soldiers, that sounds more like a terrorist tactic," Amor said, shaking her head, wondering what this world had come to.

I had left my tea nearly untouched and had had nothing to eat. Everything looked delicious, but my stomach was just not having it.

"Nerves," Amor declared. "You have purged your soul, now you have to purge your body."

This reminded me of when Alex was deployed and I puked my guts out all the way back to the Preston's. I didn't want to purge like that again. Instead I asked for some aromatherapy oils, and Amor lit up like a Christmas tree. "Oooh! I know just what you need!" She rushed to one of her cupboards and handed me a dark blue bottle with a drip nozzle. "Ten drops of cedar and ten of rosemary, five or six of mint, in a bath full of water and you'll be a new woman!" she instructed.

Twenty minutes later I was soaking in the tub, letting the invigorating steam relax my tense muscles. Unfortunately my mind wasn't so lucky. Those awful feelings kept creeping in. They were not as intense as they had been on the beach, but their memory had left an imprint in my mind. If it hadn't been for the fact that I had just had a subliminal conversation with Alex, I would have believed them, and maybe even … No. I would never do that. But at the time, my anger and my sadness were unbearable.

Those voices had lied, flat out lied to me about Alex. Why? Maybe they didn't know that I had just had a shared dream with him. Maybe those other spirits that Celeste told me about can't read minds. They seem to know so much, but they didn't know what I was thinking.

That thought gave me comfort, yet the fact remained that even though I knew that they were lying, and that Alex was alive—I still felt tempted. What would I do if Alex did die? What did Celeste do when Max died? She remarried, rather quickly, too quickly. Then she had my father. What if—? My thoughts were interrupted by the sound of voices outside my bathroom door. It was Amor and Paz who were trying to speak quietly. Then they knocked.

"I'll be going into town tomorrow," Paz called from the other side. "I would love it if you came with me. You can also check your e-mails at the computer place in town."

My aunts had no Internet connection here, and apparently the only place that did was a little store in the nearby town that had a couple of computers you could rent for fifteen minutes at a time.

"Sure! I'd love to."

"Good, I'll be here around eleven," she said before walking away.

That night, Amor gave me some of that valerian root that she was grinding up. Even encapsulated, it smelled horrible. The effect, though, was almost instantaneous. I slept soundly, too soundly, and had no dreams, except for this odd feeling that someone was watching me sleep while sitting at the foot of my bed. When I woke up in the morning, my mind still felt foggy and tired.

"Maybe I gave you too much," Amor commented as I sat like a zombie at the table.

"That stuff is strong!"

"It doesn't work the same way on everyone. What I gave you wouldn't have done much for me, but by the look of you, it knocked you from here to China."

A strong cup of tea and a walk on the beach managed to lift the fog a bit. I went back to weeding the garden. I took up another row and cleaned it assiduously for the next hour.

"It's good to see you here," Celeste commented, like a friend stopping for a visit.

"Where have you been?"

"No puede ser que un espíritu no pueda tener ni un solo minuto para si misma!" she grumbled.

"Okay, okay! I'm sorry I asked! I actually have been meaning to ask you a few questions."

"Mm-hmm."

"What happened to me yesterday?"

"Ha! Por la boca muere el pez."

"What? By the … mouth dies the fish? What does that mean?"

"It's a Spanish saying. It seems that my mouth gets me in trouble more times than I care to admit."

"Have I gotten you in trouble?"

"No, not you. I…" she sighed. *"It's hard, you know. To be in the position that I'm in, having to watch life unfold without getting involved. I've never been good at not getting involved."*

"What happens if you get involved?"

"I could be reassigned to a different mortal. One that I didn't care so much about."

On hearing her words my eyes started stinging, threatening to tear up. "Wouldn't it be hard for all Angels who are assigned to watch over their loved ones?"

"It is hard, for all of us. But the difference, Tess, is that not all mortals hear us. You do. You are aware of me. You ask questions. You want and need answers." I felt a chill brush against my forehead. She was trying to brush a strand of my hair away from my face.

"But you can't give me those answers."

"I have to let the natural course of life unfold, undisturbed."

"What's the use of a gift if you can't use it? Why would God give me this gift? What's the purpose of it?"

"Ahh ... that question, I can answer. Your gift is one that encompasses many aspects, and it has many applications. It's called, the Gift of Discernment. Through it, you can read people's natures and sometimes perceive their thoughts, like with Dorian. If you had your gift for that reason alone, it would be worth it, would it not?" I nodded. *"But that has only been one of the reasons for you having this gift. You can see people's natures; you see them because to you, they shine. That light you see, their aura, tells you something about them; tells you a lot in fact."*

"It feels more like an instinct rather than something I see. I mean, I see it, but mostly I feel it." I shook my head trying to understand it myself. It's like trying to explain what sorrow feels like, or love, or any other type of emotion.

"Seeing this in people has helped you make friends, and naturally kept you from making the wrong kind of friends." I thought of Agatha and how much I disliked and mistrusted her from day one.

"What about the voices? Hearing you ... and them." I looked up to thin air.

"Well, that my dear was a bonus ability that has been part of you since—well—always. It's a sixth sense, like seeing, smelling, tasting, hearing ... "

"What about the dreams? How come I can share dreams with Alex?" I could hear her mouth extending into a smile.

"That just happened, I guess. The Eternals, the Godhead I mean, they communicate with us through what we call the Link. They are Linked to all of us, dead or alive or unborn."

"Unborn?"

"Arrgg! There I go again! Just—just stay with me okay?" She begged and I nodded with a smile.

"Okay, as I was saying, they communicate to us through the Link. Eventually this ability can be achieved by all of us, but it's currently way out of our reach. Except for you two."

"You mean to tell me that we are the only humans who can do this?"

"No, there have been a few others. I think it's forged by

closeness and a natural tendency to openness. I think that not only are you two meant to be together, but also you have nothing to hide from each other. It seems that your love is ... very pure. Some people can love more than one mate, while other people," her voice got husky; *"never fully open their hearts like you two have to each other. So naturally, we can't Link like you two can. ... Maybe someday."*

"You mean to say that if Alex were to ... die, I would never be able to fall in love with someone else?" She was quiet for a long time. I don't think it was my plight that puzzled her, but rather her own.

"I don't think you would," she murmured. *"I didn't love him you know, I—"* She never finished. In fact, she seemed to have flown away or something, because I sat there waiting for a long time for her to finish her sentence, but it never came. Finally I stood up and went back to the house. Amor was just setting the lunch things out on the back deck. We were having another cold soup—Ceviche—raw fish cured only with fresh lime and salt. My taste buds were dubious at first, but then I realized that the fish was actually cooked, just not with heat.

As soon as my bowl was empty, Paz walked out and plopped herself down on a recliner. I don't think I ever get used to seeing a nun walking around so casually.

"Hard morning, hermana?" Amor asked with a grin.

"Agh!" Paz draped one hand over her eyes. "The girls were crazy today! Paid no attention at all! Drove me mad! I'll have to talk to some of the parents while I'm in town."

"Oooh, that bad?"

Paz nodded.

"We want to come too!" Luz exclaimed with the utmost excitement. I guess she was over the scare she had yesterday.

Minutes later, Dorian, Luz and I were climbing inside an old Volkswagen van with a hand painted picture of the Sacred Heart, and the words "Hermanas del Sagrado Corazon" written around it. Luz held in her lap, a large basket filled with bread and vegetables from the garden—corn, tomatoes, summer squashes, and jalapeños.

On the car ride over to the town, Paz talked endlessly about Dorian, and how happy they were to have him around. "He has been, not only a great friend to Luz, but also a great help to have around the house." He had been able to perform some of the heavy work that they had been neglecting for a long time. "We would love it if he stayed!" Paz said succinctly.

"I don't know about that, Aunt Paz. I can't just leave him here. Besides, I've taken responsibility for him."

"Well, it's just a thought. I wanted to throw that out there. If he wants to stay, we wanted you to know that he is very welcome to. He seems to fit in quite nicely with us!"

I turned and looked back at Dorian, who met my eyes and smiled from ear to ear. "You like it here, Dorian?" He nodded enthusiastically. "OK, we'll see. Maybe we can try it for a few months and if it doesn't work out, I can come back and pick him up." Paz agreed, and Luz started to jump up and down in her seat.

As we drove into town we passed a tall, thick, adobe wall that looked like it had been damaged by fire. It seemed to stretch out quite a ways and it was encircling something. "What's that?"

"The old burned down Mission," Paz said, "It burned down about ten years ago, and no one has bothered to fix it back up. The mission itself is much older—colonial times I think—but when I was first sent here, the buildings inside were used as a school. I worked there myself. When it burned down, the school moved to the convent, and I've been teaching there ever since. The problem is, that only girls can come to the convent," she sighed, "I would love to go in there and rebuild the school, so boys don't have to go so far to get an education. I would love to … "

"What?"

She shook her head, " … have the money to buy back this place and do all the renovations."

I turned and looked back at the mission; it was calling to me somehow. Could it be that I was destined to buy this place for my aunt? I had the money, *and* I had to spend it!

Sitting against one of the outer walls of the mission, fiddling with some junk, was a hobo. He looked up the moment the van passed by and fixed his eyes on mine. I expected to see liquor filled, blood shot eyes, but instead they were lustrous, piercing, and alert.

The downtown district consisted of just a few vendor packed-blocks that led to the main plaza, or park, that was located in the center. Crowning one end of the plaza stood an old church with a bell tower on top. There were no swings in this park, just an old fountain, benches, some trees, and more vendors. My eye caught several handmade linen blouses made after the traditional Spanish way, with a scoop neck, ruffles, and embroidered flowers. Paz had found one of her pupil's parents who was working one of the stands, so she headed right over with a determined schoolmistress, step. I wandered off to look at the goods that were being sold, while Luz and Dorian headed straight for the churros.

The shopping area was small, filling the plaza and a few side streets. I shopped leisurely, not worried about getting lost.

I hated haggling so I paid the price that I was told. This made me a quick and easy target for other vendors, who were glad to make me other offers. Before I knew it, I was surrounded by people, all trying to sell me their wares by shoving them in my face. As graciously as I could, I tried to escape them, but not before I had several bags filled with blouses, dresses, a purse, a handbag, some silver jewelry and a huge broad brimmed straw hat.

My hands were full, and I found myself in the middle of the plaza looking about in search of familiar faces, or at the very least the street I was originally on. But from this vantage point, every street looked the same to me and I saw no sign of Paz, Luz, or Dorian, who should have stood out by his mere height.

I bought myself a churro, and asked the vendor if he knew where Luz had gone. He pointed to one of the side streets and I headed in that direction. But the street was desolate and bore no resemblance to the one we came down. I would have turned around and gone straight back the way I came, but something familiar caught my eye. It was one of the corners of the mission we had driven by. I walked straight up to it and dropped all my bags on the ground.

The wall called to me. I placed the palm of my hand on the

cool, hard exterior and a strange surge of longing discharged from it. I placed the palm of my other hand on it as well and another surge shot straight through me. I leaned in and placed my cheek against it, and felt as if that wall was the dearest place on Earth. I longed to be in there. It almost felt like … like the answer to all my problems was held inside this ruin.

Could this be a sign that I'm supposed to buy this place and donate it to Paz, so it could be turned into a school again?

"You like this place?" a man's voice said with a thick Spanish accent.

I turned and found myself face to face with the hobo I had seen earlier. "I think I do," I responded.

"Maybe you should go inside, see what you find," he suggested.

"There you are!" Paz yelled from the other direction. I turned to face her and she was walking briskly toward me. Her black nun's habit rustled around her and made her look like a strange crow about to take flight. "Where did you go? What are you doing here?"

"I was just—" I turned to look at the man, but he was gone, "I was looking for you, but then I found this place, and…. Did you see the man that I was just talking with?"

"Man? What man? Was there a man bothering you?" Paz asked alarmed.

"No, not bothering me." I turned and looked again, but there was no sign of him.

"Come on; I left Dorian and Luz alone at the computer place."

Chapter 22

That night I dreamed of that mission wall. I scaled it like Spiderman. I woke up and lay awake for a while, and when I finally went back to sleep, I dreamed of that wall again. This time I was not climbing it but was stuck to it. There was a force that was keeping me attached like a magnet. Then the hobo showed up again. He was holding an ax, but not in a threatening way. He was simply holding it as someone would hold a tool they were about to use.

"What's your name?" I asked him.

"Mathonihah," he answered.

"What kind of name is that?"

"Native American."

"This ax, what is it for?"

"It's a tool; you know what it's for."

"Will I use it?"

"You are the ax; let Him be the hand ... " Mathonihah turned and walked away, after placing the ax on the ground at my feet. He had a curious face, like that of an old man, only he wasn't old. He reminded me of that policeman, John Lovell, who interrogated me after Agatha disappeared and was in that picture with my dad. They both shone differently than other people did. Their auras were brighter, but they also hinted of something ancient ... as if they held the wisdom of the ages in their hands.

When I woke up in the morning, my body was aching, as if I had been literally stuck to that wall all night, my fingertips felt raw as well, as if I had really climbed that wall. It was still early, so I thought I'd take a walk on the beach.

Instead, I found Amor doing Yoga on the sand; she was in the middle of her Sun Salutation when I joined her.

I wasn't very good at Yoga, but I followed her every move. As I stood straight and stretched my arms high over my head, and then slowly bent forward and into Down Dog, my tight muscles started to stretch and relax.

From the beach we could hear noises coming from the kitchen. It was Luz, playing the piano.

"She has played that song every day since dad died," Amor mentioned.

"Really, did he teach her?"

"No."

Luz's mind had never developed beyond the age of ten or so, and the most astonishing thing was, she looked young. Her body was like that of a grown woman, but when you saw her face, you couldn't help but see the child. She lived just like a child, who played all day among the flowers and birds. I envied her bliss. No doubt, no one would wish to have a disability, but she made it look appealing. Dorian often joined her in her girlish games, and together they did their chores and tended the garden like the innocent Adam and Eve might have before the apple incident.

That day went much as the other days had, and I was getting into the rhythm of life here with my aunts. But I felt fidgety; I hadn't had a single dream about Alex since the last one where the man promised him that help was coming. I wondered if maybe help had come and they were safe, or if they had tried to escape, but got caught and were in even more trouble than before.

During tea I asked Paz if she knew anything about the old burned out mission and if it was for sale. She told me that she had checked on it, and the mission had recently been purchased under a random company name, "International Investments", or something. You couldn't get more generic than that. The actual owner's name was a mystery.

This was a great disappointment to me, because I wanted that building more than anything else I had ever wanted. The oddest part was that acquiring it so it could be converted into a school seemed secondary in importance. So why did I want it so badly?

"Señor DeLeon."

"Are they ready?"

"Sí señor, they are ready for the exchange. You'll be here for it?"

"Yes, I'll be there first thing in the morning. I trust you kept them isolated and that you told no one about them?" The phone connection was not the best, but it was good enough to convey the threat in Eros' voice.

"Sí señor," Teodoro eyed Mathonihah, with misgiving. He had gotten drunk a few nights ago with the money that he had been paid up front. Unfortunately, Mathonihah the old Indian Shaman, had celebrated with him and later insisted on seeing the prisoners out of mere curiosity. He was harmless of course, had no family, came and went and did his odd Indian things, so Teodoro hadn't worried much about him, until now.

"The one—the girl one … she's bad." Teodoro changed the subject, "She has the fever, and might not make it."

"Well you had better do something to make sure she does make it. A lot of money is riding on this and I'm not about to lose one of them right before I get paid," Eros warned.

"But she needs a doctor; I don't know what to do for her."

"No, no doctors. Don't you have a curandero or something? Just pay one of the town's healers to give her some of those Indian homemade drugs you have down there. Just tell them it's for a cousin of yours and that you need something to give to her."

"Well…okay, I think I know just the one."

"Just make sure that they can all stand when our visitors come. If you do this well, you'll be a rich man."

"Sí señor." As soon the line was severed, Teodoro shook his head. "Mathonihah, can you cure the girl?"

Mathonihah shrugged uninterested. "Tal vez," he said, "I need to go up to the mountains and get some herbs. I come later and cure her."

"How late?"

Mathonihah shrugged again, "late, maybe midnight."

Teodoro let out a long sigh and raked his hair with his hands. On the one hand, if he didn't keep these soldiers alive, he would not get his money and might even get his legs broken by Eros. On the other, he hated to give up his sleep, especially when he had to wake up at the crack of dawn to hand the Americans over to those crazy Al Qaeda people. Why did they care so much anyway if they were healthy or not? They were going to cut off their heads regardless.

"Okay, here's the key to the gate. You just go in there and give her your medicine. Make sure you lock it up again. I'll give you part of my money, when I get paid."

After dinner, Dorian approached me with a piece of paper in hand. He gave it to me and walked back to his usual seat on the couch. The paper contained a new picture of Alex. The picture was of a small room, with three soldiers; one of them was a big black guy, with a thick bandage tied around his thigh. The other, a wounded female soldier on the ground and the third was Alex. He was sitting up with his back against the cell wall, his face was turned toward the front and it registered shock, as if he had just seen a ghost. The oddest part was that the drawing was so vivid; I could swear that he was looking right at me!

For some reason, this picture unnerved me. I called Valerie and told her about it, as proof that Alex was still alive. Then I asked Paz to pray with me, and finally, Amor made me some "tea" that she guaranteed would soothe my nerves.

"No valerian root!" I warned.

She smiled, "I'll give you something else this time. Don't worry; it will calm you, that's all." And it did. I hoped that feeling calm and meditating would help me connect with Alex again, but it didn't. Instead I tossed and turned and wished I had taken some of that valerian root after all. At some point though, I must have dozed off momentarily, because I woke up startled by the eminent feeling that someone was watching me sleep—again.

My eyes fluttered open and it took them a few minutes to adjust to the moon lit room. I could see the outline of a figure at the foot of my bed—it was a woman's silhouette—and my heart slowed its pace and I sat up.

"Amor?"

"No…Luz."

"Luz?" With her hair loose around her shoulders, and in a nightgown, she looked exactly like her sister. And why shouldn't she? They were identical. "Do you need something?" I asked, raising my pitch, as one does when speaking to a child.

"You need to trust *Him*."

"Who? Are you OK, Luz? Should I call Amor?"

"No," she said, this time her voice sounded more child-like. Then she collected herself somewhat and continued in a grown-up voice. "You need to trust *Him*, that's what I was sent to tell you."

"Him? Who? Who sent you, Luz?"

Frustrated she started to leave, but then thought better of it and sat back down. "The light that shineth in the darkness and the darkness comprehendeth it not," she said soberly. "*Him* … who came to his own, and they knew him not."

Dumbfounded, I stared at her, while warmth filled my chest and my eyes started stinging. "You want me to trust in Jesus? Is that what you wanted to tell me?"

"Follow your instincts and trust *Him*," she smiled tenderly, like a sister, and brushed her hand tenderly against my cheek. I threw my arms around her. She seemed to be taken aback for a moment, but then reciprocated and hugged me so tight that I felt breathless for a moment. Hastily, she released me and skipped off to bed without another word.

Having lost all hope for sleep, I slipped out of bed, grabbed a throw, went out to the back deck, and looked out to the ocean. The night was chilly, so I wrapped the handmade throw tighter around my shoulders. The moon was almost full and gave a beautiful muted light over the waves. There was little shore, because the tide had come in, but I managed to sit down on a dry spot and let my mind go blank.

I liked the ocean. With one exception, the ocean calmed me. It might be a combination of the soothing sound of the waves crashing against the sand, and the crinkly noise it makes as the water retreats. Or maybe it was the spray, or the wind, or the constancy of it all—like a heartbeat—earth's heartbeat.

After a few deep breaths I allowed myself to ponder what Luz had said. Charlotte had taken us to church with her on Sundays, so I knew that Luz had quoted scriptures from the Bible, but why those specifically? Was it coincidence, or did she know something?

Luz usually sounded like a child when she spoke, but tonight…while she spoke, she sounded like an adult. I groaned in frustration, rubbing my face with my hands. "I still don't know what to do! Trust my instincts! What instincts? Oh! Lord, if you are out there … and I know that you are … help me! Help Alex *and* the soldiers with him! They are dying or going to die soon, I know they are! Please don't let him die! Give us time together; let us enjoy life together, please! Is that so much to ask?" I fell on my knees and pleaded. Then I remembered what that voice had said while he gave Alex water, "help is on its way … "

"You were both given a gift. Gifts are from me, given for the benefit of others … " the thought was dropped down as it were a rain drop from above. Along with it came the memory of a story that I was taught at church. The story of the talents; to one were given five, to the other two, and one to the third. The first two increased their talents by investing them; the last one buried it—and in so doing, lost it!

Is that what I have been doing? Could it be possible that the dreams that I've always had of Alex have been a gift? Am I burying the gift? *"How?"* I thought. *"How am I burying this gift? I use it as often as I can. If it were up to me, I would dream of him every night!"*

"Follow your instincts, and I will send Angels to aid you," the foreign thought responded. And along with those words came an overwhelming feeling of love, warmth and strength.

"The wall … " I thought, and I immediately got up and started walking along the thin strip of beach toward town.

Part of me was sure that the wall held some special clue to this mysterious puzzle, and I was determined to find out why once and for all. As I walked I made plans of how to get inside. To climb the wall like Spiderman was impossible; I would have to find an entrance. I would walk the perimeter of the wall until I saw a gate or something that I could climb over. Maybe by then the sun might be coming up, so I would not need a flashlight. Once inside, I would look around for any clues that might shed some light on these mysterious messages.

"Luz, levántate! Wake up, hija," her father nudged. No longer affected by time, Max looked as handsome as ever, and exactly as he looked in his twenties.

"Vamos muñeca, levántate." Max tried to shake her leg instinctively, and was disappointed anew when the two matters were not compatible, and his hand went through the leg and the mattress in one swoop.

"Let me!" Celeste said, *" Luz, querida, it's your mother! Wake up! You need to help us again,"* Celeste whispered in her ear, and this seemed to do the trick. Luz opened her eyes suddenly and without blinking looked directly into her mother's face.

"Mami!" Luz exclaimed with a thrill.

"Listen Luzita, you need to help us again. Go wake Dorian up and walk to the village along the beach. Tess needs your assistance." Luz frowned and pouted like a stubborn child that is asked to do a chore.

"We'll be right there with you, so don't worry."

"But you never talk when you're around her! I never know what you mean!" Luz complained.

"Don't worry about that now Luz. Go do as you're told," Max said in a commanding voice.

Reluctantly, Luz obeyed, and started out the door. *"You might get chilly, grab a blanket,"* Celeste suggested, her mothering instincts still intact. Luz made a face, but obeyed.

Getting Dorian up was no problem; he was waiting for her and greeted her with his usual smile. Since coming to Mexico, and particularly to this house, Dorian finally felt that he had found his home. Luz was the dearest person to him, and he never wanted to leave her sight.

Hand in hand, the two slipped out into the night, and followed Tess at a safe distance. No explanation of what was going on ever passed between them. Whether they knew what was happening or the role they would have to play, was anyone's guess. They were simply obeying their angelic call of duty.

Why did I ever think that I could make it into town by myself? I would have gotten hopelessly lost by daylight, so it stood to reason that I would get even more lost by moonlight. Leaving the beach behind, I turned onto one of the streets that looked like it would lead to town. I hoped that it led to the plaza, and that from there I might find the street that led to the wall.

My hopes were dashed, though, when I walked and walked and the street I was on didn't take me where I had hoped it would. Instead it turned steeply uphill and followed the ocean. Frustrated and scared, I started to shiver and cry. *"My instincts are all wrong! What am I doing?"* I groaned within and fell on my knees on the cobble stone road. Pretty little white adobe homes lined the empty street, with black wrought iron balconies filled with cascading red and pink bougainvillea.

A warm hand pressed against my back and I jumped to my feet, ready to defend myself. But to my complete relief, the innocent smiling faces of Dorian and Luz greeted me instead. Neither one of them spoke, but I knew why they were here. They had been sent. They were my Angels. The words "the least of these" came to mind as I looked at them, and though not exactly what I had in mind when I thought of angelic help, they stood before me glowing with a strange light that radiated from within. I threw myself in their arms and felt secure there. My brother and my sister… an odd family we made, but that's what they were to me in this life.

"I'm looking for the mission," I told Luz.

"I know where it is," she said in her singsong girlish way.

In no time, we reached a side of the wall and skirted it all the way around until we found an entrance. The gate was solid wood and about ten feet high. It was locked with a thick padlock that looked relatively new. This I noted with interest, but made no comment. Instead we looked for a way to climb the gate and jump to the other side.

Dorian looked like he was trying to find a foothold somewhere, but even if he did, Luz would not be able to climb the gate.

"Need help?" a male voice said from the shadows. His indistinct form moved slowly toward a spot where a ray of moonlight was shining like a spotlight down on him.

It was the hobo, and in his hand, instead of the blankets and bags he had the other day, he held an ax.

Chapter 23

All three of us stared dumbfounded at the hobo, trying to decide if he was friend or foe. With a smile the man moved away from his moonlit spotlight and came closer to us. "I can break the lock with this," he offered.

We stepped back to keep some distance between us, still unsure of the man's intentions, but he didn't seem to be bothered by our distrust. He simply went to the gate, took his filthy poncho off and started whacking at the chain. After a few purposeful blows, he loosened one of the links and wiggled it out, making the rest of the chain clang to the ground. With his free arm he made a sweeping gesture, inviting us inside the mission. "There you go."

"Why did you help us?"

"I was here, I had the tools. We are all tools," he looked at me significantly.

I nodded, acknowledging my thanks to him, and led the way inside. Holding hands, Dorian and Luz followed. Inside there was a courtyard with burned down dilapidated structures near the outer walls. None of the ruined buildings reached the outer wall. The cobblestone pathway encircled the structures, separating them from the wall. All but one of the small clusters of buildings still had a roof, and at one point they would have all been connected in a horseshoe shape.

"Let's see what's inside that one," I nudged. Luz and Dorian showed no sign of fear. Their expressions were, as always, peaceful—almost angelic—as the full moon shone down on them.

There was an actual door that led to the only standing structure. It looked oddly new, as if someone had recently put it there. Dorian knocked opened with his foot, because it was locked as well. Before stepping inside, I looked around the courtyard one more time. The man with the ax was gone. Dorian, Luz, and I were alone. I swallowed the lump in my throat, hoping that the hobo wouldn't change his mind and try to trap us in here, or call the police on us, or something. But I couldn't worry about that now.

Dorian led the way and cautiously walked down a narrow corridor that looked like it would have, at one time, lead to several small sleeping chambers. Presently only five of these still stood, two on one side, and three on the other. One of the chamber doors was off its hinges. We peered inside and found nothing but a small narrow cot and an upturned table. A few rats scurried away when they saw us.

The other doors were closed and thick, reinforced with cast iron hinges. Only one of the doors had a small window, which allowed us to look inside. While Dorian tried his best to open the other doors with his shoulder, I peeked through the door with the window.

My heart lodged itself in my throat, and all the blood drained from my head. On the other side of the small window was a scene that I had seen before—not too long ago in fact. It was the exact replica of Dorian's last picture, complete with the surprised and angry look from Alex, who was leaning against the damp wall. On the floor there was the woman and standing against the back wall, was the other soldier whose face was shadowed by the light of the moon streaming in from behind him.

"Alex?" I faltered. My mouth was dry and my throat felt hoarse.

Alex's eyes grew large, but he didn't respond. I knew what he was thinking; he thought I was a vision. I was the ghost!

With two strides the other soldier stepped up to the little window, and stuck his hand through the two bars, touching my cold face.

"She's real!" he gasped.

"Amor! Maria de Amor! For heaven's sake, wake up!" Paz shook her sister, rousing her from her peaceful slumber.

The other opened her eyes and tried to focus them on the figure before her. "Que pasa hermana?"

"I've had a dream! And it's come true! They're gone and I know just where they went! Oh Amor, it was beautiful. They look young again and happy!"

"What are you talking about? Are you going senile on me?"

"Of course not! I'm telling you, I had a dream! But we have no time to waste. Hurry, put something decent on and grab that shotgun of yours!" the nun ordered, then left the room in search of a flashlight and something solid.

"But, Luz and the kids!" Amor complained.

"Exactly who we need to go get! They are gone, but I know where they are! Will you just hurry? I'll explain everything on the way."

The two women jumped into the convent's minivan and drove hastily into town.

Fixed to the spot, I started shaking. It was the oddest thing, my teeth were chattering and my whole frame felt unsteady. My mind was even a jumble and unable to make heads or tails of what was happening.

"I am real," was all I could think of to say, "Alex?"

Dorian stuck his head in front of mine and peeked inside as well.

"Brother, help us!" the big soldier pleaded with Dorian, whose only claim to brotherhood was race. Nonetheless, Dorian nodded. He turned and began looking for something that would aid us in opening the door. From inside, I heard a scuffling and a groan as Alex tried to get on his feet.

The soldier moved to let Alex have a look. "Tess?" Alex peered through the tiny window. His face looked haunted, bloody and bruised. With effort, he stuck his hand through the bars of the small opening and I reached for it as well. We held hands uncomfortably through the bars, verifying that we were both real. A surge of urgency rose within me. I wanted to knock that door down, with my own fists if necessary.

"Dorian, please!"

"You're here with Dorian? There's no police or…" Alex asked, panicked.

"Whatever you have planned, miss, you need to do it fast. It's almost dawn and the guy comes at dawn," the other soldier warned from behind Alex, whose knees were buckling.

"But—but, we have no plan. We had no idea you were here," I told them lamely.

"So … how? What brought you here?"

"I don't know … my aunts live just out of town, and since I first saw this place I felt like—like I wanted to come inside."

Alex reached his hand and touched my face again, and a small tear slid down his cheek. "For the first time in my life, I'm very grateful for your terrible lack of judgment."

"I hate to break up the reunion, but I really want to be out of here," the other soldier said impatiently while the female soldier who was lying on the ground groaned and whimpered. Alex turned to look at her, then turned back to me. "We have to hurry. She might not make it. Do you see anything that we can use to take the hinges off?"

"The ax," I breathed. Dorian rushed out to search for it. Luz just stood there with a calm and pleasant smile as she watched the scene before her unfold.

"You brought nothing with you?" the impatient soldier scolded. Right then, Dorian dashed back in, quick as lightning, with the ax that the hobo had brought with him and apparently had left behind.

Without being told what to do, Dorian started whacking at the impossibly thick door.

"This is going to take forever!" I scanned our surroundings with urgency, trying to find anything that might have an impact on the massive door.

"Try to find a nail or something that might help us push the hinges off!" Alex said with great effort. The act of standing seemed to be hard enough for him.

Dorian had stopped his useless whacking and was studying the hinges, when we heard footsteps outside. We all froze in place and held our breath.

"Luz? Dorian, Tess?" someone whispered outside.

Dorian and I exchanged glances and Luz's face brightened immediately. "In here!" Luz shouted, unconcerned.

"Shh!" the soldier, Alex, and I hissed together.

Seconds later, hurried footsteps and the ruffling of a nun's habit were heard coming into the building. Armed with a shotgun, a sledgehammer, a flashlight, and a rosary, the two women walked down the hallway, wide-eyed and cautious.

Amor, holding the shotgun and the flashlight, looking like an experienced GI-Jane, brought up the rear. She was wearing a colorful scarf around her forehead and looked like she meant business. Paz walked in front holding the sledgehammer over her right shoulder like a bat. The long string of beads that held her Rosary was pulled taut by her left hand, dangling in front of her to ward off any evil.

Luz immediately unburdened herself of the whole story, and brought her sisters up to speed on the night's proceedings. Then, after the other two ladies confirmed visually for themselves of our findings, they began to devise a plan.

"What a find! And to think they've been here all along!" Paz exclaimed after looking into the cell.

"We can now add international espionage to our obituaries!" Amor said, with a smirk. Paz nodded and studied the door. She determined that between the ax and the hammer, we might be able to break the lock. But just as she said it, the light of her flashlight reflected off something shiny.

"Let me see that." I reached for the flashlight and shone it back on the spot.

There, right next to the door, was a single key, placed there as if by providence itself. It reminded me of the night that I broke into Agatha's room. I lifted the key up, and shone the light right on it.

"You've got to be kidding me!" the soldier exclaimed.

After unlocking the door, we swiftly evacuated the building.

But our escape wasn't as quick as we would have liked. The wounded soldier had to be carried and the only one who could help with that was Dorian.

"I'm assuming that you will all want asylum from the Sisters of the Sacred Heart until your Embassy or military people retrieve you?"

"Yes ma'am," Alex tried to smile, but an inner pain quickly turned his face into a grimace. Paz nodded, putting the van into motion.

The sun was now peeking through the horizon, promising another sunny day. I uttered a silent *"thank you,"* heavenward. No one spoke while we drove, not even Alex who was leaning on me. I was sure that similar supplications were making their way up to heaven at this very moment.

Alex's breathing sounded labored and painful, and I worried for his health, but I had him! I didn't care if I had to spoon feed him for the rest of his life, I had him back and that's all I wanted. Glancing back at it, I realized that the lure of the old mission was gone. I no longer felt the insane desire to be near it. I held the former lure of the place in my arms, and stroked his dirty hair as he rested his eyes.

"Amor, you'll have to stay and do your best with these guys until a doctor comes," Paz said to her sister softly as she drove. The rest of the van was in complete silence, no one had anything to say, and none of the soldiers cared to expound on the hell they had been put through for the last three weeks. "I'll call the American Embassy and tell them that a group of American Soldiers were found by some … locals. Who do you suppose is behind this?" Paz asked.

Amor shrugged, but I had a feeling that she knew something and wasn't sharing. Her usual light pink glow was troubled and her mind seemed to be in the process of putting together a complicated puzzle. Paz noticed this too, and kept turning to look at her sister. They seemed to exchange a telepathic thought, because eventually, understanding dawned on Paz and she no longer felt the need to look at her sister for answers.

"Bastard," Paz whispered, then crossed herself, murmuring an unrepentant prayer for the swearword she had uttered. Everyone was too out of it or too tired to investigate any further into this accusation, so that particular conversation remained a mystery.

When the convent doors opened, only the injured soldiers were allowed in. They were carried by several of the sisters. I hated to let go of Alex, but I wasn't allowed in. We exchanged parting glances before the nuns obstructed his face from my view. Dorian, Luz, and I were left on the outside, looking at a closed door. Dorian wrapped his arm around my shoulder and squeezed a few times.

"I'm hungry! Who wants breakfast?" Luz smiled and rubbed her hands together. The house was a long ways away, and we had no mode of transportation other than our feet. We were mostly silent, but now and then, Luz would giggle at something or someone.

"What's so funny Luz?"

"Nothing" she snorted and laughed again.

"I'm proud of you!" Celeste's voice sounded softly in my ear.

I opened my eyes wide and Luz turned to face me expectantly. "Well, aren't you going to answer her?"

I called the Preston's right away, hoping that I wasn't doing something out of turn, but I figured that Paz had plenty of time to contact the embassy in the hour it took us to walk home. If they didn't know already, they soon would.

When Valerie picked up the phone on the other end I wasn't sure where to begin or how to explain the incredible events. Should I tell her the true story or what the Embassy and the military were going to hear? When I heard the strain in her voice, I knew I had to tell her all the details.

"We found Alex."

Silence.

"Alex and two of his comrades, just like the ones in Dorian's picture, were found this morning," I repeated.

"Tess … " Valerie sobbed and I heard the phone drop from her hands. There were a series of sounds on the other end, shuffling of feet, handling of the phone, then Katie's voice greeted me.

"Katie, is your mom okay?"

"Y—yeah … I think so … what's going on Tess?"

"Alex has been found."

"How do you know?" her voice sounded suspicious, like she was talking to a mental patient.

"Because, I just dropped him off at a convent, my aunt's convent. The embassy has been called already. I suspect they'll be picked up soon, if not already."

Silence again, then a stifled sob. The phone got passed around again; this time Dane answered, but his customary patience was gone. "Tess, now listen. I know you have been under a lot of stress lately—" he was cut off by the sound of the other line clicking.

"Answer that Dane. It might be them," I told him with confidence. I waited and waited for Dane to click back over to me, but then I realized that I was making an international call, so I hung up. I shuffled over to my bed and collapsed there. I finally slept like I hadn't slept in ages.

I woke up to the sound of music from the piano and a hot ray of sunlight on my face. In the living room I found all as if nothing had ever happened. Amor was in the kitchen grinding something to a pulp, Paz was sitting on the couch reading, Dorian was in his customary spot drawing, and Luz was at the piano, wearing an orange tutu, extra high pigtails and matching bows.

Amor smiled and winked at me as I passed into the kitchen. Paz looked up for a second from her book and smiled as well. "Good work today!" she beamed.

The table was set for tea; afternoon tea, I surmised. I sat down and wrapped myself in a knitted throw and put my heels on the rung of the chair. I closed my eyes and felt like I was in a cocoon, but when I opened my eyes something looked different. It seemed as if a thin veil had been lifted from my eyes and a new layer of vision appeared before me. I saw human forms … as if I were looking at them from behind vellum paper. They floated freely all around the room, as if they, too, resided here.

Dappled sunlight filtered through the laced curtains like fingers reaching down from heaven. A soft marine breeze made the curtains dance now and then. I blinked slowly, unsure of the reality of what I was seeing, but the transparent white robed forms remained.

Canon in D … that's what Luz was playing. It seemed fitting for this moment—soft, simple, happy. As amazing as this moment was, it was also simple, like the melody. It made me think that perhaps the figures were always here—unseen and unnoticed, but natural and normal.

Standing behind Luz was a tall man, his hands were over hers on the piano, and they both moved across the keys in perfect unison. He had dark hair, a prominent nose, dark eyes and long eyelashes. I recognized him from the pictures; it was her father, Max.

Behind the kitchen counter stood Celeste, who was interested in what Amor was doing. She hovered near her daughter and looked over the recipes on the counter. Next to Dorian, there was a woman wearing a white turban on her head, and she stroked the air above his head with motherly love. All was peaceful and perfectly natural, until suddenly, out of nowhere, two figures seemed to just rip through the wall. One was a man who had a mischievous grin on his face; it seemed to say, "Gotcha!" The other, a woman, had a more rueful look—like someone who's been chasing a misbehaving child around for hours.

The woman looked around the room, then turned her head and looked straight at me. She looked the same as she did in the pictures—my dead mother. With interest, she narrowed her eyes and came closer to me. This caught the man's attention, so he, too, looked over in my direction. His countenance changed as realization washed over his face. His green-gray eyes grew large and all kinds of feelings flooded his mind when he fixed his gaze on mine—I could see it in the ethereal light that emanated from him—happiness, love, sorrow, regret, pain, anger … revenge.

My father and my mother approached me slowly and as I followed their movements with my eyes, they noticed this and marveled. I felt like a child again. Short bursts of blurry memories came to my mind, but I couldn't hold on to any of them long enough to piece them together.

My mother placed her hand on my cheek and I felt a chill there. We looked into each other's eyes and she transferred all the love she felt for me through her light.

"Irene, I think she can see us!" my father whispered with awe.

"I'm not sure ..." my mother said, *"she feels so peaceful. If she really saw us, she would be more, more ... agitated, don't you think?"* she whispered back.

"I think she sees and hears us just fine, but," he paused, lost for words, *"doesn't care, or isn't afraid."*

My mother smiled and stroked the air right above my hair, this gave me more chills and I shivered. I felt like I should say something, but I wasn't sure what. I knew these ... ghosts; they were my parents and I knew they loved me, yet ... I didn't *know* them.

"Tess, if you can hear me," my father said as he crouched down next to me, *"you're in danger...Eros—"* Right then the music ended, and in the blink of an eye, the unseen world disappeared and the room went dark.

Chapter 24

Agatha checked herself in the mirror, making sure she looked exactly the way she intended to look—normal. For some reason this was an everyday struggle, for her Gothic tendencies kept creeping out if left unchecked. She still had no tolerance for certain colors, and dressed in dark winter tones, but practically everyone in Boston dressed in muted, solemn grays and blacks. She remained blond but wore dark red lipstick and no blush, giving her that gaunt Goth air that still appealed to her vanity.

She hadn't lasted long in college. It wasn't that school was hard; it simply was boring. What she wanted to learn, a brick and mortar school would not teach her. But she needed money, so she got a job that she knew she could do. The local newspaper needed someone to write the horoscope, and this job she easily got, after an impressive demonstration of her capabilities.

This first job was perfect for her; she was joining the real world, but on her terms. She had some money, a modest apartment, and enough time to recompile the book that she had lost.

She came to be known as 'the trippy fortune-teller chick'. She had no friends, but was respected nonetheless, due to her uncanny ability to get things right. The small buzz around the office quickly grew into a blazing fire of superstition and Agatha soon found herself writing a weekly column under her real name. When the circulation of the newspaper grew exponentially, mainly due to Agatha, she found herself being headhunted by a big magazine in Boston.

Having no scruples, Agatha quickly worked her way up the ladder in that city. Being disliked was not a bother, being reviled was no problem, and being hated was rewarding to her. She thrived on being hated, feared, and envied; she reveled in it all and found a dark amusement in it.

But working at the magazine was her daytime job; her real work started after hours. That time was spent on research for her true scheme—the reestablishment of an ancient secret society—a hybrid between a religion and a social club. She knew she had gifts and Wiccan was too cliché for her, besides … she had been there and done that already. This was deeper than mere witchcraft. This was science and power from the universe.

The world did not embrace witchcraft openly, but they would embrace solid scientific facts. The stars and the universe operated by science, and whoever understood this could control the laws of physics and nature itself. The Source had control over it, but the Source only shared his knowledge when a sacrifice was made. So Agatha started small. She used her own blood at first, then that of a rodent. Animal sacrifices had been around since the dawn of time, she thought, so why not?

She smacked her lips together and dabbed some excess lipstick off before she stepped out of the bathroom and sat at her usual table. For months now, she had been coming to this diner near her apartment. She sat in the same out-of-the-way booth, accompanied only by her books and her notes. In silence, she ate every night, while she discovered the secrets of the occult.

"Is this seat taken?" a stranger asked. Agatha looked up, surprised to hear a human voice, and tried to focus her thoughts back to the present. Narrowing her eyes, she studied the man. He was average height, long dark hair tied into a slick ponytail at the nape of his neck, dark brown eyes, and even, good-looking features. He was about twenty years her senior.

"Perhaps I should introduce myself first," the man insisted.

"Not interested," Agatha dismissed him and turned back at her work. She had gotten so many job offers lately it wasn't even funny. It was nice to hear that her particular gifts were in such high demand, but the book and her research came first, and she hated the thought of interrupting them.

Ignoring her dismissal, the man sat down across from her in the booth, "But I am interested in you, Tess DeLeon. Or is it Carleene, or maybe, Agatha?"

Upon hearing that name, Agatha looked up at the man again.

"I see I got your attention. So, which one is it?"

Agatha smiled and shook her head, finding the whole thing humorous.

"I've had my men tracking you for a while; I know you don't go by Tess anymore. I also know that somehow you were able to transform your appearance quite well with *my* money and that you used it to carve out a nice little life for yourself here," he stated simply, even amusedly.

"Is that what this is about? *Your* money?" Agatha laughed.

Eros remained silent and stone-faced.

"I'll give you your money back, if that's what you want. Consider it an … investment."

"Sure I want my money back, with interest, of course."

"Of course," she smirked, no longer looking at him.

"Still, I like knowing what I have invested in, niece."

"Niece! I'm not your niece."

"If you are Tess DeLeon, you are my niece, and I want not just the money you … invested, but all the rest of it as well!"

"If I were Tess DeLeon, I would do no such thing! If I were Tess, I would kill you and keep all of it," she said without emotion and took an unconcerned bite of her food. Several men appeared out of the shadows and discretely pointed a gun at Agatha. She noticed this without much interest and chuckled. Then with a condescending look she put the fork down and reached into her purse. The gun barrels of the armed men suddenly rose higher. "I was going for my checkbook," she said with a roll of her eyes. Eros extended an appeasing hand, and the men disappeared back into the shadows of the diner.

"Who are you?" Eros asked, as Agatha's hand moved across the check. Agatha cut it, and extended the paper toward Eros.

"Well, the check says I'm Carleene, but that's not my name either," she smiled.

Eros took the check and studied the name, then looked back at Agatha with interest. "You're not my niece, are you?"

"No. And I'm not Carleene, either. I do know them both, well, knew them. Carleene… is dead now." A dangerous shadow crossed her face and Eros knew at once by whose hand. "I just used their names for my convenience." Agatha's dangerous look passed as quickly as it had come and she was now smiling contently at Eros.

This smile of hers made the hairs on his neck stand on end, and he was no longer sure how to regard this girl. He felt both attracted and repulsed by her. She was cold, calculating and fearless. All of these things he liked in himself, but now that he saw them in the form of a woman; he found them extremely alluring.

"So, what *is* your name?" he purred.

"Agatha," she admitted, matching his tone.

"How do you know Tess?"

"I grew up with her in foster care," she answered casually, while she jotted something down.

Eros nodded and glanced at the scattered open books and the notebook that was filled with notes. "What are you working on?"

"The future," Agatha looked up, annoyed now at his nosiness, "you have what you came for, you can leave now," she dismissed him with a wave of her hand and took another bite of her cold food.

Eros didn't budge though; he was shocked at her pluck. He wondered who this creature was, but having nothing more to say, he considered leaving. His pride alone kept him there. This girl had robbed him of fifty thousand dollars, and now that he had her cornered, she was dismissing him.

"He can help you," the icy tendrils of a cast-out wrapped itself around Agatha's throat. *"Use him ... Eros ... he has many connections, and he is after Tessss."*

Agatha felt suddenly cold. She both loved and hated that feeling when it came. The chills were a reassurance to her that she wasn't losing her mind, but were indeed voices from beyond who spoke to her. Every time she heard them, she felt assured that she was indeed a gifted medium of sorts.

Eros felt the cold emptiness too, like someone had just walked on his grave. It was an ensnaring feeling that made him want to run and stay at the same time. Eros was a man who had descended pretty low, and somehow he knew that if he didn't get up and leave immediately, he would descend even lower. Agatha was not just trouble—she was certain death to him. He knew this, but his legs wouldn't move. So he stayed—knowing full well that he had just crossed a line.

Eros tossed the check back across the counter. Agatha glanced at the check then raised her eyes to meet his. "What do you want then?" she asked, with her best poker face.

"You."

Agatha laughed a mirthless, cynical laugh. However, deep inside her, she felt a jolt of excitement. She had never felt that jolt before. Everyone so far had been a pawn, not a love interest. The spirits clearly approved of this one, and she was glad.

"You have no idea what you're getting into, Eros."

Eros' hairs bristled. He hadn't told her his name. There was no way she could have known it from L.A either. His street people didn't know who he was; he operated in the shadows and guarded his name zealously.

With one word he dismissed his armed men, focusing his attention on the curious creature in front of him. She wasn't terribly beautiful, but there was something about those large eyes and thin features that felt familiar to him. He could tell that she cared about her appearance and that she could manage to look quite stunning if she set her mind to it.

Agatha examined Eros' features and build as well. She surmised that he was in his forties, but looked pretty good for his age. Obviously he worked out and was vain enough to pay big bucks to keep his hair brown. She had to admit that he was good-looking and that she would look great in his arms.

"How did you know my name?" he asked, trying to sound like he was in command of his faculties.

"They told me."

"*They*, who?"

"The spirits," she smiled. This smile of hers gave Eros goose bumps for the second time during their brief conversation.

"You hear voices?"

"From the other side, yes."

"How do you know they are voices from the other side?"

"Because they are never wrong. They told me your name just

now … " she closed her eyes and hoped to hear more information. *"Tell him that you must work together to destroy Tess DeLeon,"* the cast-out suggested and Agatha relayed the message.

"That's not very impressive," he admitted, "you already knew I was looking for Tess."

Agatha's look changed from playful to dead serious, her eyes pierced his with intensity. "What's impressive," she said poignantly, "is how you managed to kill her mother and frame her father for the murder. I wonder, though … did you mean to kill Irene, or was it an accident?"

Eros' mouth went dry. He should have left. Now he couldn't.

Chapter 25

As soon as my plane landed on American soil, my stomach gave a lurch. All kinds of anxiety filled my mind at once. I hadn't talked to Alex since the night I found him in that dingy cell. I had spoken to Dane and Valerie, and they assured me that he was recovering at a base somewhere and would be sent home as soon as he was able. They said that they would be at the airport to pick me up, but my sweaty hands and my rapid heartbeat were betraying me. I realized now that I was back to reality, and that my life would somehow be changed forever from this moment on.

After many assurances that he would be fine, I left Dorian behind with my aunts, who were thrilled to have him. I also finalized all the paperwork with Roger, effectively gifting the agave plantation and the Mexico house to my aunts. Two major chunks of my inheritance were now gone, and two more remained: the home in Spain and the home in Argentina. Roger told me not to make any hasty decisions until I saw them both, but Celeste had soured me on the Spanish house, so much so, that I had no interest in seeing it at all.

I rubbed my sweaty palms together as I walked the airport terminal toward baggage claim. Why was I so nervous? Then I knew.

As the escalator took me down, I spotted him standing below, in full uniform. He was straining his neck looking around the crowd as if looking for me. Before I knew it, I was knocking people out of the way, and jumping into his arms. As soon as I did this, however, he groaned. He had two broken ribs that were still healing, so I slid hastily to the ground to prevent further damage.

But he bent down and the world melted away as soon as my lips touched his. I lost track of time and had no consciousness of where I was, until I heard clapping, then whistling and hooting. A circle of curious strangers had formed around us and was clearly enjoying the scene. Alex bowed and thanked the crowd. Taking my hand, we made a dramatic exit.

We had a lot of catching up to do on the drive home. Neither one of us lacked for topics of conversation, until he pulled into a parking stall at a place I didn't recognize.

"Welcome home," he said dangling a key in front of me.

"What number?" I asked snatching the keys from his hand.

"Seventeen." He beamed and I got out of the Jeep and ran up the stairs to my very own home! When I walked in, I could tell that Valerie had been there. The whole apartment was furnished and decorated.

"The decorations were brought here from my parent's house. My mom wanted it to feel homier until you had time to go out and buy your own decorations." He smirked. "I hear you are loaded now." He stepped closer, cornering me against the kitchen's high breakfast counter. "This one," he pointed to a beautiful flower arrangement, "is from me."

I reached for the card tucked in between two lilies. "I love you," it said in Alex's handwriting. My heart was beating so fast, it threatened to jump out of my chest altogether. My breathing was also highly impaired and I could barely look at him without having to gulp in some air. Words failed me. They lacked the intensity and the depth of what I was feeling. His eyes mirrored my same feelings, even the note "I love you", didn't quite express the feelings we felt. I could see it in his eyes that he meant so much more than a simple 'I love you'.

Alex moved a strand of hair away from my face, then traced my jaw line with the tips of his fingers. He opened his mouth to speak, but then closed it again. Taking a deep breath and exhaling slowly he tried again.

"Te amo," he said with a smile that made me smile too. "Did I say it right?"

"Yeah, you did."

"Your aunt taught me how to say it."

"Which one?"

"The nun." This was the first comment we made about Mexico and what happened there since I landed.

"Aren't they great?"

"Yes and, they love you very much. They came up with the idea of … not revealing who found us. They wanted to protect Dorian and your other aunt, and you too. They didn't think the military would understand how you found us."

I nodded and forced in another gulp of air, to keep myself conscious. "How are the other two soldiers?"

"They are fine. Suarez is still recovering, but she'll be okay."

"And you?"

He kissed my forehead and pulled me in tightly toward his chest. "It was an experience I won't soon forget. I would like to, but—. We were all honorably discharged. The Navy is now trying to gather information on why this even happened and who's behind it. They have spies on it right now."

"What about that guy?"

"What guy?

"You know, the one who gave you water and said that help was coming?"

Alex pulled away and looked intently into my eyes. "Oh yeah, I forgot all about him!" He let go of me and started pacing the room like a caged animal. I wondered if he picked that up during his weeks of imprisonment.

"I never said anything about him when I was getting debriefed, I forgot all about him. He came while we … " he moved his hand, signaling our mental connection, "I was so out of it, I think you were more alert because I barely remember him."

"I just heard him briefly, he said help was coming. What did he look like?"

Alex shook his head, "I don't know." The subject seemed to tire him instantly, so I decided to change it by redirecting his attention. Within seconds our lips were locked and the worry was replaced by passion. Before I knew it the kiss turned into an all-consuming fire. We tripped over something and landed on the couch. Alex groaned with pain as his broken ribs sent searing pain through his body. Then he groaned again, but for a different reason.

"Oh…well…I guess I better leave." Celeste said, offended.

"Yes, leave."

"What?" Alex asked.

"Nothing," I said, and got back to the task at hand.

"Who were you talking to?"

"Si no son dos son tres ... "

"Yes, and the third one is *not* welcome right now. Come back when you're needed."

Alex sat up abruptly and scooted away a bit. "Okay, you are talking to someone and that someone is not me."

"It's Celeste. She's come to check on me and won't leave." Alex looked around the room, hoping to find evidence of ghosts.

"Ya me voy, ya me voy," Celeste said dismissively.

I waited a few minutes and tried to see if I sensed her in any way, but she seemed to be gone. "She's gone," I told Alex.

He raised an eyebrow. "Is she going to come unannounced like this all the time?"

"She usually comes whenever I need protection," I smiled.

"She thought you needed protection from me? She doesn't like me much, does she? This is the second time that she's pushed me away."

"Nonsense, she's just being ... "

"Protective?" he smirked. "She's right, you know. You do need protection from me." He smiled and pulled me close to him again, and we snuggled on the couch. "I want to stay like this forever," he chuckled. "I know sound like a cheesy love song, but it's true. Our life together starts now Tess. Nothing—nothing will separate us."

"Not even death?" I asked grimly. Why was I thinking of death now?

"Not even death. I promise." He pulled me in tighter and we remained silent for a long time.

From the living room window we watched as the sun glistened off the water and the clouds swept across the sky. My plane had come in early, so we had the whole day before us. For what must have been a whole hour we lay like this, entangled in each other's arms. I soaked in his energy and felt his breath on my neck. I relished the touch of his hand against my arm and was content to hear nothing but his heart beat.

"Will you marry me?" he asked quietly and his words transported me briefly to another time. I couldn't explain it, but I had the distinct feeling that I had heard those words coming from his lips before. The feeling was strange because I felt like I was floating in the air. I guess that's where that figure of speech comes from.

"When?" I asked.

"Right now, if you want."

"Okay, let's do it!"

"We could hop on a plane and go to Vegas," he suggested, with a joking tone to his voice.

"Okay."

"Just like that? You don't want to have a big wedding, and get a dress? You of all people would want a nice dress. Maybe you want—"

"No. I'm ready now, just like this, in jeans and a t-shirt." I thought about it and realized that I really didn't care about all that. I didn't want a big wedding, I didn't care about the dress or the flowers or the cake. I just wanted Alex. I wanted to wake up next to him every day, and see his face. I wanted to fall asleep to the sound of his steady breathing, and I wanted his arms to encircle me. That was, in fact, all I had ever wanted since the first time I laid eyes on him.

"Okay, then." He shifted his weight and put his hand in his pocket, producing a small ring from it. He held it teasingly between his fingers and watched my face as it lit up. "Your ghost would like this," he smirked, "because it was hers."

"What?"

He pulled my left hand toward him, and slipped a small but beautiful ring on my finger. "This ring was mailed to my house from Mexico, just a few days ago. Apparently it used to be Celeste's wedding ring. Your aunts thought you might want it."

The ring was beautiful, simple, yet elegant. Not your average looking wedding ring, but it fit me perfectly and it felt right to have it.

"Now the two of you have something else to talk about," he jested.

"Are you sure you know what you're doing? You are about to marry a person who hears voices from another realm of existence."

"And that gift saved my life, and the lives of two others."

"I didn't do it alone. I had help," I said, remembering parts of that night, Luz … her warning, the strange man … Dorian, my aunts … it all seemed like a lifetime ago, like a dream.

"Come on!" Alex said getting up from the couch and pulling me up as well. "We are wasting daylight. You said you wanted to marry me?"

I nodded eagerly.

"Okay then! Let's do it! I know just where to go."

"What! *Now*, now?"

"You said yes, right?"

"Right," I nodded. "But how?"

"I know people," he said mysteriously. "Come on!" He grabbed my hand and pulled me toward the door. "By the way," he added as he closed the apartment door behind him, "I love our new place!"

An old friend of the Admiral's married us. He was a retired Navy Officer, who was now the local District Court Judge. Being in full uniform helped Alex cut through a lot of red tape, so one hour later, we were standing before the judge with two witnesses from the waiting crowd who readily volunteered for the job. One was a teenage boy with severe acne and a mouth full of braces, who was there to dispute a speeding ticket. The other was a biker with a black leather vest and tattoo covered arms, who was there for a DUI.

"Would you like to say something, before I pronounce you husband and wife?" the judge said casually as he reached for the mallet.

Alex nodded and turned toward me. "Death will not do us

part," he said with an earnest look, tightening his hold on my hand.

"Death will not do us part," I echoed.

"By the power vested in me by the State of Texas, I pronounce you husband and wife!" The judge slammed the mallet once. "Son, you may now kiss your bride, and you can tell your grandfather that we are now even," the old judge said with a serious look, that caused the whole courtroom to erupt in laughter. Our witnesses embraced each other in a fraternal hug and patted Alex on the back. The judge started pounding the mallet with pretend contempt, and to no avail, ordered silence. A policewoman came to our side and kindly escorted us out of the courtroom and the judge started another round of mallet knocking, this time in earnest, hoping to get his courtroom back to normal.

Chapter 26

"Get over it, will you? It didn't work out. We have bigger fish to fry."

"Bigger fish? Bigger fish?" Eros couldn't believe his ears. Perhaps she wasn't as smart as he gave her credit. "Do you know how long it took me to make a connection with that particular faction? Do you understand how much money they were going to pay me for those prisoners?"

"They were not going to give you one cent. They were going to get their American soldiers and kill you." At least that's what the spirits had told her. She had warned Eros of this and told him not to go. He didn't listen. Luckily he got to Mexico before the terrorists did and got wind of what had happened before he showed his face. He sent his jailer instead, who, of course, paid with his life for his mistake. As expected, the terrorists didn't take kindly to one empty-handed Mexican with no American prisoners. The whole matter was done quite smoothly and no doubt the man's body may never be found. This didn't keep Eros from being furious and dwelling on his almost brilliant exchange. Agatha kept telling him that it wouldn't have worked out anyway, but he refused to believe her.

Meanwhile, Agatha tried to stay focused on her task at hand. She had been offered a television show of her own where she could communicate with her spirits in front of an audience. This was big time for her, but she was unsure of how she felt about it. What she did was not an exact science, but her gift, as a medium could not be denied, either. This opportunity could give her the platform she had been waiting for, and a springboard to her ultimate goal of being the puppet master of a nation.

"Eros, you listen to me. If I take this job, you'll have to quit. And I mean quit. You'll have to cut all ties to California and your underground ways. We'll start a new life here and we'll dive into something much bigger than anything you've ever attempted before."

Eros rolled his eyes and walked away. He didn't like being told what to do.

"If you can't do it, then it's the end of us."

This caught his attention. For some reason, he hated the thought of letting her go. "You talk of bigger things, but I never know what you mean."

"I mean getting people from all walks of life to do what we want them to do. I mean getting movie stars, business owners, law enforcement Officers and government officials eating out of our hands. Through the spirits, I can get them. I know their dirty secrets. I can also tell them when to invest and in what. I can get them elected, promoted, and I can even predict their health. I can do all this because I'm a priestess of Monad and the chosen spokesperson for The Source."

"You really believe that those terrorists were going to kill me?"

"I was told that that was their plan all along." Agatha said vehemently, amazed at the fact that she could predict even the secret plans of total strangers.

"Then you shouldn't take that job. You need to be a well-kept secret, someone who people of influence feel they can go to discretely. If you go on national television and tell the world what you can do, you'll become a joke." Eros paced the room and gathered his thoughts. "You need to operate behind the scenes, you need to discreetly infiltrate the top and you need to be a mysterious shadow. Your clout will be felt rather than seen and you should be as unapproachable as the Pope."

Agatha narrowed her eyes and pursed up her lips. "Ooh, I like that! You see…we are good together."

"You did what?" Valerie yelled as soon as we explained what we had been up to all day. From the back of the room the Admiral started laughing so loudly that it gave him a spasm and he ended up coughing.

Dane and Katie smiled and winked at us from a safe distance, while Valerie burst into an all out tirade. "How dare you do this without us there? How could you? Tess? Alex?" She looked from one to another looking for explanations.

"How did you even manage to get a marriage license so quickly?" Valerie demanded.

"I called Judge Lambert," Alex shrugged, causing a fresh wave of laughter from the Admiral, who found the whole thing as amusing as ever. "I've heard Grandpa say that he saved Lambert's a— um, life a few times and owes him big time."

Valerie shot her father a venomous look, but the Admiral ignored it completely as the lack of oxygen from laughing caused him another bout of coughing. He dug into his jacket's pocket and pulled out a key and a handkerchief. He covered his mouth with the handkerchief and tried to control his coughing. Once he had succeeded, he grabbed his walking stick and made his way toward us.

He held the key out in front of us, "I was going to give you this today, not knowing it would end up being a wedding present," he shook his head, "but I'm glad it is. Maybe you two can use it to go on a honeymoon."

"Honeymoon! Honeymoon? No. You two are staying here, until we at least have a wedding celebration of sorts. Katie!" Valerie cackled and Katie snapped to attention like a soldier, "go to my planner, we're starting a to-do list." Katie nodded once, rolled her eyes while her mother wasn't looking and headed to the desk in the kitchen where her mother's planner was kept.

"Tess, you're not off the hook, missy. You are helping me put this party together as well!" she ordered, then paused, closed her eyes and then came straight toward me, arms outstretched. "Welcome to the family, dear," she whispered in my ear as she held me tight.

For the rest of the evening, Valerie had us all busy planning different aspects of the wedding party, with the exception of the Admiral and Alex, who were planning the honeymoon aboard the Odysseus. They were being very secretive, and every time any of us went even remotely close to them, they stopped talking and covered up some sort of map or chart.

"Well … I think these might just work!" Valerie said, holding out three garment bags. She unzipped them on the sofa, and pulled each dress out. They were the dresses that I had made while Alex was deployed. The one I had made for myself, oddly, was ivory white with golden brocade—an unusual but fitting wedding dress. "Under the circumstances, I think this dress would work as a wedding dress, don't you think so, Tess?"

I came closer to it and inspected it once again; I had done a great job on this one. The dress was really a suit, with an exaggerated collar that stood high on the back of the neck, framing it, and then forming a V as it sloped down. The cuffs were also thick and exaggerated, while the rest of the jacket and the mermaid skirt was simpler. "Yes, it would make a beautiful wedding dress." On hearing those words, Alex came over and looked at the dress too.

"You made this?"

I nodded.

"Wow!" He seemed genuinely impressed.

"She made these, too!" Katie added.

"You are going to be the best designer in the world; I'll make sure of that!" Alex said vehemently.

"And what on earth will you do to make sure of that, huh?" Valerie said derisively. "She already has all she needs to be the best designer in the world—talent!"

"I'll give her my full support then, and I'll be her pincushion." He smiled and winked.

Katie had already taken out her dress and was admiring it. "I call being a model!"

"I call being the babysitter!" Dane called from his spot at the computer. This made Valerie pause and look at her husband. Then a tear slid down her cheek and she turned to me.

"I do, too," she whispered huskily.

For the rest of the week, all everyone did was plan our impromptu wedding party. Invitations were sent electronically, food and cakes were bought, decorations, tables, and chairs ordered, pictures taken, everything that anyone would expect to have at a well-planned wedding was done in only four days! Alex and I had to report for duty every morning at 9 am sharp, or we got a lecture from Valerie.

The best part of it all, though, was going "home" with Alex. Every day he took an empty suitcase to his parent's house and loaded it up with more of his things, and every night we unpacked his belongings in our new home. We had no spare time to buy him his own dresser, so we split all the drawers in half. I loved looking at our closet with his shirts hanging next to mine. I loved feeling his arms around me all through the night. We no longer had the need to dream, we were living our dreams.

Tired but happy, we reported back for duty every morning at the Preston's. Valerie had a smirk on her face when she saw us dragging our feet. Apparently the more tired we looked in the morning, the more work she gave us. But we didn't complain, we did what she asked, and the wedding was taking shape. The weather was cooperating, so we set up tables and chairs outside. Since we were married already, the temporary pergola under which we would have exchanged our vows was set up over our dinner table.

On the day of the wedding celebration, Alex and I got ready at the Preston's. I had invited Brandy and Brook to be my bride's maids and to come early to help me with my hair and makeup. They were beside themselves at the news and demanded every ounce of information on our short—to them—relationship.

After talking to them, I realized how we looked to others. We had only one date before he was deployed, and then we only wrote to each other until he went missing. We had no contact while he was held captive and I visited my aunts in Mexico. The day I get back, we elope. That's it!

When did we meet and talk? When did we fall in love? How could I marry someone I hardly knew? Better yet, how could he? I was the outcast here. They didn't say that of course, but they thought it. It hurt to see envy shining all around them. It hurt because they were pretending to be happy for me. They had no idea I could read them, and they thought they were doing a great job of hiding their suspicious glances toward my middle section.

Casually, and ignoring the exchange of looks, I told them about Roger, and what had happened this past year. Their looks changed, yet again, when they learned that I was now rich, but this only made them even more envious.

"How's Agatha?" Brooke asked.

"I have no idea. I haven't heard from nor seen her since she ran away Senior year," I lied. I didn't think it would be fitting to mention that she had sent me a card with kittens, alluding to the cat she killed in my name before she left.

"Really?" Brooke asked again, then nodded slowly as if finding the whole answer interesting. "What a strange duck she was, huh?"

"Yeah, so … Brandy, are you and Wes still … "

Brandy smiled briefly then her smile fell. "No, not really. He went to U.T. Austin; I'm at S.M.U. so we haven't seen each other that much. He called a lot at first…but not anymore. Did you invite him?" she asked with hope.

"I did, but I haven't heard back from him yet." She looked crestfallen, adding her heartache to our already somber gathering.

Fortunately, Katie showed up, bubbling with enthusiasm and energy. She eagerly explained to Brooke and Brandy how madly in love her brother was and had been since he was a sophomore in high school. Katie weaved the tale of our whirlwind romance from her brother's point of view so expertly, that I found myself enthralled by it as well.

"I'm telling you," Katie said, with a significant look. "Alex was different from that day on; I could tell the minute he walked through the door. That next summer, while we were sailing to the Bahamas, I made him spill the beans. There's not a lot to do when you're stuck in a boat for weeks at a time, so he told me how he felt about Eugenia and how he was pretty much sick of her, but that he didn't want to disappoint Mom and Dad.

"I tried to tell him that they wouldn't care, but he's always had a huge sense of responsibility toward his commitments." Katie picked up her cat and had him purring contently on her lap in no time. It was the same cat that she had rescued from school, on the day Amanda and the other Goths were torturing it.

"The ironic thing was that Alex broke up with Eugenia at the same time that Tess started dating Wes," Katie said casually, completely unaware of Brandy's tense stance. "He was so mad; he drove us nuts that year! But then he realized that perhaps it was for the best. He thought it through very carefully and told me all about it because he needed a sounding board.

"He said that he would let Tess grow up and figure out what she wanted. If she still wanted him in a year … then he would be there." She smiled sadly. "But then he got deployed, so we put together a surprise date on Tess' graduation, which was really the day before he had to leave. There was no time." She looked out dreamily. "It seemed like a cruel joke." Katie put the cat down and with a sigh, told them in great detail what our date was like, complete with our promise to spend every second together.

By the end of her tale, both Brooke and Brandy's moods had changed completely, and even I got so caught up in it, that a new surge of love for Alex swept over me, and the realization that he was now my husband hit me anew.

Thanks to Katie's explanation, Brooke and Brandy now approved wholeheartedly of our hasty marriage and they both agreed that, given the circumstances, they would have snatched Alex the moment he had proposed, too. I was so grateful to Katie for this. She literally changed the mood of the party for us, so the rest of the evening was pure enjoyment and bliss.

Brandy said a few words, and thankfully, she now meant every word she said, and no longer shone with envy. She actually looked beautiful and full of hope that someday love would conquer all. She then pointed out that all the dresses that the women from the wedding party were wearing had been of my creation. This was a bit embarrassing for me, but it effectively created a buzz about my talents, that I was grateful for.

We spent the night at a Bed and Breakfast in Austin, and the next day Alex drove us to Galveston, were the Odysseus was waiting for us, packed and ready to go on a long voyage to South America. Apparently, during the week, the Admiral and Alex had been busy planning this surprise honeymoon. Alex found out where the home in Argentina was located, and together with the Admiral, charted the trip that would literally drop us off at the home's front dock.

"Are you sure we can make it all the way to the other end of the globe in this?" I asked dubiously as I boarded.

"Sure! It's perfectly equipped! Sailing is the oldest mode of long distance travel." Alex said with a sweeping motion toward his 30-foot long sailboat.

"But they did it in big boats and with a large crew of experienced sailors," I countered.

"I'm an experienced sailor, and after one week you will be too," He smiled, then his smile turned into a pout. "You're not excited about sailing off into the sunset with me?"

"I'll go anywhere with you," I told him frankly. "But I am a little nervous. I've only sailed one time and it was on a lake."

"You'll be fine," he soothed, tucking a loose strand of hair behind my ear. "I brought medicine in case you don't find your sea legs right away. Besides, this will be good for us. I want to show you my world, for real this time."

We ended up sailing into the sunrise instead of the sunset, but it was, perhaps, more fitting. We were literally beginning our days together. For me, it was a rebirth. My life felt like it was finally starting. All that happened to me before this day seemed to be nothing more than a prelude.

As it turned out, I found my sea legs right away. The waves soothed me, and the constant rocking of the boat felt natural. Inside the cabin we had all the supplies we needed until we docked and restocked. Alex had been kind enough to bring all my sketching things, so I could design some dresses. He also packed a lot of my sewing and crochet things. He said that we could buy more as we stopped along the way.

He had downloaded hundreds of books onto several e-readers and almost twice that much in music, onto several IPods, so we could both listen to music and read to our heart's content while in open water. He also had furnished himself with several leather bound journals, maps, charts, and other navigational devices.

It took us a whole month to sail to Argentina, and though some days seemed to drag on forever, we managed to keep ourselves busy and entertained. Surrounded by nothing but blue water and his arms, I lived in a constant state of bliss. I never knew that life could be so happy, and that heaven could be experienced here on earth.

We sailed into the Mar del Plata delta and safely docked our sailboat on the old dock of *Cielo Celeste,* the house that Max had built for my grandmother. She had checked in on me a few times during the trip, but was mostly away. However, the moment we set foot on the small island where the house sat, she started jabbering non-stop.

The house looked exactly as it did in Dorian's picture. And once I looked back at the boat, I realized that it was a perfect snapshot of this moment. I shuddered as I thought of Dorian and his abilities, and I wondered anew at what a strange gift his mind was. Every picture he's ever given me has been part of a puzzle—my life's puzzle.

An older couple began walking forward to greet us. Alex had asked my aunts to call ahead and warn the caretakers to have part of the house ready for us.

"Letti! Ramiro!" Celeste exclaimed the moment she saw them emerge from their small house.

The old couple hugged us, gave us both a kiss on the cheek and started talking rapidly in a thick, Argentine-Spanish accent. I managed to understand that they had put some food in the fridge, but it wasn't much and it would only last us a few days until we recovered enough to go into town to buy more. They told us that our sailboat would not make it there but that we could use their lancha, an old, and decrepit looking motorboat. They had also been kind enough to furnish us with many different maps of the delta, El Tigre, the nearest town, and of Buenos Aires, so that we could move around with ease.

The house was big and reminiscent of the 50's, Argentina's heyday. The floors were large, with checkered black and white tile, and the ceilings had massive, dark, exposed beams. The furniture was all covered up with white sheets but this front room was big enough to be a ballroom. There was a cold, damp smell to the place, like you'd expect a house to smell after being shut up for a long time.

"We danced here…" Celeste's voice caught and I knew that she was twirling around in mid-air. *"We learned to Tango here, and we did almost every night!"*

Alex uncovered some of the furniture, and found an old record player sitting on a huge credenza table. There was a record still in it and after plugging it in, he turned it on. It was crackly at first, and the tempo was not right, but Alex touched one switch and soon the hall was filled with a mournful melodic tango tune.

We left the music playing as we continued with the tour. The caretakers showed us the large kitchen, the main dining room, and then the bedrooms. Only one had been cleaned up and prepared for us. The rest remained dusty and closed up. The last room in the house that they showed us was a solarium that was all glass, including the ceiling. After a storm, several of the panes had been broken, and debris had flown in freely. This was the dirtiest of all the rooms, but also the most beautiful. I could imagine myself here, and oddly, I could imagine Celeste here as well … both of us … drinking tea, perhaps, and talking. Spending a sunny afternoon chatting about this or that.

"We'll have to fix this," Alex said looking around the room. "It'll be our little project." He smiled and came to me. "After we do all the touring and shopping we want, we'll restore this house back to its original beauty."

"There's a lot of history here," Letti said as she cast her eyes around the room and rubbed her arms, trying to warm a chill. Her husband agreed with her, then told us how they thought that the spirits of my dead grandparents still lingered here.

I smiled, "Well, let's just hope it's them that haunt it and not someone else. Them I can live with," I joked. Alex bit his lip, suppressing a smile while Letti and Ramiro shivered.

"I suppose you're right," Letti sighed. At that moment the record ended, and the needle made a loud scratching noise. Letti and Ramiro jumped, and started to leave the room saying that they had things to do back at home, and that they wished us luck, and to not hesitate to call or, rather, come over because the phone line was dead. Suddenly the breeze picked up, and a gust of wind gushed through the broken panes and stirred all the leaves and debris around the room in a tight circle. Letti let out a high-pitched squeak, and Ramiro grabbed her hand as they both made a hasty exit.

Chapter 27

"I thought you said that it was torturous for spirits to roam places that they used to frequent while alive?"

"I said it was torturous to be around people that they love, unless they are assigned to them, not places. Besides, it's empty ... or it was until you two came."

"Sorry to crash your party."

"We don't come here that often. And it is kind of depressing to see it so run down. It used to be full of life and laughter. My sunroom used to be filled with plants and birds! There was constant music in the air. Max...he had a piano over here."

"I don't know where you're pointing."

"Oh, that's right. Well, you get the picture."

"I have a question."

"No, not again! I always get in trouble after one of your so-called questions."

"I'm curious! I can't help it; it's in my nature. Besides, you didn't get into that much trouble because you're still here. They would have reassigned you, right? Maybe sent a more...tight-lipped ghost to watch over me?"

"Go on, get on with it."

"In Mexico, I saw you and Max … and my parents. Why?"

Silence.

"Hello? Are you still there?"

"I'm still here."

"So, can you tell me why? I also saw a woman, who was next to Dorian. She looked like she might be his mother."

"That was a glimpse. You should be grateful for it, and accept it as a gift."

"I am grateful for it, but … "

"No buts, just leave it be."

"I can't stop thinking about it. Leo, my dad," I corrected. "When he realized that I could see him, he tried to warn me. He said something about Eros."

"Your father has a very hard time holding his tongue. Comes by it honestly, I guess. I'm not much different from him when it comes to that," she murmured, *"He has very little respect for Heavenly rules."* Celeste paused, then her voice softened. *"And he loves you, but his anxiety over you and your safety has him very ..."* she seemed to be thinking about her words carefully, *"very determined and single minded. This can be potentially harmful to him. He needs to understand that his time has passed, and that your mortal life has to play out without his input. He has to let go of his life, and he needs to focus on this new existence of his. If he were to do that, then he would find that he could be much more helpful to you and others. As it is, he's stuck."*

"Stuck? What kind of stuck? You mean like, purgatory stuck?"

"Something like that. There is no such place, you understand? It's really a state of being; our minds are our only limitations. Right now, his mind is keeping him from moving forward, so he's in ... heaven arrest you could say, or should be. The problem is that he's too attached to mortality and it is potentially a very dangerous situation to be in. Fortunately, your mother is quite literally an Angel! She watched over him while he was still alive, and is still watching over him now. So there's nothing for you to worry about. He'll be fine."

"It was strange, though. They came out of nowhere. You and all the other spirits were going about your business and didn't seem to notice that I was aware of you. But then my parents just showed up! My dad burst in as if he had just ripped through a piece of fabric and came out of nowhere."

"Yeah ... well ... like I said, he doesn't care much for rules. And he is a very gifted person, like you."

"You mean he had the same gift that I do?"

"No. Not the same, his gift was different. Your mother's too...all three of you in fact seem to have a different aspect of a very interesting ability."

"Well, what is it?" I asked after a few moments of silence.

"The three of you are able to poke through other realms of

existence. You can hear other realms, your mom can feel the presence of souls from other realms, and your dad can see them. Between the three of you, you could piece together a clear picture of what goes on in different realms.

"As assigned Angels, we only have access to the realm of existence that our charge inhabits. That's how I can hear your voice and see you and, to a certain extent, roam your realm while I'm on the job. But you and your parents ... you can technically rip a whole through the fabric of existence all on your own."

"Is that how my dad got through? He poked in, without permission?"

"Sí," she sighed wearily.

"What's keeping him from being with me all the time?"

"Your mother, and common sense. If he were to do that, he'd be officially haunting you, and he doesn't want to do that to you. He's just hell bent on protecting you—his way."

"Is that so bad?"

"Who are you talking to?" Alex walked in, out of breath. He had gone for a jog around the island while I stayed behind to clean up and explore the house. I looked up and shrugged, pointing to thin air.

"Oh…" he nodded, "your dead grandma."

"It sounds freaky when you say it that way."

He nodded and caught his breath while resting his hands on his knees. "It is a little freaky, but I guess I need to get used to it."

"Adios!" she said smugly.

I looked up to the spot where the sound came from and nodded. "She's gone now." I was glad that Alex took all of this craziness in stride, but I felt bad for him, too. I knew that if I didn't hear these voices myself, it would be a hard pill to swallow. I worried that at some point he would get fed up and think I was crazy.

"You don't think I'm crazy, do you?"

"Don't forget I've seen her!" He straightened and came to my side. "If you're crazy, then so am I," he declared, then kissed me.

"If it makes you more comfortable, I can ask her to be quiet; she can do that…sort of. She is very opinionated and a bit bossy, but she has held her tongue from time to time in order to give me my privacy."

"Honestly, as long as she doesn't … "

"She doesn't," I assured him, though I did wonder the same thing some times.

"How do you know?"

"They are not here all the time, just when they are needed. She has rules she has to follow, or she loses her post. If she did, she would be haunting me, and that's strictly off limits."

Alex nodded. "That's all I care about!" He leaned over and kissed me again. "I'm going to attempt a shower. Let's see if there is hot water this time."

We stayed in Argentina for a whole month, taking weekly tours into Buenos Aires and exploring everything the city had to offer. We even took Tango lessons, and practiced at home. I shopped until I almost literally dropped from exhaustion; there was so much to see and buy! Alex and I got hooked on Yerba Mate tea, and we both gained about ten pounds on pastries alone! The rest of our free time was spent on fixing up the house and restoring it to its original beauty.

We decided that, for the time being, we would rent it out to tourists, but that we would retire here some day. Or maybe even come live here, for part of the year. We could both see the allure of the place. It was well named—Cielo Celeste, Blue Heaven. We flew back home and left the boat docked there; it was too late in the season to sail back.

Four years later we graduated from college. I majored in Fashion Design and Alex in Political Science. Following in his other grandfather's footsteps, Alex went into politics. He won his first election as a local representative and, after a term, he ran again, this time for Congress; winning a seat in the House of Representatives in Washington.

I bought a boutique in town, right next to my old workplace, The Apothecary. Some of my designs got national attention, due to Alex's campaigning, so I started getting orders from all over the U.S. The fact that most of my dresses were 'recycled' and one of a kind, only made me stand out and I was soon sought out by some pretty deep pockets. Everywhere Alex and I happened to travel, I visited all the local thrift stores and consignment shops for old dresses and whatever caught my eye. Pretty soon I was adding vintage accessories and other finds.

It seemed that our dreams were all coming true and that life was perfect, but it wasn't. We lost the Admiral soon after we returned from our honeymoon. He got very sick one day and quietly passed away in his sleep. This was an ironic death for a man who cheated death so many times on the battlefield.

Alex and I also experienced several losses, in the form of miscarriages. It seemed that babies did not want to stay in me. I loved Alex so deeply. It seemed that every day that went by I loved him more, and I yearned to give him children—it was the only thing missing from our lives. This yearning—obsession almost—of wanting to be pregnant coupled with the sadness of the losses, did something to me. They added a crust of sadness that I never thought I'd be able to get over.

I also kept feeling this odd sensation of pending doom. It was like a waiting for the other shoe to drop, kind of feeling. In spite of some of the sadness I was, overall, immeasurably happy and that seemed incongruent with my life. Surely I didn't deserve this much happiness, not me … not the girl who grew up in foster care. There was something hanging over me, a promise, a sacrifice, something that would eventually unravel my whole life.

But not all was doom and gloom. In fact, I think I was the only one who felt this way. Everyone else seemed to be perfectly at peace with life. Katie, especially, who flew the coop and went off to school. After her first year she joined some "save the planet" cause that took her all the way to the Brazilian jungle. She had so much fun that summer that she did it again the following year. Unfortunately for Valerie, an e-mail came through while Katie was away this second time, saying that she had fallen in love with an Australian guy who was also working there and had gotten married. The ceremony was a beautiful aborigine wedding, performed by the local tribe leader. This was too much for Valerie, who felt betrayed by her children, especially by Katie who was her last hope for a traditional wedding. Soon after the e-mail, Katie and her "husband" Jase, showed up at the Preston residence asking for forgiveness, rather than permission.

Valerie and Dane had no other recourse than to like Jase, who was in truth, a very likeable guy. He was shorter than Katie by a few inches; had an upbeat and pleasant personality and that great Australian accent that made every word that came out of his mouth more playful. It was obvious that he adored Katie, and their romance was nothing short of love-at-first-sight.

Not being able to dispute that point, Dane and Valerie welcomed Jase to the family and made the only request that they could: "Live here in the U.S." That they did, though they traveled to Australia a few times a year.

Katie had her first child the same day I had my fourth miscarriage. It all happened in the same hospital, so once I was able to get up and walk, I headed straight for the nursery. Robyn was a beautiful baby with the promise of her grandmothers' violet eyes. I felt an immediate kinship with her, and resolved to love her as my own. I did have stiff competition with Dane, Valerie, and Alex in the mix, not to mention her own parents.

When Robyn was old enough to travel, we all took a family vacation to visit my aunts and Dorian in Mexico. Robyn got more attention than she cared for, and while Luz was taking a turn playing with her, fourteen month old Robyn tripped over her own feet and fell on her head with a thud. The floor was tile, so a purple egg quickly formed on her forehead. While several adults rushed to the freezer to get ice and Robyn wailed, Luz instinctively picked her up and started soothing her with a song.

"Duérmete mi niña, duérmete mi amor. Duérmete pedazo, de mi corazón … "

As soon as those words came out of her mouth, my senses became distorted. A tingling sensation spread throughout my body, white and black dots blurred my vision, my ears began to ring and my knees buckled from under me.

I heard a scream in my head, then voices—angry, shouting, pleading. Then a cynical laugh and a strangled, "NO!" A shot. And then another, followed by a scream. Steps retreating, crying—no—weeping, bitter weeping, then nothing.

I woke up to see Alex's concerned face hovering over me. I was lying down on our bed, and he was holding my hand. "Hi, baby," he crooned. "You passed out."

"Yeah?"

"Yeah." He stroked my hair tenderly. I knew what he was thinking, but he was wrong.

"I'm not pregnant again," I told him right of the bat.

Disappointment washed over him, but he tried to hide it. "What happened then?"

"That song…"

"What song?"

"That lullaby that Luz was singing … it … triggered something, a memory I think."

"Really?"

"I think so. It was fast, like a flash of voices, screams, and gunshots."

Alex's face showed alarm and concern. "What could it be?"

"I think I just remembered my mother's murder."

Part II ~ The Nightmare

Chapter 28

Dabbing some excess lipstick off the corner of her mouth, Eugenia examined herself in the bathroom mirror. She stepped back a few steps and smoothed the wrinkles out of her suit jacket. This was it! Her big chance to prove to the world that she was not just a pretty face, but also a serious person.

She had partied her way through college and had graduated—barely—without any significant prospects ahead of her. And by prospects she didn't mean a career, she meant a husband—a rich one if possible. Handsome was optional. But at least, she wanted someone who had a bright future ahead or a trust fund—either one. But none of her prospects ever proposed, and she had the dissatisfaction of graduating with no ring on her finger.

She hadn't expected this. She wasn't inclined to work her way up the ladder—not by earning it, anyway. Eugenia was an overgrown child, who got what she wanted the minute she wanted it. She was smart, she had the brains, but she chose to use them on manipulation and scheming, rather than good old-fashioned hard work. The thought of doing things the hard way was tedious to her.

Thankfully, her father was good enough to spare her the trouble of finding a job of her own. He pulled a few strings, and one month later, she found herself working for a large hedge fund corporation on the east coast. Nothing important, something menial that required her to dress nice and push a few papers around. She got bored of this quickly, and spent her time angling for a promotion, since working for it was out of the question. She would climb her way up the smart way—and she did—by becoming wife number three of the president of the company.

It was a proud day for her—she looked radiant. Of course, all her old high school and college friends were invited. She made sure that they were all insanely jealous. They were kind enough to play along with the whole, fake smiles and remember when's, yet secretly made bets on how long the marriage would last.

As five of her friends predicted, two short years later, that toad of a husband lost interest in her. He was currently enamored with whom she knew would soon be wife number four. So Eugenia found herself in a quandary. She was tired of playing the trophy wife. She now wanted more—she wanted to be envied for being successful. She wanted a career. If she could wave a wand and make it happen, she would do so in a second. If she had Aladdin's lamp, she would rub it raw. But she didn't, so, as distasteful as it sounded, she would have to somehow earn it.

Broadcast journalism had been a dream of hers for a long time. It was serious work, she got to look pretty, and people would see her every day! Thanks to her marriage, she now had all the right connections, but she knew that those would only be connections as long as she was married. So she took the plunge before she became ex-wife number three.

Winking to herself in the mirror, she left the bathroom and started walking briskly down the hallway, to the room where she would do her on-screen test, when a faintly familiar woman passed her going the opposite direction. For some reason, this mysterious woman left her with a distinct feeling of despair that temporarily disgruntled her. *Who was that?* Eugenia thought, bothered by the woman's face and the bad karma she left behind.

"Oh good! There you are. Are you ready?" the director asked the moment that Eugenia stepped through the doors.

"Yes, I'm ready." Eugenia took in some air and slowly let it out. She took her place behind the mock desk and looked down at her paper. The words made no sense to her and she blinked a few times.

"Don't worry, the same notes will appear on the screen right in front of you," the director said, pointing to the device.

Eugenia nodded, she knew that much. But she needed to get a grip. What was this insecurity that she suddenly felt all about?

"And … action!"

Eugenia looked at the prompt screen; the camera was right above it. She mustered an unconvincing smile and started reading. Nothing she read made any sense. She sounded nervous and her cheek was twitching.

"Cut!"

Eugenia's smile faded and she crumbled in a heap on her chair. Her only chance … and she blew it!

"I think we found our new traffic gal!" the director called with a wide grin.

Eugenia squinted. "What? Did you just say I got it?"

"Yep." The man was now gathering up some cables and moving them around. Eugenia went up to him disoriented.

"You thought that was good? … I mean … I'm flattered, but I was so nervous. I thought I bombed it!"

"You did, honey."

"Then, why—"

"Don't ask questions you don't wanna to hear the answers to. Just promise me that when you are in front of this camera again, you won't embarrass me."

"I—won't, I promise. Thank you."

"Don't thank *me*, honey."

"Who then?"

The man smiled wickedly. "My medium."

"Your what?"

"You heard me," he whispered, and looked around to make sure no one was eavesdropping.

"You have a medium? Who has mediums?"

"Lot of people have *her* as their medium. She's the real thing." He looked dead serious.

"What does she do?"

"She helps people," the director explained as he coiled a long cable around his arm.

"She helps people? How?"

"She just got you this job." His eyebrows rose.

"No, you got me this job. How did she help you?"

"Listen honey, all her clients are entitled to strict confidentiality. In fact, we all have to sign an NDA, non-disclosure agreement. She helps those she wants to help, and that's all you need to know."

"Was that her, that I passed on my way here?"

"Yeah, that was her."

"She gave me the creeps!"

"She can rub people the wrong way at first, but you'll get used to it."

"So that's it?"

The director looked Eugenia straight in the eyes and winked. "She'll be in touch."

Eros had been right; operating in the shadows had been the best move for Agatha and her future never looked brighter. They had made their union official a few years ago and he couldn't have been happier to call her his wife, though she still remained indifferent to the title. She cared about him, of course; one could even say she loved him. But the truth was, she was as fond of him as some people are of their pets. She liked to keep her emotions at bay, never letting them get too out of control. If they did, it would ruin everything—like it did with most people.

Agatha had agreed to the title, only because the spirits had approved and they said that it would make her look more established, approachable and trustworthy. They were right. For some reason, it was better for her to show up at social events with Eros in tow. He was older, much older, but he kept himself in shape and had a distinguished look that made him look reliable and solid. While Agatha was the mystic, Eros, was the good ole' boy who golfed with the clients and put their minds at ease, making everything look perfectly normal.

This combination was a success, so much so, that in a matter of a few years Agatha had a large group of wealthy and well-connected acquaintances that were indebted to her in one way or another. The whole system was based on the old tried and true system of favors and debts that tied everyone to her, leaving her with all the strings. But that was not the whole plan. She was now ready for the second phase of her master plan: the creation of an actual society where there was one more tie—an oath—a blood oath. This phase of her plan would ensure true discipleship and protection from the Source. It would enable all those who entered into the oath to create a mutual safety net of operation—a true fraternity—a society of powerful men and women who would rather die than sell out another member.

This would be tricky, she knew, but it was her dream. This society, like the secret societies of old, had been her dream from day one. Growing up, she never cared for family ties—didn't have any. One couldn't pick families, but she *could* choose the members of her secret society, and this thrilled her. Agatha wanted to be associated with only those who brought something to the table—money, talents or gifts—and these she would use to gain power until she became indispensable to those who called the shots in this world.

She was amazed sometimes at how well things were turning out for her. Nothing or no one seemed to be able to touch her. Her relations went so deep, that she was confident that she could virtually escape any wrongdoing. Only one person, the spirits told her, could harm her future—Tess DeLeon. From the beginning the spirits had warned her about Tess, and now they were particularly adamant about her. For this reason she had brought in her last acquisition: Eugenia.

As Agatha surveyed the finishing touches to the home that she had purchased as the base of operation for her society, she mused over Eugenia and her role. A smile stole across her face as she thought about bringing Eugenia into the fold. It seemed like poetic justice to her, using the one to bring the other down.

Satisfied with all the repairs and additions to the main areas of the old house, Agatha descended to the lower levels of the home, the dungeon, as she mockingly called it. It was to be the most secret part of the house, the place where the sacrifices and the initiations would take place. It was also her sanctuary, the only place where she could perform her rituals without being disturbed.

These three chambers had been finished first, and Agatha herself, decorated the rooms. With only Eros' help, she hung the scarlet drapes that covered the barren walls of the ritual room; she packed the corners with tall candelabra and crowned them with thick pillar candles. She painted the circle on the floor and placed more candles along the lines. Above the circle hung a huge rustic chandelier that also gave only candlelight.

"This room would be lit by me through the power of the Source," Agatha smiled as she waved her hand and the group of candles on the floor lit up. With another sweep she put them out.

Slowly she walked into the sacrificial room. Here the walls were exposed brick and three sides of the walls were adorned with her ancient weapons collection. The far wall held the sign of the Source and the All Seeing Eye with an altar in front of it. Feeling the cold stone of the altar, Agatha closed her eyes and tried to imagine the sacrifices that would be offered up there. This brought her as close to feeling butterflies as she ever could.

The third room was left bare, resembling a prison cell. The walls were white and there were no windows. There was only one cot, one table, and one chair in it. Feeling the walls with her fingertips she remembered that she had to set the plan in motion. Everything had to work with precision and exactness if it was going to work at all. Agatha dug her phone out of her pocket and her fingers started moving quickly across the screen as she drafted the text message.

"I hope you're enjoying your new job, Eugenia! Look sharp tomorrow; your lucky stars say you will have another break."

As predicted, Eugenia got her divorce papers just a few days after she got her first job. She wasn't surprised, but she couldn't help feeling melancholy nonetheless. She had grown accustomed to the title of Mrs. Hudson; it carried power with it, if nothing else. Now she was another ex-Mrs. Hudson, and that was far worse than having never been so.

She wasted no time in changing her name back to its original form and decided that she would make a name for herself. A name that she would be proud of and no one would be able to take away from her.

Lunch hour found her looking busy at the computer, and she decided that sacrifices such as these were the ones that would help her get ahead, until the anonymous text came through. It came just in time actually, right when her hungry stomach was giving a lurch and making an unbecoming gurgling sound. She suspected the source of the text—the mysterious woman who had taken an interest in her welfare—the reason she had this current job, her magic genie.

"I wonder who she is and why she wants to help me? Then again, the director said that he himself had been the recipient of that lady's attention and he owed her his job as well." If it was good enough for him, it would be good enough for her. So without another thought, Eugenia slammed her computer shut and left work. Who needed to work when you had Aladdin's genie on your side?

When she got back to her house, she found all her belongings packed and stacked in neat boxes outside the manned gate. She regretted now, not being kinder to the guy whose job it was to let people in through the gate. She never even noticed him until now, and even after staring at him, she still couldn't tell if he had been the only man who ever worked the gate or simply one of many. The man's stony expression told her enough, but she needed help loading some of these boxes into her car.

"Do you mind helping me?" she called tentatively, hoping that he had a soft spot for a damsel in distress.

"You're supposed to leave the car keys with me ma'am." The man poked his head out the tiny window and stuck out his hand to receive the key.

"How am I supposed to take all these boxes, then? And where

am I to go? I just got the papers this morning. I've had no time to make arrangements!"

"Sorry, ma'am." With a pitiless stare, he wiggled his fingers impatiently.

Eugenia stared at the man for a second. With a roll of her eyes, she dialed her phone and turned her back on the man, not giving him the key.

As she hung up the phone with a taxi service, she pondered who else she might call to help her haul all her stuff. But she had no close friends, no one who would actually help her move a few boxes or even pick her up if she got in a bind. She scanned her memory for times in which she might have had actual friends, and nothing but high school memories came up. Alex … he was at the center of all those memories. *"I wonder what he's up to?"* Eugenia thought longingly. She had always been able to manipulate him easily enough. It had been so long since she had seen him. Her curiosity quickly turned into introspection, and her introspection told her that she still had a thing for him. *"Well, Alex, I might just have to see what you've been up to all these years."* The honking of a cab interrupted her thoughts.

"Would you help me load these up please?" Eugenia said, poking her head in through the window.

"I'm not a moving service!" the man said, annoyed.

"Well, right now you are!" Eugenia shoved a box in the passenger seat and glared at the man daringly.

She was sweating by the time she was done stacking boxes in both cars. She told the cab to follow her to a storage unit, and then waved insolently at the man in the booth. Upon seeing that she was not about to relinquish her keys, the guard, quickly got on the phone.

Showered and safely checked into a motel, Eugenia got on her computer and let her fingers hover over the keyboard for just a moment. There were several things she needed to find, including a car and an apartment, but instead, she typed—Alexander Preston.

Rage filled her as she read about his illustrious career in politics and his fairy-tale marriage to Tess, that infuriating little foster kid. When she read that Tess had actually turned out to be the only heir to a large Spanish fortune, her seething jealousy turned into murderous thoughts. With nostrils flaring, Eugenia settled into another kind of introspection. She would take any and all help from this mysterious woman, and she would take back what was rightfully hers! She drifted off to sleep with visions of her in Alex's arms—a power couple—he in the White House, and she in the anchor chair.

Chapter 29

Valerie watched her family gaily interacting over a large pan of lasagna. Everyone was there, except for her father. She missed him terribly, in spite of the many disagreements they'd had over the years. Now that he was gone, his presence left a huge gap that no one could ever or would ever fill—his laughter, his jokes, and his stories, all gone! She was an orphan now.

In her hands she held the salad bowl, and decided that she'd better finish her errand. As she started moving forward, something made her stop. A movement off to her right caught her attention. Was it the cat?

Another movement, this time off to her left, froze her in place. *No cat is that fast,* she thought, narrowing her eyes trying to focus them. Another, and another, and yet another fast moving shadow passed her on both sides. Chills run up and down her torso and arms, as she saw actual shadows zoom by her and gather like mist around her family.

Of the entire family, only she seemed to be aware of it. Valerie let out a short cynical laugh, knowing all too well that she would be branded, yet again, as the crazy one, for noticing this. *Why is it always me that sees things that don't exist? Why can't I just be normal?* she thought. Her thoughts progressed quickly from self-pity to frustration, and then to anger.

The darkness was now high enough that it covered them completely and dark tendrils were coiling themselves around each one of them like ropes. Her anger turned to fear, a fear that spread through her, from the pit of her stomach to the depths of her heart.

A loud hissing sound emanated from the darkness; a sound that was indiscernible, but carried a message—despair. *"Give up,"* it seemed to say; *"give up and end it all!"* The suggestion sounded logical, and well within reason. She had tried that already … but failed. She had promised herself never go there again. *"They don't care,"* the eerie voices suggested again. *"This is for you … finish this miserable existence of yours. Always struggling ... always fighting to keep it together ... you're a burden ... they'll be better off without you."*

Valerie shook her head and noticed that she too was bound by the darkness. Panicked, she screamed for help, but no one seemed to hear her. They, too, were bound and they were no longer laughing. Their frames shone, but the darkness seemed to be feeding itself on their light and they were slowly dimming—Alex's in particular.

"Alex!" she shouted in warning, but a dark tendril covered her mouth, making it impossible to speak and hard to breathe.

Katie and Jase started shaking in attempts to get loose, but the harder they fought, the tighter the darkness held them. They struggled nonetheless, and right when they looked like they were about to escape, the thing tightened its grip so hard that they burst into tiny lights, like fireworks; and disappeared. The darkness laughed, and moved on to the next target, Alex. He too tried to fight it, but just like Katie and Jase, he exploded, leaving only falling lights behind.

"NO!" she screamed.

"What! What is it? Are you okay?" Dane's face was filled with alarm at his wife's blood curdling scream from right next to him in the bed.

Valerie shook her head, and tried to get her bearings. "Just a dream, it was just a dream," she told herself and tried to steady her breathing. Tears stained her face and she realized she was covered in sweat.

"That's right," Dane soothed. "It was just a dream. Breathe." He gave her some examples on how she should breathe, then watched her intently.

"I'm afraid, Dane."

"Shhh, shhh, don't be."

"Yes, Dane, I should be!" She turned to her husband with exasperation.

"No."

Valerie shuddered, and tried to put her thoughts in order. "The forces of evil are converging on us, and…"

"Val…"

"And I'm worried for our children."

"Nothing will happen to our children."

"Have I ever been wrong, Dane?"

Dane's mouth shut, then closed his eyes and shook his head. She had been a lot of things, but never wrong when it came to dreams.

Since I remembered the night of my mother's murder, displaced images of my childhood seemed to start coming out of nowhere. Dane had warned me about this, and made himself available if I ever wanted to talk, but I talked to Alex instead. Each new memory—usually a flash of something—I would tell him about, and then I would write it down. I was finally piecing together my life.

It couldn't have come at a worse time; we had very little privacy and time together lately. The House was in session and he was gone a lot. To make matters worse, word had gotten out about my father and his conviction and it was all over the media. From the next room I could hear two commentators discuss the issue of whether or not this would ruin Alex's political future.

Annoyed, Alex turned off the TV and put his arms around me as I came into the room. All the worry and cares melted away whenever he did this.

"They'll have their fun, and then it'll be over. There isn't anything more interesting to talk about right now; it'll all be forgotten as soon as something better pops up."

"I should come forward and clear his name … and yours in the process."

"No." Alex shook his head emphatically. "If your uncle finds out you were there, you're as good as dead."

"He could have come after me already, but he didn't. He must know that something was wrong when he didn't inherit. I don't think he wants to come after me."

"I'm not so sure." Alex exhaled and paced the room. "Something feels fishy about all of this. I have this feeling that he's been biding his time. He is a vicious man and he's killed two people already … one directly and another, indirectly."

I nodded and tried to warm a chill that was invading me. Roger had advised me against speaking up at this time, as well. I paced the room feeling cornered. On one hand I held all the cards that would clear my father's name and remove the cloud over Alex's political future. On the other hand, playing those cards could cost me my life, maybe even the lives of those I loved.

"Stop obsessing over her! I told you, I have it completely under control." Agatha tightened a robe around her waist and sat at the breakfast table. She took a sip of her coffee and relished the taste, before reaching for a piece of toast.

"You keep saying that, but we haven't done anything yet," Eros pointed out. He clicked the TV off. "If she talks, it's all over!" He waved the remote angrily around the room before stalking away. In the last few months Eros had gained a lot of weight and had a constant disgruntled look about him.

Agatha rolled her eyes. She was getting tired of hearing about his absurd need to have his family's estate and getting what was rightfully his. They had gone over this a million times. The money was pretty much gone. Tess had done nothing but give that money away since she got it. This whole obsession of his was ridiculous. In fact, Eros was becoming ridiculous. But she was used to him, so she kept him—managed him—rather. His whole schedule was dictated by her, his moves, his business, everything, she controlled.

Eros let himself be led by Agatha as if hypnotized. He suspected nothing of her waning feelings for him and was content to do as she said. He was even a little relieved that he no longer had to think of everything. Agatha had a vision, a master plan, and he trusted it implicitly. Everything in his life had gone better since she took the reins. Besides, there was something about her that spooked him into subservience. He was either with her or against her and the latter, he never wanted to experience.

"Trust me, dear," Agatha said acidly, between sips of her coffee, "she will not enjoy *your* inheritance much longer. But things have to happen naturally. You can't rush revenge. It gets messy." She looked ironically at Eros, who caught her drift. She was referring to his hasty pull of the trigger that killed Tess' mother.

"Do you think that she knows what happened that day?" Eros asked with a faraway look.

"I told you already, I grew up with her. She always claimed to have no memory of her childhood before she entered foster care. If she did, you'd be in custody right now." Her matter-of-fact tone sent shivers up his spine. But he pushed his fears aside and placed his trust in her, leaving his conscience clean and pure-*ish*.

"We're on our way back now, honey," Jase crooned to Robyn over the phone. "Mom and Dad miss you!" Katie added, yanking the receiver from her husband's grip. Jase smirked and grabbed it again, only to place it right between the two of them, so they could both hear their daughter's voice.

"She's fine," Dane assured the parents. "We'll see you tomorrow, then."

"Tell them I need to talk to them!" Valerie raced from the other room and stood eagerly by the phone. Dane shook his head, trying to dissuade his wife from frightening them. But she was adamant.

"Hold on. Mom wants to say something." He gave Valerie a warning look that she ignored.

"Katie?"

"Hi, mom! We got all the samples we needed, so we're heading home tonight."

"That's great sweetie, listen, I—had—" Nothing she could

think to say sounded coherent. "Please be safe." She hoped that the anxiety on her voice would translate into how safe they should be.

"Okay, Mom, of course we will."

"I mean it Katie, I have a bad feeling."

Katie knew what that meant. Something bad was about to happen.

"I understand, Mom. Please take good care of Robyn, and…" what could she possibly say? Life was life. It was unpredictable. Katie knew very well that anything could happen, to anyone, at any point. That's why she had adopted the mentality of living and enjoying life in the moment. When Robyn was born, they had asked Tess and Alex to be her godparents, because heaven only knew how much they loved her. They had a hefty life insurance policy, and they had a hazardous job that they loved. But lots of people did what they did, and they lived long and happy lives. So why did she feel like someone had just walked over her grave?

She shook her head, "Mom, we'll be fine! I'll see you tomorrow, okay?"

Valerie nodded, "Of course, dear, of course. I love you very much." A sob threatened to choke her, so she passed the phone back to Dane, who finished the conversation in hushed tones.

As the small charter plane shook convulsively and the passengers screamed, Katie felt calm. She reached her hand over to Jase, who held it tightly. They looked into each other's eyes and relived their whole lives together. Fear never gripped them as the small plane nosedived to the ground and burst into flames.

They were still holding hands and looking into each other's eyes when a golden light engulfed them. The flames that surrounded them filled them not with pain, but with love—full to the brim. They remained there, engulfed as it were, in an inexplicable love that consumed them.

Suddenly, from the corner of their eyes they saw them approaching. There were hundreds of them—a whole throng of white figures—were converging on them. Turning their heads, they watched with amazement how a few of them flew forward with unspeakable speed, and flung their arms around them.

Dazed, Katie shut her eyes, then opened them again and pulled away from the embrace to see who it was that was giving it. It was a woman she had only seen in pictures—her grandmother, Nancy.

Katie blinked a few times, hoping that the process would give her some perspective. Then she saw him hovering a distance away. "Grandpa?" she asked, confused by his appearance.

"Yes, sweetie, it's me." Russell floated to her, looking exactly as he did in his mid twenties—sideburns and all! "Do you know who this is?" He pointed to Nancy.

"Grandma Nancy?"

Nancy groaned at the sound of those words and embraced Katie again. The uncanny resemblance between the two women was extraordinary. From the cloud-like whiteness, another form appeared, a tall redhead with chocolate brown eyes. She came with arms outstretched and a wide smile.

"Estelle…" Katie recognized her from pictures as well. She was mesmerized at the love she felt coming from these two women that she didn't even know. The love consumed her, and only increased when more forms emerged, arms open and welcoming.

Not far away, Jase was being received in much the same manner. Katie couldn't suppress a smile when she saw that the spirits who surrounded her husband, resembled him in height, accent, and mannerisms. The reunion reached a crescendo when Jase insisted that they come and meet his wife. See-through forms came together, shaking hands, nodding, chatting, and laughing. No one was sad, no one lamented the end of Jase and Katie's lives— because they continued.

It wasn't until much later than Katie realized the full extent of what had happened.

"Jase!"

He turned with his dimpled grin.

"Our daughter," he guessed her thoughts, and his look darkened. Sadness spread from them to all who were assembled.

"If you'll follow me," said a spirit who wore a long pendant around his neck. "There are only a few things you need to do, if you'd like to visit her."

"Visit?" both Katie and Jase said at once.

"Yes, visit. But your influence over her can still be very powerful." He ushered Katie and Jase through the crowds, and led them along a golden path. On either side, nothing but whiteness could be seen.

"As parents of a young child, you have priority. So I'll skip a lot of the … red tape, if you will, and take you right to the Guardian Angels' training center."

Katie and Jase exchanged puzzled looks, but followed quietly.

The Angel leading them stopped in front of a huge golden gate. It was shut, and on either side huge, winged creatures stood like Sentinels.

"Before I let you through, I have to ask you … because it is granted for you to choose, since technology back on earth is sophisticated enough these days. But once you cross that gate, you cannot change your mind." The Angel waited for that to sink in. Then turning majestically around he asked, "Would you like to live, or would you like to die?"

Chapter 30

Life hung in the balance for Katie and Jase, who were both in a coma since the plane crash. Because of their severe burns it was unclear if they would survive, and even if they did, what kind of life they would have? "Vegetables," one of the doctors had predicted. "It's doubtful that they'll ever wake up, and if they do, their burned skin will be constantly threatened by infection from bed sores. Needless to say, they will need around the clock care."

I watched as Valerie stroked a single patch of Katie's hair, that hadn't been singed. Tears bleached a path down her cheek, that I was sure would never disappear.

Dane too looked as if he might never recover from this crushing blow. His usual peaceful face seemed to have aged ten years. Hollow dark circles under his eyes, and creases from worry and exhaustion marked his face.

Alex and I took Robyn home with us, and tried our best to make her life happy. As her legal guardians we suddenly became parents—not the way we hoped to be, but parents nonetheless. Even if Katie and Jase ever pulled through, it looked as if they would never be able to fully recover enough to take care of Robyn.

While Alex was busy with his work, I brought three-year-old Robyn with me to the shop. She loved being there as much as I did. Carla, my assistant, manned the storefront while I sewed in the back and Robyn played in the store with the fabric swatches, the lace and the mannequins. She showed great taste in fashion, and watched me carefully as I made her one of my famous rag dolls. I spared no details, and made the doll to resemble her mother. I even made her dress out of Katie's favorite outfit.

"This is your Katie doll," I told her once it was finished.

Robyn took the doll reverently in her arms, and cradled it. "This is mommy?" she asked innocently.

I nodded, fighting back the tears.

"Where's daddy?"

"Of course!" I said, cursing myself for being so calloused. "I'll make you a Jase doll right now."

Once that was done, she asked for another doll, a baby one. So the Robyn doll, much smaller was made. Robyn played with this little family every day. It was therapeutic for her, because the rag family had whole conversations that were very … interesting.

Laying the Robyn doll on a makeshift bed of fabric ends, she held the other two suspended in mid air. "What should we do Robyn, dear?" the Katie doll asked with a high pitch squeak.

"I don't know. I miss you, Mommy," the Robyn doll answered.

"If we stay, we may not be much help to you, but we'll be here with you," the Jase doll said in a grave tone.

"What happens if you don't stay?"

"We will watch over you, always."

"Will I see you?"

"No."

"Will I hear you?"

"No. Not really, but we'll be … around."

As predicted by the mysterious text from that lady, Eugenia had been promoted that same day to field reporter. She had her own little crew, the camera guy and a makeup person. She tried hard to win their devotion and respect, but apparently they suspected that Eugenia had gained her position through nefarious means, so they did very little for her. But right now, her crew and what they thought, was the last thing on Eugenia's mind. She was standing amid the throng of reporters, right outside the building where Alex Preston was currently giving a speech.

Like a schoolgirl she felt butterflies at the thought of seeing him again. This was the perfect place to catch him too. She was sure he'd give her an answer, once he saw who was asking the questions. At the very least they had grown up together, so he owed her that.

When the doors opened, people started coming out. Some

reporters would rush to the side of one representative or another, but Eugenia waited for her target. She wasn't alone, apparently wind of Katie's plane crash had gotten out and lots of reporters wanted to know what Alex had to say about it.

Alex stepped out of the building and shielded his eyes against the glare from the sun. He briskly started going down the steps, but didn't get too far before he was swarmed with reporters.

"Come on, come on! Stay with me!" Eugenia called to her sluggish cameraman, who didn't care much if she got a question in.

A bombardment of questions assailed Alex. He made no comment on any personal questions about his sister, but the pained look on his face said much more than words. A couple of reporters shouted questions about the bill he was working on, and these questions he did answer briefly and professionally. Eugenia wiggled her way in as Alex resumed his descent.

"Alex," she asked intimately, then she cleared her throat, "I mean, Mr. Preston." She hoped that the mere sound of her voice would make him notice her, but it didn't.

"Mr. Preston!" she called again, louder now. "I have it on good authority that your sister and her husband had third degree burns in ninety percent of their bodies. Who will take care of their daughter, your parents?" Why did she ask that? That was the dumbest question, but for some reason that's all that her mind could come up with once faced with him. He looked striking in his suit, and more handsome than ever. He was hot in high school, but he only seemed to be getting better looking with age.

"My wife and I are the Godparents to my niece. She will be raised by us," Alex said matter-of-factly, and turned in the general direction of where the question had come. His eyes glossed right over Eugenia, and then turned right back, making a hasty exit for his waiting car.

Disappointment didn't come close to describing what Eugenia felt. He had answered her question, and the cameraman pointed this out as he packed up his equipment. Then he mumbled about getting a good close up shot of his face while he was answering, and he thought that they might be able to spin his look into a nice little quip about how is so distracted with his family drama that he can't focus on his promised bill.

"We can't do that!"

"And why not? It'll get us air time."

"You don't understand, I can't show my face in the camera and say that about Alex."

"Alex? You mean Mr. Preston?"

"I know him, you idiot! I can't trash him."

"How do you know him?" The cameraman had a dubious grin on his face.

"I grew up with him!" Eugenia said haughtily, "our parents are best friends and we dated all through high school!"

The cameraman broke out in a fit of hysterical laughter. "Wow! You must have made quite an impression on him. He didn't even recognize your voice! He looked right over you like you weren't even there!" He slapped his knee and the makeup girl joined in with a giggle.

A murderous mood sized Eugenia, and she glared at the two with sheer hate.

"I thought that he had married his high school sweetheart?" the makeup girl asked amusedly.

"Yeah, I remember hearing that too!" the cameraman corroborated.

"I broke up with him during our senior year! We dated up until then!"

"You mean, he broke up with you!" They laughed again and Eugenia stormed away, too upset to face them. When had she become the butt of jokes? When had the tables turned? She thought of all the times that she had been the one laughing, and Tess the object of ridicule. Now Tess had it all, and she had nothing!

After watching the clip of the question several times, Eugenia made up her mind. She would take the weekend off and go back to Texas. She hadn't seen her parents in a long time—since her wedding—so why not go back now and hear all the "I told you so's." It might also afford her a chance at seeing Alex and wedging her way back into his life.

It was, as it always is, easier said than done—both hearing the "I told you so's" and the wedging. As it turned out, the Preston's were not seeing anyone, not even their old family friends. More often than not, Eugenia found herself more in the position of a stalker than that of a concerned friend. It started innocently enough, with her intending to go up to Alex the moment he stepped out of the car. But all that changed when she saw the exchange that took place between Tess and him.

Alex had pulled into his driveway, when Tess happened to be on her way back from a jog with a running stroller and a toddler strapped inside. The reunion between the two was tender enough to melt anyone's heart, unless that heart happened to be murderously jealous. Everything in Alex's movements and expression said that he was madly in love and completely crazy for his wife and niece.

Eugenia thought with bitterness about their moments together. He had never looked at her like that, nor had he ever touched or kissed her like that either. Clenching her jaw and pursing up her lips, Eugenia reached for the camera and snapped a few pictures. *What am I doing?* she thought, with reproach, but almost as if propelled by some unseen force, she kept taking pictures until they disappeared behind closed doors.

Eugenia stayed up almost the whole night studying those pictures. With a magnifying glass she looked closely at their faces trying to read their expressions, hoping to detect the slightest trace of trouble. But she found that, quite on the contrary, every time their eyes met, they quite literally lit up. Anger, seething and unchecked, writhed within her to the point that she had to act on it somehow.

Reaching for her cell phone, she searched for that text she had received a few months back.

"I want Tess DeLeon out of the picture and I want Alex Preston back. Can you make that happen?" She hit reply and waited in complete silence.

A few minutes later the phone chimed and showed a new message.

"I can."

Katie and Jase passed within hours of each other. Their bodies just shut down on their own and we had to abstain from resuscitating them. We decided that it would be good to get away for a while. Alex had some time off, and hanging around familiar places was just too painful. So we all decided to take a trip back to Argentina. Dane admitted that Valerie needed a change of scenery and they had never seen our home there. The only problem was that she had to be sedated for most of the trip, due to a new phobia of flying.

The whole trip she kept rambling about a bad dream and darkness that ate us alive. She seemed to be teetering on the verge of another major nervous breakdown, so Dane was scaling back on his job, just to take care of her.

Robyn on the other hand, seemed content enough. She would not part, day or night with the dolls I made for her. They had become her surrogate family and indeed they were. I heard no spiritual voices, but I knew that Katie and Jase were communicating with her somehow. It was odd to me, that at a time such as this, Celeste had chosen to remain silent. There were times in my life when she would not leave me alone, and others where she stayed away completely. There had to be a reason for this, but I just didn't know what it was.

Eugenia had no idea why the mysterious woman sent her a round trip ticket to Buenos Aires, but she knew that somehow this was connected with her earlier request. Maybe Alex was on a business trip. Maybe … she hated the thought of having to do something about Tess herself. Surely the woman knew that she wouldn't go that far. Would she?

Once she got to the hotel that was reserved for her, she found an envelope with some contact information and a picture of Tess. She was to call that number and set up an appointment with that man.

"I'm hiring a hit man?" Eugenia shook her head, "but—but—." Feeling caught between a rock and a hard spot, Eugenia thought about all the implications. If she were ever caught, the trail would lead back to her. Whoever this mysterious woman was, she was very shrewd. She was making sure that her own hands wouldn't get dirty. This thought angered Eugenia. She paced her room impatiently, not knowing what to do. Here was her chance to get what she wanted, but would she take it?

If she got caught, what would happen? Then again, she could call the man from a phone booth. She could explain this trip in so many different ways. She could actually go out and have some fun, pretending that she had always wanted to come here. There would be no way to trace this man to her.

After making the call and setting up the meeting place, Eugenia took herself out to dinner. Some very friendly guys took her dancing. Early the next morning, she stumbled into her hotel room and crashed on her bed, not noticing the outline of a man sitting by her window.

Chapter 31

We should have listened to Valerie. I, as much as anyone, knew how real these gifts are. Yet it was easy to forget, when you saw her drugged up and acting crazy. It was easy to think that perhaps she was just losing it. She had always been delicate, and something as harsh as the death of a child was excuse enough for anyone would lose a grip on reality. For someone like Valerie, it would surely be worse.

Everything happened so fast. We had made it to our home in Tigre, exhausted and sore from the long hours of sitting uncomfortably. We stayed in the island as long as we could, recuperating and watching Valerie slowly drift into madness.

Robyn was her only diversion and calming influence. She played with her and the dolls, and Valerie pretended right along with her that the dolls were real. Dane sat dismayed and helpless as he watched his wife slowly lose her mind.

"You two should go into the city, get some groceries and spend some time away," Dane suggested. He had made the decision before the trip to retire and take care of his wife full-time. The man had a bottomless well of compassion and patience. We insisted that he should go and take a break, but he would not have it. "I'm fine," he lied. "I take my breaks while she sleeps. Besides, I don't mind."

Alex and I took the smaller motorboat and headed into the city. We forced ourselves to have some fun, but neither one of us felt like laughing. Alex had been unusually quiet lately, and I left him alone with his thoughts, mainly because I knew he needed to sort a lot of things out.

"I feel like we're cursed," he finally confided. "I mean … look at us! Our family. Our parents, both yours and mine. Katie and Jase. What's this all about? How can life be so harsh? What did we ever do wrong?"

"Or right?"

"What?" He looked at me like I was crazy.

"What if we didn't do anything wrong, but all of this happened because we did something right?"

He shook his head, "Then this is one messed up world."

"What if we are a threat to those who do evil?" I thought of Agatha and the evil voices that she listened to. The idea was new to me, but I could see it taking shape in my head as I spoke. "I think that there are powers at work that we don't see, forces of evil that want to stop us from thwarting their plans."

"How did Katie and Jase fit into their plans? How did your parents?"

An ugly realization hit me hard in the stomach, like I just got punched. *What if I somehow brought this on them? What if I'm the one they're after? What if their deaths and ill-fated lives are payback for something I did ... before?* The thought knocked the air out of my lungs and I found it hard to breathe. My mind reeled and amber cat-like eyes flashed in my mind, " *... Remember Tess, remember who you are and what your mission is ... "* her soft purr-like voice resounded in some distant memory. A dream. I had a dream about that.

Alex's expression changed as well. He looked at me unblinkingly, his thoughts far away, "Whatever happens ... will happen to us." he said as if in a trance.

"What?" I breathed out feeling shivers run up and down my torso.

"A promise," he said, searching my eyes, trying to grasp something elusive. "I remember making you that promise, but ... not here."

My eyebrows knitted and I looked at him questioningly. "What do you mean?"

Alex looked around the crowded train we had been riding into the city. We enjoyed the privacy of speaking a different language, but not the privacy of personal space. No one seemed particularly interested in us, but he still lowered his voice and whispered in my ear. After all these years, these simple exchanges still gave me chills and flushed my face. My feelings for him had only intensified with time, bonding us so tightly that I couldn't imagine ever being me without him again. One flesh, that's what we have become—one flesh.

"This is going to sound crazy, but I just had the oddest memory. No, I've had this flash of memory before … the day I met you. I remember you walking into that classroom and I remembered this same thing." He looked suspiciously around again and pressed closer to me, bending his head intimately to my ear. "I remembered standing on a beach, wide and clear, unlike anything I've ever seen on Earth. It was … perfect. You were dressed in white, and looked radiant, brilliant—glorious."

I looked into his eyes and he looked back into mine with intensity.

"I—it happened so fast! I'm afraid that if I don't tell you now I'll never be able to again."

I frowned and he shook his head. "Listen, you looked like an angel, that's the best way I can describe it. We were standing on that beach and my heart felt like it would explode with happiness at the mere sight of you. One smile from you and I knew … " his voice broke and he cleared his throat. "I knew that I would endure anything just to be with you, here."

"Here?"

"Yes." He thought for a moment. "Here, in this life."

I blinked a few times, fighting back the stinging sensation of oncoming tears. "Endure anything?" I echoed.

"Anything."

We were silent for the rest of our ride, but remained standing close, perhaps even too close for public. But in this city, these eccentricities didn't seem to matter much to anyone. I remembered that day I first saw him. I had a vision of him too, but it was different. Or was it? The memory of what I saw that day flashed in my head again. I was looking at him across the room one minute, and the next he was right in front of me, bending over me getting ready to kiss me, making a promise, feeling eager, frustrated, relieved, and … promising me something,

We stepped off the train at the end of the line—Retiro, the main station—and quietly walked hand in hand toward one of our favorite cafés. It was one of those classic places that had history behind it. Everything in the place was reminiscent of the tango golden age, and indeed the furniture was from that era. The soft melody of a doleful tango played in the background, while the scent of strong coffee wafted through the air.

We ordered our lunch and we stared into each other's eyes, wordlessly. There seemed to be something hanging in the air, thick and oppressive. It felt odd, like a new chapter in our lives was about to begin.

As if reading my mind Alex leaned in and grabbed my hand, "We are turning a new page here, I think."

"What does it mean?" I asked, fear tugging at my heartstrings.

"I don't know," he exhaled. "I feel like—like we need to be strong for something."

The tears that had been threatening to fall on the train could not be held back any longer. "Alex, a lot has happened already. What more could there be?"

His response was nothing that I had been expecting. His eyes grew big, shock registering in every feature of his face. He screeched his chair back, knocking it to the ground as he stood. In a flash he reached over and forced me off my chair, pushing me to the ground. Shots, mingled with screams and shouts assaulted my hearing. Fear registered as I felt his body falling over mine. Sirens, screams, more shots, acrid, warm sticky blood ... *laughter*.

Eugenia woke up feeling stiff and sore from the previous night's events. She stumbled into the bathroom and looked into her haggard face. Something had changed; she looked different. Peering closer into the mirror she pulled the bags under her eyes taut, hoping that perhaps that would do the trick in restoring her youthfulness—but it didn't.

She checked her watch and realized that if she didn't hurry, she would miss the appointment with that man. They were to meet at a coffee shop downtown, where she would casually slip him the envelope with the picture of Tess.

Once showered, she came out to choose her outfit, and realized instead that the envelope with the picture was gone. Instead she found a note that simply said. "It is done. Meet me where we agreed, with the payment."

Eugenia's heart started beating wildly. Payment? Of course he'd want payment, but she had not been given any money to pay the man or how much it would cost. She assumed that the woman would have taken care of all that.

A sick feeling in her stomach pooled there and she rushed to the bathroom to expunge it from her system. With trembling hands and her mind racing, she cursed the day she came to this miserable country and even considered dealing with this woman. Who was she? Why was she setting her up for murder? How did she get here? Not just in body, but in soul?

She had no way of getting a hold of that woman now; she was completely on her own. After debating the matter for another moment, she started to throw her belongings back in her suitcase. She didn't bother to dry her hair or apply any makeup. She flagged a cab down and told him "Air—port." Slowly, so the man would understand.

As she rushed to the ticket booth, a man in a hooded sweatshirt and sunglasses stopped her. "Where are going in such a hurry?" he asked with a strange accent.

Caught off guard and shaking like a leaf, Eugenia mumbled something incoherent.

"You will walk to the nearest ATM and you will pay me for my work."

"How do I know it's done?"

"If you had been at our appointed meeting time, you would have seen for yourself."

"I want nothing to do with this," Eugenia muttered.

"Too late." He jabbed her in the back with something hard and pushed her toward an ATM. Trembling, Eugenia obeyed.

"How much?" she asked in vain, knowing that there would not

be nearly enough money in her account to pay the guy.

"All of it," he demanded, thrusting his gun barrel deeper into her back.

"Eugenia pushed buttons and her account balance showed way more money than she remembered having—a lot more. "This ATM will not let me cash this much money," she said in disbelief. Where had this money come from?

"Then we have a long day ahead of us," the man purred in her ear.

Alex stood up suddenly, like a spring, and frantically looked around for the assailant and for Tess, but he saw nothing. There was nothing. Just white thick fog and bright muted light. "Hello?" he called. No response.

"Anybody there? What is this place? Where is Tess?" he demanded.

From the fog and the golden light a form appeared. It was a man, tall, broad shoulders, thickly built, all dressed in white. Behind him came a woman, petite, also dressed in white. They glided forward silently. Alex stared at them and squinted to get a better look. They looked oddly familiar.

"Who are you? Where am I?"

"It's me, son," the man's voice reverberated like thunder. It sounded familiar.

Alex peered into the man's face, "Grandpa?"

"We all look young here!" Russell smiled broadly and gave him a shove on the shoulder. Alex looked at the spot where this young version of his grandfather had touched him, and marveled at the fact that he didn't feel the contact.

"What's going on?" he asked suspiciously, not really wanting to hear the answer.

"Say hi to your grandma Nancy," Russell said, pointing to the woman.

"Hi," Alex said dubiously. He didn't remember Nancy that well; she had died of cancer when he was still very young. His unconvincing greeting, however, didn't deter her from jumping up and clamping on to his neck.

"Oh, my dear boy! It's so good to see you! You have no idea how sorry I am to … "

"To what?" Alex demanded while he removed her from his neck.

"To have you under these circumstances," she finished. She looked uncertainly back at her husband.

"What circumstances?"

"You're dead, son." Russell's straightforwardness irritated Alex.

"What do you mean, I'm dead?" he spat.

"Just that. You were killed, shot. Shot dead, son."

Alex stared at his grandfather and anger seized him, propelling him forward at a speed that only his mind could create. Grabbing Russell by the shirt he pulled him forward and upwards, quite effortlessly. He held the feather-light Russell and shook him a few times. Realizing that physical contact had no effect whatsoever, he released him. He had hoped that this young Russell would at least fall down with a thud, but instead he floated smoothly down. Alex looked away from his grandparents and rubbed his face in frustration. "I'm thirty years old, grandpa! Tess needs me! I just got done telling her that I would stick by her through anything. I told her how I—we were going to go through the problems that life sent us together! How can I do that now?"

Russell and Nancy exchanged glances. "It was your time, Alex." Russell put one big hand on his shoulder and squeezed.

"Tess says we all have Guardian Angels. Hers is her grandmother, Celeste. Who's mine? Why didn't it protect me?"

"Because *he* was forbidden."

Alex looked into Russell's eyes with an accusatory look. "It was you, wasn't it? You let that bastard kill me?"

"Watch your tongue son, you're in Heaven!"

"Ha! Like you ever did!"

Nancy turned and looked at her husband through half closed eyes. Russell rolled his and threw his hands up in the air. "Okay! So I haven't always been perfect! In fact I've always fallen extremely short! But I'm trying here." He grabbed Alex by the shoulders and looked sternly into his eyes. "I could have stopped that—bastard," he whispered the last word, "but like I said, I was forbidden."

"By who?"

"The Eternals."

"Who?"

"On Earth the Eternals have many different names, but basically it's the Godhead."

"So, God told you to let me die."

"Well when you put it that way it doesn't sound right. But trust me, the Eternals would never do anything without your best interest in mind. Some people are assigned to death and that's it! If you mess with it, big problems could arise from it. I've seen it."

"He's right, dear," Nancy piped in from the sidelines.

Alex turned and looked at her again, remembering that she was there. "Where are Katie and Jase?"

As if on cue, they stepped forward from the whiteness the moment their names were called. "Were you there this whole time?"

Katie flew to her brother, and, like Nancy, embraced him tightly. "Yes, we were," she admitted unreservedly, Jase came forward and extended his hand.

"Who else is hiding back there?" Alex crooked his neck and looked in the direction where Katie and Jase had come from.

From the clouds hundreds of figures stepped forward. The sight was overwhelming to Alex. Panic filled him at the mere sight of all these spirits. "Who are you?" he breathed out.

"Your ancestors," they said, almost simultaneously, adding to his consternation.

"Well, some of us are not your ancestors. Some of us are just friends." A blond with an accent said, as she came forward with a small band of people.

"Celeste?"

"Yes, and this is my husband Max and my son Leo and his wife Irene."

They nodded in greeting.

"The shooter—he was aiming for Tess," Alex told her.

"I know. Thanks for saving her." Celeste looked genuinely grateful.

Alex frowned, "If the man was aiming for Tess, why was it my time to die? I mean, I would do it again, I would save her life no matter what, but … "

"It was meant to happen. I can't be one hundred percent sure, but you would have died some other way." Russell gave Alex a pitiful smile. "The bright side is that you died a hero's death, sacrificing your life for that of another. That actually counts for something."

"Greater love hath no man than this, that he layeth down his life for his friends," Max spoke with priestly wisdom.

"If it makes you feel better," a petite woman with raven black hair and equally dark eyes spoke up. She was the spitting image of Tess, but shorter and darker. "I know exactly how you feel right now, and trust me. It's for the better that you trust the Eternals."

Alex shook his head. "I appreciate the sentiment, and I'm sure that you—" He pointed to Tess' parents, making the assumption as to who they were, "of all people would understand. But … my mom, she's losing it! And Tess … If what we are saying is correct, there's someone out there trying to murder her!" Alex looked pleadingly at Leo. "Most likely the same person who ruined your life and ended hers," he pointed to Irene. Alex could tell that Leo wasn't sold on this passive idea of letting it be. He could see the fire in Leo's eyes, the fire he had in his own—the fire of anger and revenge.

Leo looked steadily at Alex, and moved forward, placing himself right in front of Alex. He put one hand on his shoulder and squeezed it. "I have appreciated the way you've treated my daughter, and I want to welcome you to my family." Leo's voice sounded measured and tight, as if fighting an internal struggle. Alex nodded once and looked back at Leo, wondering what was on this man's mind.

"That person to whom you are referring to is still after my daughter, but he's not the only one."

"Then we must stop them!" Alex exclaimed impatiently. "She can hear spirits! I can go back to her and protect her, or at least warn her! I'll be her Guardian!" Alex turned to Celeste.

"You can't assign yourself to be someone's Guardian Angel," Celeste cried. "You have to qualify, then go through training, then be assigned. Even then you may not be assigned to her; you could be assigned to anyone!"

"There's no time to do all that! She needs me now. She's my wife! I'll look after her!"

"It doesn't work like that," Nancy pleaded.

"Well I don't care how it works! I'm going back!" Alex looked around, searching for a door or stairs or something that would cross him over. "I get that I'm dead, but in this particular case it may still work," he mumbled as he still looked for a way out.

"I'm telling you, necio, you can't do it! You'll be haunting her if you go down without permission!" Celeste yelled. Max extended one arm and held her back.

"How could a husband wanting to help his wife be considered a haunting? It makes no sense! I'm going down, and you will tell me how."

"I'll do no such thing! I've kept her safe all these years. Even while *you* were messing with her head, and nearly broke her heart. I was the one who consoled her!"

"I never messed with her head!"

"Oh yes you did!"

"Enough!" Russell's voice boomed with authority. "Alex, she's right. You can't go down unless you are assigned. You have no idea what—"

"I'm going down, and if you won't tell me how, I'll find someone who will."

"No one will tell you," Russell said firmly.

"I will," Leo looked up and stared at Russell defiantly.

"Leo, no!" Irene gasped.

"I'm done playing by these rules! I agree with Alex. Something has to be done, and I'm through standing by and watching all my loved ones succumb to this … bastard," emphasizing this last word, he turned to Alex with a defiant grin.

Chapter 32

My mind has its own coping mechanism when it comes to dealing with trauma—it shuts down. I'm not sure where it goes, all I know for sure is that one moment Alex was pushing me down to the floor and the next I was standing by his grave site, dressed in black, listening to someone read from the Bible, "Oh death where is thy sting? Oh grave where is thy victory?"

I looked at the person speaking with anger, what did he mean "where is thy sting?" and "where is thy victory?" *It's right here!* I felt like screaming.

"Welcome back," Dane said to me as we walked back to the cars for the procession.

"What do you mean?"

"Your eyes … you looked … gone. I see life behind them now." The poor man looked tired, aged. He held on to Valerie who also looked aged, thin and gaunt.

As the car door opened I got a brief look at myself in the tiny side mirror, I too looked awful. My usual golden olive skin looked ashen. I had dark purple circles under my eyes and my hair was cut short right below my ears with blunt short bangs. It would have been a cute style, but my short strands currently hung lifeless down both sides of my face. *When did I get it cut? Why couldn't I remember that at all?*

I took in a breath and let it out in gusts. Robyn came to my side and laced her tiny hand through mine. She looked up at me and I looked down at her. Bending down so I could be eye level, I brushed some brown locks away from her face. "It's just you and me now." She nodded, then threw her arms around my neck and squeezed so tightly that I could barely breathe.

It appeared that I was now living with the Prestons. All my belongings were there. I wondered where Alex's things were and if the task of going through them all would fall to me—probably. Dane took Valerie straight to their room, and I headed to the kitchen to make myself some tea. Robyn watched me from a stool and said nothing. While the kettle warmed up, I searched the pantry for what I considered "good" tea. There was none, so I settled for mixing a couple of pre-packaged types—lemon, mint and—a chill brushed up my arm. My heart skipped a beat and I shivered as I closed my eyes.

Placing the tea bags in the porcelain teapot, I went back to the stove to wait for the kettle to whistle. The handle was warm and it felt good to place my cold hand there to warm it. But in spite of the soft steam that ascended in rivulets, another chill ran up my arm, then to my neck, softly down my other arm and all the way down my backside. I felt embraced by this chill and stood there shivering until the whistle of the pot startled me out of my trance.

"I said, is Uncle Alex in heaven too?" Robyn yelled.

I shook the chill and looked at her. I was unaware that she had spoken to me at all. "I'm sure of it, honey. He's with your mommy and daddy."

She looked at me steadily for a few minutes. "You promise?" she asked, piercing me with her large blue eyes.

"I promise."

"I want to watch something."

"Would you like some food? Are you hungry?"

"No," she climbed down the stool and headed for the T.V. After a long debate on what to watch, I settled her down and wrapped her in a blanket and kissed her forehead.

"I'll be in my room if you need me, Rob."

"OK." She smiled and seemed content with the prospect of her movie.

My room was Alex's old room; it had been re-decorated with my things—our things. I took a minute to look around as I sipped my tea, and touched some of the things that we had purchased together—decorations, mementos from trips and such. Though there was nothing of great value, they all held a precious memory.

Again, the chill embraced me from behind and I felt a great longing for Alex. With tears burning the rims of my eyes I fell down on the bed and started crying, succumbing to the grief and emptiness I felt inside.

"Alex … " I groaned.

" … *hhheeere,*" an eerie whistle like noise sounded near my ear, followed by a cool kiss on my cheek.

"Alex?" this time I asked, certain that I would hear an answer.

"Yesss … "

"Alex!!!" Tears run down freely now, no doubt smearing the little makeup I was wearing. "You came to me!"

"How long?"

"How long what?"

"I just left you…you have short hair."

"We just got back from your funeral. And yes, it appears that my hair is short now."

"I was only gone for a few minutes!"

"I—honestly, I've lost track of time … I live here now," I said, looking around the room. It seemed that his form was lying beside me on the bed, and one faint cool breeze-like hand caressed my face.

"I promised I wouldn't leave you, so I've come back."

"You should not be here!" Celeste's voice chimed in, stern and disapproving.

"You've said that already, but I disagree," Alex answered dryly.

"There are consequences, son," another familiar voice said.

"Who's that?"

"The Admiral," Alex whispered in my ear, sending even more chills and leaving me shivering. I reached for a blanket to warm me up and covered myself all the way up to my chin.

"You see! You are doing it already, you are haunting her! This is not right, and you need to leave," Celeste bellowed.

"But I don't want him to leave," I protested.

"Esta no es una buena idea. It's not good for you Tess! No good will come from this, you mark my words!" she insisted.

"Come on, son. Before it's too late," the Admiral pleaded.

"You've heard her," the chill left my side, and it seemed as if he were floating somewhere above me. *"She doesn't want me to*

leave. I'm her husband; I should be her Guardian Angel now. You leave this up to me."

"But you haven't been assigned, neither have you received any training! You are going against all the rules and this will only add to her distress!" Celeste yelled.

"This is not a game, Alex. People have lost their minds this way," Russell insisted.

"Enough! I want Alex, okay. Nothing will happen to me, I've been hearing spirits for a long time now. I think I can handle my own husband's company, even if it is … " Despair seized me and a great lump formed in my throat. I couldn't believe our lives had been reduced to a ghostly encounter. I fell in a heap on my bed, crouched into a tight ball and wept with abandon.

The days that followed were a mix of bitter and sweet. I loved hearing his voice and being able to still talk to him, but the yearning to be with him ate me alive. He too was tormented by the great chasm that existed between us now. The sting of death and the victory of the grave seemed ever present.

I also had to tread a fine line between my new life with Alex and my other life as a widow. I was careful to not let it slip that I was talking to my dead husband. More than anyone, I knew how others perceived my gift, and how cautious I had to be when talking to him.

Alex was ever present. He came with me to work, and helped look after Robyn at the store. He was there with me when I shopped, cooked, bathed, slept, everything … everywhere … all the time. After a few weeks I noticed that some of the people I worked with were looking at me funny, like I was off my rocker. I couldn't fathom why they would think that. There may have been a few times when they might have overheard me talking to Alex, but those were just a few instances, nothing to be concerned about.

I was always so cold, always wearing long sleeves and shivering, but that was not a problem for me. I was willing to put up with the constant chill I felt inside and out, just to have him near me. Eating seemed to be a problem too—I was never hungry. Food had lost its taste, it all tasted bland. Same with my teas—nothing tasted like anything anymore. Life in general seemed to lose its flavor. Work was no longer enjoyable—no designs would come to mind. No color or texture seemed to inspire me. In fact nothing about this life mattered any more. Alex and being with him became my only interest. It was easier to stay home, in my room with him than go out. That way I could avoid all the glares from strangers and the concerned stares from everyone else. Only in that little room could I speak freely and have some time with him.

"I need to talk to you, Tess." Dane opened the door suddenly, catching me in the middle of an animated chess game with— myself.

I looked up at him for a moment, resenting the lack of knock. "Sure, what about?"

He entered, looked around the room, sauntered, pursed up his lips, opened his mouth to say something, changed his mind, exhaled, sat on the edge of my bed, rumpled his graying hair and then looked at me straight in the eyes. "I've noticed that you talk to yourself," he said, coming straight to his point.

I couldn't argue with him on that. I couldn't deny that I sometimes spoke out loud, but if I told him that I could speak to my dead husband, surely that would be worse. "I know it seems like I'm crazy, but I'm not. I'm just … grieving, in my own way."

"Why did you lie to him? "Alex complained.

"See what I mean?" Russell piped in. Apparently he had just shown up.

"My dad will understand. Just tell him the truth."

"Dane has been through a lot too, and frankly, he is at wit's end. He will think she's lost it, and will feel forced to send her to someone else who will help her. You know what will happen then?"

"He wouldn't do that to Tess."

"But you are willing to take that chance? You feel perfectly fine, letting her risk it all for you!"

Their bickering was giving me a headache. I shook my head and put my hands up to my ears to shut the noise and Dane out.

"Are you okay, Tess?" Dane asked, tired and concerned. "Because Social Services just called. They want to meet with you."

"About what?"

"Who, you mean? About who?" he asked pointedly. "Robyn. They want to visit you and see how it's going with Robyn."

"Why?"

"In light of recent events, and with the death of your husband, they want to make sure you are still fit to parent Robyn."

This snapped me out of my stupor. Memories of me, vowing never to put my own children through what I was going through in foster care, flashed before me. Panic set in, as I realized that I may have become an unfit parent. I did everything she needed for survival, but….

"Tess?" Dane asked again. He was leaning forward and looked at me intently.

"Yes, of course. I'll—when? When are they coming?"

"Next Monday."

"That's in one week!" I observed as I nodded. "I'll be ready."

Dane got up with effort and started to leave the room, but then stopped and turned to look at me again. "Do you need something to help you sleep better at night?"

"No. Why?"

"Because I hear you walking around the house at night, talking to yourself or …" he looked around the room for signs of an entity, "someone who isn't there."

I had no recollection of doing this. Could it be that I would sleep walk and not remember it? *I need to get my act together.* I raked my hair with my fingers and was shocked to find the length so short. I remembered that it was short now. I rushed to the bathroom to see again what I looked like. What I saw was not pretty. I looked like a ghost myself. If the Social Worker saw me like this they would for sure think that there's something wrong with me.

Ignoring the Admiral, Alex and now Celeste who were arguing in the bedroom, I reached for my forgotten aromatherapy bag and started a bath. I mixed and matched scents until I got a steamy fragrant bath going. After closing the door I sunk in the bath and floated there with just my face out of the water. I took in the smell of rosemary and mint, letting it both relax and energize me. My actions may have clued my ghostly entourage to give me some time alone, so I enjoyed the beautiful sound of silence for a while.

Once dressed and put together, I headed for the kitchen for some tea. I also intended on making dinner for everyone. Eating together was something we hadn't done in … I couldn't remember the last meal we all shared together. I think it was before…before…I couldn't bring myself to say it. Alex was still here with us—he might be dead—but he was still here!

Thin as a rail, Valerie shuffled into the kitchen and reached for my cup of tea, claiming it as her own with a smirk. I hadn't seen her in a long time, weeks, maybe a month. She looked old, frail and weak. Her hair needed styling as well, and her usual gym fit body looked skeletal. Her skin seemed to be thinly stretched over her bones like a silk blanket.

"I don't know how you do it," she said as she smelled the tea, "but you make the best cup of tea."

"It's one of my many hidden gifts," I said with irony.

Valerie raised an eyebrow, took a sip, then closed her eyes, relishing my creation. "Mm … it never fails." She opened her eyes and watched me as I made myself another cup.

"I hear I'm not the only one who's been acting crazy lately," she sneered from above the rim of her cup, while taking another sip. "It seems Dane is running his own insane asylum right here!"

I looked at her steadily and she looked back at me unblinkingly. "He says that you have been talking to yourself, having whole animated conversations and chess games with thin air." This seemed humorous to her and she couldn't suppress a laugh. "With all the crazy things I've done over the years, you just went ahead at topped them all!"

"I can hear him," I said matter-of-factly. I don't know what possessed me to be so upfront with her. The fact that I was being considered crazy didn't bother me, but the burden of secrecy did. Telling Valerie seemed easier somehow. At the very least, she couldn't commit me to the loony bin.

Upon hearing my words, her face fell, and she put her cup

down. "Him who?"

Now it was my turn to laugh. "All of them; I can hear them all!"

"Why did you bring me here?" Alex asked, annoyed.

"I want you to see what you two are doing, from another perspective." Russell led the way to an old Victorian home, newly remodeled and immaculately decorated to the time period. They flew through the house until they came to the study. On a chair sat Eros, slumped, and staring off into no particular place. Off to one side of the room, floated Leo with a satisfied grin on his face.

"Alex, good to see you! Russell." He nodded to the Admiral. *"What brings you guys here?"*

"How's your haunt going, Leo?" Russell asked while surveying the comatose man on the chair.

"Well, it's hard to know exactly what he's thinking, but by the look of his aura, I would say that he is pretty much miserable." Leo said triumphantly.

"Hmm ... " Russell mused. *"So what exactly is your end goal here, Leo? What exactly do you wish to accomplish?"*

"To drive him insane, of course. To make the rest of his life as miserable as possible."

Russell nodded. *"Well it seems to be working well so far. What now?"*

Leo shrugged.

"Tell me this, Leo. What happens if you do your job so well that he ends up committing suicide?"

"That's his prerogative, I guess. Not mine."

"Really? Not yours? What if he does this as a direct result of your haunt? Do you think that you will not be held responsible for that at some point?"

Leo stared dumbly at Russell. This point had not occurred to him. He just figured that he would drive his half brother insane and give him a taste of what is like to feel persecuted, like he was by him. He never even made a point to hide who he was. He freely haunted him and told him who he was and what he was doing and why. He reminded Eros day in and day out of his murders, and his dirty deeds as a drug dealer and even as a kidnapper of American soldiers with the intent of selling them to terrorists, so they could be executed on camera. And all for what? Money? And what was money to him now? Nothing.

Having all his sins continually before him made Eros paranoid. He ate and drank insatiably, though nothing had flavor. Food, something that was once one of his favorite things, had lost its taste. Sleep evaded him. Agatha even tried some of her "potions" from her book and they only gave him a fitful nightmarish kind of sleep. He had even cried with real tears and begged his wife to do some sort of exorcism, but nothing she tried seemed to work.

This enraged Agatha and antagonized her even further. Revenge was also in her sights. She knew exactly who was haunting her husband, and she plotted revenge. She knew just how to hit this ghost where it would be sure to hurt the most, so she wove a new link in this chain of hate and torture that had started so long ago by a jealous and covetous man—Ricardo. He had forged the first link with his anger at losing Celeste to a poor priest. The second link came later and quite by accident when Max died, but the third and fourth…those were planned. He married Celeste under duress, then deliberately flaunted his mistress in front of pregnant Celeste.

When Eros was born, his mother Anabella, filled her son's head with nothing but entitlement and jealousy; those were additional links in the chain. Little by little this chain got longer and longer and thicker until now it weighed heavily around the ankles of many. Like shackles, those who had woven the links got tangled in them, not knowing that undoing them would be much harder than making them.

Leo was now shackled too, though he didn't know it. He could have freed himself of the whole situation, but instead bound himself even tighter to it, and deep inside he felt the weight of it.

"Leo, if he kills himself, his blood will be on your hands."

Russell said pointedly. *"This is why we,"* he pointed to the three of them, *"departed spirits have to follow strict rules when it comes to coming back to Earth. We can't just show up, untrained, unassigned, and with a personal vendetta...or agenda."* He looked at Alex. *"Tess doesn't look much better than him and she might lose custody of Robyn because of you."*

"Why does she look bad?" Leo looked at Alex accusingly. *"I thought you said you would protect her?"*

"I am! We do the same things, well not the same things, but we just talk and spend time together."

"All her time together!" Russell added. *"She hardly interacts with anyone else! That was not the case when you were alive."*

"I had a life!"

"Exactly and now you don't. So let her *have one!"*

"You two need to leave these people alone," Russell ordered. *"Before something happens that you'll both regret ... more than dying!"*

The silence that prevailed in the room was only interrupted by a crazy scream from Eros. He then reached for a bottle of whisky and poured himself a full glass. He drank it thirstily and staggered out of the room.

"Agatha! Agatha! I had a life! I had a life!" he yelled and pulled his disheveled hair out.

"What? What is it?" Agatha was out of breath as she rushed toward him.

"Shhh … they'll hear you," Eros whispered inches from her face, blowing his rank breath on her and swaying dangerously from one side to another. Agatha moved away, repelled by the stench of fermented alcohol on an empty stomach.

"Who?" she asked callously.

"The four horsemen … no, make that three," he slurred.

Agatha started to walk away, when Eros grabbed her forearm with unusual strength and pulled her back toward him. Not long ago Eros had kept himself meticulously well groomed and in shape, but in the last month or so he had completely let himself go. He now resembled a swine, more than a man. Agatha recoiled from him, grimacing with disgust. She brusquely yanked her arm free from her husband. He grabbed her again and with a malicious look pulled her back even closer now. "I know how to make him pay," he whispered, as he petted her head with a heavy hand.

The certainty in his bleary eyes let her know that he was serious.

"Fine," she responded through gritted teeth, "then get on with it." She jerked her arm free and left the room with contempt.

Chapter 33

"All of them?" Valery swallowed a lump in her throat.

"I have heard just my grandmother, since I was very young, but over time I've been able to hear more. I've been spending a lot of time with Alex; he's the one who usually comes. Your dad, your grandmother, your mother … I've heard them too."

A gurgle of laughter formed in Valerie's throat, then another and another, until she emitted a full out hearty laugh. Her laughter made me crack a smile and pretty soon I too was bent over the counter laughing.

"We'll kill Dane, you and I, with our craziness. We'll wear him out and then we'll live to a ripe old age—two old batty widows!" she laughed heartily, "We'll have lots of cats too … we need cats, you know, or it won't count." Her eyes were half shut as her laughter wore off. "How about Katie? Has Katie come to you?"

I shook my head and took another sip of my now cold tea. "Not really, I've heard her talk to Robyn, though."

"Can Robyn?" She trailed off.

"Hear her?" I thought about it for a minute, "I don't know. Not like me anyway. Children are more receptive and sensitive to those things."

Valery turned to ash and nodded slowly. "So they're still around." She waved her hand in the air above her head.

I nodded. Her eyes filled with tears now and a few drops spilled down her sunken cheeks. "Well that helps … I suppose."

"You don't think I'm crazy?"

She lifted her gaze. "I wouldn't be the best judge of normalcy, but for Robyn's sake we're going to have to pretend to be. If they take her away … "

She didn't have to say it—I knew.

"I'm sorry we screwed this up so bad for you, Tess. I was being selfish. I see that now."

"Huh? Alex?" I was so exhausted, my head had a hard time waking up. I wasn't sure if I was dreaming Alex's voice or actually hearing it.

"Alex! Russell!" Celeste burst in agitated. *"Leo! He's done it! Like I told him so many times that he would if he persisted! I told you this was a bad idea!"*

"No ... " Russell said aghast. *"Alex, I'm going to Boston. Are you coming?"*

"Give me a minute," Alex whispered.

Dinner as a family had gone well. Luckily there were no...visitors from the other side to distract me from the conversation. We talked and we planned, we even laughed a few times. Laughter felt strange leaving our throats, good, but strange. In the end, we decided that once the person from Social Services left we would all go on vacation to visit my aunts and Dorian in Mexico. It felt good to plan. Part of me felt guilty for this, but I did catch myself wishing not to be able to hear Alex so much. I loved it! I did ... but ...

I got ready for bed for the first time in—I don't know how long. I actually changed into pajamas and bathed Robyn, then read her a story and tucked her in her bed. I didn't need tea or anything else to help me fall asleep. I simply fell in my bed and lost consciousness until I heard Alex tell me something.

"Mm ... Alex?" I knew it was him because I felt a faint chill brushing against my lips and my cheek. The sensation stirred my senses, somewhat but I felt like I was down in a tunnel and I couldn't quite get out of it.

"I just wanted to say good-bye."

"Wh—where are you going?"

"Shhh ... " he soothed.

Leo? Did I hear Leo's name being mentioned? What did he do? What was Celeste all upset about? "Leo ... " My mind drifted off to sleep. After a few moments I tried to will it back to the moment, "Alex!"

"Yes, Tess. Your dad has done something. I'm going to go help him if I can." Silence. The room was perfectly silent for a long while and I drifted off again.

" … Help him? Alex?" I was trying to rouse my head awake but it was no use, I was so bone tired. Did Dane slip something in my drink during dinner?

"Tess? Good-bye, love."

"Good-bye? You'll be back, right?" Suddenly the panic that word inflicted on my brain woke me.

"No, baby, I have to go. It's for your own good. I have to let you … live!"

"No! No!" I struggled to wake myself up and willed my mind to gain its faculties. "I didn't mean it Alex, I want you to stay! It's different with us! I get that! We can make it work! I'll try harder! We can schedule visits! Just as if we were dating again! Oh heavens! … Again? We never dated! We'll do it now!"

"No Tess, I have to go. I have to undo a great wrong, and I have to prevent another one." His cool lips brushed my cheek.

My eyes opened wide and I sat up, "Alex, don't! Stay with me!" I begged.

"I'm sorry, Tess. It was wrong of me to even come. I see that now. I have made things worse for you and Robyn. Maybe a lot worse than I care to admit."

"No, no, no … that's not true. It's my fault! I can handle it! I always could, I just—it'll get easier with time. I'll get used to it, like I did with Celeste. It was hard at first too with her! Alex, don't you dare leave me!"

"Tess … "

I felt chills all over and I couldn't suppress a shiver. "What!" I snapped, but his cool touch soothed me.

"Death will not do us part." And just like that his chilly touch disappeared, leaving me shivering all the same.

"Alex?" I whimpered and crawled into bed, bunching into a tight ball. "Alex," I mumbled again and again, while tears soaked my pillow.

Now that sleep had finally left me, I wished it would return so I could spend some time unconscious. Instead, darkness descended on me—again, but this time I felt a despair that was all consuming. I could hear static all around me, like when a radio loses its signal. The sound grated on my nerves and made me feel completely and utterly alone and isolated.

Emptiness filled me and all I could envision was a future of loneliness and sorrow, much in contrast to the way I had felt a few hours ago during dinner. All that seemed to have vanished with the light of day and I felt sure that I would lose Robyn and that Dane and Valerie would not want me in their home ever again. Dorian and my aunts seemed distant and no longer part of my life.

"It's all over ... " a sound broke from the static.

"... All alone ... " another sound came at me from another angle. *"To be with him, you must die!"*

"End it!"

"Go to him now," voices assailed me from all angles. I stopped my ears, but the thoughts broke through and I could hear them better and better. *"It'll be painless ... "*

"Valerie has strong pills. Take them!"

"End it!"

"No!" I screamed. "That is not the way!"

"It was all a lie anyway ... "

"You are insane; you hear voices in your head."

"I'm not insane, they are real! They exist, just in another—"

Laughter filled the room, evil mirthless laughter. *"Schizophrenia ... that's what it's called. That's the term for people who hear voicessss ... "*

" ... And roam the house at night ... "

" ... Talking to themselves ... "

" ... Locking yourself up in your room for days ... "

" ... Neglecting your niece and your work." All kinds of different voices assailed me from different angles so I couldn't escape them.

"Admit it Tess, you are a crazy lunatic and you know it!"

"There is nothing after death, nothing at all."

"You live and you die and that's it."

"No, that's not true." But even as I said it I doubted. Could they be right? Didn't I just get done telling Valerie that they all still lived? Could I just be totally crazy and suffering from a mental disorder? That wouldn't be so preposterous after all … I did act crazy, I did freak people out with the way I behaved.

I got up and rushed to the bathroom. I looked in the mirror and I did look tortured and sick!

"You see? Your reflection doesn't lie. You are mentally ill. You imagine talking to all your dead relatives because you simply cannot accept the fact that they are all gone! Gone, Tess, gone for good, never to return."

"But they believe me! Valerie believes me!"

"Valerie is sick too. She has been committed, twice! You were catatonic during that time, so while you were checked out, she was checked in! Ha, ha, ha, ha!" The horrible laughter continued and grated at my nerves. I put my hands to my ears to stop the noise and I started humming to myself to drown out that horrible sound.

"Aunty Tess?" Robyn's little hand tapped me on the thigh. Her outline shone against the light that filtered from the open door. She was holding on to her rag dolls and a blanket. She could not have looked more angelic. Her presence seemed to dispel the darkness that surrounded me.

"Yes?" my voice cracked.

"Why did Uncle Alex leave?"

"He died, sweetie, he died." I said trying to think straight.

"I know that … but why did he leave? Will he come back?"

"I don't know."

"Is he in Heaven now with Mom and Dad?"

Earlier today I would have given her a resounding yes for an answer. But now … what if I was schizophrenic? What if I had just invented whole conversations from an early age? What if I've had a mental disorder my whole life?

"Is he, Aunty Tess? Is he with them too?"

Tears blinded me. I stretched a hand out and she rushed to my side. "I don't know," I told her as I held her.

She clung tightly to me then kissed me on the cheek. "I think so, because he said good-bye."

I tucked her back into bed and wearily made my way back to my room. I threw myself listlessly down and wept miserably, calling for Celeste or Alex, or any other spirit who cared to prove to me that I was not crazy. But the time passed wretchedly and I had no visitations.

After some time, it occurred to me how to find out for sure if I was insane or not. This would prove once and for all whether I was crazy or not.

Agatha let out a blood-curdling scream, then another, and another. Ire flowed through her veins; the cast-out devils fueled her fury as they swirled around her, happy, dancing as it were with delight. They stirred Agatha's rage and escalated the events to the point that she was now convinced that Tess was solely responsible for Eros' death.

With every new piece of malignant information, Agatha's distorted countenance reflected her rapidly darkening soul. If she was ever determined to succeed in her goal, she was more so now. If she ever hated, she hated more now. If she was cold, ruthless or murderously dangerous, she was more so now. The metamorphosis that she had undergone in those few minutes was visible as she stoically cut the rope lose from Eros' neck, letting his limp body fall to the ground with an unceremonious thud.

She walked away from the scene without another look back. Her last vestige of humanity had died with Eros; the beast was now unleashed and she was gathering purpose. Locking herself in her sanctuary, she lit the candles on the floor, stepped into the circle and began her chant. After the chant, she meditated. Her ideas were erratic at first, but then she found a way to focus them and align them in perfect order. She had always been good at this—forming a good plan and persuading people—that was her true gift. The hearing was just an ability, like a sixth sense. It was useful, but alone it was of no worth to her without the other two.

Calmly now, she reached into her pocket and took out her phone.

"Were you successful?" She texted.

"Yes, we're back now."

"Where did you put him?"

"Where you told me to." After hanging up, she left the circle and went to her bedroom. She reached in one of the cupboards and took out the wig. When she was done, she looked approvingly into the mirror.

Relief flooded Eugenia once she landed safely on American soil. She never wanted to see that awful city again; in fact, she didn't care to see any other city again. World travel had been forever soured. Bur her relief was short-lived, however, for the moment she stepped into her apartment, she found herself face to face with the cloaked figure of that mysterious woman with whom she had been dealing. An oversized dark purple hooded cloak covered her face. *"Who wears those?"* Eugenia thought, the moment she managed to slow the beating of her heart.

"How did it go?" the woman inquired evenly.

"Fine … just fine. She's dead."

"You know this for sure? You verified this?"

"W—well, sort of."

"What do you mean, sort of? Did you see Tess' dead body or not?"

"Um, he said he did it."

"And you believed a hired gun?

Eugenia plopped herself on her couch. She was exhausted and didn't want to get into this right now. She had barely slept in the past few days and all she wanted to do was to wash herself clean of this nightmarish situation.

"I didn't get a chance to see her dead body because I was too busy trying to get money to pay him."

"So you paid him."

"Of course! He said he had done the job and told me to pay him! At gun point, I might add!"

The woman's laugh was the most disconcerting thing Eugenia had ever heard. It gave her the creeps, yet sounded uncomfortably familiar.

"You truly are an idiot, aren't you?"

"What? Why?"

The woman turned on the T.V. and a recorded news flash played on the screen. With a serious demeanor the anchorman reported on the untimely death of Congressman Alex Preston, who was shot while on vacation in Buenos Aires. The gunman was said to have burst into a coffee shop and opened fire. Congressman Preston was shot and killed while trying to protect his wife from the attacker.

The woman turned the T.V. off and started for the door.

"This—is why you don't pay until you see the body."

Aghast, Eugenia wondered what was this hellish nightmare that she was living now? She had hired a man to kill the person she hated most, so she could have the person she loved. Now she was left with neither and this awful woman held her own life in her hands. Her passport would put her in the country and she emptied her own bank account on the same day of the shooting.

Anger flooded Eugenia's exhausted frame. She leaped to her feet and grabbed that ridiculous cloak and tore it off the wearer. The woman stopped stock still for a moment while Eugenia gasped for air. Eugenia had no idea why she had done this, and feared that perhaps antagonizing this person was not the best thing to have done, but she was not prepared for what she saw.

The woman turned slowly and revealed a familiar face, somewhat changed by pleasant looking make-up and blond hair, but familiar nonetheless. Eugenia peered into the woman's eyes and her mind reeled back to some elusive memory of those features.

"Remember me, Genie?"

Eugenia's mouth fell open. What did this mean? Had these freaky foster sisters ensnared her somehow? She staggered back toward her sofa and sat back down.

"Your life belongs to me, Eugenia. From now on, I say move and you move. I say speak and you speak. Understand?"

Eugenia nodded numbly.

From that moment on, that was exactly what happened. Eugenia found herself operating as some sort of assistant to Agatha. She woke up to the sound of Agatha's messages, telling her to do this or that errand for her. Then she was made to accompany the woman to different appointments and get lunches and coffee while Agatha held private meetings with some pretty important and impressive people.

But Eugenia didn't walk away empty handed; she got crumbs now and then. Agatha would give her cash, here and there, and one time she even surprised Eugenia with new clothes. It was odd, but who was she to say no to designer clothes? Besides, Agatha got showered with gifts from grateful "clients who saw no other way to please their "medium" or "muse" than through merchandise and expensive gifts.

"Why did you call me to do this?" Eugenia looked disgusted at the sight of the rope and the body on the floor.

"Because, in a way, his death is your fault," Agatha said, as she picked up the body by the arms. Eugenia moved around to the legs and with a look of repulsion, bent down and picked them up.

"I don't see how," she grunted with the effort. Why was it that limp bodies were so heavy?

"I do."

"Enlighten me," Eugenia groaned as they shuffled toward the living room.

"You're an empty headed twit who failed in a most simple task killing Tess. You didn't even have to pull the trigger. All you had to do is make sure someone else got the job done."

"I already told you, the guy I hired was the one who failed. I told him who the target was. But how was he supposed to know that

Alex would jump in front of her?" This thought was doubly bitter to Eugenia, who had hopes of winning Alex's heart back once Tess was out of the picture, and also because he had proven his love for his wife by such a heroic act. This last thought intensified her dislike for Tess.

"No, you failed, because you hired him, and you failed because you paid him."

"Well, I've never hired a killer before! How was I supposed to know how the procedure works?"

"You were not committed to the task. You cared more about what stilettos to wear on your way out of town, than how or if the work was done," Agatha said through gritted teeth. Then with a little more effort they heaved the body onto a couch and left him there while Agatha retrieved a dagger from the wall.

This wall was covered in a rather disturbing collection of this type of weaponry, all ranging from the very old and primitive to the very new and deadly. Agatha chose a small but sharp one.

"Stay! We are not done here," Agatha ordered.

"I'm not touching any more dead bodies," Eugenia said, while brushing a loose strand of hair back with one perfectly manicured finger.

"You won't have to. Just do as I say and work on your acting skills."

Eugenia let out a frustrated sigh, as she plopped on a red velvet winged back chair. "What will I get in return?"

"Hmm ... let's see ... maybe you will *not* get a life sentence and if you do it really well, you might just get the chance to become one with the Source."

"I don't care about your mumbo jumbo Source crap! I want my career back!"

"Career?" Agatha sneered, then laughed. "When did you ever have a career?"

Eugenia narrowed her eyes venomously.

"You are a twit; you'll never have a "career" until you learn how to handle yourself a little bit better. The Source can only help you so much. At some point you have to help yourself."

"The Source did nothing for me, you did."

"The Source works through me; he counsels me and guides me. But it doesn't come for free. The Source requires things … I have given all to him, and now he requires more of you."

"Like what?"

"Pledge yourself to him. Give him your word that you will obey him."

Eugenia snorted, "In return for what?"

"Your career."

"That's not enough. I want more."

Agatha narrowed her eyes. "Well, Alex is dead. You can't have him back."

"I don't want Alex. I want Tess. And I want to be released from my slavery to you! And I want money. Lots of it!"

Agatha laughed. Then she walked closer to Eugenia and regarded her for a moment before leaning in even closer. "Pledge yourself—tonight," she whispered in her ear.

Hours later, the police left with Eros' bagged up body and an incriminating tape containing footage of his murder at the hand of a woman with short dark hair. Eugenia was in the tape as well. She used up all the acting skills necessary to play the part of the person who found the bloody body and called the police.

That night Agatha inducted Eugenia into her society. The ceremony was attended by a handful of people that Eugenia would have never guessed would be this involved in suck an operation, among them the Chief of Police. He was the one who had taken the fake tape earlier that day. She also saw political leaders, major business owners and a few celebrities among the chosen hooded faces who had already pledged themselves to the Source. Soon shock turned into awe and awe turned into greed and greed into belief. These people had gotten where they were *because* of the Source. They were living proof that this … thing, whatever it was, was real.

This new reality hit a whole new level when the initiation started and she was required to participate in the ritual. She was apprehensive, yet all the others were unflinching participants, so she would have to be so as well. Each part of the ritual broke her down just a little further. Each task killed one of her sensibilities and darkened her soul. Yet she found that she desired the outcome more than her soul. Perhaps her desires were her soul, and that's all that really mattered.

Eugenia got sick a few times, like she got sick a few hours earlier when she watched Agatha stab her dead husband over and over. All the participants moved about in zombie-like trances. Their eyes had no light, no pity, just blank stares as she tried to finish all the tasks.

When it was all over, Eugenia stood in the center of a candlelit circle, naked, painted with blood and broken. It was hard to imagine that these proud hooded figures had ever endured this same treatment. But apparently they did.

Afterwards, during the party, Eugenia was greeted warmly by the elites of the group—those who had watched her sell her soul earlier. It was a well-attended event by all the members of the society, the elites who had pledged themselves, and the others, who hadn't gotten that far yet. She was patted on the back, taken in, made one of them, introduced, treated with respect and promise. Naturally under this distinguished treatment, Eugenia was able to quiet her qualms. A toast was given in her honor and she was the center of attention.

Those not part of the "inner" circle, wondered why these distinguished personalities were showering Eugenia—of all people—with their attention and respect. Like the subjects to the naked Emperor, they soon convinced themselves that there must be some good reason for this behavior, so they too joined in and took interest in Eugenia. Business cards were given, promises of lunches, dinners, parties and even jobs were offered. Eugenia couldn't believe how quickly it was all working out for her and she reached the only conclusion possible—the Source was real.

Chapter 34

Like a hound dog picking up a scent, I was led to this house in what looked to be a respected suburb of Boston. I was certain that this was the right place, yet now that I was here, it felt oddly desolate in spite of the fact that the house looked full of people.

I parked some distance down the road, and started walking up the thickly treed sidewalk.

"You've just missed him," a man's voice cut through the stillness of the night. I startled and turned, only to see the timeless face of Officer John Lovell.

"Who?" I asked, regaining my composure.

"Him," he motioned with his head upward toward the sky.

I felt like he had just punched me in the stomach and my knees buckled right there. In two strides, he was at my side and helping me up. "I don't understand anything," I said, confused and disoriented.

John held me up and led me back to my rented car. I gave him the keys and he sat me in the passenger seat. He then went around the other side and sat in the driver's seat. He didn't turn the engine on; he simply sat there and exhaled. His face looked weary, but his eyes were bright.

"Who are you?"

"I told you, I'm—"

I shook my head. "No, what are you?"

He smiled, then his smile turned into a soft laugh. "It seems we are bound to have this conversation time and time again." My puzzled look made him laugh again. "I'm an Aeonian, like Mathoniaha, remember him?

I frowned, then nodded numbly. "The hobo? I mean the guy who helped us in Mexico?"

"Yep, the same one." He chuckled. "He'll be happy to hear that he pulled it off so well."

"Pulled what off, and what's an Aeonian?"

"We are agents, if you will, humans who have sworn to spend the rest of Earth's existence in the service of the Eternals."

"Like a priest?"

"N—ot quite. We don't represent any specific church. We serve only the Eternals. By that I mean God."

"Yeah, Celeste calls them that too ... but what do you mean 'the rest of Earth's existence?'"

"We will not die until the world ends."

"You're immortal?"

"No," he shook his head, "not immortal, Aeonian. We are somewhere in between mortal and immortal. Blood still runs through my veins." He showed me his forearm and the blue veins that so clearly carried blood. "There are some perks though. As Aeoninans we possess an uncanny ability to heal. We feel no physical pain, we don't age, we do feel emotional pain and sadness but we can see the whole picture, and this gives us perspective."

"That's why you looked exactly the same in that picture." I marveled.

"What? What picture?" He asked with alarm.

"My aunts showed me a stack of pictures of my father; you were in one of them."

John shook his head, then nodded. "I tried to wiggle out of being in that picture, but your father would not have it. He insisted on me standing right there next to him." He shook his head again. "He suspected me. The little devil! He was trying to blow my cover."

I turned and looked at him with alarm. On seeing this, John laughed again. "I'll be needing that photo, by the way."

"It's one of the only pictures I have of him."

"Don't worry. I'll photo shop it, and then give it back."

"Have you always been ... Aeonian?"

"No. We all used to be mortal, but when we decided to stay and become Aeonian, we were changed."

"How long have you been alive?"

"A long time," he said with a final tone.

"So ... what are you doing here? I thought you were a detective in Dallas."

"I was a detective in Dallas, but I had to move on. I can only stay in one place for so long before people start noticing that I don't age."

"So what are you now?"

"Right now I have to see you through this. Then I'm off … back to my native land! I haven't been there in ages."

"Where's your native land?"

"Israel."

"Really? And when you say ages, you mean … "

A smile stole across his face. "I'm the John who wrote Revelations."

The phone at the Preston's rang and no one picked up. Finally it stopped, then started up again. Blurry eyed, Dane made his way to the loud thing and answered it with resentment.

"Yes?"

"Dane? Is that you? This is Amor, um … Tess' aunt. I'm sorry to call you at this time, I'm sure it's still very early there, but I couldn't wait any longer."

"Yes, yes of course Amor," Dane rubbed his eyes and tried to suppress his annoyance at the early call. Then again, it might be an emergency.

"It's Dorian, Dane! He's been taken! Kidnapped, we think," she added, coming to the point quickly, as if reading his mind.

"What? Taken? Dorian, why?"

"Oh, I don't know, I just don't know. We've been looking for him all night, and nothing! There's been a string of kidnappings here lately, all drug related, but … I don't know. We don't know what else to do. We've called the local authorities, but so far we got nothing. I feel so awful! He was left in our care!"

By now Valerie was by the phone tying her robe and looking at Dane inquisitively. He covered the receiver told her the news. At once she ran to get Tess.

Luz's hysterical voice could be heard above the loud hubbub at the other end of the line. "The empty ones took him! The empty ones!"

"What? What does that mean?" Dane asked Amor.

"We don't know. She's been like that all night. You see, Dorian and Luz were in town yesterday passing out food to some of the people we visit, when he disappeared. No one saw anything and all Luz can say is that. We've asked her to explain, but ... nothing."

"Is that why you think he was kidnapped?"

"She's gone!" Valerie shouted. She ran to Dane holding a single piece of paper. "She's gone!" she repeated as she handed Dane the note.

"I'm not crazy, and I will prove it."

Like a puppeteer, Agatha watched from the sidelines how all her strings moved in perfect synchronicity. She reveled in her power over people; she reveled in the thought that the lives of all these people—whether they realized it or not—depended on her. She was the architect of their future and the one who the Source trusted to lead his chosen people here and now. With Eros as her ally, she had built this. He had come into her life at a crucial point. He had trusted and believed in her implicitly, and had turned over to her all that he had accomplished in his life. Building from his platform was easier than starting at the bottom. Now he was gone.

The spirits had laughed and said that for once it wasn't them, Leo, Tess' father, had taken it upon himself to punish Eros. Leo had done such a great job that he had succeeded in driving the man to madness. Now Eros was gone forever and nothing would bring him back. Revenge was the only recourse now. *An eye for an eye*, Agatha thought. No one takes the man I love without feeling my full wrath.

"Watch what you're doing, you idiot!" Agatha snapped to a waiter who spilled a tray of drinks on her.

"Sorry, ma'am," the man said with a thick accent. "I'll … clean that right up," he added, while whipping out a large white napkin and dabbing some of the areas where the drinks spilled.

"Give me that!" Agatha wrenched the napkin from his grasp and cleaned herself up. "Who are you? I've never seen you before."

"New, ma'am." The man bowed and backed away.

"I didn't hire anyone new."

"Javier, ma'am; he's my cousin. He's sick and I came for him."

Agatha squinted, and peered into the man's face. "What's your name?"

"Mathoniaha, ma'am."

She stared numbly at the man, "M—whatever, clean up this mess," Agatha ordered, then left in a rage.

Mathoniaha straightened up, and watched her go with interest, his face no longer showing the submissive look of seconds past, but a sure and steady poker face.

Looking all around, to make sure no one was watching her, Agatha slipped through the pantry door and disappeared. She groped in the darkness until she found the latch and hurriedly opened the door. She rushed down the steep narrow steps and took out a key from the folds of her robes. Excitement and a rush of adrenaline surged through her veins. "Tonight will be momentous," she thought. She could feel the static and the churning of the spirits in the air. Tonight she would acquire more power—one way or another—she would gain Dorian's and Tess' gifts.

Crouched in a corner, Dorian rocked himself back and forth.

"We've never been friends … have we Dorian?

Dorian continued rocking, ignoring the sound of that voice. He still had no idea what had happened. One moment he was in town with Luz passing out food and the next he woke up here. All his senses told him that he was in deep trouble, but none of them told him what to do about it. Now she shows up. For a second he thought it was Tess, because of the hair. But it wasn't, it was *her*! He hated her.

Knowing how to respond to things had never been his strong suit; the world puzzled him to no end. People would say one thing, then do another. No one was consistent in anything. How could he know what the best way to respond would be? He marveled at the way people interacted with each other, the need to talk and express every little detail about themselves …

Luz talked a lot, but she was different. She only said what she meant and she did what she meant—and she talked with angels. He knew early on that Tess could also hear them, even before she knew it. With Tess, life had been easy. She knew what he was thinking, so she saved him a lot of grief. She also understood his need for consistency. She was in trouble now though; he knew this. He saw it in his head. He had also seen this room before … it had been in his mind last week. That could only mean one thing—death.

"She kept you from me. She was careful not to tell me of your … abilities, Dorian. But now I know. I want you to draw, draw anything that comes to your mind. Do you understand?" Agatha bent over and peered into Dorian's eyes.

He hated that, so he looked away. When people got too close he could hear, smell and see every little detail about them and it was overwhelming to his senses.

"I will provide all you need: food, water, an unlimited supply of pencils and paper," she pointed to the stack of #2 pencils and copy paper. Unfortunately it was the wrong brand of paper, so he would have no use for it. He almost said this much, to save her the trouble, but the words wouldn't come out.

"I know you like to listen to classical music, so I made sure you have your radio and all the classical music you want! You don't have to do chores, like you did over in Mexico, where Tess dumped you. I will be a better sister, Dorian. I will take care of you much better than she ever did."

Inpatient and frustrated by his lack of reaction and the lack of information that the spirits could extract from him, Agatha left him, locking the door behind her.

"Just remember," John grabbed my arm before I started going up the steps to the house. "Those who are with us, are more than they who are with them."

In the car he had explained to me what had happened. He told me how Alex and Leo got angry and came back when they weren't supposed to. He explained to me that that was considered a haunting and that it never ends well.

John told me about Eros' death and that Alex had left me and come here to persuade my dad to leave, but it was too late. He also told me that I would likely never hear Alex's voice again until my time came and I crossed over. This angered me; it seemed too unfair. What was the point in having a sixth sense if I couldn't use it? Why give me a gift like that if I couldn't reach those whom I loved?

Patiently he explained that gifts were given so that we could accomplish our missions on Earth. He said that I didn't remember this, but that I had chosen and agreed to my mission and that now it was time for me to fulfill my destiny.

"In there," he said, "resides one of the biggest threats this generation has seen. She doesn't know it, but her influence over people and what she's created will soon be out of her hands and will take on a life of its own. She may control it now, but not for long. When it gets out of control it will invade everything! It has the potential of becoming something impossible to eradicate. A secret society so evil and so entrenched in the ruling powers of the world that will expedite Armageddon.

"Trust me, I've seen the end. And this … " he pointed toward the house that held the seed to destruction, "this has to be stopped now."

"Are you saying that I'm supposed to stop her? How?"

"You also are the only one impervious to her. You have an understanding of her nature that is … unique."

"Agatha?" I shook my head uncomprehendingly.

He proceeded to tell me about her society and all the things she had been up to since she ran away from Charlotte's house. She had married my uncle Eros; she was behind Alex's death—my death gone wrong. In fact, everything he said felt like a new blow.

"And," he added, "she recently kidnapped Dorian. He is being held captive."

"What? How?" I opened the car door and was about to rush to the house.

"Rescuing him is *not* why you need to go in there," he warned, grabbing my arm. "Your job is to stop her and to destroy this society." His eyes looked intent and carried a warning in them.

"By stopping her you mean … "

He nodded.

"I can't kill anyone."

"Is better that one evil person die than a whole generation fall. Think of what I've told you. She is being led by cast-out spirits to bring an early end to this world. The time is not yet."

I shook my head emphatically. "Sorry, you have the wrong person. I can't do that. I can't believe that God would ask me to that either."

He bit his lip, then closed his eyes.

"David slew Goliath."

"I'm not David."

"It's your destiny," he said solemnly. "When the time comes you will know what to do."

I got out of the car and started toward the house. It was bustling with voices and the din of dishes and wine glasses. After his warning, or rather his assurance that I had help … more perhaps than I realized, I knocked on the door.

To my surprise the man from Mexico, Mathoniaha, opened the door. He was dressed like a butler. I turned to see John's expression, but he had evaporated. There was no sign of him anywhere.

Wordlessly, Mathoniaha ushered me in. He nodded once as I crossed the threshold and his eyes seemed to say, "Don't blow my cover. But I'm here for you."

Inside, the house was full of people I recognized from T.V. It was a wide assortment of celebrities and politicians. They were all wearing purple hooded robes, but underneath they looked as if they were dressed for a formal cocktail party. They ignored me, or let me be, as I passed through the room. Only a few people glanced at me but quickly looked away.

This place felt odd—no—not odd … bad. It felt oppressive and uncomfortable. I wanted to just get Dorian and get the heck out of here, but I knew it wouldn't be that easy. Part of me also felt duty bound to be here, to end the whole cat and mouse game with Agatha, and to do whatever I could to stop this society. No, I didn't want to kill Agatha or anyone for that matter, but bringing this world to an early and untimely end didn't sound like something I wanted hanging over my head either.

I moved through the house ghost-like, as if moved by some unseen power. The place didn't look like a home at all, though it had a parlor, a living room and a dining room. Everything seemed void of life; every item looked like a prop for a play.

I found myself in the kitchen, where lots of busy cooks ignored me and went about their jobs with unusual devotion. In front of me was a door that looked like it opened to a large pantry. Something urged me to open it and though the inside was dark, I could discern an L shaped outline of light coming from the back wall.

Narrowing my eyes, I felt my way toward that sliver of light and traced it all the way around until I found small hinges. *A door!* Jamming my fingertips on the edge of the door, I pulled it open and found narrow stairs going steeply down. The wood was old, and you could feel indentations under my feet as only years of use could have made.

At the bottom of the stairs there was a narrow hallway with closed doors at either side, I felt like Alice in Wonderland, trapped in a dream of sorts, or a nightmare. Suddenly a door opened and a woman wearing a red hooded cloak came out. She looked up and…me! It was me! I felt a scream leaving my throat, then … darkness.

Chapter 35

I woke up on a cot in a room with no windows. One of the walls was covered in drawings, familiar drawings! "Dorian!" I heard a scuffle and Dorian's head popped up beside me. He had been lying on the floor beside me.

"Dorian, hi! What? Where are we?" I rubbed my eyes and tried to focus them. Then I felt a sharp pain on my head and I rubbed that too, only to find a goose egg there.

"Ouch!" I had been hit from behind by something heavy.

Instinctively Dorian reached a hand out to comfort me.

"Agatha," he said solemnly, "and Genie."

"Eugenia? She's here? What would she be doing here? And Agatha … " My mind reeled to the last thing I remember seeing before I was hit. It was me! Or someone who looked like me."

"Agatha," Dorian insisted. Could it be? Could Agatha have changed her appearance to look just like me? If so, why?

I looked around me at a windowless room. It was set up like something between a prison cell and a nice hotel room, minus the T.V. and the coffee maker. There was a cot, a desk with a stack of papers—the wrong kind for Dorian to use—several boxes of pencils and pencil-sharpeners. There was another small buffet table with a pitcher of water, paper cups, and some crackers.

"How long have you been here, Dorian?" He shrugged. He didn't know. "Do you remember how you got here?" Again, another shrug and he shook his head no. "Do you know if my aunts are safe?" He looked at me despondently and I knew that this was one of his main worries.

"They are fine, I'm sure. I think she's after us for some reason. I don't know why she wants you, but I know that I've been on her hit list for quite a long time."

Dorian made a sweeping motion with his hand pointing to the drawings he had done on the white wall. Apparently he couldn't bring himself to draw on the wrong paper, so he took to the walls.

But all he had drawn were flames, perfect flames drawn in pencil covering one whole side of the wall. Smoldering in between the flames was this house. "Is that something that will happen or has happened?"

No answer.

His drawings were miraculous, but unpredictable. One couldn't depend on a timeline. The flames could have meant that this house was once in a fire and since restored or it could mean that it would someday be destroyed in a fire. One could never tell.

"Is this why Agatha brought you here?" I asked, pointing to his mural. "It must be."

Dorian nodded then went to the stack of paper, "Wrong kind," he explained innocently.

I got up and hugged him tightly.

"What? Did you say something?" I looked at Dorian quizzically, who shook his head.

"The—tt—time hasss come ... " A static like sound buzzed around my head making me feel dizzy and disoriented. Dorian steadied me.

"Oh, how touching," a sarcastic raspy voice with a British accent startled us. It was a heavily tattooed guy who looked vaguely familiar.

"That's right," he said cockily. "I'm Marcel." Apparently he felt that that was all the explanation I would need and that it should be obvious to me who he was by the mere mention of his first name.

The buzzing started again. They were the same voices that I heard a few hours ago after Alex left me. They spun around me so rapidly that I felt vertigo. My eyes were having a hard time focusing on any specific thing, and my stomach started churning with whatever food I had in my stomach from the night before. I felt like throwing up, but I knew that Dorian would freak out about that, so I turned to Marcel and puked on him instead.

"Oh, bloody hell!"

"Sorry," I said without apology, while I wiped my face. Instinctively Dorian stepped back and plugged his nose.

"Get out!" Marcel ordered while pushing me out of the way. "You'll pay for that you little—" He shoved me again and Dorian started charging toward him, but Marcel shut the door in his face and left him locked up in there with my vomit and that awful smell. I knew that Dorian would not deal well with that and I was proven right by his loud banging on the door.

Marcel pushed me into another room and locked the door, heaping British blasphemies and curses upon my head. The tormenting devils came back too, with more taunting words and more depressing messages as to why I should end my life here and now, intermixing them with dire assurances of the finality of death. The messages were actually contradictory and were driving me crazy.

I was left in this odd room for what felt like a long time, subjected to those unrelenting and depressing voices. The room itself was depressing, looking like a medieval dungeon or a gothic shrine of sorts. Where was Celeste? John had promised help.

"Oh … Alex!" I groaned, hoping, but knowing that he wouldn't come.

The devils laughed. *"He won't come to you, Tess. He's gone! Gone forever!"*

"No. I don't believe you. They still exist!"

"So where are they now, huh?"

"Yes, if they exist, why have they forsaken you?"

"That's because they are all in your head!" They sneered and laughed some more.

"How about you? I can hear you!"

"We don't exist either!" They laughed louder and harder and taunted some more, until finally the door opened and Agatha walked in. She paced the room, studying me as I sat in the fetal position in a corner of the room.

"Well, well, if it isn't Tess." Her hair was blond now, and she no longer looked like my evil twin. "What's wrong, Tess? Is someone bothering you? You look sick." When I didn't respond, she continued, "Did you know that there was a murder committed today?" She paused and looked at me still, like a cat toying with a trapped mouse before eating it. "And do you want to know who it was that committed this murder? You! You, Tess! You killed the only human being that I have ever loved." When she saw the puzzled look in my eyes, she sniggered, "What, you don't remember? Well let me jog your memory." She pushed a button and a projector turned on and the lights dimmed down. A horrible scene was played in the back wall, where a person resembling me stabbed Eros on the chest more times than I cared to count.

"tss ... tsst ... sss" More static sounded in my ear. A different kind but I couldn't hear it. My eyes remained fixed on the frozen image of me, holding a dagger over Eros' body.

"You see, Tess, you're in deep trouble here. So if I were you, I would listen to me carefully."

"That is not me," I said and my voice broke as I said it. "Your hair—"

Agatha shook her head and made a ticking noise with her tongue. "But this video says it is. And as you can see ... I look nothing like you. The police has been informed and you will be arrested and charged—quite ironically—just like your father was, for murder."

"This won't hold up in court. I have proof that I wasn't here when this happened."

"Oh yeah? Well I have proof otherwise, and the Chief of Police, whom you'll have the pleasure of meeting in a few minutes, thinks otherwise.

"Hmm ... let me think, the Judge also, and who else? Oh yeah, we have an additional witness too. You're about to meet them all upstairs because they are all members of my society." She grabbed me by the arm and lifted me to my feet. "And they're all upstairs waiting for their monthly ritual." She shook her head and relished some internal delight. "Tonight, they are all in for a treat. They will see for the first time how power is acquired."

"What? Agatha, you are—"

"No Tess! Not me, you! You are completely crazy. Trust me when I tell you that you need to either rot in prison or in a mental institution! Fortunately for you, I'm willing to offer you a different option."

I shook my head trying to shake this nightmarish situation away.

"Because we are sisters of a sort, I will give you a very unique option. I suggest you take it, because I'm not very patient."

I didn't respond right away. That old feeling like, Agatha was ridiculous, came back to me. "Okay, what is it?"

"You and Dorian can pledge yourselves to the Source and become part of my society, and willingly share your gifts with us, or … I take your gifts by making you and Dorian our sacrifices."

"What?"

"The ritual might not kill you, but it will definitely leave you … hampered. At that point, a mental ward would be the best-case scenario. But chances are, neither one of you will survive and I earn your powers."

"That's the most ridiculous thing I've ever heard! You can't inherit people's gifts by killing them!"

Agatha laughed cynically and I felt like I was trapped in a second rate horror film. "You know nothing of how the Source works, and how power is harnessed. But by the time I'm done with you, you'll be dead or too stupid to understand what happened to you, so I guess you'll never know."

The members of Agatha's society filed into the room in somber procession. They were all hooded and their heads were facing the ground, but I didn't need to see their faces to know that they felt like empty shells. When I saw them earlier I sensed the same thing, though they looked beautiful, prosperous, healthy and fit. However inside, they were hollow and dark, as if there was little humanity left in them.

As he passed me, Marcel turned his head ever so slightly, smiled, and winked mockingly at me. He appeared to have showered and changed since the puke incident. After him another hooded member passed and looked my way. Eugenia, too, looked contemptuously at me and suppressed a derisive smile.

The members of the society took their places around an altar. Agatha was at the head of them. Behind and above her hung a Gothic symbol of sorts that no doubt represented the Source, or whatever it was they worshiped.

The last person to enter brought with him Dorian, who jerked around as the man shoved him into the room. He tried to come to my side, but the man holding him grabbed on to him with both arms and wouldn't let him go.

"Has he drawn anything?"

"He drew a very impressive mural," the man who held Dorian said.

"Well … "

"It's a picture of this house, going up in flames."

"This house was almost destroyed in a fire nearly thirty years ago," a heavy-set older man, spoke up. Agatha turned sharply to look at him, and he cowered. I wonder who he was, and what profession he had outside these walls. He looked well to do. He looked like he was used to being in charge—this place being the exception.

"So it could be the past or the future." Agatha said, turning her attention back to Dorian, who was still writhing in the man's grasp. "Which one is it, Dorian?" She asked in a syrupy voice.

He didn't answer. He didn't even acknowledge that she spoke at all. "Talk to him, Tess!" she ordered me.

"He won't tell us, he never does. Believe me, I've tried," I said matter-of-factually.

"Very well, if he won't cooperate, we'll take the gift from him," she announced. Grabbing a thick goblet, she lifted it up and started reciting something in a strange language. The contents of the cup were red. The scarlet liquid suddenly boiled, spilling over the side. The hooded crowd knelt down on one knee and bowed their heads, repeating certain things at certain times.

When Agatha was done with the blessing, or whatever it was she had done, she took a sip. She swallowed slowly, making a big deal out of it. Then she walked around the room, and like a priest, let each of the hooded people take a sip as well.

They continued with their ritual and chanting in that odd language, then they began to shake, and their eyes rolled to the back of their heads. This fit lasted for a few minutes, before they regained control of their bodies. As the fits subsided, some of them looked slightly irked by the experience. As if this ritual was a bitter cup they had to drink in order to get whatever they got out of this organization. Others, like Marcel, looked like they had just gotten an adrenaline rush, and were jazzed up. All of them looked a little emptier.

"Bring her to me," Agatha demanded, with a low growl that didn't have her usual tenor. I looked for evidence of an electronic voice changer, but saw none. Maybe she had one hidden under her cloak.

Two members yanked me forward and roughly pushed me toward Agatha. Her eyes had changed. They were her eyes, but they seemed to reflect the thoughts of someone else—a second person. As I watched her, she shone differently. It was hard to explain, but it was as if she was ... possessed. Interestingly, she didn't like it. So why did she do it?

"I amuse you, Tess?" the foreign voice asked.

"Who are you?"

"We've met before ... a long, long time ago." The foreign voice broke out into an evil laugh that seemed to shake the room and bristled the hairs on the back of my neck. The voice was so thickly laden with dread and despair that it coated me and everyone else in the room with it. It was evil, simple and pure—undiluted. "Won't you guess my name?" it joked, and then laughed louder.

"Ha! That was a good song," Marcel piped in from the sidelines. The thing inhabiting Agatha turned its head in an un-natural way toward the sound of Marcel's voice. There was no mirth in its expression; nothing of that sort could ever be understood by that being.

"I know ... I wrote it," it commented. "I have written a lot of songs, even some of yours, Marcel."

This last comment made Marcel swallow a lump in his throat and drained his otherwise cocky face of all color. The being that inhabited Agatha now turned its attention back to me and examined me for a moment with hungry eyes.

I felt my body trembling from the inside, but something seemed to be keeping me still on the outside. All the agony that I felt inside seemed to be enhanced to the point that I felt that my strength was failing me and my eyes were becoming unfocused. I tried to fight against that feeling and tried to remember all the good things that had happened in my life, in order to counter the effects of that being, but my brain was having a hard time coming up with any.

"Interesting," the being mused. "She doesn't tremble, she doesn't fall?" As soon as it said that, Agatha started twitching and shaking unnaturally. I moved back to give her room, and in a few seconds she seemed to be rid of the thing that possessed her.

I watched as she regained her composure, and saw relief washing over her as the effects of the possession wore off and she regained command of her senses once again.

"You hate it, don't you?" I whispered. She glared at me with shock and anger. I had found her weak spot. To the rest, who acted like monkeys when they did this, Agatha looked like a supreme being who could handle anything. But the truth was that she seldom did it, and when she did, she hated it.

Furiously, and without delay, Agatha started mumbling some other words. Her followers echoed her chant in a hypnotic, repetitious way. Suddenly, my body went rigid and I could no longer feel my limbs. Everything felt detached from me, even my head! I couldn't even blink. I could see that my feet were no longer touching the ground. I could hear Dorian gasp, but I couldn't turn my head to look at him. My eyeballs wouldn't move in any direction either. All I could do was stare straight ahead unblinkingly and barely breathe enough air through my nostrils to stay alive.

I was clearly levitating. My face was staring at the ceiling's massive candelabra, and my eyes were starting to dry out from the heat the candles emanated. My eyes began to water, but the tears slid down the sides of my nose and wasted away, not giving the needed moisture to my burning eyes. I tried to speak, but I was literally tongue-tied. I wondered if this would damage my eyes permanently—it definitely didn't feel good.

"I want to speak with Eros!" Agatha demanded.

I wanted to tell her to go to hell, but I couldn't. Then I tried to tell her that it didn't work that way, but I still couldn't utter a single word. Some of the onlookers from the "society" started to laugh at my predicament.

I began to wish for a speedy death. My eyes had reached a new level of irritation, and my head throbbed with a migraine caused by sleep-deprivation.

"Make a connection with Eros, and I'll release you!" She growled. She released whatever was binding my face muscles and I was able to blink, but my tears were all dried up and I could barely close my eyes to give them the needed moisture. When I finally got them closed, I kept them shut, hoping that my tear ducts would soon start working again.

"I said, I want to speak with Eros!" she yelled again and extended my arms away from my sockets, all while I was still hovering above her.

"I—c—can't," I groaned, this time from the pain in my arms.

"I know you can talk to the spirits of the dead! I know you have been in communication with your dead husband! Now, call on mine and I'll release you!"

I shook my head to clear it, but she took this to mean that I was denying her my gift, so she started pulling on my legs now. "I—can't talk to dead people! I'm just … sick!"

"Nice try, Tess, but I know better. I've watched you since we were little, and I know that you have had visitations from an early age. Besides, they," she waved her arm in a circle, "are the ones that told me of your gift, so don't pretend with me!"

"Well, *they* are also the ones that told me that I had made it all up and that I was schizophrenic!" I protested.

"Lies!" she shouted, "lies!" She looked around the room at the invisible creatures that presently were laughing. "Don't you hear them, Tess? Can't you hear them?"

"You're right Agatha. They do lie. They do nothing *but* lie. They're lying to you right now. *This*, is *all* a lie," I say wearily.

"Sacrifice her to Monad!" Eugenia shouted from the sidelines.

"Yeah!" Marcel agreed.

At this point I no longer cared. I was done—spent, confused, tired and sick of it all. My eyes were still shut and protested every time I tried to open them. I welcomed death and I told her this much.

"I will not release you until you do as I say. I will torture you and every member of your family until you do."

Ever member of my what? What family? Then I looked off to one side and saw Dorian standing there, avoiding eye contact with everyone, unprotected and completely oblivious to what was going on around him—at least he looked oblivious. Then I thought of little Robyn. She was about the same age I was when I got to Charlotte's house. That seemed like ages ago, like a whole different life!

Suddenly and without any warning, Agatha released me from whatever was holding me up and I fell down, face first with a loud thud.

"You get to choose your path in life," a mystifying looking creature said as she swayed a lion's tail. She was beautiful and completely golden. From her torso upwards, she was human, but from her belly down, she had the body of a lioness. Her expression was calm, wise and sincere. And her eyes … I remember those eyes, I've seen those eyes before … in my dreams.

"You mean I get to choose how my life goes?" I asked, as I brushed the low branch of a huge tree with my hand. I looked disappointed at something.

It was me but I looked different, I had no substance, I was … see-through. I also radiated a soft pink glow that spoke of excitement and determination.

"Don't you wish!" the creature laughed. *"It's more like ... well, you've heard mortals talk about destiny, right? They often say that they feel like they are destined for something or other,"* she said, pausing under the shade of another large-leafed tree that sent its roots down to the ground from its branches.

"Yeah, I've heard them say that." I responded, intent on what she was telling me.

I was looking down on this scene as if I were floating in mid air. I looked around me and noticed that I was in a huge paradisiacal garden. Everything was in bloom. Everything looked pristine, like a heavenly paradise. Was I dreaming? If so, good! This was better than where I was before.

"Well, they do because of this meeting. You will decide the possible course of your life. The Eternals are linked to the High Council, and they use their abilities as seers to show you the direction your life might take. It all depends on your decisions of course, but you will be shown two possible roads your life might take, given two possible circumstances. Then they will show you the possible outcomes of either path. You choose the one you think you want to do." I saw myself being regarded by the creature as she straightened her golden dreadlocks. I knew what I was thinking; I was in awe of her ... her poise, beauty and strength. She embodied everything I wanted to be.

"I would like to be like you ... " I said, and the creature smiled.

"It does depend upon your choices while you are alive," she continued, *"but let's say that you make all the right choices...which path would you rather walk? The easier path, or the harder path?"*

"Doesn't everyone choose the easier path?"

"Some, but not all."

"Well that's silly. Why would anyone willingly choose a harder path if they could help it?"

"I chose the harder path, it made me who I am," she said, and that comment alone convinced me of the course I would choose. I determined that I would choose the harder path, so I could be just like her!

The image of this garden and this conversation faded into a

great cloud-like fog. Everywhere I turned I saw nothing but that impenetrable fog, when out in the distance I saw something shimmery move. I focused my eyes, that no longer felt pain, and I saw her coming out of the fog.

The creature from earlier was walking on all fours toward me. She radiated a beautiful golden light, like sand in a sunny beach. She had a smile on her face and a glint in her eyes that seemed to hold some secret amusement.

She stopped right in front of me and sat on her hind legs. "Are you ready?" she purred.

I wasn't sure how to respond to that. Ready for what? She found my silence or my thought amusing because she smiled as she brought one of her hands forward toward me. She turned her hand over and from her palm sprung a flame.

"Here, hold it until the time comes."

"It will burn me!" I protested.

"It only burns stubble."

I frowned and she moved her hand closer toward me.

"This is the refiner's fire, the burning in the bosom, the Eternals' gift to the pure in heart and the fire and brimstone of the wicked. It will not hurt you or Dorian—I promise."

Uncertainly I extended my hand and she dropped the flame into the palm of my hand as if it were a golden feather. She was right; it didn't burn. All I felt was a slight tickle. I stared at the flame dancing on my hand and the next thing I knew I felt some sort of liquid being poured on my face. I was brought back to the hell I had temporarily left.

"She's back," someone shouted.

"Stand her up, make her watch. Maybe this will help her make up her mind."

With blurry unfocused eyes that I think were permanently damaged by my previous torture, I saw them drag Dorian to the center of the circle. "No! Leave him alone! He doesn't understand!" I pleaded, but this only seemed to encourage them.

Sure now, that torturing Dorian would make me comply with her impossible request, Agatha started. She chanted, raising her hands high above her head. She swayed them from side to side, chanting louder. She tried to make Dorian drink something, but it spilt down his front. The whole time, Dorian stood stock still with his shoulders back and his eyes wide open, looking imposing and regal.

My vision was poor, but I could discern something shiny and white surrounding him, like a cloud made out of pearls. I blinked and tried to focus, but my sight was simply not working properly. Then a thought came to me, *"Those that are with us are more than they who are with them."*

My blurry vision finally began to clear, and I saw four giant winged creatures. Their skin radiated that same pearly whiteness that I had seen earlier in the thick fog. In their hands and between their legs, they held swords that looked like were on fire and they stood stock still as if made out of stone. They stared straight ahead, ignoring all the shadowy figures that tried to ram themselves against them. But, as suddenly as the vision had appeared, it started to fade. I squinted, trying to keep them in focus for as long as possible. Just as the point of vanishing, one of the creatures moved his eyes and winked at me. This gave me a strange sense of familiarity that left me feeling … hopeful.

"I'm not alone," I thought. I looked down at my right hand, and between the fingers of my clenched fist, I could see the flame.

My eyes, that had temporarily seen so clearly, went blurry again. I tried not to let this get to me. I needed to get Dorian and myself out of here, one way or another. But Dorian seemed to be doing just fine on his own. Whatever they tried on him simply failed, and this enraged Agatha. Looking all around me I realized that they were all filled with rage and were in some way or other actively engaged in trying to harm Dorian—an innocent—someone who had never done anything to any one.

Anger bubbled inside of me, indignation too, and a general disgust for what these people were. According to John, these people would speed up the course of evil in this world, and bring an untimely end. I didn't fully understand the ramifications that this would have, but if he was worried, then it would likely not be a good thing.

Upset with the lack of progress, Eugenia brusquely pushed Agatha aside and tried something herself. Of course, this too failed. However, Agatha did not take this mutinous act lightly. Without physically touching her, she swung her arm and sent Eugenia flying clear across the room. Eugenia's back slammed hard against the opposite wall where the exit door was. This created some sort of uproar within the group members and they all started to murmur and complain that they needed to remember what they were there for.

I was seized by Marcel and brought forward as another man reached for Dorian, but as he tried to touch Dorian, he was shocked by what seemed to be an electric shock.

"How are you doing this?" Agatha asked as she swung around with fury.

"I'm not!" I responded clenching my fists.

"Don't lie! I know you can speak with the dead! I know you speak with Alex and your grandmother; what else can you do?"

"They came to me! I didn't call them. And I'm certainly not responsible for whatever is happening with Dorian!"

"Why would Alex come to you and Eros not come to me?"

"I—I don't know! Agatha, don't you see? We are being protected! You can kill me, but you'll never get what you want." I was surprised that as those words came out I felt no anger toward her, only pity, because she was sealing her own doom with her actions.

"Join me!" Agatha looked intense and determined. She truly thought that there might be a chance that I might cave. She couldn't fathom why anyone would not want to exploit a gift such as mine and use it for gain. "Don't you understand, Tess! We could be the most powerful women alive! Why won't you join me?" She stared at me uncomprehending.

"Why don't *you* join me? I said instead. "You don't have to listen to those voices. You can shut them out! I did!"

For a second she stared at me blankly. Was she considering it? Then her demeanor changed. "I don't think so. I like *my* voices.

They get me places, and yours don't. Now, enough of this nonsense. This is your last chance to join me willingly. If you don't—you leave me no recourse but to take your powers through your death."

"Yeah!" Marcel and someone else shouted. Through blurry peripheral vision, I could see some sort of commotion toward the back of the room, where Eugenia had landed and the exit door was.

"This is *your* last chance!" I warned. "You can leave now and change, or we can all burn."

Those that were by the locked door, stopped and looked at me for a moment. "What could *she* do?" they seemed to wonder and doubt started creeping in. The guy who had touched Dorian was still on the ground, and Eugenia seem to have a trickle of blood running down her forehead. There were low murmurs all around the room and Agatha quickly started shouting some gibberish hoping to regain command of the situation.

Marcel and another guy seized me and roughly threw me on the altar. Next thing I knew the collection of medieval daggers and knives were flying off the walls, heading straight for me. Dorian saw this and screaming, threw himself in the weapon's path. One by one each dagger dropped to the ground the minute they touched his invisible force field.

"Now!" I felt the command inside of my head.

Sitting up I looked around for something that might catch on fire, and right away I saw it. Agatha's huge wooden symbol that hung above the altar! I threw the flame that I held in my palm toward the symbol of the Source and it readily caught on fire.

"Fire!" several people shouted at once.

"Open the door, Agatha, or we'll all burn alive!"

Agatha looked distracted and irritated. This was obviously not going along as planned. She took too long to move aside and her red robe caught on fire. Shrieks and screams and shouts assailed my hearing. Dorian came to my side and hugged me tightly and I wasn't shocked by his force field.

"The keys! The keys! Agatha, hurry, give us the keys!" a woman urged, yet she made no attempt to put out the flames in

Agatha's robe.

"Let me try!" a muscular man shouted. He rammed himself against the door like a bull, but the door didn't budge. The smoke was now getting to them and some were coughing. Several of them again turned again to look for Agatha, who was desperately trying to get her hooded cloak off of her—no one helped her. They all stared in dumb amazement as their priestess tried to rid herself of the flames.

Now engulfed in flames, she desperately rushed toward the door. Her subjects moved out of her way like the waves did for Moses. She had the key in her hand and as she feebly tried to unlock it, the flames from her robe caught some wall hangings on fire. The entire room burst into flames, and there was no way for anyone to escape.

Dorian and I had stayed by the burning altar. No one seemed to care weather we lived or died, so they let us be. Strangely, neither fire nor smoke seemed to touch us. We were perfectly cradled by them like an all-encompassing blanket.

Eugenia, who had regained consciousness, looked around dazedly. Suddenly, she espied something on the floor. Picking it up, she lunged forward, driving whatever she held deep into Agatha's back.

The door finally opened, and the throng of faithful followers trampled on their fallen stabbed leader to escape the flames. Amazingly, Agatha rose and turned with a wild look in her eyes. Eugenia twitched and charged forward once again. The two witches wrestled each other, Agatha with a dagger sticking out of her back.

The whole room was ablaze and had burned a hole through the ceiling. The whole house was now on fire, just like Dorian's drawing, yet Agatha and Eugenia kept fighting and throwing each other against the flames until Eugenia's hair caught on fire and she ran from the room screaming. Only then did Agatha look at us. Her fancy dress had caught on fire and the flame was quickly ascending, but she didn't seem to notice.

Picking up the single candelabrum that remained standing, Agatha walked with determination toward us and purposely tilted it in our direction. "Let this be a sacrifice to the Source!" she said acidly. But the pillar candles that were held there flew in the opposite direction as if they had bounced off a trampoline. Agatha, bleeding and burning, was thrown back against the wall. As she slowly collapsed to the floor, she shouted, "I'll see you in hell!"

Dorian and I took this as our cue to leave the burning building, which was literally falling to pieces. It was like clearing an obstacle course; beams and furniture were all falling all around us. Once we reached the top of the stairs, I saw that part of the second story was about to cave in. Instinctively I pushed Dorian forward, but it was too late for me. The upper story came down on me and all went black.

Part III ~ The Vision

Chapter 36

"Tess … Tess?" a familiar voice called.

I opened my eyes and saw a woman standing over me. She had shiny golden hair and gray stormy eyes. I rubbed my eyes, but it had no effect. In fact I didn't feel anything at all! The pain in my head, the stinging and burning of my eyes—all gone! And I could see perfectly again!

"Welcome."

I narrowed my eyes, "You look familiar."

"I'm Celeste, your grandmother."

"You look young."

"We all look the same age now."

"Now? What do you mean by *now*?" I looked around me, but I saw nothing but a thick white fog. There was bright sunlight all around, but nothing else. "Am I dead? Where's Alex?"

Celeste straightened out and gave me room to stand up. "Your life hangs in the balance," she said mysteriously.

"What balance?"

"The one between life and death. I was sent here to greet you." She swept an arm out, wanting me to follow her in the direction that her arm was pointing. Hesitantly, I followed her through the whiteness. It was thick and somewhat shimmery, like the creatures that guarded Dorian while … while … "Dorian! What happened to Dorian?"

"He is fine."

This brought me relief, but not much. I still had so many unanswered questions. "Celeste?" I inquired, but she seemed to ignore me as she floated forward with determination.

Finally a huge gate appeared in front of us. She stopped in

front of it with a grin on her face. "The pearly gates."

Indeed the gate had a pearly shimmer to it, much like metal, but unlike any metal I'd ever seen.

"So, what now?"

"You choose."

I stared at her in bewilderment. "Choose what?"

"Do you go back or continue forward?"

"Forward as in 'die?'"

She nodded solemnly and waited for my reply.

"I want to move forward. I want to be with Alex!" I said at once. Of course! What else?

She made a slight twitch with her features that warned me that there was something wrong. "What? What is it? Where's Alex? Why isn't he here?" I asked with suspicion.

"He is not here," a booming voice came from behind me and I turned to face a young Admiral gliding toward me.

"Russell?"

He smiled, and with a fatherly gesture, embraced me. "Yes, handsome, right?" He laughed.

"Very!" I couldn't help smiling. "But why do you say he is not here? Where is he?"

The two angels exchanged glances. "What?" I snapped with annoyance.

"He went after Leo, your father," Russell said with one raised eyebrow.

"Where?" I asked bewildered.

"Hell," Celeste added bluntly. "For not heeding our advice."

"Alex is in hell?"

"And your father too."

I shook my head. "Why aren't you guys getting them out? You can't leave them there!"

They said nothing. They again exchanged cryptic glances.

"I'll go then! I'll get them out!" I said, propelling myself forward toward the gate.

"It's not that simple, Tess." Russell stopped me before I

touched the gate. "Think about what you are about to do! If you touch those gates, that's it! There is no going back. Think about Robyn. Dane and Valerie are aging and tired. And they were not left in charge of Robyn. You were!"

"Alex and I were," I corrected. "Who's to say that I'll be a good mother?"

"I say." Katie came out from the whiteness with Jase right behind her.

"I'm sorry, Katie, but, Alex … "

"I know," she said with a worried look. "But what about my baby? What about Robyn? "

I couldn't argue with her. I felt all the worry and concern that she had over her daughter and I was reminded of the love I felt for her too. I thought of myself at that age. I was the same age when my parents died, and I ended up in foster care. I remembered my solemn vow not to ever let a child of mine go through that.

"You and Dorian would be great with her," Jase said with a hopeful grin. "We would like for the two of you to raise her."

"What about Alex and my father?" I looked around for any volunteers. "Celeste, that's your son!"

"I know," she said significantly. "I will do all I can, believe me."

"What is there to do? You just go get them."

"It's not that easy, Tess. Hell is not just a place; it's a state of being too. Once you're in there … " The Admiral started.

"It's hard to come back," Celeste finished. "All your darkest moments, fears and thoughts come back to haunt you and keep you from moving on. Only the most prepared and trained Angels can enter and make it out."

"Why did Leo and Alex end up there?" My heart felt like it had something tight tied around it, something that was constricting and choking it.

"Leo and Alex broke the rules—Heavenly rules, I might add," Russell explained. "They haunted two human beings, and one of them killed himself because of it."

"But Eros was already half crazy, I'm sure … "

"Crazy or not, he killed himself and it was in part because of Leo's actions." Celeste looked heartbroken over this, but not enough to risk going in there after him.

"I can't believe it! I would go in there after them. Why won't either one of you do it?" I looked at Russell and Celeste accusingly.

"Are you telling us to go to hell?" Russell leered.

"Yes! I'm telling you to go to hell! I'm telling you to go get them or I will!"

"No! Please, Tess!" Katie begged.

Trapped—I felt trapped between two very impossible choices.

"I will go, Tess." Russell closed his eyes and exhaled a breath that he no longer had. "But I have to prepare first. I won't go there to get Alex and Leo, just to get stuck there myself! Alex went in there unprepared. He said the same thing you did just now, and now he's trapped there himself!"

I shook my head and wished I could cry. How did this get so messed up?

"If I go back down and raise Robyn, Alex will be stuck in hell for years!"

"Time on Earth goes by a lot quicker than you think!" Katie put a positive twist. "Look!" She pointed to a whole or a space that had parted through the whiteness right in front of us. I could see me lying on a hospital bed, my head was bandaged up and my left hand as well. Dorian was sitting next to me; he looked intact. No doubt everyone thought it a miracle—and it was. He was drawing something. His tongue was sticking out as it usually did when he concentrated.

It was strange to be this close to my inert body and to Dorian. Could it be that the realm of the dead was right here occupying the same space, just differently? I always imagined it to be up above somewhere.

"How long has it been?"

"A whole week has passed since you were in that fire," Katie responded.

"I thought I just left!"

"Like I said, time goes by a lot quicker. That's why it's so imperative that you go back and take care of my baby," she pleaded once more.

I turned back to Katie and nodded. She jumped into my arms and hugged me. I could tell that she was squeezing me as tight as she could, but I felt nothing. Then Katie, the whiteness and the whole scene melted away. All I could feel was pain—sharp, stinging pain all over my body and especially in my head.

Oh no! I'm back! I thought with dread. I felt my lungs exhale and that too hurt. I moved my hand trying to reach for Dorian's arm. I must have startled him because he reflexively withdrew his hand. Then, realizing I was awake, he slowly enclosed his hand around mine and squeezed it gently.

"D—or—an," I tried to speak, but my throat was dry and hoarse.

Next thing I know I had a straw placed between my lips. I tried to swallow some water and I felt it go down my throat as if it were filled with sand.

"Is she awake?" a male voice asked. Having these bandages around my face was so annoying! My eyes! I remembered how my eyes were damaged during Agatha's torture.

"Tess, can you hear me?"

I nodded in reply.

"I am John—John Argyle from Social Services. I know this is bad timing, but … "

A smile spread across my face at the sound of that voice. "I thought you had to be elsewhere?"

"Well, I have one lose end to tie before I leave."

John … Argyle, as he called himself now, was my social worker. I was glad that I didn't have to explain myself to an "actual" social worker. I doubt that they would have found me, and my antics fit to parent Robyn.

Mathoniaha also came too for a short visit. He was on his way to Libya for his next mission.

"Will I ever see either one of you again?"

"Oh … I think so. We have this annoying tendency of popping up all over the place." Mathoniaha remarked.

Thanks to John, I was cleared to gain full custody of Robyn. My eyesight never fully recovered and I couldn't see without thick, ugly glasses. I tried to get the cutest frames possible, but it was hard to hide the thickness of the lenses. If I read too much, my eyes got tired and gave me headaches, so I learned to read Braille and saved my vision for sewing. Everyone at work attributed my bout with craziness as part of my grieving, and soon forgot all about it. Things went back to normal rather quickly and life continued on.

Agatha badly burned body was found in the charred ruins of her house. The surviving members of her society denied ever being members of a society at all. Any evidence of a secret society burned in the fire along with its Priestess. The survivors claimed that they had been there for a social gathering and while drinking cocktails; some candles fell down and started a fire. Though their statements had inconsistencies, no one could prove that there was any foul play.

Eugenia was among the survivors, but her hair was singed. I, on the other hand, suffered no burns. The beam that fell on me rendered me unconscious. Mathoniah, then butler, pulled me out before the firemen got there.

I was mad that so many of those evil people got away unpunished, but there was nothing I could do about it. Needless to say, I at least knew who not to vote for in the next election, and became very involved in the campaigns of their opponents. Marcel's rock-and-roll career dwindled, and he ended up a washed up druggie. He died of an overdose, ten years later.

Eugenia's hair never grew back well, so she ended up using wigs. She had no fancy career on T.V. and no fame. To get her out of their house, her parents bought her a Bed and Breakfast in Maine where she lived there the rest of her life.

The others disappeared more or less into obscurity. Somehow the fire in that house put a damper on their collective plans. Separately, they were less of a threat to the world. So in essence I did fulfill my mission. I feel more or less like Paul of old, who said, "I've fought a good fight, I have finished the race."

Of all the ones I've loved in this life, Robyn alone remains. She turned out to have a knack for fashion, like me. Maybe it was all that time she spent with me at the shop growing up. She now runs DeLeon Fashions and has taken the business to a new level of recognition. Every once in a while she runs things by me, but for the most part I am now out of it.

Katie had been right about Dorian. He turned out to be a great father figure for Robyn. They became the best of friends. He patiently he taught her a million things. He was a great gardener and kept the Preston's residence in perfect shape. He started a garden in the back and built a tree house for Robyn. He planted flowers in abundance and everything that he touched bloomed like a Thomas Kinkade painting. Valerie spent many peaceful hours painting the fruits of Dorian's labors.

Dorian never went back to Mexico, because Luz died in her sleep soon after I got out of the hospital. She simply stopped breathing and Amor found her the next morning with a smile on her face and her hands clasped around a seashell that Dorian had given her. We visited Amor and Paz frequently, Dorian would wander the beach alone and I could see him talking to himself as he did so. We left him alone; we hoped he talked to Luz. A few years later, Amor's ex-husband came to visit her and never left.

Dane died three years after the accident of heart failure. As Valerie predicted, we wore him out with our craziness. With Valerie I never had to pretend. Sometimes the house would fill with music and I knew it was Estelle who had stopped by. I would say that much to Valerie, and she would simply ask what song she was singing—then she would turn on the record player and play that song all night.

I welcome death. Not like I once did … out of fear, but rather, it feels like the next logical stage of existence. Now that they are all gone, I live alone with only ghosts for company—all but one … Sometimes, though, I can feel a yearning or a groan from Alex as if he were trying to reach me. I have tried to hold on to it, but it's always elusive and it passes by too quickly. I wonder what demons he has to face that keep him tied in hell. Is it guilt or remorse? Are they all real and valid concerns or figments of his insecurities?

I have hounded Celeste with questions when she stops by, but she has remained tight lipped and obstinate about it all. She has given me no new information and has leaked no more clues about what the other side is like. She must have gotten more training.

John and Mathoniaha have stopped by a few times. As expected, neither one of them has aged a day. While Robyn and I have grown old, they have stayed the same. Their eyes, though, give them away—their eyes look ancient and seem to hold the wisdom of centuries. I told them about Alex and Leo; John especially was very troubled by this, but they have no experience on what goes on the other side—they're experts on life, not death.

I spend my winters in Mexico now, for memory's sake. And in this solitary state, I recall my life. It seems that it has started with a dream and it will end with another.

The dappled sunlight filters from the French doors and warms my cheek while the sweet melody of *Cannon in D* reaches my ears as it once did so many years ago. My mind drifts to a distant place, a place without bodily aches, a place where Luz sits at the piano wearing a white tutu, and her dad bends over with his hands over hers, while together they follow the piano keys along the familiar tune.

The bright sunlight engulfs me now. I open my eyes and they are all there. I close my eyes again, knowing that my weak eyesight fools me and when I open them again they are all gone.

The briny ocean breeze bids me good-bye and the dining room fills once again with the familiar faces of those who quietly enjoy each other's company. They are relishing a well-deserved respite from life. Yet, I find that I miss that salty breeze and that warm sun. Part of me yearns to have it back.

"Tessss … Tesss …" his groans rouse me.

"Alex?" I ask, perplexed because his voice sounds so close.

I spent the majority of my adult life feeling his call, his anxiety, and his pleas, but have been unable to do anything about them.

Celeste recognizes my presence in that familiar room and reaches out to me. I look back at her and she knows …

"No, Tess! Not yet!" she calls after me. But I find that I'm faster than I've ever been. I charge out of the room, not towards the beckoning light, but in the other direction.

The shadows engulf me, "I'm coming, Alex! I'm coming for you!"

~In memory of Tony Scott~

About the Author

Silvina B. Niccum was born in Rosario, Argentina and raised in Buenos Aires. Her family immigrated to the US, when she was fourteen. She attended the University of Utah and studied Spanish Literature. Silvina now lives in Dallas, TX with her husband and her three homeschooled children.

Visit SB. NICCUM:

Website: www.sbniccum.com

Twitter: @veiled.com

Facebook: www.facebook.com/silvina.niccum

Blog: www.spiritualsupernaturalparanormal.blogspot.com

Veiled

The first book of the Veiled Series.

"I have always existed, not just me but all of us, the un-embodied spirits who wait to live."

Tess is an unborn spirit, who is about to embark on a much awaited journey into mortality to a brand new planet called Earth. She is chosen by the Eternals for an important mission, and is put under a rigorous training by a half-human, half-lion Seraph. This training exposes Tess to some of her darkest fears and insecurities. These experiences force Tess to work on her gift as a discerner of thoughts and reader of auras—thus helping her become one of Heaven's most powerful angels. But even angels falter, and deep inside her a gnawing fear is growing.

Available at online booksellers and at
www.sbniccum.com

What others are saying about Veiled

"This is a captivating journey of life before earth or birth. At look at before we are born where were we, what did we do, what happened before … now. The characters Tess and Alex along with the rest are so well -human. Having situations or trials even before birth that we can completely relate to, root for or sympathize with. This book captures your imagination and keeps your attention throughout. Wow a new idea, now where's the sequel!"
~ M. McElveen

"I absolutely loved this book. I am not a true sci-fi fan, I usually stick to a good romance novel, but I was intrigued by the story line. I loved the creativity of the author … the symbolism and magical elements, with just enough romance to keep me reading long into the night. I recommend this book to someone looking for a little supernatural minus the vampires. I can't wait for the sequel! Please don't make us wait too long! Well done."
~ Jen B. Cincy

"I started reading this off and on, then last night just couldn't really put it down. It reminds us of the opposition that we faced and face now and how free will is our greatest gift. I only got like 5 hours of sleep before work because I was unable to put it down."
~ Adam

Made in the USA
Monee, IL
07 July 2026

56551624R00198